LITTLE FISH

SHELLI MANNING

ISBN: 1497574803
ISBN 13: 9781497574809

For Jacob

whose mere existence made it crucial that the pattern be broken...
I always knew you'd change the world.

TABLE OF CONTENTS

One

HOOK, LINE AND SINKER

As tears spilled down my cheeks for the third time that day, I tried to ignore the panic that was pushing its way up my chest.

This is crazy. How could I have taken the wrong road?

"You can do this."

My hollow voice reverberated off the otherwise empty interior of the car. Speaking out loud did not have the bolstering effect I intended.

You have to do this.

Parked on the shoulder of an unfamiliar, snowy Chicago freeway with cars buzzing past was no place to sit pondering life decisions, so I gathered my courage, put my turn signal on and carefully pulled back into traffic.

Of all places to take a wrong exit... I had to pick Chicago.

Being a small town girl with hardly any driving experience certainly didn't prepare me for this, I had to recognize something eventually. This was the third time I'd made the trip from Wisconsin to Kentucky, in as many weeks.

After a few miles, I saw the sign for Interstates 80/94 towards Gary, Indiana.

See? One little glitch, that's all. I can definitely do this.

— 1 —

Moving five hundred miles away from the only life I've ever known – for a guy I met less than a month ago – *did* seem crazy, but I'd come too far to turn back now.

Everyone would think I was scared if I came back, that I'd chickened out.

Except Mom, she wouldn't care, she would just be relieved...

Her first reaction had been an attempt change my mind by shaming me with logic.

"Tate Parker, you mean to tell me this guy is so wonderful, you can't wait five more months until you graduate? If he's so good for you, he'd *want* that for you."

But her words fell on deaf ears and when logic failed, there was no dramatic attempt to stop me from leaving. Since I was only seventeen, she could have used legal means to keep me in Wisconsin, but she didn't. I convinced myself it was because she thought – as I thought – that whatever my new life had to offer was bound to be better than the one I had. This was my ticket out of Anders Park.

As I negotiated the turn on the slippery ramp, I was turning back towards my fate. No longer consumed with what direction I was going, I again let the dream-like memories of the last few weeks replay in my head.

Once I met Eric, it was as if my life had been put on fast forward and I was no longer in control of what was happening. On the surface I was making decisions, seemingly more in charge of my own destiny than ever before, but I suspected in reality, fate was hurrying me towards the life I was now *compelled* to lead.

It had been a strange set of circumstances that had led us to meet anyway...

I was scheduled to work that night. My job manning the front desk at the Cassden Fitness Center didn't pay much, but the perks were great and I was good at it. Getting paid to answer phones, clean tanning beds and be friendly to members – who were mostly athletic young guys – was a pretty good deal. I would have had no reason to take off that night, except that when I got there, one of my co-workers was already there to work; we'd been double scheduled. She counted on her hours more than I did; I let her have the shift.

Finding myself unexpectedly liberated, my first instinct was to call my best friend, but I remembered Jennie was at her sister's, babysitting.

I sat in my car in front of the fitness center, wondering what to do with my night when I felt a familiar pang of guilt.

Alex.

My godson. My little sweetheart. I had a big part of raising him during his first year, but now months and months had passed with little contact with him, thanks to the issues between me and his mom.

When I pulled my car up to the front of the familiar building, the façade looked as though no time had passed at all.

But time *had* passed and things had changed.

Lana and I had been friends almost our whole lives. When we were just little kids – I was six, she was eight – her step dad's sister was my babysitter. Our friendship bloomed when Lana started getting invites to sleep over when ever I would be there. Little did her aunt know how much of a catalyst she would turn out to be. By the time I was nine, my parents no longer needed babysitters because I spent nearly every weekend at Lana's.

The past summer spent living under the same roof nearly destroyed our friendship. Just three short months almost did us in. Our saving grace was that in our hearts, we were more than friends – we were family. It was only that depth of our ties kept us from walking away.

I knocked on the door and walked in without waiting for an answer. Even with all that had passed; a formal invitation to come in was not necessary.

I entered the living room at the same time – but opposite direction – as Lana. She was coming from her bedroom. Quickly scanning the apartment, more for sound than sight, I realized Alex wasn't there.

"Hey. Where's Alex?"

"With Eric and Shane, at the store. They'll be back in a few minutes."

Eric. Eric. Why do I know that name?

Then it clicked.

"Eric? Your *cousin* Eric Sheppard, from Kentucky?"

"Yeah."

"The one you've always said I should meet?"

— 3 —

"Yeah" she smiled. She looked like the proverbial cat that ate the canary.

"What's he doing here?" Excitement fluttered through my stomach. I'd never seen Eric, but if he was half as good as Lana made him sound, he was definitely worth meeting.

"Remember I said I was going to Kentucky for Christmas?"

"Yeah, you were going with your new boyfriend, what's his name? Jason?"

"Justin, only he's not my boyfriend anymore." A sheepish grin crossed her heavily glossed lips. "I broke up with him in Kentucky."

"You took a guy to Kentucky to be with your family for Christmas and then broke up with him there?"

"Well," she started, sheepish grin still firmly in place, "when I met Shane, I wanted to be with him instead, so I broke up with Justin. Then Eric and Shane decided a road trip would be fun, so Justin left and I rode back with them. They're staying with me for a few days while I pack."

"Pack for what?" I charged.

"I'm moving down to Kentucky."

"What? When? Why?"

"Soon," She waved her hand to gesture at the boxes everywhere and half packed apartment "in a few days."

How could I have not noticed the half packed apartment? What originally passed as the clutter of fading Christmas now revealed the telltale signs of the impending move mingled in.

Wait. What about Alex?

"What about Troy?" I tested, remembering that there was still muddy water here. When I'd lived here, Alex's Dad's had lived here too. Lana frequently dragged me into their drama, so I said what I really felt: a lot of times, I felt Troy was right.

"What *about* Troy?" Her tone was sharp.

Was that towards him, or me for asking?

"He's fine with it. He'll see Alex whenever he wants to. We'll work it out."

She didn't sound convinced.

She probably hasn't even told him.

— 4 —

After years of emulating Lana, living with her made me realize how different we really were.

There were at least twenty more questions that I wanted to ask her, but at that moment, I could no longer remember any of them. The door opened and there was my little sweetheart Alex with two guys I'd never seen before.

I knew instantly who was who.

Shane's eyes scanned the large cluttered living room for Lana, his eyes settling when he found her. The result was a lopsided smile that stretched across his face, adding to the roundness of it. He was cute enough, tall, broad shoulders, blond spiky hair. Not my type, but cute enough.

Then there was Eric. He was tall like Shane, but that's where the similarity ended. He was dark. Not just in color, but as if his very aura was dark. His skin was actually fairly pale in contrast to his almost black hair. His face was long and thin, with sharp, sculptured features, complimented by a neatly trimmed mustache and goatee.

Adding to the dark mysteriousness was the long black leather coat and black boots he wore. Not exactly the kind of thing you saw in Cassden everyday.

Here it was mostly camouflage and hunting boots.

Once his eyes locked onto mine and that devilish smirk appeared, I don't think I would have remembered my own name if Alex hadn't been at my feet, chanting it.

"Auntie Tate, Auntie Tate, pick me up." he said in a little sing song voice.

My heart panged. I imagined that someday when I had kids of my own, I would love them the same way that I loved Alex.

I immediately obliged him.

"Hi Baby. I missed you." I planted kisses on him, very aware that I was being watched.

"I missed you."

Then he was squirming back out of my arms.

Alex's short welcome had not given me ample to think of anything to say. Something witty would have been helpful, now that my attention was free and I was about to be introduced to the stunning man in front of me.

"Eric, this is my cou- er, Tate, you know, the one I told you about." Lana said. "Tate, this is my cousin Eric from Kentucky, and this is Shane."

She almost called me her 'cousin'. I tried not to laugh. That's how we referred to one another; we had since we were kids. It all started with a joke between our mothers.

They had some similar features: the same olive skin tone and dark brown hair and they also shared a tendency to overindulge. But in as many ways as they were similar, they were opposites, too. Lana's mom was extremely tall and thin. At over 6 foot, she was tall enough to easily shadow over a lot of men. My mom, by comparison, was 5 feet tall if you rounded up, and she was as plump as Lana's mom was thin. Somewhere, around the time I was eleven and Lana was thirteen, our moms ended up at one of those small town fireman's picnics together, with Lana and I in tow. The big joke was started that night that they were twins. Twins meant sisters, Lana and I concluded, construing the joke to be of interest to us. Our moms being sisters meant we were cousins.

It stuck.

Our ruse of family bond followed us throughout the rest of our adolescence. By the time we were nearing adulthood, every person who was not either related to us or privy to the most precise details of our lives thought we were, in fact, cousins.

He *was* her cousin though, so I couldn't expect her to have described this man the way he appeared to me, now, but even considering that, what she'd told me about him had been grossly negligent in details.

"Hi."

I intended to greet both of them, but my eyes never left Eric's, nor did his leave mine.

He extended his hand as if to shake mine. I broke his gaze to look down and put my hand in his, but when my eyes returned to his, instead of shaking my hand he drew it up to his mouth and gently kissed the back of it.

"It's wonderful to finally meet you." His voice was thick with southern charm.

I think I might faint.

"It's nice to meet you, too"

Alex was back at my feet.

"Auntie Tate, Uncle Eric, sit here." He had taken both of us by the hand, his tiny hands trying to maneuver us over to the loveseat.

"Sit here." He commanded again. He climbed up in my lap once I sat down.

Did he say Auntie Tate and Uncle Eric? Perfect.

A split second later, Alex was climbing off my lap and Lana appeared looking very smug.

"Tate, you can stay a while, can't you?" she asked innocently, as she handed Eric and me each a drink.

Clearly she'd already decided the answer.

THE CLUTTERED LIVING room soon grew even more so, with the arrival of five of Lana's friends. While she flitted about the apartment, getting drinks for her guests or ducking into her bedroom - no doubt to touch up her makeup - everyone else sat around drinking, laughing and talking easily.

Eric and I were in our own little world. The conversation between us flowed effortlessly, as did the sparks. His devilish smile and thick southern accent had me riveted.

After a few hours and one too many drinks, I excused myself to the kitchen to call home.

Lilly wouldn't be happy that I was drinking, but she wouldn't freak out either. She took a pick-your-battles approach to parenting. She'd much rather know I was safe than have me lie about it and try to cover by driving home.

After my phone call, I rejoined the gathering in the living room, and took my place on the loveseat again, only this time Eric pulled me closer to him as I sat down, his arm snaking around my waist.

"Does this mean you're staying here with me tonight?" he purred into my ear, his mouth close enough for me to feel his breath on my neck.

"I guess it does."

Then he was kissing me.

His lips were soft and tender on mine, his kisses sweet and light. I found myself wishing that I hadn't drank so much. I wanted to remember every detail of this.

There was also a part of me that was afraid of how far the alcohol would let me go.

We're in room full of people. It's just kissing. Relax.

I let myself fall back into the task of memorizing every detail of his mouth on mine, determined not to let the memory slip away.

I WOKE UP to a quiet room. Only the sound of patterned breathing indicating deep sleep could be heard. I assessed my situation, noting the details one by one.

Even before I opened my eyes I worked out that I was on the couch with Eric. We lay on our sides, facing each other, his arms wrapped around me. My face was pressed into his bare chest, making his now familiar scent fill my nostrils. I opened my eyes and waited impatiently for them to adjust to the darkness. Seeing the living room lit only by the street light streaming in through the windows filled me with a sense of déjà vu.

A thick mixture of dread and guilt crept into my stomach. The last thing I remember was sitting on the loveseat, Eric kissing me.

When did we move to the couch?

I realized that my jeans were off. I was wearing only a t-shirt and underwear.

Oh God.

Questions fired through my brain like bullets.

How far did we go?

How did my jeans get off and whose shirt was I wearing?

I made a minute movement with my leg, trying to further assess my situation without waking him up. He was still wearing jeans. Relief swept through me momentarily.

What happened?

I looked towards the VCR, the numbers read 4:27.

As carefully as I could, I untangled myself from Eric's arms and tiptoed around until I found my jeans and my purse, then slunk to the bathroom.

Once in the light, I looked down at the mysterious t-shirt.

University of Kentucky.

Okay, mystery solved, I must have asked for a t-shirt to sleep in. No big deal.

I reluctantly looked into the mirror. My reluctance was well called for.

My hair was a mess, there were uneven smears of black makeup all around my eyes, my face was puffy and my lips had the telltale smoothness and swell of too much kissing. My eyes caught on something lower, a dark spot on my neck.

"Oh no" I quietly groaned as my hand flew up instinctively to cover the fresh hickey.

Ugh! Like a dog marking his territory!

I hated hickeys.

Why did I drink so much?

This was so unlike me! I wasn't *that* girl. I was the *opposite* of that girl.

At least we didn't have sex. I was no expert, but I wasn't a virgin either, so I could tell.

Shame and regret settled over me all the same.

I thought about leaving right away, but when I returned to the living room and saw him sleeping soundly, I made the decision to wait until morning.

He wasn't quite as stunning now, but still mysterious and very attractive. Still different than any guy I'd ever met before.

I carefully wound my way back into his arms. It wasn't long before I drifted off.

⌣‿⌢

THE SECOND TIME I awoke to a much different picture. Alex was awake and cheerfully singing – not quite in unison – with the characters on the cartoon he was watching and Lana was whispering happily to Shane.

Eric's arms no longer entrapped me as they had earlier, now one merely draped heavily across my waist. I opened my eyes slowly, this time allowing my eyes to adjust to the bright morning light. Lana immediately noticed I was awake, as if she had been waiting to pounce. She smiled and opened her mouth to speak.

I held my finger up to my pursed lips and silently shushed her. Her mouth closed, leaving her looking dejected.

I lightly wrapped my fingers around Eric's wrist, lifted his arm off my waist and laid it gently onto the side of his own body. Before I could make a move to get up, he dropped his arm back down around my waist, pulling me closer to him.

"Mmmm, where are you going?" He murmured. "You're always leaving me."

I smiled. I couldn't help myself, that accent drove me nuts.

"I'm going home." I answered lightly.

"Will you come back?"

He was looking at me now.

Man, he's cute. The morning light makes his eyes look bright blue.

"When are you guys leaving to go back to Kentucky?" I asked, honestly hoping it would be soon. I liked him too much. He was too good to be true and if something seems too good to be true…

My thoughts trailed off until his response to my question registered in my head.

"Come with me."

"What?"

Crazy.

"Come with me." He said again, this time with more airiness in his voice.

"To Kentucky?"

Definitely crazy.

"Yes, come back to Kentucky with me. We're leaving tonight. It only takes about 8 hours to get there."

Crazy. No way. There is no possible way I can just take off and go to Kentucky.

"I can't." I intended that to be the end of the ridiculous conversation.

"Why?" He challenged.

"What?"

"Why? Why can't you come with me? Just for a few days?"

"Because I just can't." I replied, almost laughing. "School and work and -"

"Aren't you still off, school I mean?" he interrupted "You have a few more days yet of Christmas break, right?"

He had me.

"Well, yeah, I'm off school, but I have work."

"Come on, tomorrow is New Year's Eve... we'll have a party." His voice softened with the last part of his comment; as if when he said 'party' he *didn't* mean balloons and party hats.

I need to think.

I was starting to feel hung-over and gross.

What I need is a shower and some ibuprofen.

"I guess I'll have to think about it." I said as catapulted myself over him and off the couch before he could stop me. I turned back towards him and caught his eyes lingering on my backside as I walked away.

I stopped midway to the door when Lana chimed in "I think that's a great idea! Tate, you and Eric can ride in your car and I will ride back with Shane."

Of course she thought it was a great idea.

"What about Alex?" I asked.

"Troy is picking him up this morning. He's not going with me this time." She replied matter-of-factly.

"I thought you were moving there." I tested her as I retrieved my coat from the closet and bent down to put my shoes on. "How are you moving without taking Alex and how are you going to be packed and ready to go by tonight?"

Lana was big on great, life altering plans that she rarely followed through on.

"I'm not moving yet" she retorted as if *I* had gotten the details all wrong. "I am just taking some of my stuff down there for now. Shane is going to bring me back in a week to get more stuff and pick up Alex."

Whatever.

"Alex, come here and hug me bye." I said.

— 11 —

I pulled the little boy into a big hug and pushed my pursed lips into his cheek.

"I love you. I will see you soon, okay? I'll miss you."

"Where're you going? Stay here." he whimpered.

My heart panged again and a lump formed in my throat.

"I have to go back to my house now." I said, concentrating on not tearing up.

"I miss you Auntie Tate."

"I know Alex, I know. You be good with Daddy, okay?"

"Okay. Bye. I love you."

"I love you too, Baby." I whispered as he scurried back to his perch in front of the TV.

She uses that damn thing as a babysitter.

I looked up and found myself again the focus of those sparkling eyes. The eyes that I was pretty sure hadn't stopped watching me since I'd moved from the couch. I smiled and walked out.

MY DAYDREAM SHIFTED and changed as the flat Indiana miles rolled by, I thought about everything I'd put Lilly through over the last few weeks.

It hurt me most to leave her. It hurt to leave a lot of people, but with my mom it was different. I was abandoning her. My only hope was that with me gone, her and my step dad would have one less thing to fight about.

Through all the chaos in my life, I knew she loved me; she had done the best she could with what she had.

My mind jumped to the first time I told her I was going to Kentucky. Had she known what that trip would lead to, she may have staged a better war in the first place.

Having already showered and dressed in accordance with the ugly blotch on my neck, I stood with her in the shabby kitchen of the old farm-style house shared by our family: her and I, plus my step-dad Carl and his three sons.

"Mom. It's not that big of a deal. It's just a few days."

Deep down, I knew this trip was more than any parent should be expected to accept without issue, I would at least have to work for it.

I made it all sound as simple and wholesome as possible, reminding her that Lana was originally from Kentucky and she wanted me to meet her family.

My effort to sound reassuring was difficult, seeing as I wasn't even convinced it was a great idea, myself.

"Hey, at least it will be much quieter around here for a few days."

Judging by the look on her face, my attempt to sway her with humor had failed.

I knew the ugly fights my step dad and I habitually got into bothered her worse than anything. I shouldn't use it as a tool.

It was sad and ironic that the biggest contributing factor to my loathing was the way I saw him treat her when I was younger.

"You're leaving today? Well, when are you coming home?"

"Today, well, leaving tonight, but I'm not sure exactly what time yet. Eri, uh, Lana said it takes about 8 hours to get there." I paused, waiting to see if she caught my slip. "I will head home first thing on Sunday morning, so I will be back in plenty of time for school on Monday."

Bingo. That would be it. Any second she'd raise her white flag. School was the key. Half way through my senior year, she just wanted to see me graduate.

"Well I don't think it's a good idea."

"I know Mom, I know. I'll be fine, don't worry." I tried to placate her as I walked away, leaving her in the kitchen alone.

The sound of a bugle mourning the loss of the battle drifted through my head.

Tate, that's not nice.

In the end, we both knew it didn't really matter if she wanted me to go or not. Lilly had lost run of me a while ago. Since I'd started working and paying a lot of my own way she didn't have any way of restricting me, short of using the law and since I never did anything to warrant such extreme measures, that wasn't really an option either. It basically came down to the fact that I had more of my own money than she had to give me and my car was titled in my own name. Money was key.

Back up in my room, I stood in front of the full length mirror, surveying my appearance while I thought over what Eric was asking me to do.

Oh well, I might have picked this outfit this anyway, even if not for the hickey.

Jeans were a staple, and today I wore my favorites: low rise, dark blue denims that showed off the curves of my maturing body. The chocolate brown tone of the turtleneck sweater looked warm against my tan skin and matched the tone of my eyes and hair. Tall brown leather boots completed the look.

I crossed the room to the dresser and pulled a silver herringbone chain from the jewelry box. The petite silver cross caught the light in the mirror as I reached behind my head to work the clasp. I surveyed the mirror again as I picked silver hoop earrings out of the jewelry box's tiny little drawer and put them on.

"Not bad."

What the heck. You only live once.

Before I could get caught up again in the logic of the decision, I grabbed some clothes and made one trip downstairs to gather my beauty essentials from the bathroom. To my own surprise, I was packed and ready to go in a matter of 15 minutes.

Standing in the living room with my hastily packed bag at my feet, I said bye to Lilly with solemn promises to drive careful and be home by late afternoon on Sunday.

When I got back to Lana's, I'd no sooner stepped into the apartment than Eric had crossed the room and pulled me into a big hug.

"You're back."

He smelled of cologne, stale liquor and cigarette smoke.

Did he smoke?

I didn't remember that.

"Didn't you think I would be?" I asked, teasingly.

He took a step back, keeping his hands on my shoulders as if to survey me. I took advantage to do the same.

He looked *so* cute.

Cute but menacing. He wore a bandana, tied biker style. He had a small bottle of whiskey in his pocket.

'Hair of the dog' he called it.

I didn't know what that meant.

Whiskey for breakfast? That's... wow.

I always did like bad boys, but Eric was the *baddest* I'd ever met.

I had a few things I wanted to do before we left and he needed time to get showered and packed so we made plans to meet back at the apartment in a few hours.

⟵⟶

I FILLED MY car with gas and got in line at the automatic wash. My car wasn't much, but the little black coupe cleaned up pretty well, even if it was a little old.

I needed to call Jennie.

Jennie and I had been best friends since the day she was the new kid in Kindergarten and I befriended her. Our friendship faded in and out through grade school, but once high school started, we were inseparable.

Jennie was the type of friend who you told everything. A friend you'd *especially* have to tell if you were bailing on her for New Years Eve.

If you were bailing on her so you could spend New Year's Eve in a different state, with a bad boy you just met, and *didn't* tell her – it would be high treason.

Jennie was *that* kind of friend.

"Tate you're crazy!" She said. "Crazy, but you'd be crazier not to go, he's sounds awesome. Scary awesome, but awesome. I'd go if I were you."

"I guess it's just a little weird because of things between me and Lana." I confessed.

"Yeah, but you're not going down there to hang out with Lana, you'll be with him."

Jennie would always take my side over Lana's. There was no love loss between those two.

My whole life, it seemed, I'd been joined at the hip with one or the other, but rarely both. The three of us tried that when we were younger, but the competition between my two best friends always ended in petty fighting and me feeling torn.

"So, do you think you'll do it?"

"Do what? Go to Kentucky? Yeah, I already told you I am." I played dumb.

"Not that *it*. Do you think you and Eric will have sex?"

"I don't know." I answered sharply, as if her question hadn't crossed my mind.

I didn't want to confess that while I was afraid that Eric expected it, I didn't want to go that far with him.

"I just met him. It's not like Darrin."

Darrin was the only guy I'd ever been that close with. The first time happened shortly before my seventeenth birthday, we'd been dating for almost two years. He was always so sweet, even after we grew apart I never regretted having that experience with him and I still considered him a trusted friend.

This wasn't like that.

"Hey. You know New Years is gonna suck without you." She charged.

"Oh, you'll be just fine without me, just go to the party at *Tony's* house." I teased.

"Yeah, I'll still miss you, though. Everyone will."

"I'll be home Sunday."

"Good"

"Hey, I better let you go, my car is almost done." I lied.

I didn't want to think about Darrin anymore, or about sleeping with Eric and I sure didn't want to think about the party I'd be missing.

BY FOUR O'CLOCK we were on the road, and eight hours after that, the large, ominous looking Ohio River Bridge was looming through the windshield, the lights of Louisville spread out on the other side.

I'd learned a lot about Eric in those eight hours. Put together with what I already knew, I felt I had a pretty good picture of him.

He told me about his parents and that while he had a big extended family, he was an only child and he was adopted. That held our conversation for a long time; I'd never met anyone who was adopted. I asked a lot of questions.

I confirmed that he was only twenty, like Lana told me, though he looked closer to twenty-five or twenty-six.

Seventeen and twenty is acceptable.

Kinda.

He had a job, that part I remembered. I did learn that it wasn't just any job, it was a *good* job, at the Ford truck plant in Louisville.

As I followed Shane's little truck off the interstate and into a residential neighborhood. Eric pointed out the side street where his parents' house was, and less than a mile later, we pulled into his apartment complex.

Apartment buildings were on every side of us. I wondered how he remembered which one was his.

It was a shabby neighborhood, with even shabbier cars. I was too tired to be disappointed.

What were you expecting Tate, a gated community?

When we got inside, I mentally checked just the basics of the cookie cutter style apartment. It was clean enough, didn't smell and it had real decorations, not posters of cars and half naked women like most of the bachelor pads I'd seen.

Good enough.

Between the hangover and the drive, I was wiped out. All I wanted was sleep.

"Hey Eric, two questions: where is the bathroom, and where should I sleep?" I smiled groggily up at him.

He responded by slipping his arms around my waist, pulling me towards him. "The bathroom is there" he turned my body around so I was pointed towards the dark doorway, now revealing itself "and you can sleep in there" he slowly swiveled me back in the opposite direction and nodded to the bedroom "with me."

"Perfect, thank you." I stood up straighter to kiss his cheek.

I changed my clothes and climbed into Eric's big, comfy bed, leaving him to sit and drink at the dining room table with Shane.

Turns out, it was good that we had those eight hours in the car because for the rest of the weekend, all I learned about Eric was how much he likes to party.

Being with Eric was great – when it was just Eric, but save for a few private hours and some nice moments, most of the weekend consisted of people coming and going, lots of drinking, smoking and loud, heavy music.

New Year's Eve was a disappointment. When the clock struck midnight, Eric was almost too drunk to notice and by Saturday night, I was ready to hit the fast forward button on the trip and be home. I'd had enough.

At least I had a built in excuse to go to bed early; I had a long drive in the morning.

Lana surprised me as I came from the bathroom. "I want to ride back with you, is that okay?" she said, obviously trying to be discreet.

"No problem, it'll be nice to have the company."

Sure I would hear all about it on the drive, I didn't bother asking her what changed her mind.

I went into the bedroom without saying goodnight to anyone. It wasn't long before Eric came in.

"Hi." He said, as he sat down on the bed next to where I lay.

"Hi."

"How come you didn't say goodnight?"

"I wanted you to tuck me in." I smiled.

"Here I am." He paused and looked at me, growing more serious. "Tate, will you come back?"

"I don't know, I guess I haven't really thought about it."

"You haven't? I have, a lot. I want you to come back when it can be just us. My life usually isn't like this."

"Like drinking and partying every night?"

"Yeah, just like that." He confirmed. "I'm on vacation, so I have been partying more than normal. I know I could have showed you a much better time if there weren't people around all the time." He bent down to kiss me and nuzzle my neck.

"It's fine, Eric, it was New Years. That's what people do on New Years."

"Yeah, well I want another shot with you, just you."

"I'll think about it, okay?"

"Fair enough." He conceded after he kissed me, this time on the cheek.

"Good night Eric."

"Good night Tate."

He turned off the light and closed the door on his way out. I wasn't sure what to make of his request. Part of me wanted another chance with him, too.

I'll have plenty of time to think about it on the drive home.

In the morning I climbed out of Eric's bed leaving him still sleeping. Lana was awake and to my surprise, was showered, packed and ready to go. I followed suit quickly. By eight o'clock we were ready to leave.

"He said to tell you bye and that it was nice meeting you." Lana replied when I'd asked about Shane, who was already gone.

I went into Eric's room.

"Wake up Sleepyhead." I hummed in his ear. "It's time for me to go."

"See, you're always leaving me." He murmured, his eyes still closed. "I wish you could stay."

"I can't. I have schoo-"

"I know, school, work," He cut me off, now looking up at me intently. "I have to go back to work tomorrow, too, back to reality. But did you give any thought to coming back? Please say you will."

"Eric, I've only been awake for one hour since you asked me that the last time. I haven't really had a chance to think about it, but I will, on the way home. I promise."

He pulled me into a bear hug.

"I miss you already. I hope you come back."

"Eric,"

"I know, I know." He cut me off. "You'll think about it. Well, drive careful, okay?"

"Okay."

"Promise?"

"I promise."

On the way back to Wisconsin, the ride eventually became tedious to Lana and she drifted off to sleep, leaving me with only the radio to keep me company. I was glad for the time to think.

A list of pros and cons formed in my head. All the good things about Eric, all the sweet things he had said and done during the last few days tallied on one side of my brain, while all the partying was on the other, along with one other glaring con:

We live five hundred miles apart, this obviously can't go anywhere.

*But he's **so** cute!*

When I got home, I knew exactly what I needed to do if I wanted to sort this out.

I dialed the familiar number, the one I could have probably dialed in my sleep.

"Jennie, I'm back, can you come over?"

"Be there in fifteen."

"Perfect, bye."

"Bye."

Jennie was walking up the stairs to my room eleven minutes later. She flopped down on the bed, ready for the details.

"He wants me to come back."

"He does, really?" she said, excitement in her voice. "When?"

"Soon. Too soon." I groaned. "I don't know Jennie, he's just so, so" I struggled for words "perfect."

"And the problem is?"

I gave Jennie what seemed like every detail of my trip. I was happy to answer her loaded question this time, we had not done 'it', nor had we ever come close. I was careful to tell her about the bad parts as much as the good. If I wanted an unbiased opinion, she needed all the facts.

"I say you go back." She answered easily.

"What?"

"Yeah, go back, give the guy one more shot. What do you have to lose?"

"Uh, money, time, my heart." I trailed off at the end.

"Seriously Tate? You have to spend your money on something."

Jennie teased because she knew I was trying to save so I could move out. I didn't care where, I just knew I'd be gone as soon as I graduated and could work full time.

"And time, well, what else do you have to do?"

"And my heart? What about that?" I challenged. She was supposed to be my voice of reason and she was failing miserably.

"You're gonna fall in love with this guy in a weekend? I don't think so."

"Well, gee, when you put it like *that*. But what's the point?" I asked, then slipping into my best diva impression "Five hundred miles is very far and I do not need the drama of a long distance relationship."

Jennie laughed. "The point is fun! Just do it. Hey, take me with you! That way, you know you won't do anything crazy."

I considered it for a moment. Her being there would be helpful in several ways.

"And *you're* going to keep me from doing anything crazy?" I asked in the most skeptical voice I could muster. "You're more likely to push me over the damned edge!"

We both collapsed into giggles.

"Seriously," I said, more composed "that's not a bad idea. Would you really go?"

"Sure, why not? I made it back from our last road trip in one piece, I'll brave another one. When do you want to go?"

"Eric said soon."

"Is this weekend soon enough?" she tempted.

It was.

My SECOND TRIP to Kentucky was everything that the first wasn't.

It all started the first moment I saw him again and it ended with the conversation that led to the third one, this trip. The *one way* trip.

It was a weekend filled with easy banter and laughter. Eric was wonderful. He and Jennie got along wonderfully. He was funny and sweet and sexy, bad boy with a golden touch. From dinner at a lively little Mexican restaurant Friday night, to an afternoon of sightseeing, everything he planned went wonderfully. He was the perfect host.

Too perfect.

Too perfect because by Saturday night, emotions were starting to wash over me in waves. One minute I was happy just to be with him, the next would find me anxious about having to say goodbye and the moments in between were filled with confusion over how my feelings developed so quickly.

How had this gotten so serious? It didn't feel like this last weekend. Was it being away from him, in the sense of the cliché coming true, that absence from him made my heart grow fonder, or was it this weekend's lack of party atmosphere that was making me see him differently?

And which is the real Eric?

I knew I couldn't just keep driving down every weekend, but I could barely fathom the thought of not seeing him again.

When Saturday evening turned into Saturday night, as much as I looked forward to going to sleep in his arms again, I was dreading it, too. I still hadn't told him the truth about my desire to keep our relationship chaste, at least for now.

"I am so happy you decided to come back." He murmured in my ear. We lay together in his bed, his arms wrapped around me from behind, his breathing warm and rhythmic on the back of my neck. The full lengths of our bodies touched, and the sensations worked to wither my weakening resolve.

"You're not upset that I didn't come alone?" I asked, laying the foundation for my cop out of having Jennie in the next room.

"No. As much as I would love to have you all to myself, I would prefer you not make that drive by yourself."

"Yeah, it was nice of Jennie to come along with me. I'm sure she had better things to do this weekend than watch me fa, uh, fawn all over you."

Did I almost just say 'fall in love with you'?

"Tate?"

"Yeah?"

"Am I ever going to see you again, after this weekend?" He continued without waiting for a response, "I want to. I know I shouldn't be thinking about it yet, but I miss you already."

"Me, too." I whispered.

We lay there for a moment, silent in our shared sentiment.

"You graduate in June, right?" Eric broke the silence first.

"Yep, the first Sunday in June, why?"

"Would you consider spending some time down here with me after that? I mean more than a weekend?"

"How long are you talking? Like a week or two?" I asked my head now spinning with possibilities. The thought of being here with him in summer was exhilarating. I always loved summer, the time when everything was alive and green. I hated winter when, by comparison, everything was dead.

"Like a week or two. Or longer." He paused, "Maybe forever."

At that moment, my whole world ceased to turn and after what felt like an eternity of complete quiet, I spoke slowly, choosing my words carefully. "Eric, are you asking me to move here to be with you?"

"I think I... " he stopped.

Oh no. He wasn't.

My face flushed with embarrassment. I pushed forward before he could continue. I needed to backtrack, recall my words before he had to embarrass us both by correcting me.

"I'm sorry, Eric. I jumped to conclusions. I know that's not what you meant. It would be crazy to decide to move in together after only a we-"

"It is." He said.

My backpedaling ceased. "What?"

"I think that is exactly what I am asking you." He paused "Yes, that is what I'm asking you." as if confirming his decision out loud.

He moved back and pulled me with him, so that now I was on my back and he could see my face. The faint moonlight through the window was just enough. Our eyes locked and that seemed to be what he was waiting for.

"I have never felt this way before. I know it's not rational to feel so much so soon, but somehow I know it's too late to turn back now. Tate, will you move down here and live with me?"

There it was. I looked towards the ceiling, breaking the gaze between us. As the overwhelming reality of his question hit me, I was fully aware of his eyes, searching the dark for my reaction.

I looked back to him and could see the pleading for an answer in his eyes. I took a deep breath.

"Okay."

What? Where did that come from?

I felt like my brain was disconnected from my mouth.

I need to tell him the truth, that I'm not ready to make a decision like that and we just met and,

and...

"I don't," I tried to swallow past the lump in my throat. "Eric, I will. I will move down here, but that's over five months away. I don't want to have to wait that long to see you again."

"I think I'm falling in love with you." he murmured.

I was stunned silent.

Then he was tripping over himself to take back the impromptu sentiment.

"I'm sorry. I shouldn't have said that. It's too soon, I know. I'm probably scaring you off. If you get home and decide you never want to see me again, much less move down here, it would break my heart, but I would understand."

The words were pouring from him faster than I could make sense of them. I put my hands on his face to stop him from talking and pulled myself close so that our mouths were almost touching. The talking ceased.

"I think I am falling in love with you, too."

It took only a slight movement on my part and our lips were touching. The instant he felt the pressure of my kiss, he pulled me closer, holding me in that kiss.

I kept my hands lightly on his face and before long tears from his eyes ran across my fingers. It was a strange sensation, like I was feeling my own tears falling from his eyes.

Eric pulled away first, but only slightly.

"Is this real?" he whispered.

"I hope so."

"Tate, I have something else to ask you."

"What is it?"

What else could there be?

"I know this is going to sound terribly selfish, but if there was any way you'd change your mind about waiting until June, I would do everything I could to help you get enrolled in school down here. You need to graduate, that's the main thing but – I just don't know if I can wait that long to have you with me everyday."

"Eric, I just don't think it's possible. I want to, I mean I'd love to be here sooner, but I know my mom is never going to let me leave before I graduate." My mind raced, searching for the right words. I didn't want to make him think I wasn't serious. "I just, don't know what else to say."

"Say you'll try." He pleaded. "I know it's selfish."

"It's not selfish. Well, I guess it is a little, but I understand. I want the same thing."

"So you'll try?" he asked again.

"I'll try. I promise. I will be back as soon as I can, whenever that ends up being."

"I guess that's all I can ask for."

⟜⟶

THE DINGING SOUND of my car's low fuel warning bell pulled me sharply from the reverie that I'd been lost in since Chicago. As I pulled off the interstate just south of Indianapolis to get gas, I was grateful for the timing of the distraction.

Only eight days had passed since I'd last left Kentucky. The next part of my memories would consist of telling Lilly I was leaving, telling my friends goodbye and leaving my life as I had always known it. I didn't want to think about that part.

Besides, here you are, just an hour away from starting your new life. Be positive and believe that this is what is meant to be.

Two

PATTERNS EMERGE

I DROVE OVER that enormous bridge one more time, feeling excitement wash over me. I passed again under the sign that welcomed me to Kentucky. This time it felt as if that sign had been put there just to welcome me to my new home.

I was getting nervous. It took a lot of hard decisions to make this happen but I just needed to believe that Eric wanted it as much as I did.

Not waiting for the semester to end made the school issue a little trickier. It took some persuading, some early testing and promises that there would soon be a transcript request from a school in Kentucky before I was assured my first semester credits. Eric reassured me that I would be walking across that stage in June, it would just be in a different place. I appreciated his concern although I didn't need it. For me, graduating wasn't optional.

When I pulled into his parking lot my mind went into overdrive.

What if he's not happy to see me? What if it really is too soon but he didn't want to hurt my feelings? What if he forgot I was coming today?

Breathe.

Calm down.

He is going to be perfectly happy to see you. He probably has a nice dinner waiting.

Then I saw more than one familiar vehicle.

Seriously? People over? Tonight?

I grabbed just my purse and a bag of essentials that I had thrown together to get me through until I unpacked.

I had to knock on the door twice. Finally it was flung open to reveal Eric standing there with a huge, drunk grin on his face and about a bunch of people in the apartment behind him, mostly guys. Smoke and loud heavy music seeped into the hallway and for a moment Eric just stood there grinning.

This was not the welcome I had in mind.

"Hey Baby! Come in. Where's all your stuff?" he drawled.

"Did you think I was going to carry it all in by myself in one trip?"

"Oh, right. No, I can help you. Let's go get it right now." His voice slurred and a little hard to understand.

"No. It's fine." I insisted.

"Are you sure?"

"I'm sure." I said as I moved past him, venturing into the apartment.

He followed me into the bedroom where I put my bag down and sat on the bed.

Suddenly, a thought seemed to strike him, "Hey, you're here! You're here for good, right?"

"I think so." I replied sardonically, though at the moment it was iffy.

He pulled me up into a tight hug and smashed his face into my hair, inhaling deeply then exhaling in the same fashion. When he exhaled, the space around us was filled with alcohol fumes. It had the effect of adding fuel to the fire.

"You should really rejoin your party." I said, pulling out of his grip, but skipping the sarcasm that I was now sure he wouldn't pick up on anyway.

"I don't want to. Tate – it's your party. It's a party 'cause you're here."

"Eric, I don't really feel like partying right now. You to go ahead, have fun."

"Okay, Tate, if you're sure."

He stood just looking at me, as if he was having a moment of clarity - realizing his error - but the moment was fleeting. He moved to kiss me. I turned my head at the last second, so his kiss landed on my cheek, as did the lingering smell of alcohol that he left behind.

I followed behind him and closed the door.

Some welcome. Yeah, he's so happy he couldn't even wait until I got here to celebrate.

I yanked some comfortable clothes from my bag, quickly changed, turned off the light and got in bed. Even with the laughter and loud music blaring just on the other side of the paper thin wall, I drifted off into a fitful but dreamless sleep.

The first morning in my new home found me groggy and irritated. I was startled at first by the quiet, empty apartment that I woke up to. I ventured out and saw Eric's note on the kitchen counter.

> *Good Morning Tate,*
> *I hope you slept well. I am sorry about last night, I'll make it up to you, I promise. See you at 3:30. Have a good day. Welcome home!*
>
> *Love,*
> *Eric*

I read the note over a few times and could feel my anger starting to wane. I was actually surprised he was able to make it into work.

I unloaded my car, then spent the day getting situated and cleaning.

By three o'clock my things were unpacked and I was showered and fixed up. I felt good, I felt at home.

It was nearly four o'clock by the time Eric finally walked through the door. My irritation had returned at his tardiness, but was immediately dispelled by the roses in his hand.

He laid the roses down and sat next to me, taking my hands in his. He looked at me with what I guessed was his best effort at remorse.

"I really am sorry about last night. I told Shane you were coming down and before I knew it all those guys were here, to welcome you. I knew you wouldn't want that, but it was early, so I thought they'd be gone before you got here. I'm sorry, Tate.

"I forgive you. A little." I said, looking down at the roses that now lay on the coffee table. "Are those for me?"

— 29 —

"Oh. Yeah, these are for you." He handed the bunch of flowers to me, their aroma swirled up to greet my nose, as I bent my head and inhaled deeply.

"Thank you."

"Welcome home, Tate." He repeated the sentiment from his note. "I'm so happy you're here, that we didn't have to wait for June. I couldn't stop thinking about you. So did you get all unpacked?"

"I think so. I hope I didn't invade your space too much."

"It's your space, now too, Tate. Is there anything you need?" he asked.

"No, I'm okay for now." I smiled.

"Okay, last question: would you like to go out to dinner tonight, or would you like to go meet my parents and probably some of my family?"

"Hmmm. I think, meet your parents."

"I was hoping you'd say that." I felt like a prize he won.

I liked that feeling. I could definitely get used to that feeling.

That evening I met Eric's parents; Dell and Annetta Sheppard, plus two aunts and a few cousins who had stopped by while we were there. According to Eric, that was merely a drop in the bucket. While he was an only child, Annetta was one of ten children and Dell, one of fourteen.

It was peculiar to me that both Dell and Annetta, coming from such large families, only had one child. That was until I remembered that Eric was adopted because they couldn't have kids. They cherished Eric and it showed. Their voices were full of pride. It was *almost* implied that certain other members of the family resented him for his success, although I wasn't sure what success they referred to.

The evening passed pleasantly. Everybody I met was warm and welcoming, especially Eric's parents. The southern charm and hospitality made me feel like they were genuinely happy to have me there.

Later that night, when we were discussing plans to get me enrolled in school, Eric told me about a program that would allow me to go to school half days, since I only needed four credits. He assured me I'd still get a real diploma and have a graduation ceremony.

I asked where it was and thought about the one he'd gone to: Southern High School, just a few blocks from his parents' house. It was huge. The thought of enrolling there was scary, but exciting at the same time. It would be an adventure compared to the same small town school I'd been in my whole life.

He explained there were different options as far as what campus to attend, but when I asked if Southern was a part of that program, despite the fact that it was he flat out refused me going there. He insisted instead on a school that was in the nearby suburb of Fairdale because it would be safer. Fairdale Tap.

When I asked what Tap meant, the answer dashed any hope of excitement.

It was an acronym. T-A-P-P stood for teen age pregnancy program.

Great. That's my big adventure. I get to go to school with a bunch of pregnant girls.

I almost protested, but opted to let it go. Graduating was more important than some big adventure anyway.

The next afternoon, I went to the Fairdale T.A.P.P campus as Eric suggested, but it didn't go smoothly.

"Hi, I just moved here and I need to enroll for school."

"Are you pregnant?" the portly woman behind the counter asked me. Her words came out in a thick southern twang.

"Uh, no."

"Any babies?"

"No."

"Then you can't register for school here." She said flatly.

During the three and a half years I attended Anders Park High School there were only three girls who'd gotten pregnant. I realized that being from a small town left me a bit sheltered, but it was hard to imagine needing a whole school just for pregnant teenagers.

"I was told there was a program through Jefferson County that I could attend here. I just moved here and I only need a few credits."

"There is. Have you registered yet?"

"No." I tried to squash the irritation that was edging into my voice. "I mean, that's what I am trying to do now."

"No Honey, look. First you need to register downtown at Central High School. Then you can come here to attend class." She looked at her watch "But I doubt you'll make it anymore today. The office there closes at five o'clock."

I looked down at my own wrist: four thirty-five. I was irritated that I'd have to wait another day.

For having gone through this program, Eric sure did have his facts mixed up.

"Okay, thank you then."

"When you come back with your registration, you don't bring it in here. There are two classrooms set up for the program you're looking for. You can give it directly to the teacher in your classroom.

"Could you tell me where those classrooms are?"

"Sure. Just use the side parking lot and entrance." She gestured behind her "The first two classrooms are where you will need to be, either one is fine."

"Thanks."

"Good luck."

"CAN YOU GO with me to register? I wouldn't have the slightest idea where to go" I asked Eric when I arrived home, disappointed at my lack of results.

I felt comfortable enough navigating the back roads and side streets of the Louisville suburbs at Eric's direction, but I didn't want to brave a trip downtown by myself.

"Sure Tate, I can go, or maybe Mom can go with you tomorrow if you don't want to wait until I get home." She'll know where you need to go. She goes downtown to doctor appointments and stuff. Central is right off I-65. It's pretty easy to get to, she won't mind."

He was right, Annetta didn't mind and I was glad to have her with me. Central High School was easy to find, but it in was a very intimidating neighborhood; being alone in this area didn't seem like a good idea at any time. Buildings and houses with boarded up windows and pawn shops littered the block surrounding the large ominous school. I was relieved we got there late enough that school would no longer be in session for the day.

We found our way to the office. The woman behind the desk at this school was much older than the one I'd seen at the school in Fairdale the day before. She was wrinkled and wore a grimace that I could only assume was a permanent. She was not friendly at all. She was, however, very helpful, answering all my questions with expertise.

She explained that each weekday there were three different sessions, two during the day and one during the evening. I would work on the credits I needed, one half credit at a time, until I completed all eight. In order to remain enrolled I had to attend at least one session, at least four days per week, but there was no maximum. Each classroom had a teacher assigned for general help, but I would be working independently, which suited me fine.

She prepared my paperwork according to my word, but informed me I would have to wait for confirmation of my enrollment to come in the mail because I had not brought my transcripts with me from my last school. This could take up to two weeks, so I may have to wait until February to actually start.

When I asked about a graduation ceremony, she confirmed that there would be a graduation ceremony at the Fair and Expo Center in June and that as long as I had my credits finished by May thirtieth, I would be eligible to participate, but was not obligated to.

My mom just wanted to see me graduate; I would definitely be participating.

I walked out of that building feeling more positive than I had since I'd arrived. I hadn't given much thought to the independent lifestyle I was leaving behind in Wisconsin until I suddenly found myself at the mercy of other people in order to accomplish the simplest errand. Even with Annetta's guidance, I felt a sense of achievement.

That night Eric seemed genuinely happy that I managed to register for school, though he teased me, calling me 'Little Fish' when I told him how creepy it was.

It wasn't the first time he'd called me Little Fish, so I asked him what he meant by the moniker.

"You're just a little fish in a big ocean now, Tate. You're not in your little pond anymore."

I wasn't sure if he intended to be condescending, or if it honestly just came out that way.

My next goal was a job. Although Eric had insisted I take some time off to relax and concentrate on school, I'd already been scoping out places to apply. I didn't see how three hours of class a day would keep me occupied. Nor did I expect to find it relaxing to have that much down time, boring was more like it.

I noticed a fitness center in one of the strip malls close to Dell and Annetta's house. However, when I went to apply, I figured out right away that it was very different than the one I'd left behind.

It was huge and very businesslike. I was probably out of my league, but I asked about a job anyway. I filled out an application and mentioned to the manager that I just left a job at a fitness center. What ensued was a discussion that at first I thought had potential as a legitimate job offer, but quickly revealed itself as a generic telemarketing job disguised as sales.

"You're not working there." Was Eric's response when I told him about the fitness center.

"What?" I asked incredulously. "What do you mean?"

"What does it sound like I mean? That is not a good place for you to work; besides, I told you that you don't have to work right now, just focus on school."

"I want to work. I was going to school full time and working and doing just fine, remember? I don't think it's going to be a problem to go three hours a day and hold a job."

"Well why don't you just go to more sessions to fill your time? Then you can finish sooner and get a full time job."

That made sense, but it still really bugged me that he thought it was appropriate to tell me where I could or could not work, so I pushed it.

"What about money? I didn't have *that* much money when I came. I can't just live off you forever."

"Tate, it won't be forever. I just *said*: finish school early and *then* you can work full time. That's only a few months away. And don't worry; I'll let you know when I don't want you *living off me*." His tone was petulant and condescending.

I knew I shouldn't push because in reality, there was no legitimate job offer, none that I wanted to take anyway, but I let him do the same thing when he decided what school I would attend.

I'll have to make a stand soon, or he'll think he can control my whole life.

I WAS THRILLED, when on Monday of the next week; my enrollment confirmation came in the mail. I was happy just to be getting out of that apartment. It was starting to feel stifling. I only knew how to get to a few places, I didn't have money to go shopping and Eric had discouraged me from wandering aimlessly around. He said it made me look like I was lost and therefore a target for violence.

My new school ended up suiting me just fine. When I arrived back at Fairdale T.A.P.P. for my first day of class, I used the side parking lot and entrance like I'd been told by the portly office lady, and I found the classrooms without difficulty. I surveyed the two closed doors – and for no particular reason, picked the one on the right.

I quietly pulled open the door and was pleasantly surprised to find a bright room with only a few people, none of which looked like the juvenile delinquents I was expecting. I chose the eleven o'clock to two o'clock session to attend on my first day, hoping it would be the least populated.

I think I am going to like this.

I made my way to where the teacher sat and handed her the enrollment confirmation I'd gotten in the mail and another document containing the courses I needed to take. The woman at Central High School gave it to me with instructions to hand in.

Mrs. Bauer – my new teacher – was welcoming and gracious. She was a thin woman with short brown hair and compassionate eyes. I liked her immediately.

She looked over my papers, then bent to pull something from the file drawer of her desk. She came back up with a file folder. At the top of which, she wrote my name.

As she opened up the folder, she asked if I was familiar with how the class worked. I expressed that I was fairly sure the woman at Central had explained it well enough. She then explained my assignment.

It was math – my least favorite. It was no coincidence that as a senior, I should have been done with required math credits, but after doing miserably in Algebra as a freshman, then skipping a math elective altogether during my sophomore year, I was stuck doing it now.

"Okay Tatum."

"Tate." I corrected her. "Please just call me Tate."

"Oh, okay Tate" she said smiling warmly. "So you're just going to do the assignments in this work book, in order. This is one half credit, when you finish it, you will be given the second half credit workbook to complete." She looked back at one of the sheets I gave to her before continuing "It looks like you have four credits to complete, so you'll do eight workbooks, four final tests and a series of writing assignments. If you have questions, feel free to come up by me and get help, okay?" Her voice was hushed with a quiet enthusiasm I suspected she showed all her students.

She didn't sound as southern as most people here did. Maybe she was a transplant, like me. Maybe that's why I liked her right away, kindred spirits or something.

"Okay, thank you."

I took a seat in the middle of the end aisle, furthest from the door and closest to the window. The bright sunlight that poured in was comforting. A day this early in the year would likely be gloomy and cold in Wisconsin. That's one thing I would never miss.

I opened up the workbook and flipped through some of the pages. It looked easy enough. I flipped back to the first page and took a pencil out of my bag. Once I got going, I found the basic problems gave me no trouble and I breezed through it.

By the end of the three hour session I had twelve finished assignments. The half credit course only consisted of the fifty assignments in the whole book. At this rate, I figured I'd be done with this one in less than a week.

⟜⟶

AFTER THAT DAY, routine began to settle in and we fell into the rhythm of our new life. Eric went to work and I went to school. Most of our evenings were quiet. As for the weekends, there were still parties, but they were decreasing in frequency and even better, size. I didn't mind having two or three people over. Shane and Andy were the regulars. I especially didn't mind Andy; he was the most laid back person I'd ever met,

I spent a lot of time at school. I was determined to finish earlier than I would have in Wisconsin so I went at least one session each day, most days two. The work came easily without the distractions of normal high school and my grades showed improvement, too. I had never thought of graduating as a goal, it was just the inevitable reward for finally being done with school. But now, without a job and friends and a social life, it seemed to be one of the only things I had to do.

Eric came home at the same time each day: 3:30. Most days I tried to be sure that the apartment was neat and I was ready to head out in case he wanted to go visit someone or run errands. He was generally in a good mood, happy to see me and happy to have the work day done.

We would often stop by his parents' and have dinner, either some traditional southern fare that Annetta had prepared or we would pick up carry out for the four of us, with Dell generously footing the bill. We didn't keep much food in the apartment, so it was handy to be so close to them for dinner.

Actually the food we did have usually came from Annetta too. When she went grocery shopping, she always seemed to be picking things up for us. Either because the items were on sale or she wanted us to try something that caught her eye. I suspected she had always done Eric's shopping and was simply adding the finer points for my benefit, so I wouldn't think he was over indulged.

What I did find overindulgent was that she did our laundry. I noticed early on that there was no laundry soap to be found in my new abode, but before I remembered to ask Eric about it, Annetta instructed me to get our dirty clothes together and bring them over the next time that we came by. I'd been doing my own laundry since I was twelve, so to have someone else doing it felt weird.

AFTER SEVERAL WEEKS passed, I started to get restless again about not working. Eric gave me money a few times, thankfully he didn't make me ask. In turn I tried to spend as little as possible. It wasn't hard because there really wasn't much I needed to spend on, gas money, a little extra for essentials, and maybe to go tanning.

I really didn't even know what to look for in a job. Since my experience was limited to the fitness center and babysitting, I wasn't sure what I wanted to do. I figured any customer service job would do, but I wanted to find something that I liked. My thoughts kept coming back to the gym here, the one Eric said no to. I started to think maybe the telemarketing job could be a foot in the door. Hopefully I could eventually move on to a position that I would like better. Then there was the part of me that wanted to work there just because Eric had told me not to, a way of showing him that I'm in charge of my own life.

We were lying in bed in our usual position - his arms wrapped around me from behind - when I revisited the topic of a job at the fitness center. I explained to Eric that I just wanted to work. I needed to work, and that was a place that was close enough and I was pretty sure I'd get hired there.

Again, he flat out refused.

"Eric, I can't believe you're being like this. What does it matter to you if I work there?"

"I already told you I don't want you working at that fitness center. You're not going to like it there. They'll just take advantage of you, I know the guy who runs it." His tone told me he was tiring of this conversation, but I pressed on anyway.

"How do you know him?" It seemed unlikely to me that he knew him at all. If he did, why didn't he mention it before?

"We went to school together." He replied matter-of-factly.

"Okay, I still don't know what that has to do with me working there. You don't like the manager, so I can't work there? That's stupid. What do you think is going to happen to me?" I pushed.

I was past the point of resentment over his assumption. What I had originally seen as concern and protection was starting to look a lot like he expected compliance and it irritated me.

"I said no!" He snapped. "We don't need to talk about it any more!"

"Eric, do you honestly think I am going to let you tell me where to work? What are you my dad now?"

All at once his hands were on me, and my head was pinned to the pillow. One hand had fingers snaked through my hair, gripping me at the scalp, the other was under my jaw, pulling my head up and back towards him, as if he contemplated snapping my neck. With his warm body still pressed up against mine, he held me tightly in the awkward pose while he hissed a sharp warning, his mouth mere inches from my ear.

"*You shut your fucking mouth right now.* No I am not your dad. I'll tell you right now, I would never put up with the kind of disrespect you showed your dad." He pulled harder and harder on my hair and my neck. I wanted to scream for him to stop, but I didn't move. "Do NOT question me!" With his final words, the harsh whisper morphed into an angry bellow.

At that instant, his southern drawl had a sickening quality. I felt nauseous. Thoughts fired through my head as I struggled to grip reality.

Almost instinctually, I held perfectly still and quiet for the duration of his aggression, but the instant he let go of me, I scrambled out of bed. I just wanted to get as far away from him as I could. I started towards to door, but stopped short, feeling paralyzed. Adrenaline, humiliation and pain now coursing through my body, I didn't know what to do so I just stood there, trembling. Suddenly I felt naked, wearing just a t-shirt and underwear. Then the tears came, silent and unstoppable, they flooded my eyes and poured down over my cheeks.

The next moment Eric was out of bed and standing in front of me, sputtering apologies that sounded like he thought what he'd done was an accident.

"Oh my God, Tate. I am so sorry. I didn't mean to." He tried to put his arms around me as he spoke.

"GET away from me." I shrieked at him, ducking out of his reach. "Don't touch me."

My words came out like venom.

"I'm sorry, I'm so sorry. I know, I've probably ruined everything now." He stammered. I noticed he said it more to himself than to me.

He continued to mumble requests for forgiveness as I sidestepped him and darted into the bathroom, locking the door behind me. I leaned my back against the door and let my body slide down until I landed on the cold tile floor. My neck and head were starting to throb. While I was still struggling to make sense of what just happened, I felt a surge of anger rise up inside me, burning like stomach acid. It was the same type of anger I felt at Carl every time I'd seen him put his hands on Lilly.

In the days of my childhood, when they went out all the time, Lilly and Carl routinely ended up at home, drunk, arguing so bad that it turned physical. For the first five years or so of my life, I bore witness to a lot of it. Back then my stepbrothers served as babysitters. I often thought that was the reason they started having me stay with outside sitters.

A wave of new tears came, again without restraint when the realization hit me: it was the same anger because it was the same circumstance. The only difference now was that I was the target.

This isn't possible. I can't be in this situation. I can not repeat her history.

For as long as I could remember, I wanted my life to be the opposite of Lilly's. As much love as I felt for her, I knew I wanted so much more out of life than she had ever strove for.

I knew the statistics, that as a child raised in an abusive household, I was much more likely to seek out an abusive partner, unintentionally of course.

I always reasoned that, if that happened to me, I'd just leave.

It was an ugly family secret and I didn't want it anymore. Once I was old enough to be left without a sitter when they went out, things got even worse. I started involving myself in their drunken fights. I would intentionally get his attention off of her and onto me. At least I was sober and could protect myself - not that she didn't put up a good fight. They engaged in their clashes mutually, with alcohol always serving as the catalyst. Thankfully, the physical altercations stopped when she quit drinking – nearly six years ago – but the damage was already done.

Eric startled me when he knocked on the door. I was still leaning on it, so his knuckles rapping on the wood sent a jolt through my body.

"Tate, can I come in? I'm so sorry."

"NO." I snapped. I could still hear him breathing on the other side of the door.

"Eric, please just leave me alone."

I waited for him to plead further, but only silence followed. My thoughts turned back to what had just happened.

Eventually the trembling stopped and then the tears followed suit. When my senses calmed, that's when I started to rationalize.

This isn't Lilly and Carl. Eric lost his temper because you pushed him too hard, Tate. He's not one of the small town boys from Wisconsin; he is a grown man, and a southern man at that. Things are different here.

Then he was back at the door. "Tate, please. I'm sorry."

He really did sound sorry.

He continued talking to me through the door "I'm going to run down to the store, so you can come out, I'll give you some time alone. I will be back in a little while." He paused, maybe waiting for a response from me. When that didn't come he continued, "I'd like it if we could talk then."

I stood up and flung open the door to face him. Judging by the surprise look on his face, this time I startled him.

His face fell into a remorseful pout. His eyes shimmered with tears, making them look like little blue-green pools. He wore only jeans, having not yet put a shirt on. His bare skin drew my eyes and I found all at once, instead of being angry, I was lost in the beauty of the man standing in front of me. I knew right then I wouldn't walk away from him, not for this. It happened and now it's over.

While I was busy convincing myself to let go, I knew I wasn't ready to let Eric off the hook. I had to make sure he understood that while I learned a lesson about pushing him, I needed to know that this wasn't going to be a regular thing.

"I don't really have anything to say to you Eric." I once again side-stepped past him, this time heading back to the bedroom.

"Tate, I am sorry."

I spun around to face him before chastising him.

"I get that you're *sorry*, Eric, but sorry doesn't fix it. Don't think that this is okay. I get that I pushed you too hard, but just so you get that I don't need you to run my life."

"Tate."

"I am going to bed. I don't want to talk anymore tonight." I stormed into the bedroom, closing the door on my way in, which left him standing there, alone on the other side.

WHEN I WOKE up in the morning, all at once it hit me: a throbbing headache and a sickness in the pit of my stomach, like a hangover. But it wasn't a hangover, it was the moment that last night's incident came flooding back to me, the way that bad things do.

It didn't seem to fit that I could hear the cheerful sounds of breakfast being cooked in the next room. Eric shouldn't be here, he should be at work.

I laid there wallowing in the pain and assessing what I was going to find beyond the bedroom door. Logic would say he's trying to be nice to me. That would explain why he was home and cooking breakfast. But I didn't want his kindness. I wanted to undo what was done. I wanted to go back to before the hands I loved were used to hurt me. Since that couldn't happen, I didn't want to face him right now. I felt as humiliated as I did hurt.

I didn't really even want to get up. The more I thought about it, the more I contemplated simply staying in bed. I rolled over to look at the alarm clock next to Eric's side of the bed. It hurt a lot to move. The clock said eight-thirty, and that seemed too early to get out of bed on a normal day. My decision was made. I was staying in bed, possibly all day.

By nine o'clock the breakfast noises had stopped.

I was starting to get hungry. Maybe I could face him, just long enough to eat breakfast. I should probably take some ibuprofen, too. I laid there for a while thinking about the things I wanted to do on my venture out of the bedroom.

Eric's knock on the door snapped me from my mental planning. I didn't answer his knock; instead, on impulse I rolled over with my face away from the door and pretended to be asleep. He knocked one more time and pushed open the door what sounded like only a few inches, as he softly called my name.

I laid still.

He pulled the door back closed. The next sounds I heard were the jingling of keys him leaving the apartment. I laid there a while longer to be sure he was gone, then I got up.

I opened the door and scanned the quiet apartment. Eric left a note on the counter. It was next to several plates of food: eggs, bacon, biscuits and white gravy. I flipped the note over without reading it.

After breakfast I took some ibuprofen and set to the rest of my tasks, a return to the bedroom to get some clean clothes, followed by a few minutes in the bathroom. I emerged, teeth brushed, cleaned up and feeling a little better, though I was sick to my stomach again. Seeing the clump of hair I pulled out with my brush was very disturbing.

I walked around the apartment picking up things to keep me occupied: a pen, my journal, which I kept stashed in my closet, and the cordless phone. Luckily Eric still had a landline. I cancelled service to my cell shortly after moving here, knowing that was another regular expense I'd have to put on hold until I got a job.

When I had everything I wanted in the bedroom, I remembered Eric's note.

I went back to the kitchen to retrieve it, but instead of reading it right away, I took it back to the bedroom with me. I closed the door on my way into the bedroom and wondered how long I could hide in there.

It was nice not to have to call school and lie about being sick, but I couldn't skip two days in row. I'd probably need a doctor's note or something if I did. If I could just stay in here today, that might be enough.

I sat down right in the middle of the big bed, and made myself as comfortable as possible. The medicine seemed to be helping the headache, but the ache every time I moved my neck was still there. I grabbed Eric's note and flipped it over to read the words.

> *Tate,*
>
> *I am so very sorry about last night, I don't know what happened. I just love you so much, the thought of someone taking you from me makes me crazy. I am going to give you space today, I went to Mom and Dad's. Call me when you want me to come home. I hope you feel better. I'm sorry.*
>
> *Love,*
> *Eric*
>
> *p.s. I hope you enjoy breakfast.*

I flipped the paper back over without rereading it. His lame justification only irritated me more. What a jerk.

Won't be home until I call? Perfect, I'll call about ten o'clock tonight.

Then another thought popped in my head:

If he's really gone all day, I could be back in Wisconsin before he even realizes I left.

I let my imagination run away for a while, thinking of what home would be like when I got there. Before long, reality pulled me back.

Home would be no different now than when I'd left it two months ago. It would still be cold, I'd still fight with Carl and as far as school - I'd be worse off than when I left. There was no way around it, I wasn't going anywhere.

I reminded myself I was just angry. I really didn't want to leave Eric, but in terms of a lesson learned, if I was gone by the time he came home, it would be one he'd remember.

I shoved my journal under the pillow and laid back. I pulled the covers up to my chin, pushing the phone and Eric's note aside. It was easy to drift off, the room was warm and comfortable and I was emotionally exhausted.

I woke up several hours later, again with the headache, but thankfully this time minus the queasy stomach. I turned to look at the clock, one fourteen.

I got out bed and stood at the door listening for signs of life in the apartment. After a few minutes, I slowly opened the door and peeked out to find I was still alone. A trip to the bathroom and a few more pills for the pain and I was back to the bedroom.

When I got back in bed, I pulled my journal out from under my pillow. I opened it and dated the top of the page, but closed it again without writing a single word. Putting down on paper what had happened felt like a blaring acknowledgement, like validating the situation with written words, a permanent record of my humiliation. I shoved the journal back under my pillow and grabbed the phone instead.

I knew who I had to call. Lana.

As I dialed her number, I considered how much small talk I'd have to make before I could start fishing for information. I didn't want to give her any indication of trouble. I had a feeling every word might be repeated to Eric.

Lana answered after just one ring "Hello?"

"Hi, it's me."

"Hi Tate." She sounded surprised. We hadn't talked since she broke up with Shane.

Just as I'd predicted, she found an excuse not to go through with moving to Kentucky, but I don't think anyone expected to have it end so badly. Shane went back to Wisconsin one more time at her request and I guess they got into a huge fight. Shane almost went to jail up there.

"How are you?" I asked.

"Um, okay. We're okay."

"Who's we? You and Alex?"

"Yeah, just me and Alex."

There was something off in her voice, like she wasn't sure which side I was on, hers or Shane's. I was inevitably on hers, but being in such close proximity to Shane so often left me no other choice than to let it go as none of my business.

"Lana, it sucks that things didn't work out for you and Shane, huh? It would have been nice for you to be down here, too. He told us his version of what happened, but I am sure he was a lot bigger jerk than he made himself out to be."

That seemed to be what she was waiting for. The floodgates opened and she told me what felt like the entire recount of her day to day life since I'd last seen her, including the blow up between her and Shane.

She asked if there was any interesting gossip going on in the family. I knew it bothered her that I was now closer to her family than she was. I made it a point to tread lightly. I filled her in on some meaningless details that I had heard while at Dell and Annetta's. It all felt meaningless to me anyway, seeing as I didn't know half the people they were talking about.

"Hey Lana, tell me more about Eric." I coaxed.

"What do you want me to tell you? You live with him." She snorted.

"I know, I just, well what was he like, you know, before me? I've heard his ex-girlfriend Shayla mentioned, did you know her?"

"Shayla? Yeah, I met her a few times. Oh, Dell and Annetta *loved* Shayla. That was back when Eric lived at home. They practically had her living with them, they did a lot for her, but then when Eric got in trouble during high school, she turned on him." She said in perfect hushed gossip tone.

"She turned on him, like to the cops?" I asked, feigning surprise. I'd heard bits and pieces of that story already.

"Yeah. Eric could have gotten time if it weren't for Dell and Annetta bailing him out. That is about all I know about her, but his last girlfriend was my cousin Tara, you know Charlotte's daughter?"

"You set him up with your cousin?" This time, my surprise was genuine and the irony was almost too much to take.

"Yeah, but don't say it like that Tate. I was down there visiting and she came with me to visit Eric. The next thing you know..." she let her voice trail off.

I was almost afraid to ask any more questions. I'd already learned more than I wanted to know.

"So what happened with them?"

"Tara lived there with him for a while, but things didn't work out."

"She lived here?" I asked incredulously.

"Yep, she lived there. But all of the sudden, she moved back in with her mom and told everyone this big story that she found out she was pregnant and when she told Eric, he beat her up and punched her in the stomach to make her lose the baby. She did spend the night in the hospital, it might have really been a miscarriage, but I'm sure she made up the part about Eric, though. There's no way he'd do that."

I was afraid there was.

She continued "I think Eric probably just got sick of Tara and kicked her out. She was probably embarrassed to get dumped so she told that big story."

"Where is she now?" I was doing my best to steady my voice. I felt deflated, like I had no air, but I didn't want to tip Lana off at this point and make her think of this as anything more than harmless gossip.

Only Lana could think this wouldn't have been important to tell me *before* I moved here.

"She lives not too far from you guys. She's got a different boyfriend now. She lives with him and their baby girl."

"Oh, I see."

"Sorry, I shouldn't be gossiping about Eric to you."

"Oh no, it's fine. I am sure you're right about her making that story up."

I really wasn't sure of anything at that moment.

"Does it bug you to know that she lived there before you?"

I got the distinct impression she *wanted* it to bother me.

"No, not really." I lied. "We all have a past you know? Some people's past is just more colorful than others." I was sure she'd understand the tone I used in response.

"Yeah, I guess." She said casually, as if she had tired of the topic.

I took that as my cue to get off the phone.

We both dumped the sarcasm and shared a genuine moment as we said goodbye. I asked her to give Alex a big hug for me and tell him that I miss him. I asked that she put him on the phone, but he was taking a nap, so we agreed, next time.

I thought about calling Jennie, but decided against it. She would hear that something was off. From her, I wouldn't be able to hide anything.

I lay in that big bed for a long time thinking about what I'd learned today.

The same questions kept going through my head, like a carousel: Had Tara really been pregnant? If it was really a miscarriage, did he cause it?

As dusk settled into the apartment, it made my mood even more melancholy. I went to the living room to watch TV.

Despite not having called him, just as I figured he would, Eric was home around six thirty.

He walked over and stood next to the couch, out of the way of the TV. He spoke in a tone that was low and soft, like the edges were wore off his words.

"Can I sit down by you?"

"Sit down. I don't care."

He sat down as close as he could without touching me. Neither of us moved for what felt like a long time. We both were looking at the TV, but I didn't think he was watching it any more than I was.

My mind was much more occupied by the tension in the air. I wanted to forgive him, because that seemed the shortest route back to good, but it felt like a betrayal of my own dignity if I let it go so easily.

"Tate, can I talk to you?" he asked gingerly, as he reached his hand over and gently laid it on my ankle, obviously testing the waters.

"Eric, what could you possibly have to say that you haven't said already?"

"I'm sorry." He pled in the same fashion he'd done over and over since it happened. "What can I do to make it up to you?"

His pleading to me turned to chastising himself. "I feel like all I've done since you got here is screw up."

"That's not true, Eric."

Unbelievably, I felt a little sorry for him.

He's supposed to be the sorry one.

He used the moment to his advantage, "Will you forgive me?"

"I can forgive you as long as you understand that this isn't okay. Some things are never okay."

"I know Tate. All I can say is I'm sorry."

I noticed he didn't say it wouldn't happen again.

Then again, I didn't ask him to.

⌒⟶

I THOUGHT A lot about that day. That 24 hour period that made me question all the decisions I made leading up to moving here. I couldn't help but wonder if, in the long run, I'd only made my problems worse.

It started to bug me that another girl had lived in our apartment. Surprisingly, within a week of my first insinuation that I wasn't the only woman to have lived there with him, Eric suggested we move.

I was thrilled. I felt like that might be exactly what we needed: a fresh start in our own place.

We decided to move right away so we'd be settled in by the time I graduated and we had company consisting of Lilly, her friend Sue and hopefully Jennie. We spent three nights looking at apartments and on the third night, we pulled into Willow Creek Apartment complex. Eric pointed out that it was where his cousin Melinda lived. I wasn't thrilled with the idea of living so close to her. There was just something about her, he one time I met her, she seemed treacherous. Of course that was the complex that Eric ended up choosing.

The new apartment literally looked like a replica of the old one. Same shape, same layout. It had the same white walls, beige carpet and generic fixtures. It did have two differences and not positive ones – it was on the front side of the building instead of the back, so the patio doors faced the parking lot, and it was smaller.

I did learn to love it pretty quickly though, despite the flaws. It was a nice enough apartment and it ended up being the best deal for the money, not to mention it was about two minutes from Eric's job. Ultimately, I loved it because it was ours.

Another week went by and we were moved out of the old place into the new one and were, for the most part, unpacked and settled. Eric called a bunch of buddies, and they made short work of the task. Once we got there, it was nice. For a while, we both rode the high provided by the new surroundings. Things were good again.

MOVING INTO THE new apartment solidified my position as woman of the house and brought a new sense of adulthood, like we weren't just playing house anymore. It also brought with it new responsibilities and I knew it.

We still hadn't had sex. I sensed that time was running out on Eric's patient demeanor about it. His normal displays of affection were becoming more insistent. I decided I wanted to be the one to initiate our first time. I was afraid that if I waited for him, he'd be encouraged to make a habit of taking what he wanted.

As soon as I made the decision, I was filled with nervous anticipation. I was ready to be more intimate with him; I had been for a while. I had been so afraid that things would change between us, but now, after the positive change of a new apartment, I felt like change could be a good thing for us.

That Friday, I attended only the morning session of school. I wanted time to do all the things girls do when they want to feel their best. I timed it perfectly so just as Eric got home, I was showered, had my hair and makeup done, and was dressed in my most flattering jeans and a tight little t-shirt that I knew he liked.

I figured since he got paid he'd be up for going somewhere after work – so I sweet-talked him into taking me to dinner and a new scary movie that was playing. My love of scary movies was a sentiment I got from Lilly.

For dinner, we agreed on a popular local restaurant, the kind with nostalgic memorabilia everywhere and too many waiters and waitresses bustling around. It was crowded and noisy, but the food was good and the atmosphere was light.

The lobby of the movie theater afforded that same ambiance: crowded but fun. It seemed most of the people were there to see the newest action flick though, so as we made our way to the theater where the scary movie was playing, the excited chatter of the lobby faded to hushed suspense. We chose our seats near the top and settled in.

I tried to focus on the movie, but I was so tuned in on what the next part of the evening would hold, I couldn't pay attention to what was happening on the screen. Each time Eric stroked my hand with his fingers, or accidentally bumped my arm with his, it felt like a little jolt of electricity shot through me. By the second hour of the movie I was so lost that the ending made little sense.

I grabbed Eric's hand as we walked through the parking lot towards his car. At first he hesitated - he didn't like public displays of affection — but I looked up at him with my best puppy dog eyes, and he smiled and intertwined his fingers through mine. It was moments like this that made me love him.

Do I love him? Really love him?

Yes, I believe I do.

Although we'd both been saying it since before I'd moved here, it occurred to me that what started out as infatuation and a desire to get out of my parents' house had grown into real love, just like I thought it would. I was certain that he loved me, too. He may show his love in different ways, but I rationalized that he showed it the best way he knew how. Suddenly I felt relaxed about what I planned to do.

Once we were seated in the car, I looked over at him.

He was cute. Those eyes never failed to entice me.

"I love you." I whispered.

He looked over at me, surprised at first, before a mischievous grin crossed his face.

"I love you, too."

When we got into bed that night, he knew. I didn't have to tell him that I was ready. Maybe he read the signs I'd no doubt given or maybe he simply sensed it, but either way he knew.

As soon as I lay down, he wrapped his arm around my waist and pulled me closer to him. In one swift movement I was moved from the edge of the bed to the middle, so our nearly naked bodies were touching. He kissed me tenderly as his hands roamed, gently pulling off the rest of our clothes, first his, then mine. His kisses became more urgent as his hands continued to move over me, grazing my skin in the most tender of places. I let myself relax completely as we began to make love and all my worries were gone.

Then it was over.

"I'm sorry Tate."

We were cuddled together under the covers, still naked, in the middle of the big bed. Our first time ended just as it began.

He already apologized twice for his untimely peak. I tried to reassure him, but I really didn't know what to say. I didn't want to sound cliché and tell him that I hear a lot of guys have that problem. What guys would I know that had that problem? I had only been with one guy and he certainly didn't have that problem.

"Eric, it's okay. Please don't apologize any more."

"I don't know why it happened so fast. I guess because it's been so long and I really wanted you."

"Well, I guess we'll just have to give it another try, soon." I teased, trying to lighten his mood. It worked for a little while. He groaned as he pushed his face into my neck, kissing me and inhaling at the same time. He still seemed so full of passion, but he assured me that for him to perform again the same night wasn't possible.

As we lay there, ultimately his mood deteriorated, which led him to turn the situation around on me. Eventually, he made his disappointing performance into something that was my fault.

"If you wouldn't have made me wait so long…"

The next morning, he was sullen and avoided me as much as possible. I didn't push. I didn't know what to say to him anyway. I didn't think it was really that big of a deal, but when I tried to consider it from a guy's point of view, I decided my best course of action would be to leave him alone.

There was a tiny bit of me that felt like this was a fair revenge for when he grabbed me by my hair. It was good for him to experience a little humiliation, too.

Even so, I hoped his inept timing wasn't going to be a pattern.

Three

LESSONS LEARNED

THE WEATHER GREW warm and stayed that way much earlier in Kentucky than I'd ever experienced. By the beginning of April it was consistently in the upper sixties. There were cool, rainy days and the nights were still cool, but most days were pleasant and mild. Most people were wearing sweatshirts and jackets, while I was ready to put on shorts.

Spring brought a burst of color to Louisville. In Wisconsin, spring seemed to come at more of a gradual pace. It seemed here in the warmer temperatures and humid air everything bloomed at once. A type of tree I'd never seen before - Eric called them dogwoods - dotted most neighborhoods. They were round, mid size trees, with pink, purple or white flowers. People often planted them in groups and rows, giving the impression of candy-land houses. Even within Willow Creek, things started to come to life. There were neatly manicured courtyards spring-ing to life, and the pool, which was visible from our patio, was cleaned and filled, and now sparkled in the sunlight. It really was a nice place to live.

Outside wasn't the only thing getting a new look, while nature did her job out there, we made some improvements to the inside of the apartment, too. Eric seemed to genuinely want the apartment to look nice when my mom came down.

At first I was touched by his motivation, but as time went on it became clear he was simply using the occasion. His parents graciously offered to help us financially with new furniture, seeing as we were having company.

I realized Eric would be counting on that.

We updated the apartment with new curtains, a new lamp and a rather plain looking black couch and loveseat. I didn't care for the style much, but I soon discovered that Eric fancied himself as a decorator, so I didn't have much say in the matter

Ironically, decorating was really one of the things I'd been looking forward to the most about the new place; it never occurred to me that he would *want* to do it. I learned quickly though, it wasn't worth it to keep making suggestions, only to have them shot down or ignored altogether.

I was disappointed, but nonetheless, by the time it was done it was the nicest place *I'd* ever lived in, so I'd do best not to complain.

Adding to the energy of spring in Louisville was the preparation for the Kentucky Derby and the Derby Festival. Each year, the first Saturday in May was reserved for what is commonly referred to as 'the fastest two minutes in sports'. During the two weeks leading up to that day, the city explodes in celebration.

The topic of horse racing was never something I'd given thought to so I knew nothing about what was going to take place. It didn't take long to learn though, since the local news featured Derby stories daily. They detailed all the preparation that went into the events, the celebrities that were rumored to attend, and the history of Churchill Downs and horse racing in Louisville, which I learned went all the way back to 1783. The whole thing seemed very glamorous with its parties, steeped in tradition and attended by the world's rich and famous.

Women would wear large, overly embellished hats, the larger, the better, and they'd pair them with colorful, stylish spring dresses. Everyone supposedly sat around drinking mint juleps, the event's signature drink made with whiskey and sprigs of mint.

In my mind, the whole thing seemed right up with there with rugby and polo, except for the wild and chaotic flip side there must be to all that celebration. I imagined when thousands and thousands of people overindulge in drinking and gambling together, there'd end up being more revelry than glamour.

Nevertheless, the whole thing added a buzz to the air. While I thought it might be fun to experience some of the glamour, I knew that wasn't likely to happen, so I made myself content with watching the details on TV.

Then I heard three words that changed my mind: Thunder over Louisville.

It was the opening ceremony, the kickoff to the whole Derby celebration. The news reported it as the largest annual fireworks display in North America.

Apparently, they load barges with fireworks and close off two of the bridges spanning the Ohio River, rigging fireworks on the bridges to look like waterfalls. The news said that half a million people crowd the banks and boardwalks on either side of the river to see it. The clips they showed from the previous year made up my mind. It looked amazing.

I *had* to see it in person.

The thought briefly crossed my mind that Eric may not want to go, but he was always pointing out that I led such a sheltered life before I met him. Maybe he'd look forward to showing his 'little fish' some of what the big world had to offer.

I was wrong.

He informed me that no way was he going and neither was I.

When I asked why, his reason was that there were too many people and he made it a point not to get involved in Derby festivals, there was always too much trouble. He told me the only Derby partying we'd be doing was at a party at his uncle's house across the river in Indiana.

"When do we get to do something that I want to do, Eric? It's like I am just an accessory to your life. When is it my turn to have some fun?"

"What do you want to do?" his pleasant tone was laden with insincerity.

"I *want* to go to Thunder over Louisville. It's this Saturday."

"No."

"Why NOT?" I demanded.

"TATE. I already told you, there are too many people and too much trouble." He paused, his voice turning icy. "What, do you *want* me to go to jail?"

"What? What would Thunder over Louisville have to do with you going to jail and what would make you think I'd *want* that?"

Eric looked at me with malice in his eyes, his grin now almost ridiculing me.

"You don't seem to get it, Tate. We are not equal, we are NOT the same. You don't get what I get, you're just a woman. Worse than that, you're still a kid. You don't understand half the shit you say, so before you let your mouth get you in trouble again, try shutting it."

I turned and walked away. I couldn't fight the flood of angry tears and I didn't want him to see me cry.

This was starting to get ridiculous, I couldn't keep letting him treat me this way, it was humiliating, but what could I say? If I read between the lines correctly he just warned me to keep my mouth shut or he'd hurt me again.

I should just get out of here.

I could go. I just started my last half credit, if I bust my butt I could be done in week. Thanks to my new found dedication to school I breezed through all the courses so far.

I didn't have to stick around for the ceremony. What would it matter anyway? I don't know any of the people, and I could save my mom the trip down.

Okay, go where? Home?

What home? Back to that house?

Is that home, or is this home now?

My mind was running in circles when my conscience chimed in.

All she wants is to see you graduate.... Do you really want her to miss that?

Ultimately, that is what made me stay. I owed Lilly that much.

Plus, I knew she'd enjoy the trip. Just for the chance to get out of Anders Park for a few days. She and Carl never went anywhere that you couldn't drive to in under an hour.

The things Eric said to me ate at me inside, along with the fact that he never even apologized. I didn't bring it up again, though; it just wasn't worth the fight. I didn't even know what I would say if I did fight.

I could tell him it breaks my heart to think that he sees me as *just* a woman. I could tell him to stop threatening me or that I would leave him.

I could tell him those things, but I knew nothing would change, even if I did.

In the interest of keeping the peace, I let it go and things were okay until the Friday before Derby Day.

I DIDN'T THINK much of it when late Wednesday night Eric mentioned that he was taking off work on Friday. I figured he wanted to go fishing or something. But on Friday morning, he got up early and showered right away. When he appeared to be about ready to leave the house, he told me that he was going to Churchill Downs for the Oaks.

"What is the Oaks?"

"It's the three year old fillies." He replied, as if it were common knowledge.

"And what is a three year old filly?"

"It's a three year old female horse."

"Oh. Is that special? Why are you going? I thought you wanted to stay away from Derby events, too much trouble…"

"Dad and I go every year."

"Oh. You never mentioned that." I paused, suddenly feeling cheerful about it, "It sounds like fun. I'll go. How long do I have to get ready?"

My cheerfulness was short lived.

"It's really just something that Dad and I do. Plus, there's too much chaos in the infield Tate, it gets pretty crazy. I don't think you'd like it."

"You mean YOU wouldn't like me to be there, Eric."

Then he made his closing argument, "You have to be eighteen to get in."

That was most likely true and I really couldn't blame him for that.

I let my tone soften when I spoke again, "I'm getting bored Eric. All I do is sit in this apartment all the time."

"We'll do some fun stuff soon, okay? I promise. It's almost summer and I can show you a little of Kentucky. It really is a beautiful state and there's a lot to do here. And don't forget, we're going to Willie's party tomorrow."

From the few times I'd been to his Uncle Willie's house in Indiana, I felt fairly certain I could predict what the party would be like: lots of men, lots of drinking and gambling, and lots of meat cooked over an open flame. Four men occupied that house. Completely devoid of a woman's touch, the atmosphere was rough.

"So what time are you leaving for *the Oaks?*"

"I'm leaving in a few minutes and I'd say by six thirty or seven, at the latest I should be home."

He said 'should'.

"Fine. Have fun I guess. Hopefully you win some money instead of losing."

"Oh, I won't lose any. Dad spots me. He always does on Oaks Day." He replied, sounding smug.

"Well, that's nice for you then. That sounds like a nice father – son tradition." I said irreverently.

"It is."

He kissed my cheek and went out the door.

I was ready to scream. I was so mad at him. Like it's not bad enough that he's always leaving me behind, but must he treat me like a little kid?

There was another part of me that felt like maybe I was more upset then the situation called for. I didn't even know what was really making me so infuriated, it was just a day with his dad.

How much trouble could he really get in with his dad?

After I showered and straightened up the apartment, I decided I needed to get out of there, even if it was just for a little while.

Even if I just go for a drive.

I drove around our neighborhood in frustration for a long time before impulsively turning towards I-65. Irritated by not knowing my way around, I figured it would be nearly impossible to get lost on the interstate.

Better go south…north and I might just keep going.

Once on the highway, I accelerated up to the sixty-five miles per hour the limit allowed, and then a few more. I flipped through the radio stations and found a country song that sounded okay.

Country music certainly wasn't my favorite when I first arrived, but it was starting to grow on me. It was hard not to listen to country here; most of the stations play nothing but.

I put the windows down all the way and let the wind whip through the car, trying to clear my mind. The warm air felt good and I drove that way the full forty miles to Elizabethtown and back.

It was relaxing, but the feeling dissipated the moment I got home and saw the apartment exactly how I left it. It was seven o'clock and there was no sign of Eric.

I called Annetta but she said Dell wasn't back yet either. She told me to be patient, that they would be fine. She must have heard the irritation in my voice because she pointed out that it would do no good to start a fight, especially since Eric would probably be drinking. I thanked for her advice and hung up the phone.

It bugged me a little bit that she showed no concern for the fact that Eric or Dell would be driving home drunk.

I guess that's what thirty years of marriage does for you: nerves of steel.

Eight o'clock found me on the couch in sweats and a t-shirt and covered with a blanket.

As I flipped through the channels, I caught a glimpse of Oaks Day coverage, which was more than enough. He was right, it did look wild. It looked like lots of wild drunk guys and half naked, drunk girls.

I seriously need a distraction.

I scanned through our DVDs and picked one of my favorite scary flicks: a vampire movie that I'd already seen many times. I turned all the lights off and got comfortable on the couch, consciously trying to clear my mind and allow the movie to do its job. It worked because a little while into the movie I was having trouble keeping my eyes open.

I woke up to the continuous loop of the playback menu. The eerie music playing over and over had a disconcerting effect as I tried to assess the situation.

I looked at the clock and my heart sank. It was three-thirty in the morning and Eric was obviously not home.

I sat there, my mind racing with questions. I went back and forth between being worried: convinced that something was wrong and, being angry: convinced he was *doing* something wrong.

Eventually, after I'd got up and paced for a while, jumping out of my skin every time I heard something, I couldn't take anymore. My nerves were raw. I gave up and went to bed deciding that he would be home when he got home and if something were really wrong, I would have heard about it by now.

It was hard to fall asleep, still tuned into each and every sound, but I finally drifted off.

The next time I woke up was, shortly after eight.

Eric still wasn't home.

I felt so powerless and so irate, it was like my nerve endings were on fire.

I grabbed the phone and punched in the numbers to Dell and Annetta's house. After a three rings, Annetta's voice filled my ear.

"Hel-lo"

"Hi, it's Tate."

"Good Morning, Tate." She said in her slow southern drawl.

"Have you seen Eric?"

"No, I haven't, Hon. He dropped Dell off last night around eleven. He's not home?"

"No. He's not."

Sarcastic thoughts spun through my head as my anger ballooned.

If he was home, would I be calling you to ask where he is?

"Well, it's odd that he's not home yet." She didn't sound the least bit surprised.

"Okay well, I guess if you see him, will you please tell him to call me?"

"I will."

"Thanks."

She caught me just before I hung up, "Tate, try not to worry okay? I am sure he's fine."

I could tell she was trying to be reassuring, but it had the opposite effect. I already felt sure he was fine, that he was probably at a friend's house. Unfortunately that left my imagination with tunnel vision, charging headlong into the idea that the friend he was with might just be another girl.

A guilty little thought spun through my head.

I'd rather he be hurt.

Hours later, when he finally walked through the door, I didn't even want to look at him. He called my name, but I didn't budge.

He said my name three more times before I finally turned my head in his direction. The moment my eyes met his, he spoke.

"I'm sorry."

"You say that a lot don't you?"

"Tate, I know you're mad." As he spoke, he made his way over to the couch where I was, and sat down. He put his hand on top of mine. I started to pull away, but he slid his hand down until he fingers were in position then he tightened his fingers around my wrist.

"I know you're mad that I was gone so long, but I am here now. I am sorry and I'm asking you to forgive me."

I consciously relaxed my arm. When I felt his grip relax in turn, I yanked my hand out from his and stood up. I spun around to face him so quickly, he still had a surprised look on his face when our eyes met again.

"WHAT am I forgiving Eric? Are you sorry about the fact that you stayed out all night or are you sorry about what you were *doing* while you stayed out all night? WHERE were you?"

"I stayed at Andy's."

"Bullshit." I challenged. "Andy's mom doesn't let anyone stay there. You told me that yourself!"

"Tate, she was asleep when we got there. After I dropped Dad off I -"

"What time did you drop your Dad off?" I tested.

"About eleven."

"Fine, go on."

Of course he wouldn't lie about that, he'd figure I'd have called his mom.

"After I dropped Dad off, I swung over by Andy's to see if he wanted to go to Willie's with us today."

"That was at eleven o'clock last night and now it's almost nine o'clock *the next morning!*"

"I know, I know. Let me finish. Andy wanted to get out of the house. I guess he was fighting with Paula, she kept calling the house and his mom was getting pissed. We went down to the bar right by his house. You know, Roy's, the one right on the corner? Well it just got late. We were shooting pool and the next thing you know it was bar time and we were both drunk. We walked back to Andy's and crashed there."

"And his mom, she didn't say anything about it, huh?"

"Yeah she did." He replied matter-of-factly, "Like I said, she was asleep when we got there, but when she got up this morning she said she figured Andy has stayed at my place enough times, it was only fair."

"And you couldn't call? You couldn't pick up the damned phone and call me to let me know where you were?"

"I know, I'm sorry Hon, I forgot. I mean, I was going to, I even told Andy to remind me when we got to his house to call you. I guess we both forgot. Tate, I passed out on their living room floor.

I just looked at him. His appearance certainly looked like the drunk part was true, and he reeked of stale cigarettes and beer.

Unfortunately that wasn't the part of the story I doubted.

"I don't really want to talk about it anymore right now. I am going to shower."

I walked towards the kitchen, leaving him in the living room alone.

"What time do you want to go to Willie's?" he asked gingerly.

I stopped, barely into the kitchen, just out of Eric's view.

"I'm not going."

There was no way I was going to a party just to put on a happy face and pretend that I'm *not* furious with him.

Suddenly he was behind me.

"We are going to that party."

I spun around and looked him directly in the eyes, "I'm *not* going. You go right ahead without me, that seems to be the way you prefer it anyway."

As I turned to walk into the bedroom, I saw a flash of movement from the corner of my eye. A split-second later I knew what it was.

His arm.

His backhanded blow landed at the base of my neck. My hand flew instinctively to the place his had just been. I dropped to my knees instantly and started to cry.

"Why did you do that?" I bawled. "Why did you hit me?"

In an icy tone he spoke. "I want you to get yourself together and get ready to go to the party."

Then it was he who turned and left me sitting alone.

I sat there stunned and sobbing. I couldn't believe he actually hit me. I really didn't even know *why* he hit me. My head started to throb and a fresh wave of anguish rolled over me making the tears run fresh. I felt so trapped.

I didn't want to move, much less did I want to go to a party with him. But I didn't want to find out what he'd do if I refused again.

How did I let this happen?

TWO HOURS LATER we were on the road to Willie's and as if the hour long ride with him wasn't enough, he had to throw in a pride crushing lecture.

"Tate, I'm sorry about before, but you just need to learn to keep your mouth shut. I hate that I had to do that. I mean, you had a right to be mad about last night, I expected it, but I said I was sorry. There was no need to be smart-mouthed after I apologized."

I couldn't believe the words that were coming from his mouth. The whole time he spoke in his demeaning tone, I wondered if he really believed the crap he was saying and worse yet, if he actually expected to me to believe it.

"Did you hear me?" he asked, as if he was waiting for an answer.

I must have tuned him out; I hadn't heard a question.

"What? No, I'm sorry I didn't. What did you say?"

"I *said* I take it we won't have this problem again, that we had today?"

"What?" I questioned again, only this time I heard him, I just couldn't believe he actually expected an answer.

What am I supposed to say?

"I - take - it - we - won't - have - this - problem - again?"

I was at a loss for words. I was literally nauseous; it was as if I could feel my dignity rising up the back of my throat.

"HEY." He snapped. "WHAT is wrong with you?"

I turned my head away from him, as if to look out the window. I didn't want him to see the tears spilling out from my eyes.

"Nothing." I mumbled.

"Hey Tate" His voice was suddenly soft and comforting, as he reached across and gently laid his hand over mine, "What's wrong?"

It took everything I had not to jerk my hand away.

He is seriously crazy. He is really, actually insane.

He squeezed my hand affectionately, "It'll be okay. You'll figure it out."

He returned his hand to the wheel and we made the rest of the trip in silence.

The party was as I expected it would be: drinking and gambling. There were, however, more women there than usual since several of wives and girlfriends of Willie's sons' were in attendance, so it was nice to at least have some female companionship.

As we sat around talking, I noticed something they all shared: a blasé attitude about their men being 'the boss' in their lives. They joked about it really, like that's just the way life is. If you can learn to keep your man happy, good for you, you'll have the life you deserve, if you can't, '*well then sorry 'bout your luck*'.

⌒

AFTER THE DISASTER that Derby turned out to be, from Thunder over Louisville all the way to Derby Day itself, it was hard to let it all go, but I had to.

For a while, I hardly spoke to him. I avoided him as much as I could, but that only served to make me feel worse.

The truth was - I was almost as angry at myself as I was at him.

I knew everything that had happened should have me packing my bags and running for the door, but there was no such plan in place. The guilt of my own inaction weighed on me.

When I finally made the concession to myself that I really didn't *want* to leave Eric; I just wanted to have everything back to normal, it was a relief, as if I gave my self permission to let go of all the anger I had bottled up inside.

When Eric sensed the change in my mood he responded accordingly. We got back to planning my upcoming graduation weekend, and soon he was back to being the Eric I fell in love with. I would take it for however long it would last.

⌒

A LITTLE OVER an hour into a Monday morning session of school, I completed my last final exam. I walked up to Mrs. Bauer's desk and handed my test to her. As she had every time I handed in the final exam from a course, she looked it over, presumably to make sure it was complete, then checked the student log book to see what my next course would be. Only this time, instead of reaching into the file drawer to retrieve the appropriate file folder, she turned to me, laid her empty hands on the desk in front of her and cheerfully confirmed what I already knew.

"That was your last course. You're finished Tate, you're done with high school!"

"I know. I mean, I was keeping track. I knew that was my last one."

She beamed at me. I couldn't help but feel the pride that was radiating from her. She really had become a source of encouragement for me. We hadn't talked much, but when we did, I really felt like she was vested in my success.

"Well, congratulations and good luck!"

"Thank you Mrs. Bauer. Thank you for all your help."

As I turned to leave, she called to me once more.

"Tate, will you be attending the graduation ceremony? If not, your diploma will be mailed."

"I'll be there, my mom is coming down." I said proudly. Mrs. Bauer knew my family was in Wisconsin.

"Good for you Tate. I'll see you there."

The realization hit me as I walked through the parking lot to my car. Regardless of anything else that had happened here, I finished school. I'd been working toward this moment since I was a little kid.

I did it!

I made the short drive home and burst into the apartment, knowing I should call Lilly first, but it was Jennie I couldn't wait to tell.

"Hello?"

"It's me." I said, trying to squash my excitement.

"Hi. How are you? What's up?"

"Oh not much going on here, you know, same old stuff. Well, same ol' except that I finished school about forty-five minutes ago."

"I thought you went to school mostly in the afternoons?" she questioned me, sounding confused.

"I mean I finished. School. I'm done."

"You're DONE?"

"I'm done! Goodbye high school, *for-evah*."

"That's so awesome Tate! I knew you'd finish early. Everyone else still has like three weeks left!"

Subtle as it was, I picked up the hint. When she said 'everyone', she wasn't including herself.

"How 'bout you?" I tested. "How is school going for you?"

Silence.

"Jennie?"

"Yeah, I'm here. I, uh, damn – this is even harder than telling my parents."

I already knew what she was going to say. She dropped out.

"I quit. I quit school Tate and –"

"Why?" I demanded, interrupting her.

"I wasn't going to graduate anyway, I didn't have enough credits and pretty soon it won't matter."

My heart sank. I wanted so badly for her to do something with her life.

"So what are you going to do now? Wait, why won't it matter?"

"There's more." She said timidly.

At that point, I knew something was really wrong. Jennie didn't do timid and certainly not with me.

"Tate, I'm pregnant."

This time, my heart seemed to rise instead of sink. It felt like it was in my throat.

"Jennie, what *happened?*"

"Uh, what? I, uh –" she stammered.

"Not *that!*" I snapped impatiently. "I understand *what* happened, I mean how? WHO?" She wasn't even going out with anyone last time I talked to her. How could she have let this happen? I felt a pang in my heart as if I could see Jennie's future slipping away.

Suddenly, Jennie was choking back sobs.

"What Jennie? What is it?" I didn't know if she was crying because of what she had just told me, or if there was more.

What more could there be?

"I don't want you to hate me." Her words were staggered and muffled as she choked them out in between sobs.

"I could never hate you, Jennie, why would you even say that?"

"Because of who got me pregnant."

"Why?" I asked, now cautious. "Whose baby is it?"

There was only one answer she could give that would break my heart, but it wasn't logical. Darrin wouldn't do that. She wouldn't do that. They barely knew each other, it didn't make sense.

"Jennie?"

Her silence was deafening.

"It's Kevin's, but please don't hate me." She said it so fast the words didn't immediately register.

Not Darrin. Check.

"Kevin. Kevin who?" I questioned, relief mingling with confusion. "The only Kevin I know is Kevin Bowen."

He was the last guy I dated before I met Eric.

"Yeah, Kevin." She replied firmly. "*Your* Kevin."

"Kevin Bowen?"

"Yes. I am so sorry Tate. I never meant for this to happen. I, we, well…" she paused to sigh loudly "I saw him in Cassden one night and we got to talking about you and how we both missed you and well, you, I guess you can probably figure out the rest."

"So, are you seeing each other? What are you going to do? Does he know you're pregnant?"

"No, we're not seeing each other, well, not really and yes, he does know I'm pregnant. Do you hate me?"

"Jennie, will you please stop saying that?"

"Well, Kevin was your boyfriend and friends just don't do that." She was crying again.

"Oh Jennie, please don't cry. Of course I don't hate you. Kevin is my ex-boyfriend. To say he was my boyfriend in the first place is really a stretch anyway. We only went out for a few weeks, you know that."

"I know, I know. I just thought you'd be mad because you dated him first."

"Well, I guess I don't really have the right to be mad since I moved five hundred miles away to live with another guy, so I gave up any claim to him, first or not."

"Are you sure?"

"I'm positive. I am way more worried about you. He better not be acting like a jerk."

"He's being okay. He obviously didn't plan this anymore than I did, but it happened and I just have to deal with it. We're not seeing each other though. We were for a little while, but when he found out that I'm pregnant, it kind of put a damper on the whole thing. Who knows what will happen, maybe we'll work things out later."

There was silence between us for a moment while I tried to absorb what I'd heard.

"What are you going to do, Jennie?"

"Uh, have a baby. Geez Tate, you really should have paid better attention in health class." She was laughing a little now. It was good to hear.

"I was afraid you were going to say it was Darrin's. Then I'd have to kick your ass, I wouldn't hate you, and I'd wait 'til after the baby is born, but I'd have to kick your ass."

"Tate. Come on, you know there is no way that I would ever do *that* to you, and also, for the record, you'd never be able to kick my ass."

We were both laughing and suddenly it felt like no time had passed between us. It felt like she was just across town.

"Hey, so are you coming here or what?"

"Yeah, I'll be there in fifteen." She teased.

"I wish."

Oh how I wish.

"Seriously, are you coming down for my graduation? My mom is riding down with her friend Susie. They both said you are more than welcome to ride along. Come on, pleeeassee?"

"Yeah, I guess I can do that. I don't *think* I have anything too important going on, but I'll have to check my calendar, you know, see if I can pencil you in and all that."

I teased back, purposely sounding overly grateful. "Wow, that'd be fantastic Jennie, I mean, I'd be really honored if you could find a way to fit me in. Oh wait, are you sure you're supposed to travel, in your — ahem — *fragile condition?*"

"Very funny, Tate."

"I'm kidding. It is what it is, Jennie. I guess you're gonna have a baby. Congratulations."

"Thanks. You, too."

"Me, too, what?" I asked, confused.

"Congratulations."

"Jennie, uh, I'm not pregnant."

Thank God I'm not pregnant.

"Congratulations on being done with school, you goof!"

"Oh yeah, thanks, I forgot. Kind of stole my thunder with this whole baby thing, didn't ya?"

"You know me, I live for that sort of thing." She paused and when she spoke again she had slipped into her best mock snooty voice "I will contact your *mothuh* for the details of my travel itinerary, *Miss Parkuh.*"

"*Riiiggght*. I'll see ya soon, 'kay?"

"'Kay."

We were both still laughing as we hung up the phone.

Eric was not as forgiving about Jennie's indiscretion. As soon the words left my mouth, I regretted the decision to even tell him the details of the paternity. An icy look came over his face and he was adamant that I shouldn't talk to her anymore.

He insisted that what she did was a betrayal of our friendship and that real friends don't date their friend's exes, regardless how meaningless the relationship had been.

I tried to explain my feelings about it to him using the same logic that I had used with Jennie, but no matter what I said, he didn't agree. He felt that I should cut her out of my life for good.

The conversation was going nowhere and I quickly grew tired of it. There was no way I was going to let him bully me into turning my back on my best friend.

That he *couldn't* make me do.

Maybe I should learn to keep my mouth shut.

Four

SETTING THE STAGE

THE NEXT FEW weeks flew by as we prepared for my graduation weekend. Several more phone calls to Wisconsin and we had most of the details ironed out. Lilly, Jennie and Susie would arrive the Thursday before the ceremony. Jennie would be staying with us at the apartment, while my mom and Susie had booked a hotel room. Eric and I made plans to keep our guests entertained, and his parents jumped right on the bandwagon. They were all about being hospitable. They even offered their extra bedrooms to my mom and Susie, but I knew my mom would see that as imposing. Plus she'd want her privacy, so I joked that the ladies were really looking forward to that hotel pool so I'd be in trouble if I made other arrangements for them.

We made plans for everyone to go to Churchill Downs on Friday. I knew my mom and Susie would love that idea. While I was excited about getting to see the famous track itself, and maybe the horses, I wasn't too keen on betting. I always thought of gambling as probable loss more than potential to win and I couldn't understand how people could throw away their hard earned money when the odds were always stacked against them. The gambling bug was one thing that Lilly failed to pass on to me.

Saturday we were having a small get together at Dell and Annetta's after the ceremony, which was perfect for me. All I really wanted was to spend as much time with my mom and Jennie as possible.

When they arrived Thursday afternoon, I met them at their hotel, just off I-65.

We decided that would be easier than explaining how to find the apartment, in a complex that was filled with identical buildings.

I watched as Susie drove her white sedan into the parking lot. One word summed up my reaction: unprepared. I was unprepared for the lump in my throat and the tears that flooded my eyes; tears for how much I'd missed them and tears for how much I missed the person I was when I was with them.

I was definitely unprepared for seeing Jennie with her baby bump. I didn't know much about pregnancy, so I wasn't sure what to expect when she told me she was almost five months along. Well, she definitely looked pregnant.

I did the math. Her being that far along already meant she got pregnant about five minutes after I left, but I didn't bring it up. I thought about how drastically her life would have changed when I left — how I would have felt if it'd had been the other way around — I couldn't be mad for how she coped with those changes.

I hugged my mom, then Jennie, then I hugged Susie and thanked her for driving down. In turn, they each hugged me affectionately back. I felt loved and truly valued; I sadly realized it had been a long time since I'd felt that way.

I stood back and looked at them, they were a sight for sore eyes, indeed. I hugged Jennie again and by then we were both crying, but our tears morphed into laughter as we realized how pitiful we must look, bawling and hugging in the parking lot of a hotel.

Jennie and I waited outside by the car while my mom and Susie checked in. I asked her if she wanted to go inside and wait in the lobby where she might be more comfortable. She said she wanted to be outside to enjoy the warm weather and threatened that if I kept treating her like a fragile old lady, she'd do something really embarrassing at my graduation ceremony, so I better knock it off.

It was like old times.

Except now we live five hundred miles apart.

And she's pregnant.

We spent the evening at the apartment, eating, talking and laughing. Eric cooked a wonderful dinner: chicken fried steaks, green beans with ham and biscuits. I teased him about showing off and he said that he was just trying to impress my mom. It was, after all, the first time they'd met. It was working, so far she did seem impressed. She'd have no reason not to be though. I'd told her only good things about him and now, up close and personal, Eric probably seemed like a real prince: cute, funny, charming *plus* he cooks.

Seriously, what's not to like?

Part of me wished they knew. Part of me wanted to spill my guts to Jennie and my mom about Eric's not-so-charming side. I wanted them to know he wasn't all he appeared to be, that sometimes he was spiteful and cruel. That he hit me. But deep down, I knew that wouldn't be good for anyone. It would just make them worry about me and it certainly wouldn't change him, so I kept my mouth shut.

*Oh, you **are** learning aren't you, Little Fish?*

The next morning I woke up early, and without looking I knew Eric was still sleeping soundly next to me.

Jennie.

My heart swelled when I remembered she was sleeping in my living room. I slid out of bed carefully so he wouldn't wake up. I wanted time to talk without having to alter the conversation.

As I had laid in bed the night before, I found myself replaying the evening's banter in my mind, trying to anticipate whether Eric would have reason to chastise me for something I'd said. I couldn't decide which was worse, how he had me actually restraining my personality or how his control over me had even seeped into my relationships with my best friend and my mom.

— 75 —

When I got into the living room, Jennie was laying on the couch staring off into space. She looked deep in thought, so I spoke softly, trying not to startle her.

"Good Morning."

She craned her head back to look at me. My heart swelled again when the smile crept across her face and she returned my greeting.

"Morning."

She scooted up a bit and folded her legs, making room for me on the couch. I took her unspoken invitation and sat down, leaning on the arm so we were facing one another.

"Are you ready to go bet on some horses?" I smirked.

"Yeah, sure." She snorted in response.

It went without saying that there were plenty of other things that Jennie and I would rather do on a day together, but when Eric and I were planning the weekend, Churchill Downs seemed like a good way to entertain everyone. I knew Lilly and Susie would love it for sure as would Eric and Dell, who would be joining us. As for Jennie and me - we could have fun anywhere.

"It'll be fun, I think. It will be cool to see anyway. We figured it be something to do." I shrugged.

"I'm just happy to be here."

"I'm very happy you're here. I wish you could stay longer. I wish we had more time to talk" I paused to glace in the direction of the bedroom where Eric slept, before finishing my sentence "alone."

She picked up on my gesture.

"Are you okay, Tate? I mean, are you happy here?"

"Oh yeah, it's great." I said a little too enthusiastically.

She picked up on that, too.

"You know you could just come home." She said softly. "After tomorrow, you don't *have* to stay here."

"I guess this is my home now." I lamented. "What's that saying about making your bed?"

"Now you have to lie in it." She finished the quip sardonically. "Yeah, I know."

"You still have a bed at your parents' house." She said, twisting the metaphor into a literal fact.

"I can't Jennie. Believe me, some days I'd love to." I lowered my voice so it was barely a whisper "Some days I'd love nothing more than to throw my stuff in the car and head north. But I can't. I'm stuck, at least for now."

"Why?" She demanded. "Why are you stuck? What makes you stuck here?"

"Well, there was school and now —"

"Yeah, now, what?" she interrupted. "You're graduating tomorrow. So now what is holding you here? If you're not happy, you should come back."

"I just can't. It wouldn't be any different. Carl and I would probably fight even more. Maybe eventually, I don't know. I just need to get a job so I can start saving some money." I let my voice trail off.

As much as I wanted to confess everything to her, I couldn't. Not now, not when she was here and had to be around Eric for the rest of the weekend. I knew the moment she found out he hurt me, she'd hate him and it would show.

"Okay, okay I get it. I'll drop it. But just so you know, I would love it if you came back and so would a lot of other people."

"Thanks Jennie." I smiled feebly.

I knew she was telling me what she thought I wanted to hear, trying to make me feel better, but in reality it only made me more sad and confused. She was right, there probably were a lot of people who would be happy if I came back, but if I left now, it would feel an awful lot like tucking my tail between my legs and running back home. I'd talked and talked about leaving Anders Park. To come back less than six months later would mean I couldn't make it in the big bad world. It would mean that I couldn't make it outside my sheltered little pond.

"So" she smiled "are you ready to go bet on some horses?"

"Yeah, sure."

We both laughed a sad accepting kind of laugh and silently agreed to move on. Things were changing and we could both feel it. In a very sad way, life was spurring us forward whether we wanted it to or not. Neither of us had even turned eighteen yet and already she was pregnant and I felt stuck in an abusive relationship.

Off to a great start, aren't we?

We spent little more time chatting, mostly about the baby and what being pregnant was like. It was interesting to hear about her experiences. I'd never given any thought to being pregnant. Since I was a little girl, I always knew that I would eventually have kids, but at seventeen, I hadn't given the actual process a lot of thought, other than how to prevent it.

CHURCHILL DOWNS WAS so much more than I expected. It was a beautiful place filled with history and excitement. The stands weren't packed full like they would be on Derby day, but there were still a lot of people there. It was a beautiful eighty-two degree day, perfect for me, perfect for Lilly, too. She loved the sun. She arrived at the apartment wearing a pretty white summer top, jeans and gold jewelry that glinted off her tan skin in the sunlight. She had obviously taken more time than usual on her hair and makeup, too. It made me happy. She seemed to be enjoying her vacation. I hadn't seen her get that fixed up in a long time.

One thing that amazed me was the horses. They were the most muscular creatures I'd ever seen. You could see each and every muscle rippling with force as they ran. From a distance the jockeys – who are typically very small in stature – looked more like little kids than adults on the powerful animals. When I laughed and commented about how small they looked, Eric pointed out the obvious. As if I couldn't figure out the lighter the burden, the faster the horses could run.

I brought only twenty dollars to bet with. I couldn't really afford to lose that much, but Eric told me the least you could bet on each race was two dollars and there would be ten races so twenty would be the minimum if I didn't want to just sit there not betting. As Jennie and I looked over the lists of horses in each race, we both found the betting to be very confusing. I figured you just had to pick the horse you thought would win in each of the ten races, but I kept hearing words like win, place and show from the more experienced gamblers. Fortunately, Dell offered to help Jennie and me with our bets. He taught us a little of the lingo at the same time, enough so that we could go to the window and place our own bets. Before we went though, he shoved a twenty dollar bill towards each of us. Jennie looked hesitant at first, but I simply thanked him and looped my arm through hers and gently pulled her with me. Jennie thanked him as well before I pulled her away, and we made our way up the steps of the stands.

Then she turned her surprised look on me.

"He does that. I know better than to argue." I said, making it a non-issue.

"Sounds like a good guy to have around." She mused.

"For the most part." I said, as I winked at her.

Once our bets were placed and the racing started it was exciting for the first few heats, as each of us cheered and yelled for our picks to run faster. Unfortunately the horses I chose continued to show up fourth, fifth and even last, at the finish line, so I was fairly bored with the whole thing after the fifth race or so. I continued to watch the leader board as the results of each race came in to see if I'd won, but during the races themselves, I was content to sit back and watch everyone else. It felt good to see Lilly, Jennie and Eric – my three favorite people in the entire world, having a good time together. Despite the problems, I loved Eric. This weekend he was reminding me why.

When he was good, he was *so* worth it.

After the racing was done, we all went back to Dell and Annetta's for dinner. Since Eric would be cooking out on the grill the next day, Annetta took today to be her only opportunity to prepare a traditional southern meal, namely her famous fried chicken, along with southern sides like cornbread, pinto beans and home made macaroni and cheese. Dell and Annetta were gracious hosts. The evening passed much too quickly.

My graduation day started out just like the day before, and it would pass as the day before had as well: too quickly. On this morning, when Jennie saw me, she was all smiles and this time she spoke first. In her most cheerful voice, she asked if I was ready for my big day. I could feel her happiness for me, but I sensed a sadness in her, too. I presumed her sadness was similar to mine. Today should have been entirely different. Today should be a day that we experience together in an entirely different fashion. We should be in Anders Park celebrating a graduation day that belonged to *both* of us and to the group of kids we'd both known nearly our entire lives.

Neither of us mentioned our sadness. It wasn't perfect, but it was a day to celebrate nonetheless.

My mom and Susie arrived at the apartment just as I was finishing up getting ready. Jennie and Eric were ready to go, and all I had left to do was get dressed. I was having trouble deciding what to wear. I really didn't have much to choose from for dressy clothes. I would have liked to buy something new for the day, but I figured it really wouldn't matter in the long run. I'd be covering up my clothes with a graduation gown as soon as I got there anyway. I ended up in a simple black pencil skirt, strappy black heels and a pretty white floral jacket.

Once I'd put on jewelry and fixed my lip gloss, I stood back and surveyed my appearance in the mirror, trying to memorize the moment. I felt good, but still on edge.

I stepped out of the bedroom to find everyone in the living room waiting for me, including Dell and Annetta. Everyone stopped talking, they all beamed at me. I felt my face turn flush at all the attention, then Lilly walked over and put her arms around me. She pulled back a little and looked up at me.

"I'm so proud of you." She whispered.

"Thank you." I leaned down to return her hug.

Eric's voice broke the moment "Are we all ready to go?"

There was a murmured collection of 'yeses' as everyone started to get up and gather their things.

"Mom, Dad, Lilly and Susie can ride with you, and Jennie can ride with Tate and me." Eric addressed the room.

Everyone agreed to the plan as we went out the door.

When we arrived at the Fair and Expo Center we easily followed the signs to where the Jefferson County Public High School graduation ceremony was being held. It was a huge place, but the buildings were clearly labeled and parking was fairly simple, too.

Signs continued to direct us all the way into the building and then indicated the point when I needed to separate from the group. I paused for a moment as they all turned and wished me well, then I continued down the hallway leading to where we would receive our gowns and hats. I didn't even know what color the gowns were. Orange and black had been my school colors all my life. It was ironic that a half hour before I was due to walk the stage I didn't know what color I'll be wearing.

Following another sign I turned down a hall to the right. The question of color was immediately answered as students milled in and out of a room with both of its double doors propped open.

Blue.

Blue is okay.

As I made my way into the crowded, noisy room I saw people carrying hats with blue and yellow tassels. I scanned the room trying to figure out where to go when I heard someone calling my name.

"Tate!"

I turned all around, trying to gauge where the sound was coming from. Then I saw a girl I knew from class, Valerie. I only saw her in school a few times so we certainly didn't know each other well. Had I thought about it before now, I wouldn't have really expected her to even be here. It didn't seem like she was in school enough to have completed her credits. Seeing her now though, she was obviously pregnant, so maybe she went to the other part of Fairdale T.A.P.P.

"Hi!" she yelled again, waving frantically. She was always nice enough to me, but she seemed a little wild, so I never pursued a friendship with her. I realized this would probably be the last time I would ever see her, so it felt harmless to hang out with her today. It would be nice to have someone to talk to.

"Hi, Valerie." I said as I made my way over to her. She wasn't wearing a gown yet either. "Do you know where we go to get our gowns and hats?"

"Yeah, I was just going too, over here." She said as she started to lead the way, cutting through the crowd with a loud series of 'excuse me's. I followed her lead, smiling politely at the people who bothered to look. I even exchanged smiles with a few of them, but nevertheless, I couldn't get over how indifferent people all seemed towards each other.

We each got our gowns and hats and were instructed to proceed to the area marked with the first letter of our last name to prepare to line up. Valerie turned to me.

"What's your last name Tate?" she asked.

"Parker. What's yours?"

"Polk." She replied smiling.

"Cool." I said, as we head off to look for the 'P' section.

Our social time was limited though, as shortly after we got to our designated area, a teacher came around and started calling off names in our section in alphabetical order. Soon I was back to not knowing the people standing around me. There were five people positioned between Valerie and I, causing our brief bond to quickly be for naught. She began chatting with the person next to her and I stood silently, looking around.

Ten minutes later, we were seated on the stage, staring out into a sea full of shiny beaming faces. It took me a while, but I finally located the faces I was looking for. They were half way back on the opposite side of where we were seated, but at least I could see them. I wondered if I'd be able to find them while I walked across the stage, or the moment after they hand me my diploma. I'd love to see the look on Lilly's face, but as easy as that sounded, I had a feeling it may require more grace than I possess. Being clumsy by nature, I could end up flat on my face.

They were already at the M's. Two more letters and I'd be there. All of the sudden I was nervous. I honestly didn't expect it and I didn't know if it was simply walking across the stage or the literal future that was before me, but suddenly my palms were sweaty and stomach felt like it was doing somersaults.

Then I was hit with another wave of regret, this one over the fact that my brothers weren't here to see me accomplish this. Danny, Ben and Joey had always been a big part of my life, especially Ben. I'd learned a lot growing up with them and I wished they could be here now.

I'd do well to take the biggest lesson they've taught me over the years: Don't Panic.

"Pamela Ann Meadows" the loud voice came through the speaker. A girl with long dark brown hair, two rows up, got up and walked across the stage. My eyes followed her as I calculated how long before that would be me.

I'd watched the other students, one by one, after they got their diplomas, they walked down the steps, off the stage and circled around the back. There was another set of chairs in place, floor level on the side of the stage where students were to take their seats and wait for the ceremony to finish.

Don't panic.

I took a deep breath, then another. The rate the names were being called seemed to be speeding up.

"Cynthia Lynn Olson"

I doubted there would be another 'O' name, and there had only been one 'P' before me: Jeremy Pacer, I'd heard the teacher call his name during the line up process.

I tried to ready myself, and took one more look at where my family was seated.

"Jeremy Thomas Pacer."

My hands were sweaty, I wanted to wipe them off, but I was afraid I'd leave marks on my gown so I shook them a little bit and rubbed them together instead. I could see something crazy happening, like the diploma slipping out of my sweaty hands and skidding across the stage.

"Tatum Lily Parker"

I stood up and took a brief second to steady myself, before making my way past the now empty chairs to my right. Once I cleared the chairs, I focused on the podium where the man to whom that loud voice belonged – the Jefferson School District Superintendent – stood. Next to him was a woman handing out diplomas to the students. I now realized the woman was none other than Mrs. Bauer. I remembered her final words of 'I'll see you there' as I left her classroom on that final day. A wave of relief passed over me, maybe just from seeing a familiar face. As for the other familiar faces in the audience, now that I was actually up here on the stage, I didn't dare to actually attempt to look.

As I shook the superintendent's hand he congratulated me and I thanked him, in turn. I then shifted my eyes to Mrs. Bauer's, which were glassy like she was fighting back tears. No doubt she had a lot to be proud of today. I'm sure without her help and encouragement, a lot of these kids wouldn't be graduating at all.

"Congratulations, Tate." She beamed.

"Thank you, Mrs. Bauer."

"Good luck."

I saw a camera flash out of the corner of my eye. The moment was very surreal.

I did it. I graduated from high school.

I made my way around the back of the stage and took a seat next to Jeremy Pacer once again. He smiled at me when I sat down and we shared an unspoken bond of relief that our moment was over.

Shortly after I sat down, I heard Valerie's name called. I smiled and waved at her as she made her way to her new seat, she enthusiastically returned my gesture.

None of the other names that were called registered with me. I sat there, lost in thought and once again trying to memorize the moment.

In the end, it really didn't matter what school I was at, or what color my gown was. I graduated high school and Lilly got to witness her child accomplish a goal that she had long since abandoned herself.

Once everyone had walked the stage, the superintendent issued a brief closing statement congratulating the class and wishing everyone success. Then it was over.

We students were issued back to return our gowns after we took pictures, but the caps and tassels were ours to keep. I was happy on both accounts: that the pictures would be with gowns and that we got to keep the smaller items. Those will all make good keepsakes for this once-in-a-lifetime day.

Amongst the crowd, I spotted Jennie first. I yelled her name only once before she heard me above the commotion of all the people. It was an awesome thing having a friendship like ours. We just seemed to be tuned into one another.

When I caught up with them, we made our way out of the building and found a nice spot to take pictures. I got my lip gloss out of my purse, which my mom had been holding for me during the ceremony, and tried the best I could to straighten my cap.

We took pictures of what seemed like every possible combination of people, all featuring me in the center. Each person took their moment to hug and congratulate me. Everyone laughed when I took off my shoes before the pictures with my mom. Without heels I was nearly six inches taller than her, I didn't want to tower even higher over her in the pictures.

We wrapped up the photo session fairly quickly and I went to return my gown, planning to meet them at the car.

This time the classroom was filled with friendly smiling faces. Everyone was talking and laughing, enjoying their shared moment. I smiled back at people as I made my way through the crowd to return my gown.

Again I heard someone calling my name, but this time I recognized Valerie's voice right away. I turned to her just as she threw her arms around me in an impromptu hug. I was taken aback by the gesture, but she pulled back quickly anyway, like the whole hug had been in high speed. She excitedly congratulated me and wished me well. I did the same to her and we parted ways. She darted off to assail someone else with affection and well wishes.

I dropped off my gown and left.

The party that followed wasn't what I would have expected my graduation party to be, but it was a fun, lighthearted celebration of my achievement, nonetheless.

Eric cooked on the grill while we all talked and laughed the evening away. The only quiet moments were when everyone was too busy eating to converse. After dinner Andy and Shane showed up, they said to make sure I was celebrating properly. It was a great ending to a great day. My heart was warm and full.

I had honestly forgotten about the concept of gifts until one by one, guests handed me cards, most had money in them. By the time I'd opened them all, there was over two hundred dollars. Dell and Annetta surprised me the most with their overly generous gift: a one hundred dollar bill. I felt a little funny accepting that much from them, but I reminded myself what I had said to Jennie at the track. Besides, the money would definitely help until I found a job.

As expected, the evening was ending before I'd have liked it to. Eric's friends left first and we were next. Dell and Annetta bid fond farewells to Susie, Jennie and an especially fond farewell to Lilly, with vows to see her again soon. They wished Jennie good luck with her pregnancy and thanked Susie again for driving down. As usual, they were the picture of southern hospitality.

THE NEXT MORNING Susie and Lilly were at the apartment promptly at eight-thirty. Jennie wasn't quite ready yet because she and I were up late talking, which made it a little harder for her to get up and moving. While she finished up in the bathroom, the four of us sat in the living room biding time.

The lump started to form in my throat as soon as I heard Jennie come out. I didn't want our time to be over yet. I found myself resenting Eric for imposing on these last few moments that I'd have with them, even though I knew he was just trying to be hospitable by sitting around making small talk with us.

When Jennie appeared to be ready, we all just kind of sat there for a moment, quietly looking around at each other when Susie finally broke the silence.

"Well kids, I hate to be the bearer of bad news, but I think we better head back."

"Yeah, I think you're right." My mom chimed in. "We've got a long drive."

My fight to hold back the tears was in vain, as we walked them out. Eric tucked Jennie's bag into the open space in the trunk and closed the lid. There was nothing more left to do, so he said his polite goodbyes to everyone, and excused himself back to the apartment.

Finally.

I hugged Susie and thanked her once again for driving down. As she got in the car, it was as if the floodgates opened. First I hugged Jennie, whose eyes were as flooded with tears as mine were, and with promises to talk soon and to take care of ourselves, she got in the car.

Lilly was last. I walked over to the passenger side of the car where she stood with a look on her face that was a mixture of pride and sadness. I wanted to be strong for her, but the tears kept coming.

"You know you can always come home, right?"

"I know, Mom. I'm fine. Things will be fine." I tried to sound cheerful, but more than ever, I wanted to tell her the truth. I just felt like if anyone would understand it would be her.

"I love you, Mom."

"I love you too, Tate. I hope you know that I am so very proud of you."

"Thanks. I know you are, I can tell." I said smiling through the tears. "I'm pretty proud of me, too."

I gave her one last hug and she got in the car. When I got to the door, I turned to wave and they all waved back. I went inside, I couldn't stand to watch them pull away. I was suffocating, my last chance to escape something was slipping through my fingers. I knew that when I walked back into that apartment, they would be gone and reality would snap back into place.

Five

WHO SAYS YOU CAN'T GO BACK?

THE REST OF June, and into July found me waiting.

Since we moved to the new apartment, I'd been scoping out places to work. Just a few miles from Willow Creek was a section of Fern Valley Road filled with different stores, restaurants and hotels; all potential employers. Since I didn't want to push Eric's buttons again, as much as it spurned me, I had to consider the prospective public I'd be serving and his potential jealousy.

I applied for jobs at four different places: two department stores, a gift shop and a dental office, but so far I hadn't heard back from any of them and I was becoming less optimistic each day.

Eventually, I decided I'd have better luck with getting a job after I turned eighteen, so I was basically waiting until after my birthday to do more serious job hunting.

I was also waiting for the fun of summer that Eric promised. It turned out his idea of fun was to spend every weekend fishing or drinking, or both. Usually both.

I missed summer in Wisconsin. My summers had always been filled with local small town festivals, swimming, cookouts and baseball games. So far, my first summer here was passing with only those same walls and not much of anything else.

The last weekend of June brought Eric's twenty-first birthday. Most of his friends were already past the legal drinking age, and he'd been getting served for a long time now, so he didn't even opt to go to a bar. There was, of course, a party at our apartment.

Once all the partiers cleared out, a drunken Eric very crudely announced his self-made rule that I *owed* him sex on his birthday. The alcohol undoubtedly compelled him to be more obnoxious about it, but his approach to sex had been starting to get that way, anyway.

His advances left me longing for the sweet closeness we had shared in the beginning.

Now he treated sex like it was just another one of my responsibilities. After the first few times, he had stopped any effort to please me and he no longer apologized for the swiftness of his climax, which was invariable.

What I'd hoped wouldn't become a pattern, did, and the result always left me frustrated.

As the end of June approached, I had hope. Fourth of July meant fireworks; we'd finally do something that would be fun for me.

On Friday, July 3rd, when Eric got home from work, he found me curled up on the couch with the makings of a rotten weekend: achy muscles, headache, sore throat and the chills which were the worst. Even though it was ninety degrees outside, the air conditioner was off, the patio door open, and I was wrapped in a blanket, I still couldn't stop shivering.

When I told Eric that I thought I was probably getting strep throat, that I'd had it several times before and recognized the signs, he was less than compassionate. He said he didn't want to get sick so within a half hour of coming home, he'd made plans and left again.

I silently added 'hurt feelings' to the list of my ailments. While I certainly didn't expect him to sit here and nurse me back to health, all we had to drink were tap water and beer, there was little food in the house, and there definitely wasn't any kind of medicine.

He didn't even *offer* to help.

I woke up hours later in a dark, quiet apartment. I staggered to the bathroom and then to the bed, too sick to care where Eric was.

The next morning was more of the same. I woke up after nine o'clock and Eric still wasn't home and I still didn't care.

I wanted so desperately to enjoy the holiday I thought I could force myself to feel better, if I had some medicine.

I got up and made my way to the bathroom. I looked in the mirror and it was obvious I'd need more than a little medicine to function. I looked like death. My face was pale and puffy, my eyes glassy and a closer look revealed white spots all over my throat. I couldn't remember if that meant strep or tonsillitis, but whichever it was, it sure hurt.

Eric finally meandered in about twenty minutes before two o'clock. I wanted to scream at him, but I didn't have the strength. My contempt was easily overshadowed by illness, so peace ensued.

He sensed the calm - even though it was forced - and he used the opportunity to avoid reproach for staying out all night. He drew near to me, smiling kindly and softly asking me how I was feeling.

He was being very sweet.

His dual personalities never ceased to amaze me. Sometimes, he could be the biggest jerk, but every time he turned on the charm, I melted all over again. If only he'd stay like this, the Eric I loved, instead of the one I resented.

"Could you go get me some medicine and maybe something to eat?" I asked gingerly as he got up from sitting by my side and walked towards the door. I watched as he picked up two twelve packs of beer – one in each hand – and carried them to the kitchen. I hadn't noticed him carry them in.

"Uh, sure Hon, maybe in a little while, okay?"

Like it would make a difference if I said it wasn't.

"What's all the beer for?" I asked trying to sound as non-accusing as possible; despite the feeling of dread was building in the pit of my stomach.

There was only thing that could make this day worse: company. Unfortunately, there was only one reason he'd have that much beer here: company.

"Just a few people coming over."

"A few people? Are you kidding? Eric, I'm sick. Do the *few people* coming here know that I'm here, sick?" I challenged.

"Yeah, I told 'em." He said with annoyance. "Shane and Andy are coming and they're bringing a, uh, someone."

"Eric, couldn't you go someplace else? I need rest."

"Tate, it will be fine. You can go in the bedroom and we'll keep it down out here, I promise."

I didn't believe him, but I knew I was fighting a losing battle. Who was I kidding? Fourth of July was another perfectly good reason to drink.

"Well, can you please go get me some food? I'm starved and I could really use some juice."

"You know what would really help you - knock that cold right out? Whiskey. I cured myself of pneumonia once with whiskey and honey." He said warmly.

"No." I shook my head at him. "Food. Juice. Please?"

"Soon." He replied, still smiling warmly.

I got up and went to the bedroom.

He seriously doesn't get it.

Within an hour, there were at least ten people in our apartment. From fever or anger, I wasn't sure, but I felt like my blood was about to boil.

The music was blaring. At one point, I walked out into the living room, purposely ignoring the faces of our guests, to very sarcastically ask Eric if he could please turn down the music just a *little*. He obliged, giving me a forced smile, and then as soon as I was back in the bedroom, the volume went right back up.

Jerk.

I got so aggravated with all of it that I decided the only way I was going to get any food or medicine was to go get it myself.

I was in the process of pulling myself together enough to go out in public, when I heard a new voice above the rest: Dell's.

A moment later, there was a knock at the bedroom door. I was standing in front of the closet, pulling a sweatshirt down over my head, so I was only two feet from the door. Dell looked surprised, probably because I answered so quickly, but he simply smiled and followed me as I walked back to the bed. I sat down and pulled the covers up around me while Dell sat at the foot of the bed.

"How ya doing, Kid?" he asked softly.

"Not so good." I struggled to fight back the tears.

Maybe he can talk some sense into Eric, make him get rid of these people.

"Wanna get out of here?"

I looked over at him to see a sympathetic smile and a knowing in his eyes. I was afraid that look meant that he'd seen this before, that it was normal for Eric to treat people like this, and that he felt sorry for me.

"Yeah, I do."

He stood up from the edge of the bed. "You do what you have to do. I'll be ready when you are." He said, as he walked to the door.

Now it took everything I had to keep the tears from spilling out.

"Dell?"

He turned back to look at me, raised his eyebrows in response, but didn't speak.

"How did you know I was sick?"

"Eric called Annetta."

"Oh. Okay. I'll be ready in a few minutes. Thank you."

He smiled that same sympathetic smile and closed the door behind him.

He got his parents to take care of me, just like all his problems.

I hastily grabbed some clothes and threw them into a bag. Short of having my own mom to take care of me while I'm sick, Eric's mom would be my next choice.

I opened the bedroom door and walked straight out of the apartment without saying a word. As the door was closing behind me I heard several people say 'bye' and 'hope you feel better'.

I hope you all get sick.

A few minutes later, Dell got in the car, where I was waiting for him.

"Thank you." I said.

"You're welcome. You look like you could use some quiet."

I ENDED UP staying with Dell and Annetta for the better part of three days, most of which I spent asleep. They picked up some kind of flu medicine for me, that seemed to help a lot, cough drops to soothe my throat and they kept me supplied with plenty of juice and good comfort food. They both had been wonderful to me and I was very grateful.

When I woke up Monday morning I laid in bed for a while trying to gauge how I felt. My throat was still a little sore, but all my other symptoms seemed to have gone.

"Oh Tate, you're up." Annetta said as I walked into the kitchen. "Good Morning."

"Good Morning." I said, smiling weakly.

"How are you feeling, Hon?"

"Much better, thank you. I think I'll head home this morning."

"Are you sure? You're welcome to stay."

"Thank you, Annetta, but I think I'm okay now. I'm sure there's a lot that needs to be done at home anyway, but I can't thank you enough for letting me stay and taking care of me."

"Oh, that's okay. When Eric told us you were sick, Dell and I were worried that he wouldn't... well, you know how men are."

It was a little sad, that she was crediting her son's inconsiderate nature to a simple Y chromosome. I knew there was no point in arguing with her southern logic about men and their entitlements.

"I know, it's fine. I mean, it turned out fine, thanks to you."

"Oh that reminds me: Eric called last night to talk to you, but you were already asleep. He didn't want to wake you."

"He didn't end up sick did he? Is he home now?"

I made sure my question sounded like concern, but I was actually fishing. If he was home, I wanted to know *before* I got there.

"No, no. He wasn't sick. As far as I know he's at work today."

"Oh good." I said, feigning the reason for my relief. "I was hoping I didn't get anyone sick. Maybe I'll call just to be sure. If he's there, I can see if he needs anything."

"That's a good idea Tate. Maybe he'll learn a thing or two about being considerate from you." she laughed.

Fat chance.

I called home and was relieved when I got the machine. I gathered up my things and thanked Annetta once again for her hospitality before I left.

As I drove home, I was also grateful that Dell had retrieved my car. Sometime on Sunday he had Annetta drive him to the apartment, then he drove my car back to the house so it would be here when I was ready to go. The freedom to leave early in the day was an important part of the plan that had been budding in my mind since I left the apartment three days ago.

Everyone has their breaking point.

When I got home I immediately took a shower. Once my hair and makeup were done and I was dressed in something besides sweats, I finally felt back to normal.

I sat down on the couch to survey the apartment. Despite the mess that had built up over the last few days without me here to clean, this place was nice, comfortable.

It's still not worth it, Tate.

Without any more thought, my decision was made. I jumped up and started to pack.

It went quickly. Most of my decorative items were left in boxes from when we moved into the new apartment. While it angered me at the time, when Eric insisted that my stuff didn't match the new decor, it certainly helped now.

I wanted to be on the road long before he got home. I wanted to be as far away as possible when he realized that I was gone.

I backed my car into the empty first stall, which was right out side our patio doors, and once again found myself grateful for something that had been a nuisance in the past. The apartment facing the parking lot meant that I had less than ten feet to cover with each trip to the car.

I loaded the boxes into the trunk first, along with the duffle bag that now held all my stuff from the bathroom. I loaded my clothes, leaving the hanging clothes on their hangers while the folded clothes ended up in a garbage bag. Another garbage bag held my two blankets and my pillows off the bed, and a small shopping bag held a mixture of odds and ends that I needed to keep track of: my journal, my camera, things I just didn't want to lose in the mix.

I did a quick check around the apartment – being sure to look in closets and cabinets – to make sure I wasn't forgetting anything. Upon checking in the kitchen, I remembered the dishes I had brought with me, but decided they weren't worth the time they'd take to pack.

When I was sure I had everything of importance, I locked the patio doors, grabbed my purse and keys, took a final glance around the apartment and walked out. I'd have to mail his key back, since I needed it to lock the door.

I stopped at a gas station right by the interstate to fill up and get toll money. As I stood filling up my car, I noticed a hotel set back off Fern Valley Road that had a big, red 'Now Hiring' banner stretched across its roof. To see that now felt sardonic. It hadn't been there when I'd been out looking for a job.

A little after twelve thirty I got on the ramp leading onto north-bound I-65, heading home.

Traffic was lighter than I expected and I was making good time. As the uneventful miles stretched in front of me, I found myself daydreaming and wondering what it was going to be like when I got there. I hadn't even taken the time to call Lilly and tell her I was coming. I wondered if that would work for or against me with Carl.

I was excited about being around Jennie again, but then I remembered that she was pregnant and selfishly thought about the fact that things were never going to be the same for us because there would always be the baby to think about.

As the drive wore on, my thoughts continued to bounce from optimistic to melancholy and back again. I had been trying to keep Eric off of my mind, but it was difficult.

About two hundred miles into the trip, when the reality of actually not seeing him anymore, not being with him, set in, I almost turned around. It was true - he had treated me badly – but I still couldn't help loving him. For every bad trait he had, I could find a good one, too.

I kept driving and told myself that it had to be this way. I rationalized that the option might be open to go back eventually, but there had to be some changes first.

I don't get it, it's like the double standards are bred in.

Even with the issues my parents had, there was a certain parity between them. I hadn't met any couples here that showed any equality. Here it was always the man and the 'little woman'. If the woman was smart, she knew her place.

I guess that worked for some people, but not for me. To me it felt like I was being diminished.

I was raised a tom boy. My brothers didn't treat me like I was some little princess of the family; they treated me like I was one of them. Anything they could do, they challenged me to do, whether it was eat something gross, throw a ball, or lift something heavy. I may not have always risen to the challenge, but no one could accuse me of not trying. Maybe the fact that I was challenged to be as *good* as a boy was just another form of chauvinism, but at least it was the kind that rewarded strength, instead of punishing it.

As I slowly made the sharp left into my parents' driveway, I was immediately taken aback. It was exactly as I left it, like absolutely nothing had changed. While everything else in my life felt different - including me - here, in this place that had always been the center of my world, it was as if time stood still.

It had a reassuring effect on me, like I'd done the right thing by coming back.

If I could just hit the reset button on my life somehow, maybe things would start to make sense again.

I was nervous about Carl. While I doubted that anything would have changed between he and I in the short time that I'd been gone, I hoped that at least the bickering wouldn't start immediately.

I didn't have to wait any longer to find out what kind of reception I would get; before I'd even turned off the engine, Lilly and Carl were heading toward me, both wearing inquisitive looks on their faces.

As I climbed out of the car, I stretched my sore muscles and realized of how exhausted I was. The long drive, being sick and undoubtedly the emotional upheaval was a lot all at once.

I forced a smile at my approaching parents. I was bracing myself for the questions that I wasn't prepared to answer, but as they got closer, I could see the genuine happiness on both their faces and my apprehension disappeared. My forced smile relaxed into one that felt as genuine as theirs looked. Problems or not, they were my parents.

"Trouble's here!" Carl said in a mockingly cheerful voice.

Trouble; he'd always called me that, from the time I was a little kid. Even now, when I'd call from Kentucky, if he answered the phone he would tell Lilly that 'Trouble's on the phone for you'. It was a little corny, but I didn't mind it.

Lilly immediately pulled me into a hug, while Carl stood back.

"What are you doing here?" she asked, trying to cover the uneasiness in her voice with enthusiasm. She would know something was up, since I hadn't called first.

"I thought you said I could come home anytime." I teased. "You don't want me here?" I let my eyes graze past Carl's as I asked my mock question, he looked away from my gaze, but the smirk on his face told me things were okay for the time being.

"I was sick and I wanted you to take care of me. Annetta did a pretty good job, but it just wasn't the same, so here I am."

"Really, you're sick and yet drove all the way here, just so I could take care of you?" she asked skeptically.

"I really was sick, Mom. I don't know if it was strep again or what, but it had me out for a few days." I confessed, before I'd considered the

consequences. She could let a lot of things go, but when it came to illness, she was a serious worrier.

"Are you still sick?" she asked, immediately moving toward me to
press the back of her hand to my forehead.

I knew I was fine, but it felt good to be worried about anyway.

"I think I'm okay now. I started to get sick last Friday, I had the chills
really bad and a bad sore throat. Then Saturday I went to Eric's parents'
house and I just left there this morning. I'm feeling a lot better today. I
slept a lot."

"Why did you go over there? Why didn't you just stay at your
apartment?"

"I, uh, I just figured I would be able to rest better there. Eric isn't a
very good nurse." I laughed to cover, but it came out sounding phony.

Carl was looking over my car. My little black coupe was starting to
look worse for wear. While I waited for him to reprimand me for not
taking better care of it, I realized he was now looking *in* the car.

Oh. Here it comes.

"Plan on staying long?" he asked curiously, without taking his eyes off
the pile of clothes stacked in the back seat.

The tone of his question made Lilly look up at him. But instead of
the dirty look she no doubt planned to give him for his tone, she saw that
something had caught his eye. Her eyes followed his gaze to the interior
of the car.

"Is that *all* your clothes?"

"Pretty much, yeah." I said quietly, turning my head to look around
again.

"Uh, okay. How long *are* you planning to stay? Are you home for
good?" she sounded hopeful.

"I'm not really sure yet." I mumbled. "Hey, I really have to pee, can
we talk about this later?"

I started walking towards the house without waiting for an answer.

I hadn't even considered the need for an actual explanation about
why I was back when I'd packed and left so hastily. I wasn't ready to say
that I was back for good, but to try to pass my sudden appearance off as
a simple visit seemed a little implausible.

I knew eventually I'd have to come clean, but as for now, dusk was quickly fading into night and I'd have to get some stuff out of the car before it got too dark. Then I could just go to bed. That would get me through until tomorrow, anyway.

As I stepped through the back door into the mudroom, I stood looking into the kitchen and the lack of variation was now emotionally overwhelming. It was as if I was just returning from wherever I'd been for the evening. As if I'd never really left.

As if I've never gotten out of this place.

The kitchen always had an orangey glow at night, no matter what color Lilly painted the walls. The glow came from the old fashioned ceiling light fixture; time plus Carl's cigarette smoke had stained it over the years.

The counter top and window sill were still littered with wallets and mail, odds and ends that all belonged to my brothers. It was all the same.

As I walked through the rest of the rooms to the opposite end of the house, I found the rest of the house was just as littered with their stuff as the kitchen counter.

When I climbed the last stair and stepped into my room, I was overwhelmed all over again.

The room was hot; the stagnant air was thick and smelled like dust. It dawned on me that just because the rest of the house seemed like I'd never left, didn't mean my room would be the same.

I wasn't here to live in it.

It seemed like such a silly thing to not have occurred before, but it truly hadn't.

I carefully made my way around the bed, to the dresser, where I could see by the shadows the lamp was still located.

I clicked the lamp switch and as light flooded the room, my heart felt like it sank even lower. Everything seemed to be in the same places that I had hastily left them in, nearly seven months ago, with one exception: now the furniture and all the left over belongings that I hadn't bothered to take with me, were all covered in a thick layer of dust.

I felt my cheeks warm and no doubt, turn red, followed by hot, stinging tears that flooded my eyes without warning. I sat down on the bare, dusty mattress and gave in to the unwanted emotions crashing down on me.

I didn't know what I was expecting, but this wasn't it. Being here, in this room filled with unwanted remnants of my old life made me wish I was back in my nice clean apartment in Kentucky, which in turn made me feel guilty that I wasn't happier about being home. The run down farmhouse already had me feeling stifled and the fact that there had been no mention of a call from Eric had me feeling panicky, on top of everything else.

Does he even care that I'm gone?

A few minutes later, I quickly wiped the tears from my face as I heard Lilly climbing the stairs. I turned back to look at her as she appeared over the banister, with clean sheets in one arm and in the other, a dust rag and furniture polish.

"I wish you would have called." She said wistfully. "I would have had your room ready for you. Are you hungry? I could make you something to eat."

She walked over to where I was sitting, set the items down on the bed, and sat down next to me; close enough so that she would no doubt notice the telltale signs that I'd been crying.

"Are you okay, Tate?"

I simply shrugged in response.

"Okay, I won't push, but you are welcome to stay as long as you want. I hope you know that. Whether it's a week or a year, it's fine."

"Thanks." I said, sorrowfully.

Now I've involved her feelings in my mess. She's hoping I'll stay.

"You didn't answer me before. Are you hungry?"

"No, not really. I haven't had a huge appetite since I've been sick."

Actually my appetite had been failing for a long time, now.

"Well you need to eat. You look like you've lost weight." She got up off the bed and immediately started spraying furniture polish on differ-ent surfaces.

"Wow, I didn't realize how dusty it's gotten up here. I haven't come up here much since you left." There was a sadness in her voice now. "Why don't you go get whatever you need from your car, and I will clean up in here a little bit. I'm off tomorrow, so we'll clean it better then, but right now you look like you could use some rest."

I smiled appreciatively and walked down the steps.

While most of the reality of being back here was a disappointment, seeing my mom, being genuinely taken care of felt every bit as good as it should.

By the time I passed through the house and climbed the stairs for the second time - this time with my pillows, some clothes and my bathroom bag in tow - Carl was in bed and Lilly had my room in much better shape. The bed was made with crisp clean sheets that smelled like they were dried on the clothes-line outside. The stagnant dust smell was all but gone; in its place was a mixture of the fresh laundry smell from the sheets, furniture polish and the warm night air, from the now open window.

Much better.

Lilly gathered up the now filthy dust rag and furniture polish and stopped at the top of the stairs.

"Don't stay up too late, okay? Get some rest. Tomorrow is another day." She smiled sympathetically.

"Okay."

She was halfway down the stairs and already out of sight when I called to her.

"Mom?"

"Yeah?" her voice floated up to me from the stairwell.

"Thanks for helping with my room." It felt funny to say the words 'my room'.

"You're welcome." She said warmly. "I'm happy you're here."

"Me, too." I lied.

Maybe it was a lie, maybe it wasn't, I wasn't really sure, but it seemed like the right thing to say.

"Goodnight Tate."

"Goodnight Mom."

I changed my clothes and got ready for bed, putting my pillows and a blanket in place with the clean sheets. As I looked around the room, I was impressed at how far Lilly had gotten on the cleaning in the few minutes I was outside.

Without anything left to do, I flipped off the light and got into bed.

There was a warm breeze coming through the window and the room was now lit only by moonlight. I'd forgotten how peaceful it was here, without car stereos and police sirens blaring into the night. I closed my eyes and the last thing I remember thinking was Lilly's words running through my head: 'tomorrow is another day'.

I woke up to birds chirping and the occasional semi barreling past the house. There was no television, no kids splashing in the pool outside, no thumping car stereos or car alarms. It was nice. I felt better than I had in a while. Judging by the sunlight in the room, I'd slept late.

I flipped back the covers, sat up and stretched. I really did feel good, lighter even, like the weight of something had been lifted off me. There was a small nagging sensation in the back of my mind that I was missing something, but I forced it out by reasoning that right now, Eric should be at work, so the only thing I was missing was another boring day sitting alone in that apartment.

When I got downstairs to the kitchen, I opened the fridge to survey the contents: nothing that looked appetizing.

Maybe I could grab breakfast somewhere...

I looked up at the clock: eleven forty-five, too late for breakfast.

I settled for a can of diet soda from the fridge and went outside. I knew exactly where my parents would be: in the garden.

As I walked through the break in the long row of tall lilac bushes, the stepping stones leading out to the back yard felt warm under my bare feet. I stepped clear of the bushes and the expansive back yard opened up in front of me. I'd forgotten how beautiful our country yard was in the summer.

I looked to the left, and just as I figured, both my parents were in the garden, bent over pulling weeds.

I reached the row where my mom was weeding and the sudden shadow I cast over the spot she was working in caused her to look up at me. A warm smile spread across her face, as if she'd just remembered I was here.

"Good Morning, Sleepyhead." She hummed. "You must have slept well, you look a lot better."

"She must have slept well since she slept 'til noon." Carl chimed in. He had walked up behind my mom and joined her in weeding radishes.

"I did sleep good. I feel a lot better."

"What are you going to do today?" my mom asked casually. She didn't do casually well, she was fishing.

"Do you mean am I driving back to Kentucky today?" I laughed at her transparency.

"Well?"

"I don't know when I'm going back, if I'm ever going back, but it definitely won't be today." I tried to answer in a tone that wasn't impolite, but conveyed the message that I didn't really want to talk about it right now.

For now, I just wanted to enjoy the freedom of being here.

That was it, freedom. That is what felt so good about right now. It just hit me that right now, I could say or do or wear whatever I wanted. There were no expectations and no obligations.

Ironic for a teenager to have a sudden onset of feeling free in the presence of her parents.

Lilly was still looking up at me, smiling curiously. She had her head cocked to one side, like she was trying to figure me out.

Good luck with that. I can't even figure me out.

"I'm going to shower and unload my car. For now." I added, in effort to prevent any more questions about how long I'd be staying.

"Did you eat anything?" she asked, thankfully changing the subject.

"I looked, but I couldn't find anything. I am pretty hungry, now that you mention it." It was a little blatant basically implying that if she didn't make me something I'd starve, it just felt nice to have her take care of me.

"I will come in and make you some lunch in a little while. Are you going to call Jennie? She'll be happy to know you're here, I'm sure."

"Yeah, after I get cleaned up. I'll probably go over by her today. I haven't even talked to her since you guys left Kentucky, maybe I'll just show up at her house and surprise her."

Lilly laughed and went back to her weeds. Carl had already moved to a different part of the garden to tend to the tomato plants.

I looked back towards the far right corner of the yard. Our yard was dotted with mature trees, but there, in that back corner, stood one lone tree and for the first time in my life I felt sentimental about it. We always called it the 'little tree'. It was by that tree that my mom and I always laid out in the sun when I was a kid, before I discovered indoor tanning.

We would drag blankets and magazines, tanning lotion and snacks out to that spot and lay there for hours just soaking up the sun.

Only now, the tree wasn't little anymore. In my memory, it was a sapling barely taller than me.

In reality the tree stood probably thirty feet tall and while it used to barely cast a shadow at all, it now provided a shady spot big enough to park a vehicle in. It made me sad. That tree certainly didn't sprout twenty feet in a year; I was just *realizing* it was grown. It felt like a sign.

Life changes whether you want it to or not; sometimes, without you even noticing.

After I unloaded my clothes, I lugged the vacuum up the stairs, along with a clean dust rag and the furniture polish to finish what Lilly started last night. I had no intention of taking her up on her offer to help; she'd done enough for me last night. I was certainly capable of cleaning up my own room, seeing as I just showed up here unannounced.

It went quickly, compared to cleaning a whole apartment.

I fished my shower stuff out of my bathroom bag and went downstairs. The bathroom was another part of the house that never failed to disappoint. It was about as big as a postage stamp; it didn't even have a bathtub. The inside of the plastic single shower stall was always stained with rust from the hard water. I thought a water softener would be a simple solution, but when it came to home repairs, Carl always seemed to opt for the cheapest and least effective method possible.

By three o'clock, I had my room cleaned, my car unpacked, was showered and had eaten the grilled cheese sandwich Lilly left on the stove for me.

I CALLED JENNIE, but her mom said she was gone for the rest of the week. She was staying up north by her sister's house, near Green Bay. She asked how long I was staying and when I told her I wasn't sure yet, she said I was welcome to call Jennie because she'd be sorry she missed me. I wrote down the phone number to Janelle's house with intention to call later. I didn't want to disrupt her plans and I wasn't sure I wanted to make the drive two hours further north to Green Bay.

I'll just have to stay long enough for her to come back.

I thought of Darrin.

Should I, or shouldn't I?

My mind raced with 'what ifs'. Talking to Darrin was always cathartic to me. He and I had often turned to each other for relationship advice. Why should this be any different?

What Eric doesn't know won't hurt him, besides; it's just a phone call.

I dialed the number to Darrin's house, my heart thumping inside my chest as I waited for him to answer.

"Hello?" a woman's voice answered.

It was Darrin's mom, Stacey.

"Is Darrin home?" I asked gingerly.

"Uh, no he's not. Can I ask whose calling?" she sounded suspicious.

"Hi Stacey, this is Tate."

Her voice warmed instantly. "Oh hi, Tate! I didn't recognize your voice, we haven't heard from you for a long time. Darrin actually doesn't live here anymore."

"Oh." Seems I wasn't having any luck getting a hold of people today.

"He lives in Racine now. He got a job at the prison down there. He's a guard." She sounded happy for him.

"Oh." I was surprised. I couldn't picture Darrin bossing around hardened criminals. He played the bad boy pretty well, but underneath, he was a softy.

"I guess a lot has happened since I left. I am actually at my parents' house now, so I just thought I'd check in with him, see how he's doing."

"Yeah a lot has changed. I'm sure Darrin would love to hear from you though. He mentioned that you were moving out of state, Tennessee? Are you visiting or are you back for good?"

"Kentucky actually and I'm visiting right now, not sure how long for yet."

"Oh, okay well, I could give you his cell number."

"That would be great."

She gave me the number and we exchanged pleasant goodbyes and hung up.

I dialed the number she gave me. I was disappointed when after four rings, it went to voicemail.

"Hey Darrin, it's Tate. I am here in Wisconsin, um, visiting. Not sure how long I'll be here, but give me a call when you get a chance. Your mom gave me your number; she told me you've got a new job. I'd love to hear about it, so give me a call. Oh, I'm at my parents' house. Talk to ya later."

I hated leaving messages; I always sounded so dorky.

I sat at the kitchen table not sure what to do next. Besides Jennie and Darrin, there really wasn't anyone else I wanted to talk to right now.

I didn't have to think about what to do any longer. I heard the screen door open and Ben walked in. He had a smile on his face that told me he was glad to see me, though his verbal greeting was lukewarm. My brothers weren't the most emotional guys.

"Hi. What are you doing here? I thought you moved." He said, in mock sarcasm.

"I did, but I just missed you guys so much, I couldn't stay away. What, a little sister can't come to visit?"

"Yeah, I guess that's okay. Are you by yourself?"

"Yep."

"Where's what's-his-name?"

"You mean Eric? He's in Kentucky. He lives there."

"And you? Where do you live?" he asked bluntly.

How could I have not thought that everyone was going to ask me that? How could have not been more prepared to answer that question?

"I don't know where I live right now."

He wouldn't push. It wasn't in his nature.

Ben and I had always been close. Some people didn't get Ben. He had a sarcastic nature about him that a lot of people took as being a smart ass. He was, but I knew better than to take offense. I found him funny. I couldn't help it.

"What are you all doing tonight?"

"Ugh! Stop talking like that." He demanded.

"Like what?" I honestly wasn't sure what he meant.

"With that accent! You're not down there anymore, so don't talk like that."

"Okay boss. I'll try. I mean, I've only lived in the south for almost seven months now, but I'll do my best to get rid of my southern accent in a day."

"Good." He sounded as if he actually expected me to comply.

"So?"

"So what?" He'd obviously forgotten my original question.

"So what are you doing tonight?" This time I carefully over annunciated each word so I sounded like a computer generated voice, with perfect diction and no hint of the accent he apparently despised.

"Oh yeah. We have baseball at seven."

"Cool. Maybe I'll come to the game."

I grew up going to my brothers' baseball games. That actually sounded fun.

"Cool." He mocked affectionately as he walked out, leaving me to resume my post of sitting by the phone, wondering what to do next.

At least now I have an option for something to do.

Then the phone rang. I silently cursed my parents for not having caller ID. If it was Darrin or Jennie, I wanted to talk, but if it was Eric I didn't, not yet. I didn't know what I wanted to say to him.

I plucked the phone out of its cradle.

"Hello?" I said cautiously.

"Tate? It's Darrin."

My heart skipped a beat; it was good to hear his voice not to mention the relief that wasn't Eric calling.

"What are you doing home?" He sounded a little too eager. "Are you here for good?" His normally soft, deep voice was higher pitched and he was speaking faster than usual.

"Uh, I'm just here for a visit. You know, things happen and, well, I'm not sure how long I'll be here yet."

I really need to work on a better answer for that.

"So. How 'bout that new job?" I blatantly changed the subject. "I have to say, when your mom first told me that you're a prison guard now, I was shocked. I still don't know if I can picture you doing that. Isn't it kind of scary?"

"It's alright. It was at first, but you get used to it. You just have to walk the walk. If you act like you're afraid, the inmates will push you, but I do okay. For the most part, if you're decent to them, they're decent to you."

"Huh. So you like it then?"

"Better than Quad." He said quickly. Quad was a printing company he worked at since even before I'd met him.

"What about you, Little Miss Tate? What's up with you? What are you doing in Wisconsin?"

"What a girl can't visit home?"

"Yeah, a girl can, but that's not what's going on here and you know it. What's up, Babe?"

It warmed my heart to hear him call me 'babe'. He was always such a sweetheart.

"I don't know Darrin, things just got messed up."

"So are you and -" he stopped.

"Eric." I took his cue for me to fill in the blank.

"So are you and Eric broke up, or what?"

"I don't know." I said dejectedly. "Things just weren't how I expected them to be."

"Like how?"

"Like, I don't feel like I get to be my own person there. I feel like I am just a kid and he's the dad. It's like I'm an accessory to his life."

"That doesn't sound like something you'd let happen, Tate."

"I didn't have a choice. I mean, it happened before I even realized it. It's weird down there, Darrin. It's like all the women are happy to let their men take the lead in everything, to be *the boss*."

"So did you tell him that was why you were leaving?"

"Well, I actually didn't tell him anything. I left while he was at work and I still haven't talked to him."

It sounded really bad when I put it all together like that.

"You haven't even *talked* to him? Tate, what are you going to do?"

"I don't know yet."

"He hasn't hurt you, has he?" he asked launching into protective mode. He would be so upset that Eric hurt me the way that he had because Darrin was a gentle soul. He would never consider raising his hand to a woman.

"No, it's fine. Nothing like that."

I couldn't tell him the truth, no way.

"Well, do you *want* to go back?" His tone was softer.

I sat quietly lost in thought, wondering what the answer to that question might be, when he called my name to pull me back.

"Tate?"

"Honestly, I don't know yet."

"You could come live with me. You know I would never treat you like you're *just* a girl. That's how he treats you?"

"Yeah, I guess that's a good way to put it." I confirmed.

"Darrin, I really don't know what I'm going to do yet. I appreciate your offer, but I really just need some time to think."

"Tate, you know I love you, right? I mean, we've been through a lot together and, well - I think part of me will always love you and I think you feel the same about me."

"I know, Darrin, and I do feel the same."

"Do you love him?" he asked gently.

"Yeah, I do. That's the problem."

I knew that confessing my love for another man would diminish the indulgent feelings Darrin had for me, but I also knew I owed him the truth.

"I figured."

"Darrin, I should probably get going."

"Please take care of yourself, okay?" he pleaded with me. "And call me, keep in touch with me, either way, I just want to know you're okay."

"I will, I promise."

"You have my number and I'll give you my e-mail address too, so no excuses. Just keep in mind that I'm here and I would love to have you with me."

"I know Darrin. I just have a lot to sort out right now." I felt like I kept telling him that over and over, but I just didn't know what else to say.

"I love you Tate."

"I love you, too."

Only not the way you need me to.

I suddenly felt like there was so much more I wanted to say, but I knew I was out of time.

Once we hung up, I walked outside and let the tears come. I kept walking until I was under the little tree.

I just sat there, under that tree crying. In my head, I kept hearing his words when he said 'I love you'. That was probably the last time I'd ever hear him say those words to me.

When I finally got up I realized that was the last page in that chapter of my life. What Darrin and I shared would forever be a part of my past and there would almost certainly be no going back.

Six

A WHOLE NEW BALL GAME

"OH THERE YOU are." Lilly said as I came in the house to find her in the kitchen washing dishes.

"Hi. Did Eric call while I was outside?"

"Yes he did."

"Who answered the phone?"

"Me."

"So how did he sound?" I queried cautiously.

"Honestly? He sounded sad. You need to call him, Tate. I don't know what happened to bring you back, but I think you owe him a phone call at least. What did you tell him when you were leaving?"

"I didn't."

"Didn't what?" she was puzzled by my vague answer.

"I didn't tell him anything. I left while he was at work. He was a jerk!" I said, letting my anger bubble to the surface.

"I was really sick, and when he got home on Friday, he left me there without anything to eat or drink, he stayed out all night and when he finally came home, he had the gall to invite friends over for a Fourth of July party. That's why I went to Annetta's. They felt bad for me, so Dell picked me up and took me back to their house. Monday morning I felt better, I went back to the apartment, packed all my stuff and left while Eric was at work. It was just the final straw."

"Oh. Well he shouldn't have done that." She said, now empathetic instead of judgmental of my methods.

"I just couldn't stay there. Honestly, I'll probably go back if he asks me to, but I just needed a break."

Wait.What?

"I figured you were going back." She said knowingly. "What do you mean by the final straw?"

"Just -" I halted for lack of an explanation I was willing to give. After a long sigh, I put my best effort to pass it off as nothing serious.

"Just stupid stuff. It's just different living with someone, I guess."

"Are you sure? Something seemed off when we were down there for your graduation, too. You weren't really yourself…" Her voice trailed off as if she were getting caught up in recollection.

"I'm fine, Mom. I guess I need to call him and get it sorted out. Who knows, maybe he won't want me to come back."

I knew if that were reality, I would be crushed.

"I doubt that." She mumbled as I left the kitchen.

Once I had some laundry going and had eaten dinner, I decided to call Jennie at her sister's after all. At this point, I didn't know if I'd be here a week and I didn't want to leave without at least talking to her while I was here.

"Hello?"

"Hi, this is Tate, is this Janelle?"

"Hi Tate, yeah, this is Janelle. You want to talk to Jennie?"

"Sure."

"It's good to hear your voice, Tate. Here's Jennie."

"Thanks, Janelle, yours, too."

I waited for Jennie's voice to take the place of her sister's.

"What are you doing?" Jennie inquired sharply, without even saying hello. "What's wrong?"

"Nice to talk to you, too, Dork." I teased.

"Cut it, Tate. Mom called me; she said you're in Wisconsin. What happened?" she demanded.

"How much time ya got?"

"All the time you need. How long are you staying?"

"Not sure yet. When are you coming home?"

"Not sure yet." She mimicked sadly.

If I was going to spill my guts to her, it was going to be in person.

"Well, I guess my only choice is to come up there tomorrow." I was dreading the drive already.

"Can you stay over? There's plenty of room, Janelle wouldn't mind."

"Ahh, I probably shouldn't. I think I just want to hang close to home, ya know?"

"Okay, seriously?" her tone told me she was tiring of the cryptic answers.

"If I tell you everything now, I won't have to come up there and I have to 'cause there's a lot to tell."

"Okay, okay. Hey, I can meet you somewhere, so you don't have to drive all the way. I imagine you're a little burnt out on driving."

"I am. That'd be great."

"Do you want to meet in Oshkosh? We can meet at the front of the Outlet Mall and then we'll find someplace to hang out, a coffee shop or something. Then you can fill me in on *all* the details, 'kay?"

"Kay. When? How about noon?"

"Noon it is. See you then." She confirmed.

I DIDN'T EVEN get halfway through the details of the problems I'd had in Kentucky before Jennie and I both had tears streaming down our faces.

Once we found each other in the busy mall parking lot, we window shopped for a while, chatting casually – just catching up. Later in the afternoon, we proceeded to the little coffee shop at the end of the mall. It ended up being perfect, because it was just busy enough that the noise from other customers kept our conversation private.

I told her everything. The possessiveness, the control, the sex and that he had hit me. I told her about some good parts, too, but as the details rolled out, I realized there wasn't much good to tell.

"Tate, why didn't you tell me any of this?"

"I didn't want you to worry about me."

"Well, I do. What are you going to do? You can't be thinking of going back?"

This was what I was afraid of.

"I don't know yet, Jennie. I do love him, and I know it sounds all bad, but there are good parts, too. I just don't know if it was fair to leave without giving him a chance to understand where I'm coming from."

"It doesn't sound like he *cares* where you're coming from. Tate, listen, it's like he's in your head. You haven't even talked to him yet and you're already turning yourself into the bad guy. So you left without telling him, big deal. That's nothing compared to what he's done to you!"

We just sat there, both of us silent, for a moment. The sting of her words left me feeling deflated. I couldn't even deny what she was saying; it was true.

"I'm sorry Tate. I know this is your life and I won't judge. I love you no matter what you decide and if you see good in him, then I'm sure it's there."

Just before seven o'clock the two remaining coffee shop employees started turning off lights and we sadly knew it was time to leave, but after almost four hours and two sodas each, we were both sufficiently caught up on each other's lives, it was like therapy.

It felt so good to be able to really talk to Jennie without censoring the details, I felt like a gigantic weight had been lifted from me. As for her details, I was happy to know she was in a good place about her pregnancy. She was due in September, and she was starting to get excited for real about the baby. She rattled on and on about all the cute clothes she'd been seeing and how the nursery was decorated. Despite the lack of planning, she was happy and I was happy for her.

Back in the parking lot, we hugged and cried some more as we said goodbye to one another, again not knowing the next time we'd get to visit. She promised to call me as soon as she had the baby and I promised to keep being honest about how things really were.

The drive home gave me time to appreciate how much better it felt to have gotten everything off my chest and it seriously made me consider telling my mom all the details, too.

It would be good to have her as a confidant, but ultimately I still decided against it.

She'd understand, but she'd certainly put up a bigger fight to get me to stay and I didn't want the battle right now. I already knew that I was going to go back; there was no point in telling her now.

I called Eric as soon as I got home. I was glad the kitchen was empty. During the day, it was the busiest room in our house, but at night, the most private.

My heart raced in my chest.

"Hello?" his deep southern twang filled the receiver.

"Hi." I said sadly.

"Hi." He said, echoing my sadness.

There was long pause where neither of us spoke, until Eric broke the silence.

"Tate, I'm really sorry. I know I was a jerk. I can't believe I treated you that way when you were sick. Will you forgive me?"

"Eric, it's mor-"

"I know, Hon, I know you don't like when" he paused "I get mad."

"It's all of it. You're too possessive and bossy, you have to relax. Stop smothering me." "Do you still love me?" he asked softly.

"Of course I do, Eric."

"Good. When are you coming home?" his voice almost sounded whiney. "I miss you."

"I miss you, too." I replied. "I'll come back on Friday."

"Why Friday? Why not tomorrow?" he whined again, but his tone was harsh when he spoke again. "What's so important that you have to be there tomorrow?"

"Eric, it is too late to pack and get on the road tomorrow morning."

"It didn't seem to take you much time to pack and get on the road on Monday when you left here."

"Seriously? Are you sure you *want* me to come back?"

"Yes." He urged apologetically.

"Well, this is exactly what I'm talking about. Relax alright? Don't freak out, I just want to spend time with my family before I leave again."

"Fine, I'm sorry."

"I am my own person you know, I get to make some decisions, too."

"Alright, I know, you're right." He agreed, though I wasn't convinced it was more than just lip service.

"I will see you on Friday night, okay?"

"Okay."

"I love you."

"I love you, too. Bye."

It felt like I just raised my white flag to surrender before I'd ever really gotten to the war.

Lilly and Carl weren't surprised the next morning when I told them I'd be leaving on Friday. They exchanged a knowing glance between them and then Carl set about checking over my car's fluids while I sorted my stuff and carried it downstairs, leaving out only the items I would need before I got back to Kentucky.

I spent the rest of the day with my family. First, Carl helped me carry my stuff back out to my car. We agreed that'd be easier to do it today than hauling everything out Friday morning.

Once we had the car loaded, I volunteered to help my mom in the garden with some weeding, even though I hated that chore. I wanted to do something nice, since she'd been so patient about me popping in and out of her house all week, probably being a nuisance. We talked and laughed the whole time. I told her funny things about living in Kentucky, like pay lakes and some of the crazy southern sayings. She seemed to enjoy our time together very much. It made my heart feel full.

My family day was rounded out with an evening hanging out with my brothers. I went to watch them play baseball. Afterwards, we ended up sitting around the bleachers long after the game, talking and laughing with some of their teammates.

I'd known most of the guys on their team my whole life.

By the time we got home from the game, Carl was in bed and my mom was on her way there, too. I got there just in time to catch her on her way from the bathroom, dressed in her nightgown and robe. Her robe had a floral pattern that made it look like it would be far more suited to a much older woman, yet she'd been wearing it for years already. For some reason it comforted me to see that hadn't changed.

The reset button was Lilly all along.

It hit me that as long as things were normal with Lilly, then I could be brave enough to venture back out into the world. Like somehow, she was a safe zone, but I needed reassurance that she was still here, still the same.

We shared a brief, light conversation before I hugged her and went to bed.

Once there, I looked around the room, once again lit only by moonlight. Sadness settled over me like a blanket. While Lilly was the same and most of the house was the same, I was not and this room was proof. It was as if I had emotionally outgrown it.

⌒

AROUND SIX O'CLOCK Friday evening, I backed my car into the empty stall right in front of our patio doors. Eric's car was parked in the next spot over, so I assumed he was home and I grew even more nervous. I didn't really know what to expect: the charming Eric or the mean Eric.

He pulled open the sliding glass door and greeted me with open arms.

"Welcome home, Hon." He purred in my ear as he hugged me close.

I was happy to be back, but I wasn't sure how much of that was because of Eric or how much came just from being back in my nice apartment. It was even clean. I assumed Annetta had been over to do it, because not only was the housework done, the cabinets and fridge were full. I didn't even care where it came from; it was just good to feel like I could get back to normal.

We spent the rest of the weekend enjoying our reunion. That night it was a home cooked dinner in, followed by sleepily cuddling on the couch, sleeping in on Saturday morning and Saturday night was dinner and a movie.

If he always treated me the way he did that weekend, I would be the happiest woman anywhere. He was sweet and gentle and funny and he couldn't take his eyes or hands off me. He seemed so genuinely happy to have me back and when we made love, he devoted more attention to me than he had in months.

Sunday morning we lay cuddling in bed until he got up to make breakfast. While he prepared the usual southern meal, I lazily dragged myself out of bed. I pulled on a pair of cute cotton shorts and chose a little tank top instead of a baggy t-shirt, as had become my norm around the house. I felt better and sexier than I had in such a long time, no doubt from all the attention and affection he'd been lavishing on me all weekend. As I passed by the mirror on the way out of the room, I stopped to admire it for just a moment.

Lilly was right, I have lost weight.

Only, what she saw as a negative, I saw as a positive. I hadn't really paid as much attention to myself lately as I used to, so I hadn't even noticed before now, but my curves were becoming much more noticeable as I slimmed down.

I smiled and walked out into the kitchen, kissing Eric on the cheek as I maneuvered around him in the tiny kitchen to get to the fridge for a soda.

He smiled and returned the kiss as I passed back by, before playfully swatting my behind.

"Breakfast will be ready soon." He hummed.

"Okay, I'm just going to make the bed and clean up."

During breakfast, I broached the subject of how we should spend our day. I felt like I owed him an activity that was of his choosing, since he took me to a scary movie the night before

"What do you think?" I asked cheerfully. "Would you like to take me fishing? How about the place in Indiana by your Uncle's house? We could go there, if you want."

"We could probably do that. Are you sure you really want to go fishing though?" he asked skeptically.

"Sure, it looks nice out and I don't think it's supposed to be too hot today. I'll go as long as you'll bait the hook for me." I said making a gross face that made him laugh.

"Okay, it's a deal." he chuckled.

We got everything ready to go, including ourselves and we set off to have another great day together. The weather was perfect, Eric was attentive and happy, which in turn made me happy and while I didn't catch anything, Eric did. It was fun.

I was convinced that I had made the right decision about coming back and that things would be different from now on. I didn't expect to live in bliss all the time, that wouldn't be realistic, but as long as it was still a possibility for us to be this happy, I couldn't give up on it. I could deal with a little possessiveness for this.

On the ride home, Eric talked about how he planned to prepare the fish he caught for dinner. Cajun style was his favorite way to eat fish, and he had a new seasoning to try out.

"You really like to go fishing don't you? You'd like to go fishing in Wisconsin; there are a lot of places to go." I said absentmindedly. "I thought of you when my brothers were talking about going fishing this weekend."

"They fish for Walleye up there, don't they?" he asked.

"I think so. One of the guys on their team was talking about a Walleye he cau-"."

"What team?" Eric interrupted.

"My brothers' baseball team." I replied casually.

"Why were you talking to a guy from their team?" he pressed, his voice filling with suspicion.

"Because, I went to their game on Thursday night."

"And you talked to them about fishing during their game?"

"N-no." I stammered, flustered. "It was after the game, a bunch of us were sitting around talking, that's it."

"Is that why you wanted to stay until Friday morning? So you could go a baseball game and hang out with a bunch of guys? Were you drinking?"

"No Eric." I said, exasperated. "I went to the game because I wanted to see my brothers for a little while before I left, just like I wanted to spend time with my mom, so I helped her in the garden on Thursday afternoon."

"Oh, I see."

The spell was broken. We were still civil to one another, but the laughter died down and the loving atmosphere we'd been enjoying all weekend ceased almost immediately.

Back at home, Eric cooked in silence while I set the table and put the fishing stuff in the hall, next to the closet.

Dinner was bittersweet. The fish was excellent, as were the cornbread muffins and garlic mashed potatoes he'd prepared, but the ambiance was cold as we ate in unrelenting silence. Afterward, I simply thanked Eric for the meal and set to clearing the table, while he went to organize his fishing stuff.

I was bent over wiping off the table when he walked back into the dining room.

"Hey Tate, there's something I wanted to talk to you about."

"What is it?" I asked absentmindedly, without looking up.

Without my notice, he moved around the table to position himself right beside me.

As I moved to stand, to face where I *thought* he was still standing, his hand connected with the back of my head, hard. The collision caused my head to snap back down towards the table.

I jerked to a standing position and stared at him through tears that were instant and stinging.

"What was that for?" I cried. "What's wrong with you?"

He looked at me, and his voice was cold and raspy when he spoke:

"Don't you ever even fucking *think* of leaving me again."

"Leave me alone." I ordered as I moved backward to get away from him.

He followed toward me and struck again, this time the blow landed on the left side of my head, above my ear. I cried out in pain as I dropped to my knees.

"Please just leave me alone. I'm sorry. I'm sorry I left, alright?" I wailed, desperate to make him stop.

As he towered over me, he leaned in and grabbed my hair, twisting his fingers through it, and used his grip to yank my head backwards. He bent down toward me, so our faces were mere inches apart. "I don't know how you thought this would go, but make no mistake. The next time you leave, I WILL come to get you and I WILL take out anyone who tries to stop me. GOT THAT?"

"Yes" I murmured, trying to be still, despite the fact that I was shaking violently.

"Like your family *or your baseball team*." He snorted. "What a fucking joke." His words were dripping in sarcasm.

"DO NOT leave here AGAIN!" He roared through gritted teeth as he stood up, flipping my head forward as he jerked his fingers from my hair.

The adrenaline he'd provoked kicked in, but my revolt was short lived.

"You're CRAZY!" I screamed.

He had already taken a step away from me, but instead of stepping back, he simply extended his arm its full length and leaned in as he swung.

This time, because I was facing up at him, the bulk of his back-hand came down across the bridge of my nose.

It happened so fast. I instinctively shoved my face into my open hands to cover my nose and eyes.

The warmth that touched my hands a few seconds later confused me. I pulled my hands away from my face. Each palm had a streak of blood.

The next sensation was the thick warm liquid dripping down my mouth, mingling on my face with the hot tears.

All I could think of was that I'd never had a bloody nose before.

While I was slowing figuring out what happened, Eric had already gotten a towel from the kitchen and was on one knee, at my side, spewing apologies all over me.

"I'm so sorry. I didn't mean to hurt you Tate, you have to believe me." He begged, handing me the towel to catch the blood.

I was bawling. "Just, I, please just get away from me."

I accidentally smeared blood across my face as I wiped my nose with the back of my hand.

"Tate, no" he said gently as he tried to put his hand on my shoulder, but withdrew, apparently thinking better of it. "I'm so sorry. When you were talking about being in Wisconsin, I got so mad because, well, I'm just afraid that you might leave me again and I don't want that to happen. I just lost it, I didn't know what I was doing, I just love you so much, Tate, *please*."

"This isn't the best way to keep me here." I snapped, or rather tried to but my voice sounded hollow in my own head, and came out sounding weak.

"Please just leave me alone." I pled again.

I just wanted him out of my face.

"OH MY GOD, please just let me help you at least. I feel horrible!" He leaned in, extending his arms toward me, to help me get up off the floor.

I jerked away from him, which triggered one of the knots on my head to start throbbing.

"JUST get AWAY from me!" My voice cracked as a fresh sob ripped through me.

He backed away and put his hands in the air with his palms facing me as to show me that he meant me no harm. He looked oddly hurt as he turned away and walked into the kitchen.

I sat there trying to get a hold on my emotions. I felt like I was drowning and there was nothing I could do.

How could I have been so stupid?

The crying finally slowed to sporadic sobs and I managed to pick myself up. I glanced in the mirror that hung over the dining room table as I passed it on my way to the couch, instantly sorry I'd done it. The glance turned sickeningly long and set off a whole new torrent of tears.

My cheeks were flushed and streaked with tears and blood in various directions and my hair was a tangled mess from where his grip had been. It felt like he had ripped it from the scalp.

It was awful to look, but morbidly difficult to look away.

I got to the couch just before Eric reappeared carrying a bag of ice wrapped in a towel, wet paper towels, some ibuprofen and a glass of water. Again he tried apologizing, but I stopped him.

"Thank you for this" I said, motioning with sudden composure, to the items he'd brought, "but please just leave me alone now."

It sickened me that he knew exactly what to bring.

He mumbled "Okay.", and walked away. I heard what sounded like him gathering some clothes from his closet in the bedroom. When he walked to the door, I watched him and he stopped with his hand on the doorknob to look back to meet my gaze.

"I'm sorry." He whispered.

I looked away without speaking, focusing instead at the blood on my hands.

The next sound I heard was him closing the door behind him as he left.

Once I was sure he was gone, I went to task wiping the blood off my hands and face as best I could without getting up. Then I swallowed two of the pills he brought, lay my head back with the ice across my eyes and nose and cried myself to sleep.

I WOKE UP cold and my head was throbbing.

The memory of what happened didn't come rushing back to me, the way bad things usually do, it was just there, like it never left the surface.

When I opened my eyes the living room ceiling came into focus. I wasn't sure if the dim light coming from the window was dusk or dawn. I had no idea what time it was, and I didn't want to move, but I had to use the bathroom.

Slowly and painfully I moved off the couch and through the apartment, noting that the clock on the microwave displayed 5:27 - meaning it was morning, and that mercifully the bed was still made - meaning I was still home alone.

When I reached the bathroom I braced myself against the door frame while my fingers searched blindly for the light switch. I squeezed my eyelids closed to avoid the sudden light. When I opened them, what I saw made my stomach lurch in disgust. As gruesome as my face was the last time I saw it, I wasn't remotely prepared for the macabre reflection that now stared back at me.

I stepped forward to hold onto the vanity and as my face came closer into view, a wave of nausea crashed down over me.

The middle of my face looked bloated and flat. The contours of my eyelids and sockets were distorted, as if my face had been inflated, and the bridge of my nose looked much wider than it should. Ugly red and purple streaks covered my swollen eyelids and curled around the inside corners of my eyes and continued, forming two bruised semi-circles. There was dried blood crusted around the edges of both my nostrils and the mess of tangled hair on top of my head was starting to separate into what was attached to my scalp and what wasn't.

I sat down on the toilet lid and let the silent tears drip from my face for a few minutes before confronting the mirror again.

I gingerly wiped my face with warm water and a washcloth, getting rid of the blood. Then I gently pulled the ponytail holder from the back of my head and used the brush to detangle it, section by section, staring unbelievingly at my reflection the whole time.

What I ended up with was a clump of hair the size of a softball and tears borne equally of pain and humiliation, streaming down my face.

By the time I was done, I couldn't stand to look at my own reflection anymore, so I procured another round of meds and ice, changed my clothes and went to bed. I lay there feeling like the world was crashing down around me and all I wanted to do was sleep it away.

In one way or another, that feeling lasted for over two weeks.

ERIC WAS APOLOGETIC and overly nice the first couple days, but then, thankfully, he just left me alone. He still cooked for us, though I hardly ate.

Most days got minimum effort: cleaning, and showering, just the basics. Some days didn't even get that. As a rule, when Eric was home, I stayed in bed. I didn't know how, but I was getting to the point that I was able to sleep sixteen or seventeen hours a day.

For more than two weeks, we barely spoke, had no company, nor did I leave the apartment.

I imagined it was what depression felt like.

ONCE THE BRUISES were gone completely, I slowly re-entered the world. I felt like a different person. I felt smaller, like I was more vulnerable and the whole world could see it.

All this, even though my trauma had taken place at home.

I started small, out just running errands like picking up carryout food or going to Dell and Annetta's. They never saw the black eyes. Eric kept them at bay while I healed. While the bruises were still evident, I secretly wished they would stop over unexpectedly. Part of me wanted them to see what their son had done to me, despite the shame.

One afternoon, when I stopped to get gas I saw that the 'Now Hiring' banner was still hanging on the hotel roof, as it had been when I left for Wisconsin. I went home and thought about it.

I knew the best thing I could do for myself would be to get a job and that seemed like as good a place as any, so the next day, I spent the morning psyching myself up and mid afternoon, I finally made the four mile drive to apply.

The young woman at the front desk snidely informed me that informed me that yes, you did have to be eighteen to work there. I asked for an application anyway.

Although there were tables in part of the lobby, I filled out the application standing at the counter. If I moved from that spot before I finished the application, I might turn around and never come back.

When I looked up from the now completed form, the girl wasn't there.

I saw an open office door off to the left of the front desk. The plaque on the wall next to the door read 'General Manager: Glen Davis'. As my eyes traveled to the inside of the office, I saw a man sitting at the desk engrossed in the computer screen.

I saw the opportunity and took it. I walked over and knocked softly on the open door.

"Mr. Davis?"

"No, I, uh – he's not in today. Is there something I can help you with? I'm Paul, I'm the Assistant Manager of the hotel."

"I just wanted to hand in my application. I saw the banner outside."

He had curly reddish brown hair and a round, friendly face. He looked young.

"I can take it for you." He said, standing up to reach out for it.

I handed him the application and he immediately turned his eyes to it.

"Tatum?" he read.

"I prefer Tate."

"Tate." He confirmed, smiling broadly. "I will be sure Mr. Davis gets this."

ONE WEEK BEFORE my eighteenth birthday, Mr. Davis called me, only he insisted on Glen. He said he knew my eighteenth birthday hadn't arrived yet, but asked me to come in for an interview anyway. We set it up for the following Monday.

I WALKED THROUGH the front doors of the Bowman Park Inn and straight up the front desk Monday morning promptly at nine am. In place of the snotty girl who'd given me the application was a different blond. She looked like she belonged on a beach playing volleyball somewhere.

She smiled warmly as I approached the desk.

"Hi, can I help you?"

"Hi. I have a nine o'clock interview with Mr. Davis."

She took a step backwards and glanced toward the office door on her right.

"Sure, he's not in his office, so let me just call him for you."

She picked up the phone and punched a few numbers.

I looked around and for the first time I noticed how upscale the hotel really was.

The front of the entire building was glass, the view being obscured only by the large, pillared overhang that provided shelter for arriving and departing guests and the wide staircase with glass side panels and stately looking burgundy carpet that separated the lobby from the front desk area.

I could handle working here.

A moment later, a man walked through the door behind the desk. I knew he had to be the manager, the man I had spoken to on the phone. He just *looked* like a figurehead.

The man disappeared through the door he'd came through, then appeared seconds later, emerging from his office. I watched as he approached me and sensed the professional demeanor was through and through with him.

"Tate?" he said, questioning me.

I extended my hand to his and grasped it firmly

He instructed me to come with him into his office.

"Okay, first things first: You'll be eighteen when?"

"Next week." I said. "Wednesday."

"Okay, okay. That works."

He asked a lot of what felt like standard job interview questions and I gave what I thought would be the best answers, the ones most likely to get me hired, though I didn't lie. I did make my job at the fitness center sound a little more sophisticated than it was.

Then he told me a little about the job. It would be answering phones, directing calls and taking care of guests when they check in and out, when they need something which usually would consist of sending maintenance or housekeeping. It sounded easy enough.

Twenty minutes after we sat down, Glen was offering me a job. He said we could go ahead and get everything taken care of today and I could start after my birthday.

He informed me that as a full time employee, I would be started at $8.50 per hour and that health insurance and paid vacation time would follow later.

It all sounded great to me.

Once I'd accepted the job, things moved quickly. Within an hour, I'd had the interview, the tour of the hotel, gotten uniforms from house-keeping, learned how to punch in and filled out my tax papers. It all went so fast, that as I walked out of the hotel, I couldn't believe it actually happened.

I was happy, but nervous.

I was also relieved to finally have a job, but I still had Eric's opinion to contend with before I let my hopes get too high. The only thing that I thought might help was the fact that his wallet was feeling the pinch with me not working. He'd already made a few snide comments about it.

Financial reasons or not, that night at dinner, when I told Eric that I'd gotten hired at the hotel, he was totally fine with it. He didn't even put up a fight.

"That sounds like a nice place to go to work every day." He replied, once I'd told him about the upscale lobby and how nice the people were.

"I'm happy for you, Tate." He said.

I almost believed him.

Since that awful night, things weren't the same between us. The balance of power had shifted completely to his side. I suspected that it had been that way all along - almost back to when we'd first met - but I just didn't see it until now. I was stuck. I didn't know if I'd ever get away from him, or if I'd even take the opportunity if I had it. I sort of started to think of leaving as something I would do 'someday'. As long as I kept that someday in my mind it didn't feel like as much of a self betrayal to still be with him.

As for how that someday would turn out, I didn't know how or when but I knew the time for me to be at my parents' house was over, there was no doubt in my mind of that. I needed forward movement, not backwards. That meant that I needed money, so a job was the first step.

AUGUST TWENTY-FIRST PASSED almost like any other day. If it weren't for going to the bank to open a checking account and the half hour celebration at Annetta's house, you wouldn't have even known it was my eighteenth birthday.

Eric and I sat at the table while Annetta was in the kitchen getting the cake she'd made for me, along with plates and forks. Dell was stuck at work, and I declined having any kind of party, so service for three was all she needed.

Eric picked up an envelope off the table and handed it to me. It was from Dell and Annetta. I opened up the card and read it silently, clutching the fifty dollar bill that had fallen into my hands. Then he gave me a box and Annetta said that went with the card from them.

I opened it and found perfume that looked expensive. It smelled nice but wasn't something I'd really like to wear. I made a point of raving about how much I liked it to Annetta anyway.

The next gift Eric handed me was from him. He told me to close my eyes and hold open my hand. The moment he set the small, square box in my hand, my heart started to pound. It was obviously jewelry and when I opened my eyes, I saw that it looked too small to be anything but a ring box.

Please, Dear God, do not let this be an engagement ring.

There was no doubt in my mind that if he asks - or more like tells - me to marry him, I would be stuck forever. There would be no someday for me, just this.

I looked at his face to see it full of excitement.

"Open it." He said eagerly.

I unwrapped the box and flipped open the lid. My heart felt like it was on a yo-yo in my chest. First my mind only registered that it was, in fact, a ring, but the next moment I realized it was not a diamond solitaire, but a ring with lots of small diamonds.

I looked to Eric, expectantly, for clarification.

"It's called a waterfall ring." He said proudly.

"What *kind* of ring is it?" I asked hesitantly.

"What?" He looked confused. "Oh. It's just a ring Tate, it's not an engagement ring if that's what you're thinking." His words ended flatly.

I breathed a sigh of relief and looked back at the ring with renewed interest. Without the panic over what it meant, I saw that it really was beautiful.

"Thank you very much, Eric. I love it." I smiled warmly, though the thought of being tied to him still had my blood running a little cold.

The last gift was a package from my mom. It was a framed picture of her and me at Churchill Downs and card with twenty dollars in it.

Then Annetta set the cake down in front of me and lit four candles.

It was a cherry cheesecake. Tears immediately sprung to my eyes and I put my head down to hide them.

"I'm sorry Tate, I forgot to get candles at the store today, I remembered everything else, but forgot those and when I got home I found that I only had those four." She rambled.

"Annetta, it's fine. This is great." I tried to steady my voice.

My mom made a cherry cheesecake every year on my birthday; she had since I was about ten.

Annetta had done this for me. I remembered a casual conversation a few weeks prior, when she asked what I usually did on my birthday back home. I mentioned the cherry cheesecake to her, but never thought that she would make me one. It seemed like such a simple gesture, but it meant more to me than she could know. It made me appreciative but sad, too.

"Thank you, Annetta, thank you very much." I said, tears still shining in my eyes when I met her gaze. "This was very thoughtful of you."

Eric snapped. "Why are you crying?"

"I'm not, it's nothing." I said, rubbing at my eyes angrily, mad at my tears for betraying my emotions.

"Eric, maybe she just misses home. It's her eighteenth birthday and she's not with any of her own family, you have to just be patient." Annetta said as if I weren't even in the room. Her words said she meant well, but her tone was a little condescending.

"Whatever." He mumbled.

I made a wish and blew out the candles, and a fresh wave of tears flooding my eyes, but this time I wiped them away before Eric noticed.

I wished for someday to come soon.

⌒

THE FIRST DAY of my new job I arrived at ten minutes to seven, dressed in my uniform which consisted of a navy blue pencil skirt and blazer with a white collared shirt underneath.

My birthday money paid for the most stylish pair of comfortable shoes I could find, some good pantyhose and some updated makeup. All the front desk staff I'd seen so far had been well groomed, so I wanted to look my best.

I felt good.

The only negative so far was that although I was hired to work second shift, I'd be spending two weeks working each shift before my hours would be consistent. Glen said the idea was for me to have a firm grasp on what each shift consisted of for emergency scheduling and for the overall concept of the job. I had mixed emotions about it. My only consolation was that it was only two weeks.

I walked up to the front desk to find the beach girl - whose name I learned was Jamie - talking to an African American girl. She was very pretty, tall and voluptuous. Where Jamie and I both looked a little shape-less in our uniform, hers was taut in all the right places. Her black shiny curls were arranged and pinned in a pile on the top of her head and her makeup and nails were done to perfection.

Jamie stopped talking and they both looked at me. Jamie recognized me immediately. I was surprised when she remembered my name.

"Hi, Tate." She smiled warmly before turning back to the other girl. "This is Monique. Monique, this is Tate. She's the new second."

"Hi, Tate. It's nice to meet you." Monique's accent was thick compared to Jamie's. It was funny here, everyone sounded like they were from a different place.

"It's nice to meet you, too."

Jamie pointed around the corner to her left and told me to meet her at the door and she'd unlock it for me.

I did as she instructed and walked into the back office to find Paul sitting at one of the desks in the large room and another unknown face at the other desk.

The girl at the desk had long dark brown curly hair and olive skin. As she stood to shake my hand, her tall thick frame was revealed.

"Tate, this is Megan, our Front Desk Manager." Jamie again did the introduction.

"Hi Tate. Welcome to Bowman Park Inn. Glen told me you were starting today."

"Hi Megan, it's nice to meet you." I replied.

"Well, we've got a lot to cover, so let's get started right away, okay?" she asked pulling an extra chair around so it was sitting next to her. "First we'll go over the handbook quickly and then I will get you started on the computer system you'll be working on."

"Sounds good" I replied, as I moved to the open chair next to her. Jamie excused herself to the front desk.

Paul looked back at me when I passed behind his desk. He looked busy.

"Hi Tate." He said mischievously.

"Hi Paul." I replied, smiling coyly back at him.

I sat down next to Megan and we jumped right into my training.

BY THE END of my six week stint of shift jumping, I loved my new job and I felt confident doing it.

I learned how to operate a multi-line phone system, check people in and out, take reservations and take care of guest services. I'd learned to navigate the hotel which consisted of six different hallways, two entrances besides the main one, plus the two large conference rooms at the top of the stairs, the pool, the maintenance room and housekeeping.

Through my rounds, I met all the front desk staff - most of whom felt like friends already. I was even getting to know some of the regular guests.

There were five front desk girls in total, plus Megan, who was really more like one of us. She shared the commonality the rest of us did: we were all well groomed and well mannered young women. I was the youngest among us, the oldest being Monique at twenty-five, though she could easily pass for younger.

I learned that Megan had only recently been promoted to management from working the front desk when the previous manager left. That's how my spot opened up.

Making up the five were Monique who worked third - the solitary shift, Jamie and the snotty girl, whose name was Leah, who covered first and Anna, a petite girl of Middle Eastern decent who I would be working with.

So far, Anna was the one I felt the most connection with. When we were first introduced, there was a tension between us that worried me, but after working together for only a few nights, the tension faded and we started to get to know each other.

She was born in India, but was raised primarily in the States. Her voice sounded more like mine than anyone. Her lack of accent showed no trace of her heritage and only little of her time in the south. She lived in Michigan for a time, but returned to Louisville to be back with her family.

Things at work were good and things at home were quiet.

I hadn't seen much of Eric since I finished my two weeks on first shift. I slept most of the evening away when I worked third, and now that I was permanently on second, I didn't see him at all. He was usually asleep by the time I got home, and I stayed in bed long after his six am departure time.

I was more content than I'd been in a while. As a result, my thoughts of 'someday' fell to the back of my mind and I settled into a new rhythm and tried to make the most of what I had.

Seven

FRIENDS IN LOW PLACES

MY FIRST HOLIDAY season in Kentucky brought with it a loneliness the likes of which I'd never felt before. I spent most milestone days lamenting the companionship and camaraderie of my childhood traditions. Each holiday pushed me further and further into acceptance of what my life had become, and how short it fell of my expectations.

Thanksgiving brought a big family dinner to Dell and Annetta's. It was mostly Annetta's family, but some of Dell's showed up later. At one point, there had to be at least twenty-five people crammed in their house. It was a festive day with all those people; it was the biggest holiday gathering I'd ever been a part of.

Growing up, holidays were pretty small. Thanksgiving wasn't much more than a typical meal for our family. A few extra items for dinner and that everyone made it a point to come in from hunting and eat dinner at the same time were the only things that marked the day as unique. Usually, we had a goose for Thanksgiving dinner instead of a turkey, thanks to the hunting skills of my brothers. Even our Christmas Day was just the same small crowd: my mom, Carl, my brothers and I. We'd open presents in the morning, and follow that up with a big lunch that usually put Carl and Danny into sleep mode for a few hours and the rest of the day would be spent playing with new presents and hunting.

At Dell and Annetta's that November day, the conversation never waned. Everyone spent the day talking, laughing and enjoying the holiday and seemingly, each other's company. Everyone treated me with warm, welcoming compassion, but I felt like an outsider nonetheless. Loneliness hung on me like a cloak.

Christmas was another big event with Eric's family. We had three different gatherings to attend, including a Christmas morning breakfast at Dell and Annetta's, just for the four of us.

Christmas Eve was spent with Dell's family, at Eric's aunt Patsy's house. Dell's siblings were considerably more southern and much rowdier than Annetta's and it amused me. There was a lot more drinking and debauchery involved in a Sheppard family get together than a Willmont gathering. They got drunk and loud, gambled and argued about who was cheating. It was funny.

Christmas morning, Eric and I got up and opened our gifts to each other before we left for his parents' house. We had agreed not to spend a lot on each other since I had only just gotten back to work, but he went overboard and bought me a beautiful gold necklace and a leather jacket among other little things.

I was irritated by the guilt I felt when he opened my gifts. Mine were mostly small, inexpensive items related to fishing, coupled with a few sweatshirts, but I pacified the guilt by reminding myself that *he* was the one who had broken the agreement.

We went to his parents' house where we gorged ourselves on the breakfast spread that Annetta had put out for us. As usual, the dining room table looked like she was feeding an army, instead of just four people. After breakfast we opened gifts. Eric bought his mom a bottle of her favorite perfume and a new robe, and tools for Dell. Eric put both our names on the gifts despite the fact that he paid for them alone, although I suspected his mom may have actually footed the bill.

Dell and Annetta spent way too much on us, which wasn't surprising but it did make me uncomfortable. I'd already seen the gifts she bought for Eric because I wrapped them. I volunteered to help, so the week before Christmas she had me over wrapping what must have been a hundred gifts for various family members.

They got Eric a new shotgun and a lot of clothes, plus they gave him money. For me, it seemed like she had picked up at least one of everything I put on the list she asked for. Two pairs of my favorite Levis jeans, a pair of athletic shoes, perfume – this time in a scent I liked, and gift card to a local discount store so I could buy whatever I wanted.

We went home to get cleaned up before going to his cousin Jodi's house for the big family gathering. While there, I wanted to take a private moment to open the package my mom had sent. It came in the mail three days earlier, but I saved it for Christmas day.

While Eric was in the shower, I sat down on the couch with the package, carefully pulling off the brown paper she had wrapped it in to mail it. I opened the cardboard box, revealing another box, a decorative one made from hard cardboard that was laminated with glossy navy blue paper. It had angels all over it. It was about twice the size of a shoebox with a silver handle on either side and silver corner protectors. It looked like a treasure chest.

I knew instantly I would treasure the box itself, regardless of what was in it.

When I lifted off the top, I saw that it was filled to the top with smaller presents, each individually wrapped and there was a card on top that had my name written on the envelope, along with the words 'Merry Christmas, we miss you!'. Seeing her handwriting alone was enough to flood my eyes with tears. I meticulously unwrapped each gift, revealing the most thoughtful little trinkets. It was clear she had spent a lot of time and care on this.

There was an angel ornament that was pale green and held a peridot – the birthstone for August, two candles, a beautiful journal that had stars and moons all over the cover and lined pages, some little bottles of lotion: one apple scented and one peach and two cans of mandarin oranges, which made me laugh because that was something only she would do. That was a favorite treat of mine and I couldn't remember the last time I'd had any. She used to buy them for me all the time.

By the time Eric was ready to go, my eyes were red and swollen from crying. I missed my mom so much. At that moment I would have given anything to be in Wisconsin with her.

"What's your problem?" he snapped when he saw my face.

"Nothing, I'm just a little bummed."

"Seriously Tate, you need to get over it." He said as he looked around, seeing the unfamiliar wrapping paper scattered all around me. "Grow up."

"Like you?" I snapped. "You barely go a day without seeing your mommy and daddy!"

I regretted the words as soon as they left my mouth.

In a heartbeat, Eric was over by me and had his hand around my throat.

"Shut the fuck up. I didn't hear you complaining about *my mommy and daddy* when you were opening the gifts they got you!"

He just held me there, staring into my eyes. For once, I stared back.

Then I was starting to gasp for breath. I bucked and clawed at his hands, sending the gifts sliding off my lap. A split second later he pushed me back into the couch, releasing his grip on my throat, only to back-hand me in the back of the head when I leaned forward to put my face in my hands and cry.

"Besides, looks like they spent a lot more on you than what this useless shit is worth." He said, referencing the gifts, now scattered on the floor at my feet.

"Clean this shit up, we're leaving."

I couldn't help but feel a little sorry for myself. It was Christmas. He hit me on Christmas. At that moment, he seemed even more depraved than normal.

I didn't want to go by his family, but I knew better than object.

We both put on our fake 'life's wonderful' faces and went to his cousin's. Our rouse of perfection worked on everyone except Dell and Annetta who could tell that something had changed since they'd seen us just a few hours prior.

Just like Thanksgiving, the merriment never waned, the façade was carried out and the irony of being around all those people and feeling so lonely was stifling.

BEING SO ENTRENCHED with Eric's family throughout the holidays only added to my feeling of being trapped. On the inside I felt like I was screaming for someone to notice, someone to see that our happy little life was all a lie. For around his family, Eric was charming and playful, even loving towards me. It was all so far from the truth. It made me feel even more double crossed, that Dell and Annetta perpetuated the façade. They were so very proud of their only child, they, more than anyone, would never want his true nature to be revealed because that would be a poor reflection on them.

Working at the Bowman Park Inn became the only form of self preservation I had. The people with whom I worked were becoming a substitute family to me and it was a place I could be myself, a place where I took part in conversations freely without fearing the fallout. Although, occasionally I did get the feeling that Eric was lurking around some corner, spying on me.

I signed up for a free e-mail account, which I'd been using to keep my friendship with Darrin alive, an electronic version of it anyway. The trouble with keeping in touch with him was when I was truthful about my happiness, he was vigilant in reminding me I was always welcome to come and stay with him. I knew that wasn't an option.

The holiday season rounded out with a New Year's Eve that was almost identical to the one I had celebrated with Eric just a year ago: too many people in our apartment, to much drinking and smoking and Eric being too drunk to notice me, which this time was just fine.

What was immensely different from the last one was how I felt about him and how I felt about myself.

About eleven-thirty, I went into the bedroom and closed the door to get away from the noise and smoke for a few minutes. I sat down on the bed and began to think about how different things used to be, how different I used to be and I got caught up in the self pity and regret over the decisions I made around this time last year. I ended up sitting in there at midnight, alone, thinking about how differently it could have all gone.

What would my life be like today if that would have been my last trip to Kentucky?

WITH THE HOLIDAY season over, life started to resemble normal again, at least back to our version of normal. The exception was a new feeling that I just couldn't shake. I felt hollow, like a piece of me was gone. He was in complete control of my life and I had already lost a year.

He'd only hit me once since Christmas and thankfully it was limited to one smack on the back of the head rather than a beating that would leave me covered in bruises or being choked. The smack was out of the blue, at least to me. He said it was because I'd been sarcastic - or 'popped off' as he called it - when I brought up the subject of a cell phone. The smack made me mad more than anything, but the horrible, demeaning things he said afterwards cut deeper.

The topic wasn't new, he'd already told me lots of times that I'm *just* a woman, I should learn my place, but he did keep the lecture current by asking 'what the fuck' I needed a cell phone for and who did I think was going to call *me*. With this tirade he reached a whole new level of degrading. He told me what a piece of shit I was and added that if I'd just keep my mouth shut, he wouldn't have to *correct* me so often.

When he was done screaming at me, I felt like exactly what he had called me.

After that, when Eric was around, I didn't say much. I was less likely to get in trouble that way. We carried on conversations - I knew better than to avoid him completely, that made him irritable - but I held my tongue. I no longer sought out attention from him. At home, I was quieter than I'd ever been in my life.

On the weekends Andy was usually around to hold Eric's attention, which I came to appreciate. Andy was a good choice as any, out of Eric's friends, to have around. Truth be told, the more he was around, the more I actually started to look at him as a friend to me, too.

The drastic contrast between work and home led to two different personas. At the hotel I was happy, engaged in life and confident. I laughed and joked and I enjoyed my work.

However, even on good days, when I was about as happy as I figured I was going to get, that hollow feeling never went away. When I'd walk into that apartment at night after work, it was like stepping into a heavier atmosphere, like the tension and animosity literally made the air thicker. It was stifling.

When I wasn't at work, I spent most of my time sleeping or cleaning. When there wasn't something to clean, I'd reorganize something. It didn't take a degree in psychology to tell me that tendency most likely stemmed from all the clutter of my childhood home.

Some days, when I'd get caught up feeling sorry for myself, I reasoned that the changes I was going through were all a part of adjusting to adult life, part of growing up. The feeling of shrinking into the world was simply adolescent buoyancy fading away.

I tried to convince myself that my relationship with Eric was no better or worse than anyone else's. Sure, Eric could be a real jerk, but maybe that was just my cross to bear. He could be a little cruel sometimes, but he was cute, had a job, he provided a life for us. After all, Lilly and Carl had demonstrated the same thing, to a point. They lived their days out together and were fine on the surface, but at the core neither of them seemed happy either.

Why should I expect anything different?

I resigned myself to thinking that this was just how adult life worked, but in the back of my mind, there was a nagging knowledge that Eric had issues that were far from normal and a refusal to let go of the idea that there was better out there.

AT WORK, ANNA and I had a lot of time to talk and had subsequently gotten to know each other pretty well. Our jobs consisted of a lot of things to take care of, but on weeknights the typical business travelers that we played host to were pretty quiet. Once we got past the six o'clock check in time, finished up all but the end of night paperwork, the guests were mostly settled into their rooms leaving us with little to do but talk.

We found quickly that we had a lot in common. Besides having lived in Michigan – which, in my head, was at least a connection to outside of Kentucky – I learned that she had moved north to be with a guy who was from there, just as I had moved here to be with Eric. She met him, Chad, while he was in Kentucky visiting colleges, and she was visiting her older sister on the University of Louisville campus. Long story short: He ended up not going to school here and she ended up married to him and living back in Michigan, much to the chagrin of her very conservative parents.

Our friendship reached a new level when Anna confessed to me that her first husband had been abusive to her. She said he was insanely jealous, always accusing her of cheating. He routinely beat her up, but the turning point was when he did to her what Gina accused Eric of: he caused her to miscarry. Chad repeatedly punched Anna in the stomach while she was pregnant, with the intention to cause a miscarriage. After the fact, he told her he didn't think the baby was his, and if it was, he didn't want it anyway, end of story. She left a year later.

Anna was now happily remarried. Her husband, Tom, worked as the manager at the restaurant across the street from the hotel. He was everything her first husband was not. Tom treated Anna like a queen. He respected her, complimented her and did nice things for her all the time. Just in the few months we'd worked together, he'd sent her flowers at work twice.

It was only days after Anna told me about her past, that I confided in her about what my present life was like. She didn't seem surprised. She said she could tell there was something wrong at home, maybe, she figured, she recognized some of the signs of an abusive relationship. The fact that I never went anywhere with anyone from work, despite the frequent invitations was one clue. I didn't talk much about Eric, and never about the future, she said had been another hint. It made me sad to hear her say that.

Knowing what Anna went through made me see Tom's treatment of her and their happiness in a whole new light. Deep down, it added to the draw of having her as a friend. She was living proof that there could be a 'someday' for someone like me.

It felt good to have a confidant, especially one who really understood. Anna listened with empathy. She understood that the words hurt worse than the fists and while she knew that the best thing I could do was leave Eric, she also understood that it wasn't that simple. I could be completely honest with her.

I still confided in Jennie, but we hadn't talked as much since the baby was born in September. She now had a healthy little boy, but there had been some pretty serious complications during her delivery, she ended up needing an emergency c-section and her recovery was a lot harder than she expected. Our conversations became limited to what her life was like, and the difficulties that she was going through with a new baby. I didn't mind, she needed my compassion right now more than I needed hers, so I was content to listen.

I began to hold back from her for another reason: when I told her about hard times I had with Eric, her answer was always the same: come home. I loved her for caring about me and giving the only advice that was logical, but it served to push me away. The reality of our friendship now was that she couldn't understand what I was going through any more than I could understand her new situation.

Babies were a common topic among my friends, it seemed.

Anna was thinking of adopting a baby. She told me that she and Tom were just starting to consider it. Because of Chad's assault, the doctors told her they weren't sure if she ever would get pregnant. It made me think about Gina and what she might have gone through at Eric's hands, and how devastated I would be if that happened to me. Granted I didn't want kids now, and not ever with Eric, but I would be devastated if I knew the choice was gone.

Working with Anna wasn't all disheartening conversations; we laughed a lot too, most of the time actually. We talked about some of the goofiest things and bonded over similar impressions of guests and our co-workers. We discussed how Paul tries so hard to be professional, but just can't help being a hound dog around the girls and how Leah can be such a snot.

Jamie was a lot of fun to work with, too. She and I worked the second shift together on Mondays, when Anna was off. I genuinely enjoyed her company and was thankful that it wasn't Leah I had to work with.

There was one conversation that I had with Leah that was almost devoid of her typical pretentiousness, but she was asking me for something, so I didn't expect it to last. She wondered if I could switch nights with her later in the month. If I would work Tuesday night for her, she would work the following Saturday night for me. She said she was standing up in her cousin's wedding in Ohio, if I would switch with her, she could wait until Tuesday night to come back. I didn't care – one day was the same as the next as far as I was concerned.

When I mentioned to Eric that I would be off on a Saturday night, in a rare moment of generosity, he suggested we go out to dinner and movie that night.

The week arrived and I worked Tuesday as planned. When I saw Leah back at work on Wednesday afternoon, she said she appreciated me switching with her and asked if I had any plans for my Saturday night off. When I told her about our dinner and movie night plans with a little too much enthusiasm I ended up feeling lame for being that excited over something so simple.

UNFORTUNATELY THE NIGHT that I had been so excited about went horribly astray from the plan.

Instead of spending my Saturday off going to a movie or to dinner with Eric, I sat home alone, not having any idea where Eric was. By nine-thirty, I had given up on our plans all together.

It was after ten o'clock when he finally walked through the door to find me sitting on the couch, staring at the television that was not turned on.

I was so mad and disappointed, I was afraid to speak, afraid of what I would say if I opened my mouth. At first I wouldn't even look at him. Then I heard him speak; the words were muffled, but he was obviously in conversation with someone else. I looked over and saw that Andy was with him, and that Andy was very drunk.

At that moment, Eric glanced over at me and saw what must have been a hateful look on my face, my anger seeping into the air; he returned my look with one of his own that told me I had better keep my mouth shut.

He seemed to have a clear mission to get Andy to the bathroom. Once he had, he walked back through the living room on his way towards the door and spoke without looking at me.

"I'm running over to Melinda's, I'll be back in a few minutes to get Andy."

Then he was gone.

I just sat there, staring at the door, stunned, and a new surge of anger exploded in me.

Are you fucking kidding me?

A half hour later, nothing had changed. The apartment was quiet, I still sat seething with anger, Eric still wasn't back and Andy was still in the bathroom. The last part was starting to worry me because there was no sound coming from the back of the apartment. I debated for a while on whether or not to check on him, afraid of what I'd find. He probably puked all over the bathroom or something, but after forty-five minutes had passed, I couldn't take it. I was worried he passed out and hit his head on the bathtub or something.

I knocked and knocked on the bathroom door, eventually yelling Andy's name, getting no response. A twist on the knob revealed that it wasn't locked, but as I tried to push the door, it wouldn't open. Andy was passed out on the floor, in front of it.

Wonderful. This night keeps getting better and better.

Anger threatened to take over and finally I let it.

I threw on my shoes and coat, grabbed my keys and went to my car. It was a short drive around the apartment complex, so within five minutes of knocking on our bathroom door, I was knocking on the door to Melinda's apartment.

Melinda opened the door looking glaze eyed and suspicious.

"Oh, hi." She said flatly.

"Is Eric here?" I asked, out of contemptuous civility, my tone drenched in sarcasm. His car was outside and I had already heard his voice, I was almost daring her to deny me.

"Yeah, he's here." She turned and walked back into the apartment, not inviting me in, but not closing the door in my face either.

Eric appeared quickly. He stood in front of me as he pulled the door closed behind him, as if purposely obstructing my view into the apartment. He was just a moment to slow. I had seen, on the table, a CD case with four lines of white powder, and a razor blade lying next to the case.

My heart seemed to sink and rise up into my throat simultaneously. Before I could rationalize what I saw, Eric was speaking to me.

"Yes, what do you need?" His tone was polite, but condescending.

I was determined to hold my ground and not letting him pilfer my rage.

"Can you please come and get your drunk friend out of my bathroom?" I snapped. "He's passed out in front of the door."

Eric's face turned cold.

Without waiting for an answer, I turned away to leave the building. "I'll be right there."

When I got in my car, I was feeling self satisfied about standing up to him. I tried to put the scene of what I could only assume was cocaine out of my mind. I had no proof that Eric was doing it. No doubt Melinda was though. She seemed like the type of person who would do just about anything.

Eric must have left Melinda's right after me because I was back in our apartment only moments before he walked in. When I saw him, I knew immediately that I had grossly underestimated what I'd just done.

I was standing at the edge of the kitchen; he walked straight toward me, never slowing down. He looked deranged, like he was out for blood. I instinctively backed up against the wall, trying to avoid being thrown or pushed down. My mind was racing, trying to figure out what I did to make him this mad.

He raised his hand as if to strike me. I turned away to shield my face and squeezed my eyes shut, but the strike didn't come.

"What the fuck do you think you're doing?" he bellowed as he slammed both hands on the wall on either side of my head. I had to either look at him or look down. I chose down.

"I just wanted you to get Andy out of the bathroom, he's passed out." I spoke meekly, all the sarcasm now gone from my tone.

"I don't give a fuck!" he screamed.

By reflex, I turned my face away from his overpowering voice, and impulse pushed me to try ducking under his arm, out of his trap.

That was a mistake.

When I stepped away from the wall, he punched me in the lower left side of my back. Pain immediately began shooting through my midsection, starting where the blow had landed and radiating inwards. He grabbed me by my hair and threw me down like a rag doll, twisting me around in the process so that within seconds, I was face down on the kitchen floor and he was sitting on top of me, straddling my waist, with his fingers still twisted through my hair.

He leaned down toward me and pulled my head back so that the stench of his alcohol soaked breath filled my nostrils. He dug the heels of his boots into the side of my legs - as if to hold me still - despite the fact that I wasn't struggling.

"I don't give a fuck what the reason is, DON'T YOU EVER COME LOOKING FOR ME! NOT EVER! I don't fucking care if someone died, I don't care if *you're* dying, when I leave here it is none of your mother fucking business where I go or what I do! As for when I'll come home, I'll come home when I'm good and fucking ready, you got that?"

He was holding my head in an awkward position, back towards him, but at an angle, so when he once again pushed my head forward as he yanked his fingers from my hair, the side of my head crashed into the linoleum floor. I let out a cry which seemed to anger him even more.

I thought that would be the last blow. I thought once he released his grip, he'd get off me and leave me alone, but I was wrong.

The next feeling was that of his fist striking the back of my head. My hands flew up, and covered my head as I tried to protect myself, so when he hit me again, the blow landed on my hands. My audacity of trying to protect myself must have angered him even more because he muttered 'stupid fucking bitch' and the last blow, the most painful and disturbing blow, landed at the base of my neck. I screamed as my head bounced once more off the floor.

Then he was off of me and calling Andy's name from outside the bathroom door, five feet behind where I lay, as if nothing had happened.

I was scared to move. I was disoriented, and my head was throbbing harder with every sob. My neck didn't hurt which scared me that there might be something really wrong, because I thought it should hurt.

I was sobbing uncontrollably. Inside I was panicking, trying to figure out what to do.

'Move before he comes back for more' said a voice. It sounded like someone else speaking from inside my head.

I slowly rose up so that I was on my hands and knees. Just as I made a move to crawl forward, I heard the bathroom door open and Eric ask Andy 'what's up?' in the most nonchalant way. He was laughing a little, no doubt at Andy's lack of staying power under the effects of so much alcohol. Although I couldn't see Andy, I could picture his sheepish grin as he took Eric's teasing lightheartedly. That was Andy.

Andy's sudden rousing caused the situation to advance faster than I was prepared for. While I was glad he was awake - thinking Eric wouldn't hit me anymore with him there - I knew they wouldn't stand there in the bathroom doorway for long. I *had* to move.

Without concern for potential injury, I pushed myself up from the floor. I tried hard, albeit unsuccessfully, to stifle the sobs that were escaping me again as pain burst from my neck and lower back. I got as far as the couch.

Eric and Andy came into the living room. Andy was stumbling a bit, obviously still very intoxicated, but aware enough, so that when he saw me, he knew something was wrong. He wouldn't cross Eric by sticking his nose into our business, but I could tell by the look on his face - sympathy mixed with drunken helplessness - that he wished he had not suddenly found himself in the middle of this situation, whatever it was.

Eric walked over to where I sat, and just stood there towering over me for a moment before he spoke.

"You're coming along." He ordered.

"Coming where?" I pleaded. "I just want to stay here. Please."

"I said you're coming along, let's go."

I had no choice but to do as he instructed. At the door, I tried to hang back, wishing he'd change his mind on making me go, or that I could become invisible, but neither happened. Quite the opposite, he stood back and waited for me, telling me to follow Andy. It was as if he thought I'd try to run, which was stupid since I'd have no place to run to.

As we approached the car, I was more afraid than I'd ever been. Through all the previous times he'd hit me, he'd never been this violent, and the hatefulness never lasted this long. I continued to follow Andy so we both approached the passenger side of Eric's two door car, as Eric went to the driver's side. Andy opened the door, leaned in to flip the seat lever but before he could climb into the back, Eric looked at me barked "NO, YOU get in BACK."

Andy stood up and looked at me, as if for confirmation. I simply put my head down and painfully climbed into the back seat, starting to sob again. I didn't want to involve Andy anymore, but I was terrified of what Eric planned to do to me once he had dropped Andy off. For him to be so blatantly hateful in front of someone else was another blaring confirmation that this time was different.

The drive to Andy's never went as fast as it seemed to that time. In what felt like only a few minutes, Eric was pulling the car into the driveway.

My heart was pounding, I felt like I might throw up. I was silently screaming inside for Andy to help me. I knew that once he closed that door, I'd be left alone to feel the rest of Eric's wrath and the more time that went on, the more I had the impression he wasn't quite done with me yet.

Eric put the car in park and Andy opened the passenger door. It was like I could see freedom, but I just couldn't reach it. I knew I couldn't fit through the space between the seat and the door frame, and by the time I would have pushed the lever located near my feet and pushed the seat forward, Andy could have already closed the door. I'd be trapped with Eric, who would then even more furious that I'd tried to get out.

If I did nothing, I was stuck anyway.

Panic burned through me as I saw my chance slipping away.

Andy got out of the car and turned to look back at me. I said more to him with my eyes in those few seconds than I could have possibly spoken aloud. Silently, I pleaded with him to let me out, to keep me from whatever was in store for me at Eric's hands.

Without a word, he broke our gaze as he leaned back into the car, pushed the lever and pulled the seat forward in one continuous movement. His eyes met mine again and this time it was he who was silently communicating to me. Even through the drunken haze, I could see in his eyes compassion and an unwillingness to let this go any further as he stood there, holding the seat forward, clearing a path for me to get out.

Despite the pain, I darted out of the car and out of Eric's reach. Instinct took over as I walked towards the house. I knew the closer I was to other people, the safer I'd be. No amount of rage would make Eric hurt me in front of Andy's mom, because ultimately that would tarnish his image.

I heard Eric say 'whatever dude' as Andy closed the door. He pulled out of the driveway and left without another word.

"Thank you Andy." I gushed as tears flooded my eyes again, a mixture of pain and profound relief.

"You're welcome." He said quietly. He seemed much more sober than he had been just minutes earlier in our apartment.

"Do you need to go to the hospital? You seem like you might really be hurt."

"I don't know." The sobs were coming faster now, making it hard to get the words out. "Eric punched me in the back of the neck."

"I'll drive you," he said, fishing his keys from the pocket of his cargo style pants "but I can't stay. I think they'll nail me for drunk driving."

"O-okay."

The ride downtown was as long as the ride to Andy's had been short, and other than sound of my sobbing, it was quiet.

I felt bad for Andy, too. It wasn't fair for him to be dragged into this and I knew he usually didn't drink and drive, that was more Eric's thing. What he'd done for me tonight was a big deal. He could have just turned his back and went into his house. He could have gone to sleep in his bed by now.

I was so glad he hadn't. As bad as I felt for him, I felt worse for myself.

In a way I'd never felt before, my world was crashing down around me. I could see no further ahead than the moment, and as crazy as it was, I'd never really considered the possibility that Eric would seriously hurt me. Yet here I was on my way to the emergency room.

I wondered what this would do to Andy and Eric's friendship. No doubt that at this moment, Eric was considering this a betrayal, which would not bode well for Andy at all. Who knows what Eric would do? I didn't think he would beat Andy up, that seemed to be a special privilege kept just for me. For all the talk about the fights he'd gotten into, I was the only person he'd laid a hand on in the year we'd been together.

At the very least, he would give Andy the cold shoulder for a while. Eric tended to surround himself with friends who had less than him so that he could feel superior. At twenty-five, Andy was three years older than Eric, but still lived at home with his parents, had no job, little money and didn't seem to do much but hang out and drink with Eric or be with his girlfriend who, from all accounts was an overbearing nag. Eric could simply punish Andy by not getting him out of his parents' house.

Andy pulled his little car up under the concrete canopy at the University of Louisville Hospital. There were big red letters painted by the door that read 'ER'. All of the sudden I was terrified all over again.

I looked over at Andy and for the final time that night, I knew the message would have to be clear without words. I had so much gratitude for him, but I knew it would only make him uncomfortable for me to speak it out loud, so with a simple 'thank you' and a look that I hoped conveyed the rest, I got out of the car and walked through the emergency room doors.

THREE AND HALF hours later, after I'd been admitted, had my vitals checked and had my neck x-rayed, they said they had one more area of concern. Apparently when they had me pee in a cup, there was a little blood, and they were concerned that my kidney may be damaged. They subsequently needed to use something that I had never heard of - a catheter - to test my urine. That would tell them if the blood came from my kidney, or if I was just spotting.

The catheter was the single most God awful thing I had experienced in my life, thus far. Right in the ER room, with only curtains dividing us from people on either side, I had to remove my underwear while the doctor took out a long, very skinny metal tube that he then used to 'collect' my urine.

I scathingly found myself thinking that had I known this would happen, I may have opted to stay with Eric.

When all was said and done, they determined that while I was injured, I was not injured enough to warrant a stay in the hospital. My x-ray came back normal and as did the urine test. I was free to go.

When they asked me who they should call, I froze.

Calling Eric was out of the question.

I didn't want to call Anna either. Having the knowledge of something ugly and seeing it up close and personal are two different things. Plus, I wasn't willing to subject her to Eric's wrath, should he choose to direct it at her.

There was only one person left: Annetta.

When I gave them Annetta's phone number - because they insisted that they needed to make the call - I wondered how much they would tell her.

When I'd been admitted, the nurses asked me a lot of questions, questions that I really didn't want to answer. I confessed that someone had beaten me up, but I wouldn't give them his name.

Eric had already told me once that if I ever called the cops on him, he'd be out of jail before I got out of the hospital. The last thing I wanted was to make more trouble for myself.

It was almost another hour before she got to the hospital. I was dressed and sitting on the gurney in my curtained room. The doctor led her in and then gave her some instructions about my care, which irritated me.

I am an adult; I think you can explain the concept of ice and ibuprofen to me.

I was glad however, when he took a few moments to explain what tests they had done, because that meant he had to indicate to her where I had been struck and to what severity. I wanted Eric's mom to know what he did to me. I wanted him to feel the shame, like I did.

I went home with Annetta. The ride to her house was fairly quiet, too. Other than casually asking me a few ridiculously impertinent questions, like how long did I have to sit in the waiting room and did I think the doctors were nice, Annetta didn't speak.

It was dawn before I finally got to sleep. The light of day made the whole thing seem like a nightmare. Annetta put me up in one of their spare rooms and after a little of her caretaking, I was comfortable enough to rest. She had some cold packs which were much more user friendly than bags of ice. Luckily, some of our laundry was at her house, too, so I even had clean clothes to change into. I lay there in that big comfortable bed, feeling lost and hopeless, and I finally drifted off into a flat, dreamless sleep.

I woke up to the sound of Eric's and his parents' voices, drifting down the hall to where I lay. At first, through the grogginess, I couldn't understand what they were saying, but as my mind cleared, so did their topic of conversation. They were arguing about what happened.

Really, Eric wasn't arguing, he was getting lectured. Dell was telling him how stupid he was to risk getting into trouble like that and how lucky he was that I didn't just call the cops and throw him in jail. Annetta was shaming him with how embarrassed she was, having to pick me up at the hospital after he beat me up. She asked him how she was supposed to feel the next time that she talked to my mom, for I surely would call her and give her a fully detailed account.

Eric just kept saying 'I know, I know.', like he knew he had messed up, but he was tiring of their sermon.

I didn't move a muscle during any of it. I held perfectly still. I felt as though the instant I moved, he'd somehow know I was awake. I did not want to see him. I could not face him.

I stayed poised to simply close my eyes and turn my face toward the pillow should anyone walk in.

I heard Annetta recounting the tests the doctor had told her about and what the doctor said had been done to me, including the catheter.

Then the kitchen door slammed and everything was quiet for a minute. When the door to the room I was in opened I quickly closed my eyes and turned towards the pillow, concentrating on breathing deeply to put on a convincing show of being asleep.

I assumed it was Eric who slammed the door on his way out and that Annetta was checking on me, so I was startled when Eric lay down on the bed next to me. He wrapped his arm around my waist pulling me toward him.

My heart was pounding so hard, I thought for sure he would hear it and know immediately that I was awake. I felt sick. I didn't even want to talk to him, much less did I want him there, touching me.

I should puke on him, right here.

"I'm so very sorry."

His whispered words were followed by muffled sobs.

"Please forgive me." He spoke again in a hushed pleading tone.

The longer I lay there, his words echoing in my ear, the more I realized there was something different about him. He wasn't just quiet; it was like he was ashamed of what had happened, like it had gotten out of control, even for him.

I wondered what that would mean for me.

Had he scared himself? Would things be different now? What would be my best reaction to this new level of regret he was displaying, self serving though it was?

Here he was with his arms wrapped around me, apologizing; yet all I felt for him was contempt.

Eventually, I gave him what he needed: forgiveness, but in words only. The damage he'd done this time was irreparable.

A FEW WEEKS later, it was all but forgotten. No one talked about it. Things went back to normal with Andy. My injuries had all healed and the cycle had reset itself.

I now understood that there would most certainly come a day when the ugly part came around again, but I also knew that at least for now, it was done.

I was starting to learn to navigate the terrain.

Smart Little Fish, smart.

Life did fall back into routine as it had before, but things were changing. I was changing. For a while, Eric was as sweet as he'd ever been, but none of it rang true anymore. I was starting to see Eric for what he really was: a coward.

Each time that he hit me, called me names or exerted unreasonable control over me, the more anger I held on to. I lost the idealism that I had about him, and my 'someday' became inescapable. I was no closer to knowing what that someday would consist of, but the longer I was with Eric, the tighter I clung to my secret, that there *would* be a day that I would be free of him, if it *was* the last thing I did.

Eight

PILOT SEASON

SPRING ARRIVED IN Kentucky with an explosion of colors and blooms, just as it had during our first few months in our apartment. The familiar feeling of it made me feel attached. Kentucky was becoming my home, whether I was with Eric or not.

Sadly, I had all but lost the connection with Wisconsin. Sometimes as I talked about it at work with guests that hailed from there, too, my former Midwestern home became a place that was dreamed and not really lived, as if I had read a book about the state and memorized the details. Just as would be in a book, in my mind, the details did not change. I kept it memorialized as a childhood place full of long summers and even longer winters, baseball and swimming and time spent with friends.

I knew on some level, my childhood home would never live up to the image I now kept. I could never again return as anything other than a visitor.

Lilly was the only connection I held onto. Contact with Jennie had all but stopped and I e-mailed Darrin less and less. He had a new girlfriend and was finally moving on. I felt a little jealous, though I knew I had no right to. Ultimately, it wasn't good for either of us to keep in contact.

In contrast to losing connections in Wisconsin, I was making them at work.

Anna was always there to listen to what details I would offer about my troubles at home, with discretion and without judgment. I was there to listen while she relived the emotional details of trying to have a child, either her own or through adoption, as both were proving unsuccessful.

It was a similar friendship to the one Jennie and I had, but on an adult level. Though we were both quite young – which often showed - we were both living adult lives, which set us apart from some of the other girls we worked with.

ONE THING THAT all the staff shared was our feelings about certain guests. Fridays and Saturdays were filled with tourists, which no one particularly liked. Weekend travelers were often frazzled; not knowing how to get to where they were going, and usually with kids in tow. It made them cranky and expectant.

Weekdays were much calmer. We had more regulars than anything, so they all knew how to get what they needed. Some though, were so particular that we'd share tips on how to deal with them.

Then of course, there were the *cute* guests, which were everyone's favorites. We shared notes on them, too. It definitely kept things more interesting.

Being so close to the airport, it wasn't unusual to see uniformed pilots walking through the lobby. This led to my ability to appreciate the typical fondness for a 'man in uniform'.

In late March, there was a whole group of pilots who checked in to the hotel. When they arrived, one by one, Anna and I realized that they were all checking in for extended periods of time, some up to three weeks. That was odd because pilots were usually one niters. If a pilot flew into Bowman Field, and their next flight was cancelled for some reason, they might choose our hotel for the night and fly out the next morning.

When the fourth pilot arrived – a portly, distinguished looking middle aged man – Anna asked.

"Mr. Russell, do you mind me asking what brings you to Louisville?" she asked sweetly.

He seemed happy to oblige, as he launched into a ten minute speech all about how they were pilot instructors who would be using the flight simulator near the airport to train fledgling pilots on specific types of planes. When he'd finally finished, we thanked him for his time and sent him on his way to his room.

Then the gossip began.

We summarized what he'd told us:

A group of five pilots would be staying there, (two of whom we'd seen had been cute already).

Another group of ten would check in, these being student pilots (i.e. younger), who would stay for two weeks and leave just in time for the next group to arrive.

This procession was scheduled to take place all through spring and summer.

Needless to say, we were *pleased*.

Mr. Russell was the last one to check in that night. The two remaining instructors hadn't arrived before the end our eleven o'clock shift, but it didn't stop us from gossiping about it all night, all in good fun.

It was just all in fun. We knew we were dreaming in vain anyway. Anna was happily married (though at times her tendency to admire other men did amuse me). As for me, I was stuck.

As much as I would love to think of meeting a cute guy who would sweep me off my feet, one who had the means – both emotionally and financially – to take me away, it wasn't going to happen. I'd have to engage in some kind of affair to make it happen. Morals or not, there was one clear fact standing in the way: To cheat on Eric would be a death wish.

It could still be fun though, Anna and I agreed, to *look*.

What girl wouldn't want to spend her time at work talking to rich, hot pilots?

By the end of that week, all fifteen pilots were there, coming and going through the lobby in shifts. I got to know several of them by name, and enjoyed talking to them on a regular basis.

They didn't wear pilot uniforms, as they were just training, but they did dress in business attire and they were sufficient eye candy to keep the all of us front desk girls entertained. Glen was happy with them being there simply because it meant fifteen more rooms booked each night. In fact, the only person not pleased was Paul. He apparently didn't like the attention we gave to the pilots and not to him.

The timing of a memo Glen sent out was laughable. It stressed a renewed mission of unsurpassed guest satisfaction at the hotel.

Our pleasure.

The first Friday in April, Eric came home from work and announced that the following week, he was permanently going to second shift. At first I took it to be horrible news. He'd be there all day long with me, everyday. That was *not* something I wanted.

When he mentioned that his second shift was from two o'clock until eleven, I considered what it would actually mean.

Eric would most likely sleep well into the morning, get up and have little time before he'd have to get ready and leave for work at one-thirty. He needed a half hour to get there and walk from the middle of the huge parking lot to his line. That still left me plenty of time to get ready for work alone and I'd most likely be home before him. The new schedule also meant that I'd have Tuesday nights all to myself.

Maybe this will actually be better...

It was better. After just one week of us both working second shift, I felt better. I felt just a little freer at work. With him tied to being at his own job, I no longer worried that he could be right around the corner.

Nor did I talk to him on the phone like I used to. He'd call me at work sometimes, no doubt to make sure I was there, but now he couldn't even do that. They weren't allowed to make phone calls at his work unless it was an emergency.

There was a little voice in my head, who mentioned that it did happen at a particularly convenient time, considering the pilots and all.

Mornings went exactly as I figured they would, too. I saw Eric less now than I ever had and it was good for me. Not only was I not pissing him off every other minute, but when I wasn't around him, it was easier to tell myself that I was just there until I saved up enough money to move out. That had become my goal.

I knew it wouldn't be that easy to get away from him, but I had to have money before I could do anything, so I was determined to tackle that one first.

Saving money wasn't my strong suit. Now that I was finally making money, it seemed like there was always something to pay for. I took over paying for the utilities: the cable, electric and phone.

After I paid my first phone bill, I asked again if we could get cell phones, pointing out that it would be cheaper than a land line, but instead of a cell, I got smacked in the back of the head and ordered to stop asking.

Another chunk of my money went to putting gas in my car, now that I was driving every day. That, plus tanning and buying my own beauty products, and there wasn't much left. When I did have a little extra money Eric sometimes reminded me that I owed him for all the time he'd paid my way.

ON MONDAY, TWO weeks before Derby week started, a flurry of activity took over the Bowman Park Inn.

For starters, it was time to start getting ready for Derby week. As for what that would consist of, the newbies – Anna and me – got the full scoop from the girls who had been through Derby week at the hotel before.

The hotel would be cleaned from top to bottom; some things that only got cleaned once a year were done at this time. The phones would start ringing a lot; people would start calling to confirm their reservations. I was shocked at the rate that people were paying for their room during Derby. It was like paying double the normal rate for every night you stayed. I asked why it was that way and Megan explained that, simply put, every hotel does it and people will always pay it to have a room in Louisville that weekend.

Adding to the buzz about Derby, we had a new group of student pilots coming in sometime in the next few days.

Sadly, once the pilots were checked in, Anna and I didn't actually have much opportunity to talk to them, although they did continue to pass frequently through the lobby. We joked with Megan that we'd like to work first shift now, since her and Leah made a point to let us know that they talk to the guys all the time. But it was actually Monique who talked to them most. When she came in each night to start her shift, she'd tell Anna and me about the previous morning, when the usual bunch came down for early breakfast. Her stories always left us cracking up.

To hear Monique tell it, she'd like to have a few of *them* for breakfast.

There was one pilot instructor in particular I kept hearing about: Adam Ballard.

One afternoon, I poked my head into the back office and asked Megan to describe him to me. He was the only one of the original five that I hadn't met so my curiosity was piqued.

Why haven't I seen this guy? I thought I'd seen all of them by now.

She obliged, when, mid description, she stopped, lowered her voice and said "Turn around, you'll see him."

I looked up to see two men in business casual attire heading toward the desk. At first glance I already knew one of them was Joel Levine – tall and lanky, cute, but in a nerdy way, definitely not this hot guy I was hearing about.

Then I focused on the other one. He wasn't just cute, like they'd said, he was *gorgeous*. Megan and Leah had grossly understated how gorgeous this man really was.

I realized that I had seen him before. He'd passed through the lobby a few times when I was here, but he was always with other people, and was usually in conversation. That's probably why I didn't pay much attention to him.

But here he was now, standing at the counter not two feet from me. I knew there would never be another time that he would go unnoticed by me.

Physically, he was literally like a vision of a fantasy come true.

He was about four inches taller than me, and he was built. His broad shoulders and well developed arms showed through his white oxford shirt. His hair was dark brown, cut short with just a little natural curl to it. Clean shaven, nice white teeth and big brown eyes that sparkled when he smiled at me.

He smiled at me.

Wait.

How long have I been staring at him?

Joel called my name and it pulled me sharply from my spell.

I stepped forward and smiled at him.

"Yes Joel, what can I get for you this afternoon?"

"Can I get a wake up call for seven tomorrow morning?" he asked, polite as always.

"No problem. I'll take care of that for you right now." I said, still smiling at him, not daring to look back over at Adam. I was afraid I might forget how to speak if I made eye contact with that beautiful creature again.

Joel thanked me and the two walked away, leaving me at the counter, staring after them. The view of him leaving was pretty nice, too.

Just as they reached the door, Adam turned back and looked at me. He smiled at me again before he walked out.

I hoped he couldn't see me blushing from across the lobby.

I turned back to Megan, who was sitting at her desk with a smug look on her face.

"See? We told you he was hot!" she teased.

I poked my head further in the office and looked around, to be sure Paul wasn't there.

"Megan. That is the *hottest* man I have ever seen in my life and I am not even exaggerating. *How* could I have not noticed him before?" I mock yelled, making Megan collapse at her desk in a fit of giggles.

When she composed herself, she said "Yeah, Leah thinks so too. But it's —" her words trailed off into mumbling that I couldn't understand.

"What was that, Megan?" I asked, now laughing myself.

"He's noticed you."

"What? What do you mean?"

"I heard him talking to Joel."

"And?" I demanded.

"And, he thinks you're hot, that's all I know."

She was rebuffed that I'd forced her game of coy to end so soon.

"Oh my God, he does not. Shut up, Megan." I said incredulously.

"Fine, don't believe me, I don't care. But it sure pissed Leah off when she heard it."

"Leah heard it too?"

"Yeah." Now apparently happy she had gotten me to play along once again.

"Seriously Megan, *what* did he say?"

"Well, I didn't actually hear him talking, but I heard Joel."

At that point, I imagined the sound of a bubble popping loudly as I began to doubt her big reveal would be anything other than speculation.

She continued "Last Tuesday, when you were off. Joel came up to the desk to ring Adam's room to tell him that he was waiting in the lobby. While they're on the phone Joel says 'no, not today' to Adam, started laughing and handed the phone to Kristy to hang up, then he asked her if you were coming in. She told him you were off and asked why and Joel told her 'Adam wanted to know if she was here, he thinks she's hot'."

I was speechless.

From that point forward, going to work took on a whole new meaning for me. Instead of not noticing Adam Ballard when he passed through the lobby, I made it a point to watch for him. I would have gone out of my way to make sure he noticed me, but I didn't have to. Whenever I saw him, he was already looking at me, and he always had a big smile waiting for me the instant we'd make eye contact. We really hadn't spoken yet, other than saying 'hi' to each other, but we would. I knew it.

I tried to hide my new enthusiasm for work from Eric. If he even slightly suspected the real reason I was so happy to go to work all of the sudden, I'd be sorry.

I imagined making me quit my job would be the *least* of what he'd do.

While I didn't see Adam too often, I did find out a little more about him simply by looking at his guest information. While the pilots were booked under their company name, they had to provide personal information at check-in time in order for the hotel to verify their identity. Just from our computer system, I knew that Adam lived in Atlanta, he was twenty eight years old, and he always requested room two-seventy-two. It made me wonder what was special about that room, if anything, or if he just preferred the familiarity. There was a lot I wondered about that man.

Adam started coming to the front desk more while I was working. I loved just being in the same room with him, but it was frustrating because now we were swamped with Derby. The instructors would be checking out in about a week, not to check back in until three weeks after the race. Even though I knew he'd be back (I'd already made sure by checking the reservations) I felt like I was running out of time.

It helped that whenever he did come around, Anna would mysteriously disappear. She knew the deal and because, she said, she wanted to see me have a little happiness; she would do anything I needed her to in order to get closer to him.

We talked a lot about him. With her prodding me to 'go for it', I came to the conclusion that while I didn't know what would happen between Adam and I - if anything - I was going to follow wherever it would lead. Anna also pointed out that I should not feel guilty if I cheated because if Eric treated me the way he should, I wouldn't even be open to the possibility of being with another man. I liked that. I didn't know if it would actually work that way, but it sounded good.

At first, Adam just asked me for things like wake up calls or shuttle rides to the airport and made a little small talk with me, though he seemed nervous. It was good for my ego to see him be so self assured and poised when he was around his co-workers, but when it was just him and me, there at the front desk, he didn't know what to say any more than I did.

One night, during the week before Derby, the night maintenance man called down to the desk asking if we could take a box of tissues and some cold medicine up to room two-seventy-two because the guest in there had requested it. He was busy cleaning the pool.

As soon as Anna said the room number, I knew who it was.

"It's for Adam! You should go. This is your chance!"

My heart was in my throat.

"My chance for what, Anna? He's obviously sick, he probably would be annoyed if I show up. He seems a little vain you know, he probably doesn't look his best right now." I argued.

I really wanted to go, but I was terrified.

"Seriously, do you think he cares? He just wants some cold medicine; so really, he'll be thankful to you for bringing it to him. You could call him first to give him a heads up." She said hopefully.

I got the distinct feeling that Anna was living vicariously through me. Maybe it was just the excitement of a fling, or maybe her way of exacting revenge on her own past abuser, through me.

Either way, I didn't mind a bit, as much as she'd been there to share my bad times, the least I could do was share the details my illicit excitement with her.

"Hey! You could call him!" I said, excited as the plan formed in my head. "Yeah, you could call him, as a courtesy, to apologize for the delay in his request. Tell him that the maintenance man is cleaning the pool, but that I will be up with his items shortly. Then he'll have a heads up that I'm on my way, but it won't sound dumb, like 'ready or not here I come', like it would if I called him. That would totally work!"

Anna grinned at me. "Yeah, I guess that *would* totally work." She conceded slowly, laughing.

I was already on my way to the breakfast room to get a small basket and some orange juice. I decided to put a little extra touch on his request. I got a box of tissues and some cold medicine from the back office. Once I'd put together the little care package, I wrote a quick note that read:

Adam,

Sorry you're not feeling well. Please let me know if there is anything else I can do for you. Remember, keeping the guest happy and satisfied is my job...

Hope to see you feeling better soon.

Tate

For a brief moment, I second guessed adding the note because it was a little obvious, but I impulsively shoved it in the basket anyway. He'd be leaving in two days and wouldn't be returning for three weeks. If I expected to make any headway, it needed to be before he left. If not, he might lose interest all together. Obvious might just be the key.

I did a quick touch up of my make up and smoothed my hair as best I could, grabbed the basket and headed towards the stairs. On my way back around the front desk, I saw Anna standing there with a huge grin on her face. She wished me good luck and laughed.

I got to the top of the stairs and my heart seemed to thump harder and harder in my chest with every step closer to his room.

It seemed Adam had become somewhat of a legend in my own head over the last two weeks.

I knocked on the door to his room. A moment later he answered, wearing just a pair of black athletic pants.

It was a little like getting the wind knocked out of me.

His hair was wet and there were little droplets of water that clung to his chest and shoulders. He looked more gorgeous than I'd ever seen in real life.

I think it's illegal to look that hot.

For a moment, neither of us spoke. We both just stood there staring at one another, like we were just absorbing the energy that seemed to be flowing between us. I knew as soon as I walked away from that door that the feeling would pass, and that by the time I got downstairs, I would begin doubt that it was even real, but for this moment, there was no denying the sparks that flew between us.

If he wasn't sick, I might've just stepped up and kissed him right then.

"I brought you some things to make you feel better."

"Can you stay? That would make me feel better." He softly teased, making me blush.

"I wish I could."

My eyes stayed locked on his and I could tell he knew I meant it.

"Feel better Adam." I smiled sympathetically and walked down the hall the way I'd came. I could feel his eyes on me as I walked and didn't hear his door close until I had almost reached the main hall where I had to turn.

THE NEXT TIME I saw him was as he was checking out. Just after five o'clock, he came down to the lobby. He was in uniform, which once again, left me stunned by how amazing he looked.

After Anna commented to me on how hot he looked and said 'hi' to him, she expediently disappeared.

"Hi Tate."

"Hi Adam. Feeling better I take it?"

"Yeah, thanks to you and your care package."

"Oh, I think you probably would have made it okay with out me." I was blushing again. Busying myself with the papers in front of me, I was remembering how it felt to stand face to face with him without the massive counter between us, and wishing I could be that close to him again.

"So I'll be back in a few weeks. Save my room for me?"

"I'll tell you what, if there's someone in room 272 when you get back, I'll personally kick them out." I said with a conviction that almost made it sound like I wasn't kidding.

My loyalty was rewarded with a huge, dazzling smile.

We just stood there staring at one another for what felt like a full minute.

"I guess I better go."

"You don't want to miss your flight." I said, realizing only after the words left my mouth that it was dumb to say. He obviously had something to do with when the flight left. I laughed and started to correct myself when he looked down at his uniform and interjected.

"Yeah well, they'll be looking for me. They won't leave until I get there." He laughed.

I felt my face blush and decided to use my faux paus to my advantage.

"Good point. Um, since we're kind of on the subject, you look awesome."

"Thank you." Now he was blushing.

"I'll see you in few weeks, Adam. Take care.

"You too, Tate."

He walked away and just as he did the first time we met, he turned back and flashed a gorgeous smile just before he reached the door. I smiled back and gave a little wave, trying to look cheerful.

In my mind, I was already dreading the next few weeks and how slow I knew they would go.

Later that evening, as I was staring out through the enormous windows of the hotel, I saw a plane that had just taken off from Bowman Field. I watched it climbing higher and higher until finally it was out of sight.

I decided that Adam was the pilot who was flying it.

THOSE WERE THE slowest three weeks of my life. If it hadn't of been for the chaos of Derby, I may have died from boredom.

At work the preparation for Derby was making life move at a faster pace and kept things interesting, but at home, I dreaded the chaos I knew it would bring. Eric had already reminded me that he and Dell would be attending The Oaks again, and that there was a party at his Uncle Willie's house again.

Lucky for me, I had to work both nights.

The thoughts of Adam that kept swirling around my head kept me from being too bothered by anything Eric might be doing. On Friday night, when I came home to an empty apartment at eleven fifteen, I was neither surprised nor upset. By the time Saturday's shift ended, I'd found that I'd forgotten he was even gone until I got home before he did.

The ironic thing about it was the less concern I had for what Eric was doing, the more he seemed to want to include me in his life. I worried maybe he knew, somehow, that I had thoughts of cheating on him with Adam.

Yeah, like you'd still be alive if he did.

I resolved that it was just him sensing me pulling away. I was beginning to realize that while he could control my life in a lot of ways, force me to do a lot of things, he couldn't force my feelings. When I was angry at him and showed it, he rebelled and proved to me that he could do whatever he wanted, but the moment I started to become indifferent, his attitude changed, too.

It was definitely an epiphany.

Another thing that I realized I had power over - something he couldn't possibly control -was my weight. He'd noticed that I'd gotten thinner, and had taken to commenting on it. But like Lilly, to him it wasn't a positive. He started telling me all the time how I looked like a 'fucking bone rack' and that I needed to eat. The more he insulted me, the less I consumed.

He tried forcing me a few times by implying I'd get hit if I didn't eat what he put in front of me. I put an end to that fairly quickly. I'd eat what he dished out, excuse myself to the bathroom and stick my finger down my throat so I'd throw up and I did so loudly. He got the point pretty fast.

I knew that was messed up, but the twisted reward of having control over a part of my life – a part that Eric couldn't control – was worth it.

Nine

FLYING HIGH

FINALLY THE FOURTH Wednesday in May arrived. The day Adam was scheduled to check in. I put extra effort into getting ready that day, the whole time my heart was racing. I felt like a school girl with a crush and I started to worry that I had imagined the whole thing. Maybe there wasn't any real chemistry between us; maybe it was just Adam being polite. There was probably a girl at every hotel he frequented that had a crush on him and no doubt a man like him could figure out how to work that in his favor.

I had no grand illusion about him or where things would go between us, but I didn't want to be the butt of a joke either. I decided to hold back and let him set the mood between us.

When he checked in that night, I knew immediately my concerns were unfounded.

He walked in the front door of the hotel and a huge smile crept across his face as he made his way towards me. By the time he reached the counter, I could see the twinkle in his eye and there was no longer any doubt that the chemistry was real.

It felt almost as if there were *actual* arcs of electricity shooting between us.

"Hi."

"You're a sight for sore eyes." He said, the smile still fixed on his chiseled face. "Tate, I swear I've been counting the days until I could come back and see you again. Can I see you alone?"

Taken aback at his bluntness, I just stared at him, not knowing what to say.

Say yes. Say YES!

"Sure." I said casually, like it was no big deal. "Where? When?"

"Anywhere. My room, a park, a bar, I don't care. I just want to talk to you and – "

I looked around, suddenly feeling awkward that someone may be hearing this conversation, but no one was around. Anna had already disappeared into the back office.

"And? And what?" I wasn't letting this one go.

"And I want to kiss you. I just want to be alone with you Tate. I want to see you without this counter between us."

It was as if he'd read my mind.

I looked down at the switchboard to check the time. Seven-thirty. Then I glanced over at the late arrivals list and saw that Adam was one of the last ones. I could probably get away for a few minutes.

"I'll come to your room." I whispered. "I'll try to get away at eight-thirty. Is that okay?"

His tone was more breathless than whispered. "As long as you show up, any time is okay."

I looked back down at the computer and realized I hadn't even checked him in yet.

"I guess I should give you a key to that room, then huh?" I said, now laughing. As I turned to the back counter to code the electronic key card for room 272, I could feel his eyes on me.

"Make a key for yourself." He said teasingly.

"Uh, I don't think so. I don't want a key to your room. How about I'll just knock when I get there? "

Right then, Anna emerged from the back office, a smile on her face and mock surprise in her tone when she greeted Adam.

"Oh, hi Adam. I didn't even know you were getting in today." As if she could have forgotten he was coming when I'd been counting down the days, everyday, to her.

"Hi Anna." He smiled knowingly. "It's good to see you again."

I handed Adam the little cardboard folder with the two key cards in it and proceeded with my check in duties.

"Here you go Adam, your keys to room 272. I'll see if maintenance is available to bring up those extra towels to you, but if they're busy, I'd be happy to bring them up myself. Is there anything else you need?" I asked sweetly.

"Nope, I think that should do it for now." His tone laden with innuendoes. He smiled innocently, picked up his bag and turned around, heading for the stairs. Anna and I watched him as he walked away then looked at each other in struggled silence.

She was firing silent questions at me with her eyes and it was all I could do to keep from screaming like a giddy adolescent the moment I thought he'd be out of earshot.

"Extra towels, huh?" she hissed. "I'm guessing maintenance won't actually get that call?"

"Your guess would be correct." I giggled.

"Tate, did he even *want* extra towels?"

"No. That was for your benefit." I replied proudly. "Don't you think it's a good cover for when I go to his room and he kisses me?"

"WHAT?"

"Anna, I swear I could have fainted." I lowered my voice. "He said he just wants to be alone with me, to talk to me and —" I paused to build suspense. "to kiss me."

Now it was Anna who looked like she might scream.

"So? When are you going?" she prodded.

"I told him about eight-thirty. Is that okay if I leave you for a few minutes?" I pled.

"It's only okay if you stay for longer than just a few minutes! I'll be fine and there is no one in maintenance until ten tonight so you don't even have to worry about the cameras as long as you're out by nine forty-five or so."

"Oh! I didn't even think about the cameras!" I said, now worried about my plan. I could seriously lose my job over something like this.

"Don't worry. If there's no reason to look at it, no one does, you know that. You'll be fine."

"Yeah, you're right." My worries give in to the excitement building in my chest.

At eight-thirty on the dot, I grabbed two of the fluffy white towels from the supply closet and made my way up the stairs. Once again, one last glance at the front desk had Anna standing there wishing me luck. This time, she gave me a thumbs up and mouthed 'have fun'.

I made my way to down the hall until I was standing outside the door with the room number that was permanently etched in my brain. I took a deep breath and knocked. I looked down and was suddenly painfully aware of my drab attire.

Even given the relatively small size of the hotel room, as fast as he answered, I figured Adam must have been standing within arms reach of the door. He swung it open and once again that big beautiful smile was the first thing I saw, then the eyes.

As I let my eyes wander down, I saw he was still in business clothes, though the tie was gone and his crisp white shirt was unbuttoned a third of the way down, revealing just enough of his tan skin.

"I have your towels, Sir." I said teasingly, breaking the silence between us.

He leaned forward and looked right, then left to be sure the hall was otherwise unoccupied. When he saw it was, his right arm snaked around my waist and he pulled me towards him, taking my breath away.

"Get in here, you."

The next instant I was in his room, the door was closed behind me and his lips pressed hungrily to mine.

After just a moment, he released his grip on me and pulled back so he could see my face.

"Do you know how long I've wanted to do that?" he asked.

"About as long as I've wanted you to?"

I leaned back in towards him and initiated the next kiss.

I parted my lips and let my tongue tease his lips before I pulled away, just enough to keep him wanting more.

I pulled out of his embrace and sat on the bed. He stood there, looking stunned for a second before he turned towards me and looked down at my face, studying me. It looked like he was trying to figure me out.

"You know I shouldn't be in here, right?" I wanted him to give me a reason to stay longer.

"I know but I'm *so* glad you are." He sat down next to me.

"Tate, you are so beautiful. You're eyes. You have the most beautiful eyes I've ever seen."

"Ah, I bet you say that to all the front desk girls." I tried to hide my skepticism with humor. I couldn't be under some grand illusion that I was special to him. What we felt was obvious, but I could not for a second let myself think this could go anywhere in real life or I'd be crushed when it didn't.

"I don't have any other front desk girls, Tate, just you."

There was something I had to do. I knew it could break the spell between us, but I had to get it out in the open.

"Adam, you should know that I have a boyfriend." I confessed.

"I know, Anna told me." He said, sounding not concerned. "She said it's kind of a bad situation for you."

"It is."

"Do you want to talk about it?" he asked tenderly.

"No. That's not why I'm here. I'm not looking for you to save me."

"Why are you here?"

"Do you want me to go?" I asked mockingly, starting to rise off the bed.

His arms found my waist again as he pulled me to the bed, but this time, he didn't let go. He kept them wrapped around me as we sat side by side.

"No, I don't want you to go, but I do want to know what you're looking for – from me, I mean."

I shifted around so that I was looking in his eyes. He kept his arms wrapped around me and I laid my hands on his arms.

"Okay. You want to know why I'm here? I'll tell you the truth. You are the hottest man I have ever laid eyes on, and I am not just saying that. Yes, I am in a bad situation, one that I will get out of on my own. Right now? You? You are someone who gives me something to look forward to. I like you Adam, I want to get to know you better. *That's why I'm here.*"

I couldn't believe I'd found the nerve to be that blunt, but there it was.

Then his lips were on mine again. He kisses were still soft, but even more aggressive than before. All the while, the only thought going through my mind was that I couldn't believe I was here, kissing this gorgeous man. It was like the rest of the world had floated away. For a little while, it was like my own private fantasy world.

Reality crept back into the room as I pulled away from him and sighed. I knew I had to go soon; I felt guilty leaving Anna down there alone the way it was. I looked back at the clock and shocked that it was already nine fifteen. The night maintenance man would soon be passing by this room on his way to housekeeping to punch in and then back to his room where he had a clear visual of the cameras that monitored all the goings on in the hotel hallways and entrances.

Adam was kissing my neck.

"I wish you didn't have to go. I wish you could just stay the night with me." He said, his words muffled by his mouth pushing against my skin.

"Sorry, that will never happen." I said sarcastically.

He pulled away and sat just looking at me for a while before he spoke.

"Tate? Are you okay?" His wounded tone had the effect of pulling me mentally back to him. I instantly regretted my tone.

"Yeah, Adam, I'm sorry, I didn't mean that at you. It's just —"

"Home?" he asked.

"Yeah. Home."

"Can I ask you another question?"

"You can ask, not sure if I'll answer" I teased.

"Are you safe?" He sounded almost timid, as if he wasn't sure he wanted the answer.

"Right now, I'm safer than I've been in months." I replied cryptically. With him I did feel safe.

Suddenly I felt panicky. I turned to him and spoke with a seriousness I didn't have before.

"Adam, this has to stay completely private. Not just for work reasons, okay?"

"Sure, I know. Tate, I could lose my job over this, too." He said, as if to reassure me I wasn't the only one at risk.

"I would never want to risk your job or even mine right now, but it's more than that. For – for my safety, this *has* to stay secret." I implored.

"You got it." He said smiling. "Whatever it takes to be able to spend time with you. I want to get to know you better."

"Oh, you didn't just want to kiss me?" I teased, my mood returning to its former lightness.

"Well, there was that too." He leaned in to kiss me again.

I giggled while he was kissing me, leading him to pull away and look at me, obviously puzzled at what could be funny at that moment.

"You know, the secret does make it a bit more exciting, doesn't it?" My voice was filled with guilty pleasure.

"It does," He said, putting his lips back on mine before repeating "it does."

The clock seemed to call to me that it was time to go. Another glance revealed it was now nine twenty-five.

"Ooh, I have to go!" I said, jumping up. "I'll get busted by the maintenance guy!"

"Tate, when will I see you again?"

"Adam." I couldn't help but laugh, "it's not like you don't know where to find me!"

"I mean, when can we get together again?" His impatience turned to seduction.

"Soon, I promise. I'm off on Tuesdays and he works second shift." I knew I didn't have to explain who 'he' was.

"Okay, I will see you tomorrow and we'll get something planned then."

"That sounds good." My smile felt permanent at that point.

He pulled me back into one last kiss for the night.

I floated back down to the front desk.

ALL THROUGH THE next week, the secret that Adam and I had kept me in a kind of suspended reality. When I wasn't talking about him to Anna, I was thinking about him. I kept a constant lookout for him.

The only difficult part about it was being around Eric. I tried to act as normal as possible, but I always felt as though he could just look at me and see that something was going on, that I was happier, almost lighter. I made sure to keep as quiet as usual, especially as afternoon approached and it was time for me to go to work.

The following Monday, Adam came down to the desk shortly after I got to work.

"Can I see you tomorrow?" he asked, without bothering to make small talk.

"Um, yeah, but where?"

"I've got it all figured out. Where is someplace you'd normally go for a few hours? Someplace you can park your car?"

I tried to think, but nothing was coming to me.

"Here."

"Besides here, Tate. It wouldn't make much sense for you to be parked here when you're off."

"Good call. I don't know, how about the mall? Do you know where that is? Wait. You don't have a car."

"I do. I have an old pick up I leave at the airports sometimes. I flew into Cincinnati and drove from there this time so I'd have it. And yes, I know where the mall is, you mean the one up on Outer Loop?"

"Yeah, Jefferson Mall."

"Okay, what time should I pick you up?"

"Three o'clock. What kind of old pick up should I look for?" I was laughing at this point, purely from the covertness of our plan and serious look on his face.

"A gray and red old pick up. You'll know it when you see it. Three o'clock then."

"See you then."

He dropped the seriousness only long enough to return my smile. He looked around each shoulder, and walked away, leaving me there laughing.

Anna caught just the tail end of our conversation and now just stood there looking puzzled.

"What was that about?"

"It's our secret plan." I said winking at her.

THE NEXT DAY when Eric got up, I casually let it be known that I was planning on going to the mall that afternoon.

"Well, if you have extra money –" he retorted.

"Eric, I need some new underwear and bras and stuff." I said, with the hopes that would shut him up about the money.

It did.

"Oh. Well, what time will you be home?"

"Depends on how long it takes me to find what I want. Shopping for bras sucks."

Apparently that made him uncomfortable enough to drop the subject.

"Fine."

I got in the shower just as he was leaving, I wanted to be on time for Adam, but I didn't want Eric to see me putting too much effort into getting ready to go to the mall. Once my hair and makeup were done to perfection, I went to my closet to choose my outfit carefully. This would be the first time that Adam would see me out of that awful uniform. I chose a flattering pair of denim Capri pants, a simple white tank top and a pair of wedge sandals.

I pulled into the mall parking lot at ten minutes to three. Adam's old pick up truck was no where to be found, so I sat waiting. The minutes seem to drag on and on.

At five after three, a truck fitting the description Adam had given me pulled right up to the driver's side of my car. I looked up at the truck and as the tinted window moved down, his beautiful smiling face was revealed.

In a flash I was out of my car and had hopped up into the passenger side of his truck.

It was certainly beat up on the outside, but the inside was clean and the scent of his cologne filled the space inside the air conditioned cab. He put the window back up and the dark tint made the cab cool and private.

I scooted over, sliding all the way along the bench seat until I was right next to him. Without even speaking he started kissing me.

He pulled back as if trying to restrain himself.

"I can't do this yet."

I giggled. It made my ego soar, the way he couldn't keep his hands off me.

"You look amazing by the way." He said as he backed the truck out of the stall.

As he pulled away, leaving my car innocently parked there for all to see, I looked around and decided I felt about as comfortable as I was going to, being with another man in broad daylight. This was a pretty good plan.

"Where are you taking me?"

"You'll see."

As we headed towards the airport, I just kept staring at him. It was a strange sight to see him driving a vehicle like this one. He seemed more the type to drive a very expensive, very fast sports car, or a luxury sedan or something.

I'm sure there's one of each parked in his garage.

After just a few minutes, we were parked on what seemed to be a frontage road to the back side of the airport.

Puzzled, I asked him "What's special about this place?"

"You'll see." He repeated.

We started kissing again and he told me how happy he was to be with me. We talked for a while about ordinary life things. I asked him about being a pilot, did he always want to do that and if not, what changed his mind.

He was telling me all about how he had actually planned to go to medical school and was working as a med-flight EMT when he discovered a love of flying.

Just as he got into the details about completely altering his plans, I heard a roaring sound that was getting louder coming from the right.

"Look, now you'll see." He pointed over me, out the passenger side window. My gaze followed the direction he was pointing just in time to see a huge airplane lift off the ground and take flight. It was still so low, it seemed like the wheels would scrape the roof of the truck cab.

"Oh! That was awesome! It was so close!" I was laughing like an excited child.

He seemed very pleased with himself at my reaction.

He lifted his arm as if to invite me to cuddle close to him. I took his invitation and we stayed that way, talking, kissing, laughing and watching the planes land and take off until it was almost dark.

"I should get you back; the mall will be closing soon, huh?"

"I guess so." I said sadly. I didn't want this day to end. I didn't want to go back to reality.

"Tate? Next Tuesday will you spend the evening in my room with me? I know you can't stay the night, but —"

"Yes Adam, I will."

I knew exactly what he was implying. It was the same thing I wanted. The difficult part would be waiting another whole week.

I was home by nine-thirty and in bed by ten-thirty. I didn't want to see Eric. Being in that apartment was enough of a reality check to almost break the spell the way it was. Being forced to face Eric and speak to him would bring me crashing back down altogether.

THE WEEK PASSED more quickly than expected, with the exception of Sunday - the only day I didn't get to see or talk to Adam. Sunday was painfully long.

When Tuesday morning finally arrived and I still hadn't quite worked out a plan in my head of how I was going to get away with hiding in plain sight at the hotel, I decided that my plan was not to have a plan at all.

Once Eric left for work, I got ready as fast as I could while still doing everything that needed to be done. When I stood in front of my closet deciding what to wear, it seemed a little pointless.

Something easy take off.

I felt guilty for the blatant approach, but when I'd accepted Adam's invitation to spend the day in his room, I knew what he had in mind.

I ended up choosing a black short sleeve button down shirt, a black cotton skirt that had a drawstring waist and black slip on sandals, no jewelry. My outfit covered my best black lacy bra and panties, a set that rarely saw the light of day.

I arrived at the hotel and parked between two trucks on the side of the hotel in effort to hide my car. My heart was pounding in my chest.

I am so getting fired for this.

I gripped the key card that I had made the night before to get me into the side door. I coded it for the conference room, so as long as no one else had made one and cancelled mine out, it should work fine to get me into the building. My only hope was that I could get through the door and past the camera in the hallway without anyone noticing me on the monitors behind the desk. Anna was working, but so was Leah. I reassured myself with the thought that while I had no doubt that Leah would tattle if she saw me, luckily Anna mentioned that Leah could usually be counted on to hang out in the back office flirting with Paul until five o'clock when he left.

I got out of the car and walked with my head down, my long hair covering my face until I was safely inside the hotel and past the first camera. I walked quickly and quietly up the stairs, down the hallway and around the corner to the right, taking care to keep my face covered again as I passed the second camera.

I got to Adam's room and didn't hesitate to knock this time and he didn't hesitate to open the door and let me into safety.

"Hi." He immediately pulled me into an embrace.

"Hi." I returned his greeting, but pulled back from him. "Call down to the front desk."

"What? Why?"

"Just call down there and if Anna answers, tell her I want to talk to her and give me the phone."

"And if Leah answers? Or someone else?"

"Just ask for a wake up call or something." I said impatiently.

"Okay, okay."

He picked up the phone and pushed the '0' to reach the front desk. After what was presumably a greeting on the other end, he smiled and said "Hi Anna, Tate wants to talk to you."

He handed me the phone looking puzzled, but smiling.

"Hi, I'm here. Am I good?"

"I'm out here alone and have been for fifteen minutes and maintenance is on an airport run. You're clear."

"Awesome." I breathed a sigh of relief.

"I'll call before I leave."

"'Kay."

"Hey Tate, have fun." She said, a devilish playfulness in her voice. She knew.

"Thanks."

I hung up the phone and looked at Adam.

"Hi."

He laughed. "Feel better now?"

I slipped my shoes off and walked over to where he was standing, wrapped my arms around his neck and kissed him lightly on the mouth.

"Now I do."

He looked so sexy. He was wearing a pale blue polo, khaki pants and no socks. It made me think of a male model in a beach photo shoot.

He smiled and led me to the bed, where he sat down and positioned me so that I was standing in front of him. He put one hand on each one of my hips and looked up at me, his eyes full of wanting.

"Is this okay?"

"This is okay." I said smiling. I knew exactly what I was agreeing to, despite the fact that he hadn't spoken it out loud.

I bent over to kiss him then I stood back up to wait for him to take the next step. He seemed like the kind of man who liked to seduce a woman. After so many months of being with Eric or rather *not* being with Eric, I honestly longed to be seduced.

As a pang of guilt ran through my mind, I reminded myself of what Anna had said when this all started: if Eric treated me the way he should, I would never have been open to something like this happening in the first place.

I owed him nothing.

Adam toyed with the bottom button on my shirt before finally unbuttoning it, then moved to the next one up. He worked the buttons at such a slow, steady pace that by the time he got to the last one my heart was racing.

He stood up and slid my shirt over my shoulders, letting it fall to the floor while I stood motionless. He left a trail of soft wet kisses from my neck down all the way down to my stomach as he resumed his position on the bed. He looked up at me and gently started tugging on the drawstring in front of him. A moment later, he slid my skirt down over my hips and it joined my shirt on the floor.

I realized I was holding my breath.

Breathe Tate. Now would not be the time to pass out.

He took my hand in his and gently led me to the left, one step, out of my clothes.

"Will you turn around for me?" he asked softly. "I just want to look at you."

I spun slowly on the spot, feeling his gaze on me as if there was actual heat coming from his stare. Once my back was to him, he placed his hands lightly on my waist and on cue I stopped turning.

"God, you're so beautiful."

I felt his fingertips travel lightly up my back, sending shivers through me that had nothing to do with the temperature in the room. When his hands reached my bra strap, in a flash he had effortlessly unfastened it. Without really moving, I let my arms fall forward so the bra would slide off.

I held my position, my back to him. Next his hands were back at my waist and he ran his fingers gently inside the waistband of my black lace panties before hooking them on either side and sliding them down over my backside and hips as he had done my skirt.

He took my hand once again and gently turned me back towards him, taking a moment to survey the parts of my body he had just revealed.

Somewhere in my mind I thought I should feel awkward or self conscious about standing there naked in front of this man.

I didn't feel awkward at all. I felt completely at ease.

More than anything I felt eager to please him and anxious for him to have his way.

He stood up, took me by the hand and led me to the side of the bed, where he leaned over and pulled the bedspread back. I sat down and leaned back into the pillows, wondering what kind of show I would get in return.

He didn't take quite as much time in undressing himself as he had undressing me, but it was incredible nonetheless.

He gripped the bottom cuff of his polo shirt and pulled it up and over his head in one slow, continuous movement, showing what seemed to be every muscle in his stomach, chest and arms. It was the second time I'd seen him without a shirt on, and it had the same effect, I felt breathless.

He unbuttoned his pants and slid them off, revealing a pair of white boxer briefs that were form fitting and left little to the imagination. Now he looked even more like a male model.

The rest of that afternoon and well into the evening was spent enjoying one another's bodies. I had never in my life known the sensations that I knew that day, not with Darrin and certainly never with Eric.

Adam was gentle all the while but aggressive at exactly the right moments. He asked me several times if I was okay, what I liked and what I wanted him to do. I spoke without embarrassment and didn't hold back. In return, neither did he.

It was incredible.

As we lay in bed, arms wrapped around each other as the moments ticked by, I was sad to see darkness begin to fall over the room. That meant it was time for me to go. I wanted so desperately to stay with him - to fall asleep and wake up in his arms - but I knew there was just no way that was possible.

Adam got up first and brought me my clothes and excused himself to the bathroom while I got dressed in private. He was such a gentleman.

A true gentleman, not a fraud like Eric.

When he emerged he was dressed as well and we both knew what was next.

We said a sad goodbye with a promise to make plans for the next Tuesday. Caught up in the moment, I almost forgot to call downstairs.

"Oh, you have to call for me, same as before." I laughed.

He picked up the phone without needing further instruction and called down to the desk. A second later he was handing me the phone with Anna on the other end.

"Perfect timing, Leah's in the back eating and the van's on another airport run. See you tomorrow. Oh, and I'll be expecting details." Her voice trailed off into a little singsong when she said the word 'details'.

"'Kay, see ya tomorrow. Thanks Anna."

"You're welcome, Tate."

I kissed Adam one more time and told him I had to go right then, that I had the perfect window of opportunity.

"I'm so glad you came here today, Tate."

"So am I. More than you know.

I got home and showered without washing my hair. Eric would be home in just under an hour so I had time, but if my hair was wet or if I looked like I'd just gotten fixed up, he'd be suspicious. After my shower, I sprayed a little perfume in my hair to cover up any smell of Adam's cologne. I decided to again avoid Eric all together and went to bed, dreaming about the blissful day I'd shared with Adam and not feeling a bit of guilt.

THE FOLLOWING TUESDAY could have gone exactly the same way for all I was concerned, and it would have, if Eric wouldn't have taken off from work.

The days following the tryst Adam and I shared showed a change in how we responded to one another. It was even more fun, more intense and thought consuming than it had been before we slept together. I was loving it. I knew it may not last much longer, so I was determined to have as much fun with it while it did.

When we were making plans for the following Tuesday, Adam told me he wished there were more options for things we could do. He figured I'd had my fill of watching airplanes, but he didn't want me to think that all he wanted was sex. I quickly let him know that I *didn't* think that was all he wanted, and that being said, I would be perfectly happy to spend our next time together in his room.

So that's what we planned. He said he'd pick up dinner and a movie and that it would be almost like a real date. I laughed and told him that if it was going be our first date, we may be doing things a bit backward.

The plan was all set, until Eric came home from work on Monday night touting the fact that he had taken off the next night to spend time with me. He thought maybe we could go mini golfing or something.

I tried to be excited about his plan, if for nothing else but to keep the peace. Inside, I was completely disappointed and panicking over the fact that I had to get a hold of Adam somehow to cancel our plans without Eric noticing. My only option was to have Anna give him a message.

Tuesday morning, before Eric woke up, I grabbed the cordless and called Anna at home. Just in case Eric woke up without me knowing, I tried to sound really casual about how nice it was that Eric had taken off work and how we were going to go play mini golf and go to dinner. I teased her about having to work with Leah and how it was nice to know that *someone* would miss me that night. That was all it took. She figured out the rest and I discretely confirmed.

ERIC WAS DISTRUSTFULLY nice all day. I had his undivided attention, he was playful and funny, even encouraging when we played golf. He even let me choose the spot for dinner. Of course the thought I kept coming back to was that he knew something and this was the lead up to the wrath that would follow. But as the evening wore on, no wrath came.

On the way home from the restaurant, I complained of the onset of a migraine, just in case he'd want to finish this evening off with us sleeping together.

In what I recognized as extreme irony, it felt wrong to sleep with Eric while I was involved with Adam.

Eric and I hadn't had sex in months. He showed no interest and the last time I had showed any, he shot me down in a very rude, hateful way, so I hadn't tried since. There was no reason why tonight should break our streak.

The night ended with no split personality, no anger, no wrath. I was still left wondering what suddenly caused him to be so interested in me, but I figured it must not have anything to do with Adam.

There was only one Tuesday left before Adam would be checking out for the fourth of July holiday. I was a lot sadder than I should have been.

I have to keep in mind this isn't permanent. This is a summer fling, nothing more.

"So what did you do on your surprise date?" Adam asked me mockingly the next afternoon at work.

The lobby was empty, all the management was gone and Anna was on the computer in the back office so it was like we had the place to ourselves.

"You really want to know?" I asked sarcastically.

"I don't know, do I?" He seemed a little sorry he'd brought it up.

"I'm just kidding, we went mini golfing and to dinner. It was nothing, but it was weird."

"Why was it weird?"

"It was weird because we don't do stuff like that."

"Well, what kind of stuff *do* you do then?"

"He has friends over, they drink, I clean up. That's what we do."

The words came out more bitterly than I had intended.

"I see."

"You know what? Let's not talk about it, about him. Okay?"

"Deal. It's just that, well, I wish *I* could take you mini golfing and to dinner. Hell, I'd be happy just to take you to dinner." He smiled playfully.

"Oh yeah, why's that?"

"Because I would get to enjoy your company while everyone else is jealous that I'm with the most beautiful woman in the room." He replied matter-of-factly.

"Smooth, very smooth, Adam."

"So what do you want to do next Tuesday? Or is he going to make every Tuesday date night now?"

"God, I hope not!" I snapped.

"Tate, why do you stay with him?" he snapped back at me. "I'm not trying to save you, I couldn't even if I wanted to, but can you explain to me why you're there? Why don't you go home to Wisconsin?"

"Adam, it's complicated. It's, well, I don't even know how to explain it."

"Do you love him?"

"Why do want to know this stuff?"

"I don't know, because I care about you. Quite frankly it seems like the smart, beautiful young lady standing in front of me is wasting her life with a loser who hits women."

"Okay, okay, I'll answer you, at least the best way I can.

"Yes, I do love a part of him. I don't love the abusive part, but I love the other part, a part that I'm not even sure is real anymore. As for why I don't go back to Wisconsin, well honestly, there's nothing better for me there either. Why do I stay with him? Partly because right now I can't afford not to and even if I could, he would find me. Right now it is easier to stay than it is to go. I'm fine, I can handle this and believe me, I will get out s-" I stopped short of finishing the word.

I didn't know if I could say that word to him. He couldn't possibly understand what that very ordinary little word meant to me.

"What Tate? You'll get out what?"

"Someday." I said quietly.

"Oh." His reply rang with sad acknowledgement. Maybe he understood more than I gave him credit for.

"Hey I know, let's go back to that part when you tell me how smart and beautiful I am."

"You are smart and beautiful Tate, you really are, probably much more than you realize."

"Thanks Adam." I said, smiling warmly, despite the lump left in my throat from our conversation.

"I should probably get going; I have to be at the sim in twenty minutes."

BY THE FOLLOWING Tuesday things had gotten back to normal both at home and at work. Adam was back to being fun and lighthearted and Eric was back to ignoring me and being rude. I didn't even bother making an excuse up for where I was going that day. As long as I was home before he got home, he'd never even know I was gone.

Thank God he'd never made friends with any of our neighbors.

Adam and I planned our date night again, which made me happy. I enjoyed watching the planes and being in the truck with him was nice, but cuddling in his hotel room was much better.

The instant I was safely in Adam's room, I threw my arms around him, squeezing him hard. "I've missed you."

"I missed you, too." He said, returning my hug. "I'm sorry about last week, about making you talk about him."

"It's forgotten." I said cheerfully. "What did you get for dinner? It smells good."

"I got bacon cheeseburgers and fries. Your burger has barbeque sauce and pickles, just the way you like it."

I was thoroughly impressed that he'd gotten that from one casual conversation weeks ago.

"You know, you'd better be careful." I warned.

"Why's that?" he said, not looking up from his task of taking the food out and making a little setting for us at the small hotel room dining table.

"If you don't quit being so nice to me, I might follow you back to Atlanta and stalk you until you take me in."

He suddenly looked up at me, with what almost looked like panic in his eyes.

"Tate —"

"Relax, Adam, I'm kidding."

He still looked spooked, so I tried to recover.

"Adam, have you noticed that I've never asked you what *your* situation is at home?"

"Yes, I have noticed Tate." He replied quickly. "and I —"

"That's because it doesn't matter to me." I said, interrupting him. "I don't need to know because if you're happy being here with me and I'm happy being here with you, then right now, that's all that matters."

"Believe me," I continued "I know that sounds terribly selfish, but I guess I don't care. If you're cheating on someone with me, well, I guess I think like this: if you weren't with me, you might be with someone else. It may as well be me."

I wrapped my arms around him from behind and whispered in his ear.

"Relax, everything is fine. You're not hurting me, you're not leading me on. My eyes are wide open here, okay?"

He put the food down and turned to face me, twisting inside my embrace. He put his arms around me and looked into my eyes.

"You're amazing, you know that? I wish things were different. I know I shouldn't, but I do." He said remorsefully. "I wish there was a way."

"I don't think there is, Adam."

"I don't think so either."

"Then stop feeling bad about what can't be and enjoy what is right now."

"Deal, let's eat, I'm starved."

We ate dinner together and it was peaceful. We looked out over the parking lot, watching people come and go from the hotel and the restaurant across the street where Anna's husband worked, where Adam had gotten our food.

"Well, there's no one else here to make jealous, but is this still okay?" I teased.

"Yeah, even better I think. I like having you all to myself and you're still the most beautiful woman in the room."

"Adam, I'm the *only* woman in the room."

"Even if you weren't Tate, even if you weren't."

After dinner - which I did my best to eat most of, despite my shrunken appetite from the power struggle with Eric – we cuddled on the bed and watched a scary movie that had just come out on DVD.

When he'd told me he'd gotten a horror flick, I reiterated how smooth he was.

"You're impressed that I remembered you like barbeque bacon cheeseburgers with pickles and scary movies?" he said incredulously. "That doesn't sound like too much to remember."

"I think I'm more impressed that you listened in the first place."

It was almost six thirty by the time the movie was over. Adam fell asleep before the end, but the loud music that the credits were set to woke him up.

"Sorry, I think I fell asleep for a minute there." He said sleepily.

"Don't be sorry. That's one more thing I got to experience with you. You look very peaceful when you sleep, by the way." I giggled.

He squeezed me closer and laughed with me.

"So now what do you want to do?" he asked. "Watch TV or something?"

"Or something." I said as I rolled over on top of him.

"Oh really? That something?"

"Yeah, I think that something." I murmured, my mouth already pressed to his.

AT NINE O'CLOCK Adam was handing me the phone with Anna waiting on the other end to talk to me.

"Wait five minutes. Someone just called for an airport pickup, so maintenance will be leaving soon and Leah just got back with her food."

"Five minutes, got it. Thanks Anna. I'll see you tomorrow."

I hung up the phone and sat down on the bed next to Adam.

"So you check out on Friday, huh?"

"Yeah, but this is a short break Tate, not even two weeks." His cheerfulness sounded painfully forced.

"Okay well then I'm only gonna miss you a little bit this time."

"Hey!" he said, feigning injury.

"I'm kidding. I'll miss you a lot, Adam. Unfortunately, I'm sure of it."

We sat there quietly, looking, studying one another. He was so gorgeous, I could look at him forever and never get tired of it.

Before I let myself get caught up in moment I knew I shouldn't be having, I stood up and hugged and kissed him one more time before I made my discreet escape and went home.

When I opened the door to get into the apartment, I had a rude surprise.

The light from the hallway illuminated the small space just enough for me to see Eric. He was sitting in the dark, waiting for me.

Ten

THE END OF THE WORLD

WHEN I CLOSED the door the apartment was once more plunged into darkness, so when Eric spoke, his voice seemed to come from thin air.

"Where the fuck where you?"

I am so dead. Think Tate, think.

Keep it simple.

"I was at work." I said, giving my best effort to sound casually offended.

I walked over and flipped on the light. Eric squinted his eyes in reaction to the sudden brightness of the room. He looked deranged.

I am so dead.

"Why the fuck would you be at work on your day off, wearing *that?*"

I looked down at the light blue tank top and khaki shorts I had on.

Thank God I'm not wearing the mini skirt.

I purposely moved to a spot far away from where he was sitting at the dining room table. I knew I probably reeked of Adam's cologne.

"I was there talking to Anna." I said matter-of-factly. "It's not like I have any other friends you know and what's wrong with what I'm wearing?"

"That's funny because Anna told Mom you weren't there." He snapped, ignoring the question about my clothes.

"*What?* Why was your mom talking to Anna?" I snapped back. Now I was as mad as he was.

Wait, Anna would have mentioned that Annetta called, he's trying to catch you up.

"She called here to see if you wanted to go to bingo with her and since you weren't here, she was worried about you." I could tell his tone was meant to sound caring, but it rang false, it only sounded condescending.

"What, because I'm not allowed to go anywhere?" My fear was quickly succumbing to the injustice of being searched for. "Do you people get that I AM NOT FIVE?"

"What are so worked up about, Tate? Do you have something to hide?" His tone laden with suspicion and insinuation.

"No Eric, I don't have anything to hide, but newsflash here: I am an adult. Yeah, I went to work to hang out with Anna because she gets bored on the nights she works with Leah. All Leah does is sit on the phone. Anna's been having a rough time with the whole trying to get pregnant thing and could use a friend. Yes, I went to work, on my day off, not in uniform and hung out with my friend. Is there something wrong with that?"

I was actually starting to believe my own story.

"What are *you* doing here anyway?" I snapped. "Where the hell is your car? What you take off work now to spy on me? Hide your car and sit here in the dark like some kind of freak stalker?"

That was too far, Little Fish.

In a flash he was up from the table and standing in front of me with his fingers clenched around my throat.

"DO NOT talk to me that way you little fucking bitch. Yeah, my car is around the building and I sat in the dark waiting for you. Don't fucking worry about it."

His grip was tightening, I was running out of air.

"Eric, let go." I gasped, clawing at his fingers.

"If I find out you're lying about where you were tonight, you will be sorry and if I find out you're screwing around, I will *fucking* KILL you! Do you understand?"

I didn't speak. I didn't think I could.

"I SAID DO YOU UNDERSTAND?" he bellowed.

He wasn't going to let go until I answered. Adrenaline was starting to pump through my veins, it took everything I had but I answered him.

"Yes" I gasped. "Let go."

He pushed me backwards as he released his grip. I flew back and landed on the floor with a thud.

"Now get the fuck to bed."

I got up off the floor and walked straight to the bathroom, not even daring to look at him.

As I stood looking in the mirror at my own reflection, my mind raced with questions. Could someone have seen my car? Did Annetta really talk to Anna?

That part would be easy enough to find out at least. I'd just ask her tomorrow.

If I had a cell phone, you'd be able to find me, asshole.

I resigned myself to the fact that if he really knew anything, I'd have gotten a lot worse than I did.

I sprayed a little body spray on my clothes and hair to try to cover up any trace of Adam. I hoped it would be enough because there was no way I could shower without raising more suspicion.

I quietly unlocked the bathroom door and opened it slowly. I didn't want any more confrontation from him. I could hear the sound of the TV, so figuring he was in the living room and out of sight, I turned off the light and crept quietly into the bedroom.

As I lay there in bed, thoughts swirling around inside my head, a profound thought occurred to me.

I didn't cry.

The next day Eric got up and treated me with his normal indifference. Other than a comment he made that 'I'd better hope he doesn't find out that I'm lying', there was no mention of the previous night's incident.

As soon as I got to work, I told Anna everything that happened.

"Oh my God, Tate! You have to be careful."

"I know, I know. Anna, did Annetta really call here for me?"

"Oh, you know, someone did – a woman, but she didn't say who it was. I thought it was just a guest you had helped with a reservation or something. I'm so sorry Tate, I would have told you right away if I knew it was her!" she said.

"It's fine, Anna. Don't worry about it. There's no reason why they should be calling here for me anyway. It's bad enough that I have Eric to answer to, much less his parents."

"Tate, are you okay?" she asked compassionately.

"Yeah, I'm fine. It was nothing. All he did was choke me for a minute, he didn't even hit me. It definitely could have been worse - considering." I said, looking at her with wide eyes.

"I have a few bruises on my neck, but they're easy enough to hide with my hair." I continued, pulling my hair back to show her Eric's fingerprints on my neck.

With perfectly *bad* timing, Adam walked up at that moment.

"Hi Ladies, whatcha looking at?" he asked cheerfully.

I spun around to face him.

"Hi. Oh, uh, I'm thinking about getting my hair cut short." I lied, cheerfully.

That may have been perfectly believable if Anna wouldn't have spoken at the exact moment I did.

"Earrings." She fibbed.

We looked at one another for a second, while my mind scrambled to recover. I did not want Adam to know what happened.

"Yeah, what she means is that I was wondering what kind of earrings I should buy if I cut my hair short. I think the ones I wear now would be too big."

That sounded believable, maybe.

Yeah, maybe to a moron.

"Oh, I thought you loved your long hair, Tate. I'm really surprised you'd think of cutting short." He said incredulously. He obviously knew I was lying.

"I haven't really made up my mind yet." I said smiling. "So how are you today?" I asked in attempt to change the subject.

The phone rang. The moment Anna stepped away to answer it, Adam took a step closer to the desk, and looked me in the eyes, now looking serious.

"Want to tell me the truth now?" he asked

"The truth about what?" I asked lightly.

"Tate, what happened? Did he hurt you last night? Did he find something out?" His voice sounding more panicked with every question.

"No, Adam. Everything is fine. Don't worry, okay?" I said reassuringly.

"Pull your hair back, let me see." He demanded.

"What? Why? No. It's nothing, I told you." I insisted.

"If it's nothing then let me see. Please?"

All of the sudden, Anna was hissing my name. I looked up just in time to see Eric walking through the front door of the hotel.

I looked back at Adam.

"You have to go, but act normal, please. Just follow my lead." I pleaded.

"What? W-" he started to look around, but I interrupted him.

"DON'T turn around." I hissed.

He followed my instruction. Just as Eric was approaching the desk I looked up at him, then back to Adam.

It was quite possibly the most surreal moment I'd ever experienced in my life.

This can not be happening. These two men can not be in the same room. It's impossible; they don't even exist in the same **universe***.*

I felt like my two worlds were about to crash together and I was terrified of what would be left in the aftermath.

"I'm sorry Mr. Ballard, I don't think maintenance will be able to do an airport run at that time, the van is scheduled for service. Could we arrange cab service for you instead?"

Adam looked confused for a moment, but recovered quickly.

"Um, no, that's okay. Maybe I can catch a ride with one of the guys."

Anna stepped up to the desk and politely asked Eric if she could help him. They'd never met, but I had showed her a picture of him. At that moment, I was so thankful that I had.

"No, I'm just here for Tate." He spoke in that fake southern gentleman tone I knew so well.

The sound of him saying my name caused Adam to turn and look at him. He turned back towards me and continued our charade.

"Thanks anyway, Tate."

"Sorry I couldn't be more help."

"It's no problem." He said. As he turned to leave, he and Eric made eye contact. They both gave each other a polite 'hey'. My heart was in my throat. Adam walked away and I turned my focus onto Eric.

"Are you on vacation or what?" I snapped. "What are you doing here?" I did not like him invading my world here. With or without Adam, this was the place I was free of Eric.

"What's wrong with you?" he sounded offended. "There was a problem with the line, so they sent us home tonight. I just thought I'd stop by and see if you wanted me to bring you some dinner."

Yeah, right.

"No, I'm fine. I can just eat when I come home."

"Okay, well, I just thought I'd check. I'm going over by Mom and Dad's. We're getting that good fish you like."

"Oh, I guess you could just take some home for me."

(It really was very good fish.)

"Sure. I'll see you later. I love you."

"Okay, see ya." I said mindlessly, looking down at the reports in front of me.

"Tate? I said I love you."

I heard him the first time. I was trying to ignore it. He never said it any other time, why bother now? Just for show.

"Oh, sorry. Love you, too." I muttered.

He turned dejectedly and walked away.

The instant he was out the door and out of sight, Anna dropped what she was doing and looked at me, her eyes wide.

"He has to know something, he just has to!" she said.

"No, I think he *thinks* he knows something, but he doesn't actually have anything." I said, giving her my honest take on the situation. "Anna,

I think that was the craziest thing I've ever been through. I swear I half expected a brawl right here in the lobby."

"It was weird. Thank God I saw him coming."

"You're telling me. I guess I better call Adam. I'm sure that was more than a little weird for him. Anna, he was telling me to show him my neck and I was about to. Can you imagine what would have happened if Eric would have walked in ten seconds later?"

"I don't even want to!" she exclaimed. "You are just going to have to be very careful. I mean, if you plan to keep seeing Adam, do you?"

"Yeah! I'm not giving him up until he's not here anymore. I know it's not going anywhere, but you were right all along. I deserve to have a little happiness in my life and if right now this is all I can have, then I'm going to take it as long as I have it."

"I figured you say that." She said. "I'd do the same thing. Just please be careful, Tate."

"I will. He's leaving Friday for two weeks anyway, so that will give things time to calm down. By the time he comes back, Eric will hopefully have gotten the suspicion out of his system."

"I hope so, for your sake."

I picked up the phone and dialed the three digit extension to ring Adam's room, but got no answer. Maybe he didn't want to talk to me, maybe this was all too close for comfort for him. A man like Adam could have pretty much any woman he wants, even if it is just on the side. He certainly didn't need all this drama.

I didn't hear from him again that day.

Or the next.

Friday afternoon when I got to work, I went immediately to the computer to see if room 272 was available. I prayed it wasn't. If things were going to end between Adam and I, so be it, but I didn't want things to end the way they had.

My heart seemed to leap inside my chest when – before I'd even gotten to the screen to check if he was still there – I heard his voice.

"Looking for something?" he asked playfully.

I looked up at him and let out a big sigh of relief.

"Yeah, you." I said, smiling gratefully. "I thought maybe you left already. I didn't want you to be mad at me."

"Tate, first of all, I wouldn't have left without saying goodbye and secondly, why would I be mad at you? You didn't do anything wrong."

"Yeah, well, I just figured it might be too much drama. Not sure I'm worth all the work." I laughed nervously.

"Hey, you are worth it, and so much more." He smiled warmly, my heart leaped again.

"Besides, I thought you covered the whole thing very well. You're quite the actress."

"Why thank you." I said, taking a little bow.

His tone was different the next time he spoke.

"He didn't hurt you did he? I would hate to ever think that you got hurt because of me."

"No, he didn't do anything. Maybe he was checking up on me, but my acting must have worked. He was his normal inconsiderate self when I got home." I tried to ease his mind. "Besides, you're not holding a gun to my head here. I *want* to spend time with you. You're worth the risk."

"Oh yeah, well you're worth the drama." He said, laughing again.

"So you have to go now, huh?"

"Yeah, my flight leaves in an hour. I'm not flying this time, so they *can* leave without me."

"You're flying out of Bowman? What about your truck?" I asked.

"My truck will be safely parked here in the parking lot. Glen has graciously offered to let me keep it here until I get back in two weeks, so it will be here everyday when you come to work to remind you of me." He said, a grin spreading across his gorgeous face.

"Yeah, 'cause I need something to remind me of you. The fact that you're on my mind constantly isn't enough already." I said in mock sweetness.

"Bye Tate. See you in two weeks."

"I'll be here." I replied cheerfully as he turned to walk away.

I hated that he was leaving, but I was so relieved that things were okay between us before he left, I couldn't help but be happy.

———

IT TURNED OUT two weeks was plenty of time for me to ease Eric's suspicions. The next Tuesday, I spent my whole afternoon and evening cleaning the apartment and the following I went to bingo with Annetta. When Eric was around, I still stayed out of his way, but I was much more cheerful when I did talk to him and on the weekends, when Andy and Shane were over, I happily catered to them. All the while, I was careful not to overdo it.

Adam was right, I am a pretty good actress.

———

TWO WEEKS AND two days after Adam left the Bowman Inn, he returned. He walked in the hotel with the biggest, brightest smile I'd seen on his face yet and made a bee line right for me. Despite the fact that there were three other people standing behind the counter with me, one being Leah, when he got to the counter, he spoke – obviously to me.

"I missed you." He breathed.

I felt warmth spread over my body like someone had poured warm oil on my skin.

Happiness Tate, that's happiness.

Brazened by his bluntness, I returned the gesture.

"I missed you, too Adam."

It was almost as if my co-workers sensed they were intruding on a private moment, because one by one they disappeared. The whole world could have disappeared for all I cared. After two weeks of not seeing that beautiful face, I would have been happy just staring at him for hours.

"Can I see you tomorrow?" he pleaded.

"Yeah. Maybe I'll even pop up tonight. Are you going to be around?"

"I have to be at the sim by eight o'clock, so if you can make it before seven-thirty I will be." He said hopefully.

"I will see what I can do, if not tonight, tomorrow for sure. Same plan, I think. I'll just have to come up with a better story." I looked around at Leah who just emerged from the back office. She was packing up her stuff to head out for the day.

"You better go, people will start to *talk*." I said quietly, laughing under my breath.

Like they're not already..

I never was able to get away from the desk that night to see him, but the next day - my day off - went perfectly. It was a cookie cutter replica of our last time together - our 'dinner and movie date'. Thankfully, the only thing that wasn't repeated was the part where Eric was waiting for me when I got home.

⌐⟶

As the end of July approached, I stared to wonder how long the pilots would continue to hold residency at the Bowman Inn. I knew Adam would be checking out the last Friday of the month, but there weren't any more reservations booked under his name.

Our affair continued through the month, and life outside the hotel held the same pattern as well. Eric seemed to be convinced of my innocence in general and he was content to leave me alone as long as I didn't gripe or question him when he was out on the weekends doing who-knows-what. At point, I wondered if maybe he wasn't cheating on me, too. If he was, I knew I'd never have proof. The ironic part was, I didn't even care.

Adam and I could tell the end of our relationship was near. He started making comments about 'finding me someday' and 'it wouldn't be this way forever'. It took everything I had to keep it all in perspective. I clung to the fact that it was going to be hard enough when he stopped coming to the hotel, if I let myself dream about a 'someday' with him, my heart would break.

No, my someday had to be my own.

THURSDAY, THE DAY before Adam was due to check out, everything changed.

I talked to him that night, before he left for the sim and he told me he'd see me the next afternoon before he left to fly out. He was scheduled to be back in another two weeks. He said that would be a short stay – only one week – and he wasn't sure when, or even if he'd be back after that, but at least we'd have one more week together.

When I got home from work everything was normal. I changed out of my uniform and sat down on the couch to watch TV for a while, but I got so involved in a movie I found, I didn't even notice that the time Eric should be home came and went.

It was twelve-thirty when he stumbled in the door, reeking of booze. My heart sank.

"What are you still doing up?" he mumbled.

"I was just watching a movie, but I'm going to bed now." I said getting up off the couch.

"NO, you're not." His words were slurred badly, I hadn't seen him this drunk in a long time. He'd been drinking whiskey.

"You're gonna stay right there. I gotta talk to you."

I sat back down as he walked over the couch. He sat down, and landed hard, misjudging the height of the seat below him.

"You're gonna quit that job." He stammered.

"What? Eric, what are you talking about? We can't affor-"

"I don't like you working there." He interrupted. "You're getting too chummy with people there." His eyes were starting to droop. I could only hope he'd pass out soon.

"Eric what do you mean?" I used the most comforting voice I could muster. If I rebelled against him, it would only make things worse.

"You'll get another job, somewhere else."

He is not doing this. He is not going to make me quit.

"Eric, I'm not quitting my job. It's a good job, I have benefits there."

A lot of benefits.

"You're quitting." He said, firmer this time.

"I'm not. You're drunk, I'm not talking about this anymore." I started to get up off the couch, but he grabbed my hand and yanked me back down.

"Eric, please let me go. I'm tired and I just want to go to bed." I pleaded. "I don't want to quit, I don't understand why you want me to, but we can talk about this in the morning, when you're sober."

"I said you're quitting that fucking JOB!"

Then he was on top of me.

He'd pushed me over so I was laying almost flat on the couch. He was straddling me and had both hands wrapped around my throat, pushing and squeezing the life out of me.

It was as if the rage had sobered him up in an instant.

"I don't like how chummy you're getting with people there, like that fucking guy who was at the counter when I came in the other day. I don't like fuckers like that standing there just gawking at you. I don't like how you're big buddies with those trampy fucking girls that work there. YOU'RE QUITTING THAT FUCKING JOB!"

I couldn't breathe at all. The room was starting to go dark, my field of vision was closing from the outside in.

He's choking me to death. If I pass out, I'm dead.

Panic and adrenaline took over. I bucked my body – still trapped under his – as hard as I could. He lost his balance and tumbled off the couch unceremoniously onto the floor.

Oh shit.

I scrambled up off the couch as fast as I could. All I could think of was to get to the bathroom so I could lock the door. He grabbed for my foot right as I took off, but my momentum kept him from getting a good grip. I kicked out of his grasp and ran, banging into the wall as I rounded the corner.

I got to the bathroom and slammed the door shut, fumbling with the lock as fast as my trembling fingers would move. Two seconds later he was pounding on the door and screaming at me to let him in.

Please Dear God, let someone call the cops.

I put my back against the door and let my body slide down, just as hot tears started to slide down my face. Every time he banged on the door the blow seemed to go right through me. With every pounding blow, I was afraid the cheap-grade lock wouldn't hold.

I stretched my legs out and put my feet on the bottom of the cabinet to use the strength of my legs to hold the door closed in case the lock gave way. I had to keep him out, no matter what. Quitting my job was the least of my worries, if he got a hold of me now, there was no telling what he'd do.

After a few minutes, the pounding turned to knocking and the shouting to pleading.

"Tate, please open the door. I'm sorry, I won't hurt you, I promise." He begged.

"Eric, just go to bed. Please, just leave me alone and go to bed."

"No, I don't want to go to bed without you. I'm sorry. Please let me IN!" The rise in his tone gave him away. I knew he'd hit me the instant I opened the door.

"Eric *please*."

"Fine Bitch. But you're still quitting that fucking job."

Then it was quiet.

I WOKE UP in the same position with no idea how long I'd sat there. I figured I'd fallen asleep with my legs flexed holding the door, because they were stiff when I moved. My left hip was throbbing from where I'd hit the corner of the wall and my throat felt like sandpaper.

I stood up slowly, giving my legs time to adjust to my weight. When I looked in the mirror, I was once again thankful for the lack of black eyes and blood. The only evidence was the tear streaked makeup on my cheeks and purple bruises on either side of my neck, this time marking the spots were *both* of his hands had been. They were much darker than the last time, and there was a line starting to form right across the center of my neck. By tomorrow, it would be obvious what had happened.

I crept quietly out of the bathroom, being careful to turn off the light before I opened the door. The apartment was quiet all except for the sound of him snoring in the bedroom. When I passed through the kitchen I saw that it was only shortly after two a.m., so at least I hadn't slept like that for too long.

I grabbed a blanket from the hall closet and curled up on the couch, shivering, although I wasn't cold.

⸻

THIS TIME, WHEN I woke up, it was to the sound of Eric quietly calling my name. My eyes flew open and he was kneeling on the floor in front of the couch, his face no more than a foot away from mine.

I jerked back from being startled and he immediately apologized.

"I'm sorry; I didn't mean to scare you."

The irony of that statement was enough to choke on.

"Listen we need to talk." His breath reeked like stale booze and cigarettes.

I rolled over and turned my back to him.

"I don't want to talk, I want to sleep." I muttered.

"I know, Tate, I know you're tired. But we need to talk about this now. I am so sorry about last night. I was drunk, I didn't mean to hurt you."

"Hurt me, Eric? Do you remember what you did? Do you remember choking me? You could kill me doing that shit!" I snapped.

"Tate, I think you might be overreacting just a little." He retorted.

"Eric, just please leave me alone. I just want to go back to sleep"

"Tate, you're quitting that job. Today." He said firmly.

I rolled back over; in an instant I was sitting up, facing him.

"What is the matter with you? Where is this coming from?" I asked incredulously. "I like my job, I don't want to quit. What about money?"

"You'll get a different job. I know you like it. That's the problem." He said softly.

"Are you kidding me? You don't want me working there because I like it? You seriously don't want me to have any happiness do you?"

"No, it's not like that. I don't like how wrapped up you are in that place. It's not normal to be so involved in job like that." He said quietly.

His delicate tone made me want to scream.

"You are crazy, you know that? How can *YOU* talk about what is and isn't normal? Do you think coming home plastered and choking your girlfriend is *normal?*"

"I said I'm sorry. We need to get this figured out. I want you to go to the hotel and tell them you're quitting. I promise I will work on being better to you, but I need you to do this for me."

I was stunned. I couldn't believe he actually expected me to go along with this. He needs me to do this for him? Is he kidding? This was bizarre, even for him.

"And what if I don't?" I challenged.

"Hon, I don't want it to come to that."

"To what?" I demanded.

"If you don't quit, you will find all your shit outside on the patio and your car not working, ahem, properly, and if you fight me, I'll kick your skinny little ass and dump you out there, too."

"You are seriously fucking crazy, Eric." I snapped. I knew I was pushing my luck, but at that point, I didn't even care.

I really couldn't tell if he'd hit me again or not. I didn't know if we were past the violent part of the cycle, in which case he wouldn't, or if we were still in the thick of it and he was just using that condescending tone to get what he wanted, for whatever reason he wanted it.

"I want you to do it now." He insisted.

"Eric, if I don't give a two week notice, I'll never get another job. I don't have any other work reference besides the fitness center and that was over a year and a half ago, in a different state!" I was trying to appeal to his common sense, assuming he had any.

I could see at this point, quitting was inevitable, but I needed time. I needed time to say goodbye and hopefully make arrangements to see Adam just one more time.

"It'll be fine. Just do it today." He murmured as he got up off the floor and walked away, telling me there was no point in arguing any more.

"I hate you." I spat out. At that moment I meant it. I really did hate him.

It only irritated me more that he didn't even acknowledge that I said it.

I sat there seething and for a minute I actually considered the alternative. So he throws my clothes outside, beats me up and messes with my car. That would actually be a fair price to pay if I thought I'd be truly free of him afterwards.

Once I calmed down and began thinking about what had to be done, a plan came together in my head.

I waited until I was positive that Eric was in the shower and I grabbed the phone to call Anna.

"Hello?"

"It's Tate. Listen, I can't talk long, I need your help." I said, my words coming out in such a rush I was surprised she understood.

"What is it, do you need me to come get you?" she asked, alarmed.

"No, I'm okay. Eric is making me quit my job. I don't think he knows anything, I just think he's effed in the head. He thinks I'm too *happy* there and too *involved* in my job."

"What is that supposed to mean?" she asked, sounding as confused as I had been.

"I don't know. I think anything that makes me happy or gives me the slightest bit of independence worries him. You know the deal."

"Yeah, I get it." She acknowledged. "So what do you need me to do?"

"Well, he's making me quit today, no notice, nothing. I have to go in and tell them, but I need you to have Adam call me before he leaves if he can. He said he'd be down to the desk to see me before he flew out, so actually, when he gets there, can you call me?"

"Yeah, that way if for some reason Eric is there and he answers the phone, it will be me not Adam." She said, putting the final details on my plan.

"Perfect. Thank you so much, Anna."

"You're welcome." She said.

I heard the water stop.

"I gotta go. I'll talk to you later." I whispered.

"Wait, I want you to know something. This doesn't change anything between us Tate. We're still friends, okay? I got your back."

I could hear the sincerity in her voice. It brought tears to my eyes and I wanted to hang up before she noticed, and before Eric came out of the bathroom.

"Thanks Anna. That means more than you know."

I hung up just in time.

I PURPOSELY PUT off going to the hotel until I knew Eric wouldn't have time to accompany me. I hated waiting until the last minute, leaving them in the lurch with no one to work, but the last thing I wanted was him there.

I had every intention on blaming him completely for what I had to do and if he was there, I couldn't do that.

I pulled into the parking lot and tears that I wasn't prepared for filled my eyes. I thought my biggest loss would be Adam, but that wasn't really what I was feeling at that moment. I knew the loss was so much bigger than just him. This had become my safe zone, my place to have friends and be myself. All that would be gone now.

The whole thing went exactly how I expected it to. When I walked in at two o'clock, uniforms in hand, and tears in my eyes, Leah and Megan, who were behind the desk knew immediately that something was wrong. I didn't know how much they knew of my situation, but they were about to find out. I could hear Paul and Glen talking in Glen's office, so I turned to go in there, nodding for Megan to come in. Leah would just have to hear it second hand.

I knocked lightly on the open door. Paul and Glen both looked up, but Glen spoke.

"Hi, Tate. What's up? You're early, aren't you?"

"Glen, I need to talk to you."

"Sure, come on in, have a seat." He said, professional as usual.

Paul made a move to get up and muttered something about giving us privacy, but I told him I wanted him to hear this, too. Just then, Megan appeared at the doorway that connected Glen's office to the back office and I motioned for her to come in.

"I am so very, very sorry to do this to you guys. I can't work here anymore."

I was crying, so whatever anger they would have had over me quitting without notice gave way to concern.

They all seemed to speak at once; I heard a mixture of 'Why?', 'What happened?' and 'Are you okay?', though I wasn't sure who said what.

It was as though someone had turned on a faucet, the tears started to flow freely. Through the sobs I managed to choke out an explanation.

"I don't even know why, other than I am too happy here. I am not in a good relationship right now and I'm sorry, I know that's not your problem, but he's making me quit."

I was aware that it was coming out all jumbled, but I couldn't help it.

"Tate, it's okay." Glen said. "I understand. You have personal things going on that are bigger than your job here. It's okay. Don't worry about us, we'll be okay. Won't we guys?" he said, directing his words at the other two managers in the room.

"Paul, why don't you go give Jamie a call and see if she can work the second tonight, okay?" he said calmly.

"Sure, will do." Paul replied. He put his hand on my shoulder as he walked towards the door leading to the lobby. "Hang in there, Kiddo."

"Megan, I'm going to go get some forms for Tate to sign from the back office, why don't you see if there's anything else she needs before she leaves us." Glen said as he rose from his chair.

I remembered I was holding my uniforms.

"Here are my uniforms. I still have one skirt and one shirt at home. I have to wash them, I'll bring them back though." I said, still sobbing.

Glen took that in stride, too.

"No problem, Tate. You can set them right there on the desk and we'll take care of them, okay?"

I'd never heard him use such a fatherly tone with any of the staff. It made me even more sad because I felt like he genuinely cared for me.

Megan took the seat next to me and put her hand on my arm.

"Tate, I'm so sorry. I knew things weren't great for you at home, but I had no idea. Why is he making you quit?"

"Because he's a jerk." I spat. "I honestly don't know, other than like I said, because I'm too happy working here."

"I'm going to ask this with no judgment. Is there anyone that you want me to get a message to?"

I knew she was talking about Adam. She wasn't blind, neither was Paul. I figured they knew something was going on between us, but they'd always kept it to themselves. I just didn't want anyone to think that me quitting had anything to do with that.

"No Megan, thank you though. That's been taken care of. I want you to know, that's not what this is about."

"Are you sure?" she asked softly.

"If it was, believe me, I wouldn't be sitting here talking to you, you'd be getting a phone call from the hospital." I reassured her. "No, this is way more pointless than that."

"If there is anything you need, please call, okay?"

"Okay." I agreed.

Glen came back in carrying some papers that had to do with my insurance and a standard resignation form. I signed everything without even really realizing what I was signing. I didn't care about anything at that point.

As I left the building, I couldn't bring myself to turn and look back. I knew Paul and Leah were probably both standing there and would have given me a sympathetic smile and wave on my way out, but I just couldn't do it.

It had started to rain while I was in the hotel. That fit perfectly. I cried all the way home.

At three-thirty, the sound of the phone filled the quiet apartment. I knew it had to be either Adam or Eric, checking to see if I'd actually quit. This would give him ultimate satisfaction, he'd showed me – yet again – that he had ultimate power over my life. I was relieved when the caller ID confirmed it was Adam.

"Hello?" I said sadly.

"Hi, it's me." Anna's voice filled the receiver. "I have someone here who wants to talk to you, is it a good time?"

"Yes" I said appreciatively. "It's a good time."

"Hi." This time it was Adam's voice I heard. "Tate, what happened? Are you okay?" His words were filled with concern and sadness.

"I'm okay." I choked out. The tears came again, against my wishes. "I don't really want to get into a big explanation right now, but just know that I'm okay, alright?"

"Alright. Can I see you when I come back?"

"Absolutely." I said with conviction. "Can you just have Anna call me from the hotel when you get back in? That would be safest for me."

"I'll do that then. Tate, please take care of yourself, okay? A lot of people care about you. More than you think."

"Thank you, Adam, I will, I promise."

"Someday, right?" he asked.

I knew he meant that well, but it sounded hollow in his mouth.

"Yeah, someday." I said sardonically. "I'll talk to you soon."

"Okay, bye."

I hung up the phone and laid it on the end table next to the couch, then I laid back and let the sadness wash over me until finally I fell asleep.

LESS THAN TWO weeks later, I had another job lined up. Turns out, Glen gave me a glowing recommendation when the owner of the small paralegal firm that was looking for a receptionist called to check my reference.

I found the ad in the paper and when I saw the address said Fern Valley Road, I thought at least it was in the right neighborhood. When I went looking for the place to apply, I found it almost exactly halfway between our apartment and the hotel.

The whole process went fairly quickly. I didn't get hired on the spot like I did at the Bowman Inn, but the day after my interview, Marc

McKinney called me to tell me I was hired and I could start in two weeks.

A Clean Slate was a company that consisted of a father and son team of paralegals who prepared divorce, bankruptcy and adoption papers for people who didn't want the expense of hiring an attorney. I didn't even know that was possible, but I learned during my interview that not only is it possible, there's even a name for it: it's called 'pro se'.

Their offices were located in a nice, but non-descript two story building that housed automotive bays on the ground level and offices on the top floor. There were a total of four offices on the floor; the only one not occupied by A Clean Slate was rented to an insurance company. There were his and her restrooms located at the very end of the hall. All in all, it was a pretty decent set up.

They told me that the dress code was business casual, with an emphasis on the casual. There were no benefits, but I would be making $9 per hour and I'd work nine to five with a paid hour lunch everyday. They figured that was pretty good for me, because I could go home for lunch if I wanted to. I didn't tell them I wouldn't want to.

The best part about it was that I would have my own office with a huge window.

Once Marc called to tell me I had the job, I couldn't wait to start. Being home with Eric all morning, every day, plus all day on the week-ends was getting to be too much, especially with him silently gloating over his success at making me quit the hotel.

ONCE THE JOB situation was taken care of, my thoughts turned back to Adam. I knew he should be arriving soon and I honestly wondered if he would call or just leave things alone, now that I wasn't easy access. I talked to Anna a few times, but I never asked her exactly what day his reservation was for because I didn't want her to think I was using her. I wanted to maintain our friendship job or no job, Adam or no Adam. She was the only real friend I had in this state.

He did call, or rather Anna did, as soon as he checked in.

It was Thursday night around five o'clock. Anna did the same as before: called the apartment, told me there was someone there who wanted to talk to me and asked if it was a good time.

When Adam got on the phone, he informed me that he'd called the minute he got in and that he hadn't even gone to his room yet. I gave him my number and told him to go get settled and call me back.

The phone rang ten minutes later.

"Hello?"

"Hi." He said, the warmth in his tone filling the receiver. "I miss you."

"My heart swelled and I felt happier than I had in weeks. "I miss you, too."

"Tate, when can I see you? I know it won't be as easy, but I don't think I'll be back after this week. I have to see at least once more, please." He pleaded.

"You can see me. I mean, I want to see you, at least one more time." I let my voice trail off. The reality of saying that out loud hit me hard and a lump formed in my throat.

Don't do this Tate, you knew this was short term.

"Hey, I got another job." I said cheerfully, trying to change the subject.

"You did? That was fast. Tell me about it."

I told him all about my new job at the paralegal company. He sounded impressed when I told him I had my own office with a window. He joked that he didn't even have a window in his office. I pointed out that his office had a *windshield*, and I was sure one hell of a view.

We made plans to meet the following Monday. He said he hated to wait that long, but he had to be at the sim all afternoon and most of the evening on Friday and he knew the weekends were no good for me. When we got to the subject of how and where, I told he could just let me in the side door of the hotel and we could have one last date night. I said he'd just have to be there waiting for me. He agreed and we planned to meet at four o'clock on the dot. That would give me time to get ready *after* Eric left for work.

When I told him that was the day before my birthday and that spending the day with him would be the best birthday present I could have, he promised to make it extra special. I told him any time I could spend with him was special enough.

That Friday, Saturday and Sunday all dragged on painfully slow.

Monday arrived and I took care to be as sullen and moody as I had been since Eric made me leave the hotel. I didn't want to give him a reason to suspect I had anything to be happy about.

At three fifty-five I pulled my car right up next to Adam's truck. He had purposely parked it close to the door so I could use it for cover and not have far to go.

At that moment, it hit me how this started out as a fun secret to keep, but now everything had gotten so covert and serious, like we *had* to see each other. As much as I knew I would miss him, I thought a part of me might be relieved not to have to work so hard at staying safe.

He was waiting by the door for me and as usual, he looked fabulous, no doubt without even trying. He was wearing khaki pants, with a crisp white shirt unbuttoned a third of the way down and again his hair was still damp from the shower.

That evening was a reunion and a farewell jumbled together. A couple hours after I got there, he jumped up and said he'd almost forgotten something. He told me to close my eyes and keep them closed.

I did as he instructed and just listened. I heard the door open on the little hotel room fridge and the sound of a match being lit. Then I felt him sit back down on the bed and he told me to open my eyes.

"Happy Birthday Tate." He said. I opened my eyes and he was sitting in front of me holding a little cake, with one single candle.

His face was even more beautiful by candlelight.

I was very touched by the simple gesture.

"Make a wish." He whispered.

"Adam, you and I both know that what I'd really like to wish for can't come true." I said sadly.

"Then wish for a miracle."

That's exactly what I did. I blew out the candle and then he got up and set the cake on the table. He came back to the bed and pulled a small box from his pocket.

"What is this?"

"It's a present, you open it."

I opened up the box to find a charm and a necklace. It was a dragonfly, the most beautiful, dainty little silver dragonfly I'd ever seen. It was hooked on a delicate silver chain.

"It's beautiful, I love it Adam."

"I know you can't wear it right away, but you can wait a little while and just say you bought it for yourself. I hope when you wear it, you'll think of me. It was the closest I could get to anything flying-related." He started laughing and added "I couldn't find an airplane charm."

We spent the rest of our time cuddled up together on the bed, kissing and talking and just looking at each other, like we were each trying to memorize the other's face. It was very bittersweet.

We talked mostly about how glad we both were that things happened the way they did, that circumstances allowed us to meet and have this time together. He told me he'd always wonder about me and he hoped that my 'someday' would come sooner, rather than later. He said if his circumstance ever changed, he would find me, no matter if I was here in Kentucky or back in Wisconsin.

That led me to ask because after all this time I really did want to know.

"What is your circumstance Adam?"

"I thought you didn't care, didn't want to know?" he said suspiciously.

"Well I didn't, but now I do. Isn't a woman's prerogative to change her mind or something like that?" I teased.

"Yeah, I guess it is. Funny you put it like that, though."

I suspected the sarcasm in his voice had nothing to do with me and everything to do with his circumstance.

"I'm married, Tate."

I felt like I got punched in the gut.

Married. Married? I never thought married, girlfriend probably, but not married.

"I see." I said, trying not to let my disappointment come through. "Kids?"

"No. There are no kids. I wouldn't be here if there were." He said firmly.

"Good. That makes me feel a little better. I don't want to have to think of myself as some kind of little home-wrecker."

"Tate, you are not a home wrecker. You said it yourself. If I wasn't with you, I might be with someone else. Would I? I don't really know, maybe, but I *can* honestly say I didn't think of it until I saw you, but –" he stopped short.

"But what?" I persisted. "What, Adam?"

"I'm not acting, I'm reacting." He said, anger creeping into his tone. Suddenly, it was all clear.

"She cheated on you then." I said, sharing my suspicion.

"Yeah, she cheated on me. Then, when I threatened to divorce her, she promised that she'd take half of everything. I just built a five hundred thousand dollar house and Georgia is a marital property state, she'd get half."

"Wow that sucks. Now I understand why you said 'if things were different'."

"Tate, I want you to know something. I know you don't want to be saved, but if things were different for me, I'd save you anyway. I would take you away from here and I promise you that creep would never get to you. I would give you the life you deserve." His voice was filled with passion and conviction.

"Thank you Adam, not just for wanting to save me but for everything. For helping me to believe in myself again and for giving me a few months of happiness. I wish you could have known me the way I was before I was with him. Actually, that's not true. This is me. The person I am when I'm with you *is* the real me. The person I am with him, that girl is the shadow of me, nothing more." I said sadly.

When the time came to say goodbye, Adam offered to walk me out, but I declined. I told him that it would be easier and safer if I left alone. We stood by the door, locked in an embrace that I prayed didn't have to end, but it did. When we pulled apart after one last kiss, we both had the shimmer of tears in our eyes.

"I'll look for your beat up old truck and I will wear my necklace all the time." I said smiling sadly.

"And I will find you someday." He promised.

I went home and climbed into bed. I tried to fight back the tears, I tried with everything I had, but they forced their way through. Adam was the epitome of the man of my dreams and I was never going to see him again.

Finally, I couldn't fight anymore. I gave in to the pain. The pain I tried to protect myself from, the pain I promised myself I wouldn't feel.

Once I let go, it felt like my heart was being ripped from my chest. As far as I was concerned, it may as well have been.

BY THE END of the week, my sullen mood was wearing on Eric's nerves. My birthday came and went with about as much fanfare as the one before it and I didn't even care. It really only made me more depressed that at nineteen my life was even more pathetic than it was at eighteen and I had wasted another whole year.

I missed Adam terribly. I promised myself after the night we said goodbye, I would let it go – let him go – but everywhere I went, I looked for that stupid beat up truck. Of course I never did see it.

I was wearing the necklace all the time. I told Eric that Anna had given it to me for my birthday. He asked what the significance of the dragonfly was. I pointed out that we're girls; it was pretty, that *was* the significance.

At that point, the only thing I had to look forward to was starting my new job. At least that would get me back out of the apartment.

I did find it ironic that letting go of Adam was made at least a little bit easier by not being in the hotel every day. Funny that Eric ended up helping me when his intention was the opposite.

On the weekend before I was due to start my new job at A Clean Slate, Eric blew my world apart. Again.

His dad had stopped over by the apartment on Saturday afternoon to talk to Eric about a house that was for sale. I thought the last thing we needed was a house. Eric didn't even take care of his own car, the last thing he needed was more responsibility.

I made the mistake of voicing my opinion on the subject.

"Why don't you shut the fuck up and mind your own business?" Eric snapped.

Dell looked at me then back at Eric.

"What's the matter with you, Son? You don't need to talk to her like that." He said calmly.

Humiliated, I walked into the bedroom, leaving them sitting at the dining room table. Through the paper thin walls, I could still hear their conversation as if I was standing right there.

"What's wrong?" Dell asked Eric.

"Nothing, it's her. She's been a bitch all week." He snapped.

"Hey, don't *call* her that." Dell said.

"I can still hear you, you know!" I shouted. "Maybe I'm such a bitch because you made me quit my job!"

I sat down on the bed, with my back towards the door, so I was at a disadvantage when he came storming into the room, Dell hot on his heels.

Eric pushed me down on the bed, got on top of me and once again put his hands around my throat.

"Don't you talk to me like that in front of my father, you ungrateful little bitch!"

I screamed at him to get off me and I heard Dell yelling at him to do the same.

In a moment of panic, for the very first time, I hit Eric. I punched him. I was aiming for his face, but the commotion of Dell now pulling at Eric from behind, trying to get him to let me go, made the blow miss his face and hit him in the shoulder.

Then Eric did something he'd never done before. He punched me in the face. Even if the last thing I saw hadn't been his fist coming down towards my eye, I'd have known it was a punch by the impact. It wasn't anything like a backhand.

Dell yelled at the top of his lungs and yanked Eric off me. I had my hand covering my eye and I could feel it already starting to swell. I was disoriented and stunned. I couldn't believe what'd just happened.

Eric stormed out of the room with Dell chasing after him.

"I gotta get out of here." Eric said as he walked out, slamming the door behind him.

"Son! Son wait!" Dell yelled.

The second slam of the door was the last sound I heard before I passed out.

Eleven

There's No Place like Home

When I woke up I didn't remember what happened.

I didn't know why I was laying sideways across the bed.

I didn't know why my vision was distorted or why my face hurt.

I didn't know why, until I instinctively put my hand to my left eye and what I felt wasn't recognizable to my touch. Then the whole thing came rushing back.

What should have been the indentation of my eye socket felt like a protrusion under my fingertips and when I turned my head to look around, the pain in my face exploded like I'd just been punched again.

I lay still for a few minutes just trying to figure out what to do, which was difficult because I could barely focus on anything but the pain.

I knew I needed to see what I was dealing with to know if I needed medical attention or not. When I finally got to the bathroom, what I saw in the mirror was enough to make me throw up, which in turn made the pain explode all over again.

My left eye was nearly swollen shut.

When I was done getting sick, I sat down on the toilet seat without looking in the mirror again.

I just need to get my bearings.

Maybe there was nothing that could be done medically. Maybe they'd simply tell me to ice it and let it heal on its own.

Maybe I could just call the hospital and ask if I need to be seen. Surely an ER nurse could give me some advice over the phone. If I could handle this here, it would be better since I had no one to call and no insurance.

Slowly I made my way through the apartment, gathering the phone and phone book and sat down on the couch.

My head was spinning and the room around me was coming in and out of focus. I hurried to find the number I needed, but before I found it, the pages of the phone book were splattered with blood.

I jerked my head back up and put my hands to my face. By the time I figured out the blood was coming from my nose, the phone book and my hands were covered.

My trembling fingers found the digits 9-1-1. Ten seconds later I was crying into the phone to a dispatcher that I'd been hit in the eye and now my nose was bleeding and I didn't know what to do.

She calmly instructed me to relax and tilt my head back. She explained that the blood was most likely from the pressure of the swollen eye. She said an ambulance would be on its way soon. Her soothing tone calmed me down enough that when she asked if I wanted her to stay on the line with me until help arrived, I declined.

Ten minutes later there was a knock at the apartment door, but when I opened it, instead of the EMTs I expected, there were two uniformed policemen standing there.

"I didn't call for the police." I stammered.

I could only imagine what they thought when they saw me. My nose had stopped bleeding, but between my horribly swollen eye and the blood now covering not only my hands and mouth, but the front of my shirt as well, my appearance must have been disturbing.

"Ma'am, you called for an ambulance due to an assault. Any time an assault takes place, the police respond first." the older of the two officers said calmly. He looked friendly. His salt and pepper hair and laugh lines probably would have had a calming effect on people in some situations, but I was panicking on the inside.

"Before we go any further, is there anyone else with you here in this apartment?" he asked.

"No, I'm alone."

"Who did this to you?" the younger officer asked angrily.

"I –I don't want to press charges. I don't –"

I didn't know what to say. If I lied to the cops, I could get myself in legal trouble, but if I told them the truth my troubles would be even bigger than that.

"Do you know the person who did this, was it your boyfriend?" he asked gruffly.

"Yes, no, I mean, yes I know the person, but no it wasn't my boyfriend."

A big fat lie came started to come together in my head.

"It was - it was an ex-boyfriend. My ex-boyfriend did this, but if my boyfriend now - the one who lives here with me - finds out my ex did this, he'll want to retaliate." I cried. "I just want it to be over. I don't want him to end up in jail for something stupid that I did."

"Why did your ex-boyfriend do this?"

"Because I was telling him that we were over for good. I'd been seeing him again, but I was trying to break it off with him today and he got mad."

"What's his name?" he pushed.

"I don't want to give you his name. I don't want to press charges; I just want this to be over."

"Okay, well what is your current boyfriend's name?" the older one stepped back in.

"Eric Sheppard."

"And where is he now?"

"I don't know. I mean, I think he's with his dad. I think they went to go look at a house or something."

Just then, two men dressed in EMT uniforms showed up.

"Do we need a stretcher here?" One of the EMTs asked the cops.

"No, I think she'll be able to make it to the ambulance on her own." The younger cop said disapprovingly. He knew I was lying, but it didn't matter; I couldn't risk telling the truth. As long as I stuck to my story, they couldn't do anything.

"Ma'am, I'm going to ask you one more time, will you please give us the name of the person who did this to you?" he pleaded, changing his approach. "He needs to be punished."

I put my head down and shook it side to side and muttered "I can't".

Then the two emergency techs took over. One asked me if I needed to grab anything to take along, a purse, keys, anything.

I told them yes, that I needed my purse. I went into the bedroom to grab it and when I came back, I saw the policeman looking around the apartment and making notes on his little notepad. I followed his gaze around the room and wondered what he was writing down.

Then the ground seemed to give out from under my feet.

When I woke up, I was strapped to a gurney in the back of the ambulance. I could tell by the speed we must be on I-65 heading towards downtown.

There was an EMT on either side of me.

"What happened?" I asked weakly.

"You passed out." the EMT on my left replied without looking at me.

It felt like only a few minutes after I woke up in the ambulance we were at the hospital, but it was hard to tell because of how surreal the day had become.

Once I'd been transferred me to a hospital gurney, the EMTs disappeared and the nurse wheeled me into a curtained room, just like the one I'd been in last time I was here and set about taking my vitals. When she finished, she told me the doctor would be in shortly.

Before a doctor, came a different woman dressed in scrubs. She said she was an X-ray tech and she was there to take me down to radiology and X-ray my face to make sure nothing was broken.

I found the radiology lab to be the loneliest of places, just like when they'd x-rayed my neck, the last time I was here. It was so cold and dark in there, compared to the bright glare of the rest of the hospital. That room was a jolt of reality.

Look where you are. Look how far out of control this has gotten.

The tech had me lay flat on my back on the cold table and positioned the X-ray machine over my face. She told me not to move and explained that the machine would move around my head to take pictures of my bones from different angles. I let her go on with her speech, already knowing that she'd then leave the room, take the X-rays from behind a thick window, return for me and take me back to the room, same as last time.

Once the X-rays were done, she wheeled me back and deposited me in the same room I'd started in. That's where I waited for what felt like an eternity. I dozed off and woke up several times, always waking up startled because I didn't instantly recall where I was.

When the doctor finally came in, he examined me briefly and then told me there was nothing that could be done. He reassured me that while it was very swollen and no doubt painful, the x-ray showed no damage to the facial bones. I asked him if he could just cut it open to release the pressure or something, the way boxers do. He laughed in a warm, sympathetic kind of way that told me he was not making fun of me, but my request was not realistic. He said he wished there was something else he could do, but if he made any kind of incision, the skin under my eye would burst and leave me with a huge scar on my face.

"My best advice is to stay away from whoever did this to you." He said gently. "I'm going to give you a prescription for something for the pain. Keep ice on it to help make the swelling go down and you should be okay in a week or so."

When the nurse came back in to give me my release papers and an ice pack, she asked the question I knew would be coming.

"Who should we call to pick you up?"

There was nobody to call because I didn't want anyone to see me. I wanted to hide out in that curtained room long enough to look normal again.

"What time is it?" I asked the nurse, trying to stall.

The portly nurse looked down at her watch and replied "Eight twenty-seven."

"Can I just have a few minutes to get dressed? I'm not sure who I want to call yet." I said quietly.

"Sure, Hon. You just take your time and I'll be back in few minutes."
She said kindheartedly.

She probably thinks I'm pathetic.

A little while later, she returned to find me sitting on the gurney
fully dressed in my blood stained clothes.

"You can call my friend Anna." I told her as an answer to the expectant look on her face.

I told her the number as she wrote it down on the paper attached to
her clipboard and she disappeared again.

I laid back and closed the eye that wasn't already swollen closed.
My face was throbbing and felt like it could burst from the pressure any
moment. As I gently lay the ice pack on my face, I was wishing the doctor
wouldn't have told me about the big scar that could be left. Now I was
afraid it would happen on its own, that my skin - swollen and stretched
beyond its limit - would just burst open, spewing blood everywhere and
leaving me with a permanent, ugly reminder of what had happened today.

When the nurse returned and pulled back the curtain, Anna slowly
stepped into the room, not sure what she would find. She was looking
cautiously at the blood on my clothes when I lowered the ice pack that
had been covering my eye. I watched as a look of horror came over
Anna's face as she focused on mine.

"Oh my God Tate, are you okay?"

The lump in my throat gave way. On the right side of my face, tears
made a little trail down my cheek, on the left they slowly seeped out
from between the folds of my swollen skin.

"Let's get you out of here." She said. "You can come home with me."

I got off the gurney, gathered my things and followed her out of the
hospital to her car while neither of us spoke.

A few minutes after we got on the expressway, she repeated her
question.

"Tate, are you okay? What happened? Why did he do this to you?" she
asked incredulously.

"I don't even know, I mean, I don't know why he did this. He punched
me, right in front of his dad.

"What did his dad do?" she asked even more shocked.

"Nothing. He chased after Eric and then left. I had to call the ambulance because I couldn't see and then blood started pouring out of my nose. I guess it was nothing though."

"Nothing? How can you say that? Tate your eye is swollen *shut*." She said in disbelief.

"I just mean the doctor couldn't do anything. They x-rayed my face and said there was no damage to the bones, I just have to ice it and let it get better."

"Oh."

"So what are you going to do?"

"I think I'll just go home for now."

She looked at me and I could read the question on her face.

"I'll be fine." I continued, answering her question before she even asked it. "He probably won't even be there and if he is, he'll be sorry now. He won't hit me again. I just want to go to bed."

"If you're sure."

"I'm sure."

She dropped me off at the apartment, offering to come in with me, but I declined.

"Call me, okay? Let me know how you're doing." She insisted.

"I will, I promise. Anna, thank you for picking me up, thanks for understanding."

"I do understand, Tate."

When I got into the apartment, Eric was sitting on the couch

"Oh my God, I am so sorry." He broke down into tears immediately. My tears, however, did not come.

"I'm going to bed."

As I walked towards the bedroom, I could hear him sobbing and saying how sorry he was over and over. He sounded like a child who had accidentally broken his toy.

I felt nothing but hate.

THE FOLLOWING WEEK was spent lying on the couch, holding ice packs to my face. By Monday night the swelling had gone down enough for me to see normally again and by Thursday all that was left was the ugly bruising of a black eye.

There were two dozen roses in my living room, one from Dell and one from Eric. I scoffed every time I looked at them, as if flowers would make it better. Dell's flowers had come with $200 cash, his attempt to buy my forgiveness. That didn't help their cause either, but I took it anyway.

Eric treated me like a princess all week. He doted on me with anything I wanted to eat or drink; made sure I had ice at all times. I let him take care of me with quiet indifference. Each day I was thankful when he went to work so I could be alone.

Friday afternoon, before Eric went to work, Dell and Annetta came over. That was rare because we were usually the ones who went to their house, not the other way around. Although the purpose was to pick up our laundry and drop off some groceries, I suspected it was morbid curiosity that actually brought Annetta to us.

Dell had no doubt told her all about what had happened. He wouldn't be able to keep something like that from her, not something about their precious Eric.

When they walked in the apartment, Annetta's reaction to the remnants of what Eric had done made me feel like I'd gotten punched in the gut.

"Well it's not *that* bad. Roy gave Dotty one much worse than that!"

I didn't hear anything else she said. I got up and went to the bedroom, closing the door behind me.

Eric came in to get my laundry from my closet and tried to apologize for his mom's insensitivity.

"She didn't mean anything by it Tate, that's just how she is." He said apologetically.

I simply rolled over and ignored him.

AFTER STALLING MATT and Marc for a week by claiming to have been in a bad fender bender, the ugly bruise that was left was mostly hidden with makeup. I started on Tuesday, the day after Labor Day.

My first day went smoothly. Marc and Matt were very welcoming. Matt's wife Sara stayed for a little while to show me the phone system and how they liked messages to be taken, their specific abbreviations and stuff. It was simplistic compared to what I was doing at the hotel. Here, all I had to do was answer the phone, find out what the person was calling about and transfer the call to whomever was available or take a message.

A MONTH LATER, I had completely reorganized their filing system and was not only answering calls, but explaining the processes of both pro se bankruptcy and divorce to clients when they called. I was setting up appointments, handling the questionnaires Marc and Matt used to get client information during initial office visits and doing callbacks for missing information. Marc and Matt didn't even speak to the client until they'd booked their first appointment and had their questionnaire filled out.

They were so pleased with my progress and the changes I'd made, they raised my pay up to $10 per hour on my one month anniversary.

Over the course of the month, I'd also developed a bond with both of my bosses.

Matt and I would sit in his office and talk for hours. He was a nice looking guy, tall, blond and clean cut. He had a friendliness about him that made him easy to talk to and he was very intelligent, so that made him interesting.

Neither of us spoke too much of our home life. I certainly wasn't going to tell him about my situation with Eric. I didn't want him to pity me and I didn't want to hear how I should leave. We mostly joked around.

Appropriately, Marc took a fatherly approach to our relationship. He was a big man and could have been intimidating, but his warm nature — obviously inherited by Matt — had the opposite effect.

THINGS AT HOME were back to a tolerable pattern. Working my new hours, I saw Eric only on the weekends and then he was pointedly pleasant. The incident with my eye seemed to jolt him into awareness of what he was capable of, which was ironic because it only served to make me numb.

Knowing that both his parents had witnessed first hand what he did to me and that it was no doubt gossip amongst his family, gave me a sense of sad acceptance. No one was going to save me from him. No one was going to stop him from hitting me again.

Dell did seem to be on a mission after that day though. He was convinced that the problems with Eric and I lay with the fact that we had no room to breathe in that apartment. He was sure that if we could just buy a house, we'd get along much better because we'd have room to spread out and not be in one another's face all the time.

About two weeks before Halloween, Dell stopped by the apartment after I'd gotten home from work. He said there was a house for sale that he thought would be perfect for us. He wanted me to see it.

I rode with him out to the part of town where Andy lived, called Fern Creek. On the way he explained that we had to move fast on this house. The sellers first attempt was to a young couple who, after a month of stringing the sellers along, ended up unable to get financing.

He continued to head out of town and I found myself wondering how far out this house would be. Fifty feet after we'd turned off busy Bardstown Road onto a little side road, trees seemed to swallow us up and it suddenly felt like we were miles and miles from the city atmosphere. The country road snaked up hill and after we'd made a sharp right followed by a sharp left we came upon a simple white house with two big pine trees in the front yard and lots of land surrounding it.

"This is the place." He said excitedly. "What do you think?"

"It looks okay, so far." I said, being careful to reserve judgment. I didn't want Dell to buy the house based on my first comment. That was the type of thing he'd do.

We pulled into the driveway and got out of the car. I was surveying the property while Dell was excitedly chatting away about all the great features of the place.

It had a nice yard, surrounded on two sides by trees, with a small clearing that led to farm fields. There was a house next door that was similar in style and size, the two yards being separated by a fence. Judging by the toys scattered through the neighbors' yard, they had kids.

I followed Dell as he walked to the front door, stopping to grab a key from under the door mat.

When he opened the door, we stepped into the living room and I fell in love with the house.

The front room was huge, much larger than the outside of the house would have it appear. It had a window on one side, looking out towards the driveway and a huge picture window that let in light filtered through the giant pine trees in front. The carpet was dark green and looked brand new.

Along the back wall, the room opened up to reveal a hallway that led to the kitchen and bedrooms. Further inspection revealed a kitchen that was almost as large as the living room and twice as bright. It had two full size windows and a smaller one over the sink. In contrast to the crisp white walls of the living room, the kitchen had an old fashioned feel due to the mint green paint that covered it. Dell seemed to read my mind as he chirped something about how simple it would be to paint the rooms whatever color we wanted.

There was a door from the kitchen leading down to the basement. Dell started to go down the stairs while I looked around at the rest of the place.

I backtracked through the kitchen and found a hall closet, two bedrooms and a small bathroom. The size of the bedrooms and bathroom apparently gave way to the large kitchen and living room, but each bedroom had two windows, the bathroom one, which gave them a bright, airy feeling.

I could see us living here.

I was on my way to join Dell in the basement when someone opened the front door. A man who looked to be in his fifties smiled warmly at me.

"You must be Tate."

"I am." I said, having no clue who this man was or how he knew my name.

"I'm Cliff. This was my dad's house." He said, with a touch of sadness in his voice. "Dell told me he wanted to bring you by to see the house. You're his daughter-in-law, right?"

I wondered if Dell told him that because that's how he feels about me, or if it was to save face at the fact of his son living with a girl before they were married. Either way, I didn't want to complicate things by making a liar out of him.

"Uh, yeah."

"So what do you think of the house?" he asked hopefully.

"So far, I really like it."

I knew that my opinion had little to do with whether or not we got this house. I figured out from Dell's conversation on the way over that my name would not be on any of the documents, which suited me, *just* fine.

Just then Dell came into the living room. He echoed Cliff's question.

"So Tate, what do you think?"

"I like it, I guess I'll go look at the basement." I replied. I figured Dell and Cliff would stay upstairs talking, but they both followed me down into the basement. Dell pointed out that it was a good solid basement and could easily be finished. I realized that the lower level of the house was exposed in the back when he showed me the large sliding door that connected the house to a one stall garage. At the end of the garage was a cistern that'd been used as a storage cellar. There was a service door that when opened revealed the big back yard and a car port that I hadn't noticed when we pulled up.

I kept telling Dell that I liked it, but was cautious to not sound too excited. Cliff stayed with us the whole time so I didn't want to appear too eager. I knew next to nothing of buying houses, but I figured that since there wasn't a realtor here with us, there may be some bargaining going on.

The three of us trooped up the stairs and stood around in the kitchen talking. I just kept trying to picture what it would look like with our things in it. The black and glass furniture certainly wouldn't match the styling of this house, but maybe Dell was right. Maybe having some room to spread out would be better for us.

Dell once again repeated the question, but this time, the tone of his voice told me it was decision time.

"So, what do you think?"

I looked out the window, wondering how much my opinion mattered anyway, when I saw a groundhog in the back yard.

"Does the groundhog come with the house?" I asked smiling.

Cliff took a step forward to look out the window at the animal in question.

"Yep, sure does. You want him, he's all yours." He said laughing.

Dell took his cell phone out of his pocket and dialed a number; I wondered who he was calling.

"Hello, this is Dell Sheppard, chief steward from building four; I need to have my son Eric Sheppard paged. I need to speak with him. He should be on the line in building two. Yes, I'll hold."

A minute later Dell was handing me the phone, with Eric presumably on the other end.

"Hello?"

"Hi. How do you like the house?"

I was aware of two sets of eyes boring into me as I resumed my post looking out the window. The groundhog had disappeared.

"I like it." I replied quietly.

"Do you really?"

"Why?"

"What do you mean 'why'? Why, because we'll live there."

"What do you think of it?" Suddenly I was confused over when he would have seen it.

"I haven't seen it." He replied matter-of-factly.

"Well, you'll have to see it, I guess." I said, resigning myself back to the fact of my opinion not mattering anyway.

"No Tate, we don't have time. Dad says Cliff wants an answer today or he's putting it on the market. You have to decide. If you like it, we'll buy it."

I was stunned.

"How? How that fast?" Again, my lack of home buying knowledge plagued me, but I suspected you needed more than a day to buy a house.

"Dad's going to pay cash and then I'll go to the bank and get a mortgage to pay him back."

I spun around to look at Dell, surprised that anyone could pay cash for a house. My step-dad didn't even pay cash for used cars.

"How much is it?" I asked, lowering my voice.

I got my answer in stereo as Eric answered me on the phone and Dell answered me in person.

"Ninety-two thousand." They said in unison.

I was stunned again.

Ninety-two thousand dollars in cash? Must be nice.

"Oh. Well, I guess I'll take another look around just to be sure then. The closets are a little small."

That was all I could think of that wasn't great about the house.

Eric laughed. "Is that it? Is that all that you don't like? I think we can work with small closets, don't you?"

"I guess so." I said, letting the excitement start to take hold.

We're going to have our own house?

Oh my God, we're going to have our own house!

"Tate, I have to get back to work. I guess you can just tell me when I get home, if you're still up. Or leave me a note or something."

"Yes."

"Yeah? You want it?" he asked cheerfully.

"Yeah, I think I do."

"Well then tell Dad. He'll take care of the rest. I gotta go."

"Okay, bye."

"Bye Tate. I hope this makes you happy."

I flipped the phone closed and it hit me that this was a pay off. They figured that this would make up for the abuse.

It didn't, but I wasn't giving up the house anyway.

"I guess we'll take it." I said to Cliff, smiling happily. I looked to Dell for confirmation, after all, for me to say I wanted it was about as useful as saying I wanted to sprout wings and fly. It was Dell who would have to make it happen.

The look on his face told me it would.

WE MOVED IN to the house right away and whatever paperwork Eric had to do at the bank to get the mortgage and pay Dell back was done without my involvement. I knew that meant that I had no claim to the house but I also kept in mind that it meant I had no legal obligation either, so the benefits outweighed the downfall. It kept me free to bail someday, whenever someday arrived, although my someday seemed to float further away with the purchase of our home.

Maybe I could actually be happy here.

Eric seemed happier. We'd spent a lot of time making the house the way we wanted it. After several arguments about colors, we finally got some paint on the walls in the kitchen. We ended up choosing a warm tan color with white and a prettier pale green as accent colors. The house had beautiful natural woodwork throughout, so there was no need to paint the window or door frames. We'd bought a farm style kitchen table and chairs, agreeing that the black and glass did not suit the house.

The rest of the house got purely decorative touches for the time being. We kept the white walls, figuring the kitchen was a big enough ordeal to get through.

For some of the larger things or the things that took more talent than just paint, Dell helped us out. He talked to us about turning one of our kitchen windows into a door and building a deck off the back of the house and finishing the basement. It all seemed a little ambitious to me, but Dell seemed convinced it wouldn't be too hard. We decided we would start to tackle the bigger projects in spring.

We hosted Thanksgiving dinner in our new home. It wasn't as big of an event as it had been the year before at Dell and Annetta's, but it was festive nonetheless. It felt good to have people over to our house. Eric and Annetta cooked a wonderful dinner and everyone raved over the food and how much they loved our little country house.

Andy was the only friend who visited on a regular basis. It seemed now that we weren't right in the city, we weren't convenient for most of Eric's friends. The location of our house worked out well for Andy though, he was even closer to us now than before.

Once Thanksgiving was over, my thoughts started to turn towards Christmas. On one lazy Saturday morning, while we both laid in the living room watching TV and talking about Christmas decorations for the house, I uncharacteristically confessed to Eric that I was feeling homesick. I told him that I wished there was a way we could spend Christmas in Wisconsin.

I was shocked when he said we could. I started planning our trip right away, before he could change his mind.

When I called my mom to tell her that we were coming, she jumped right on the bandwagon, too. She told me that my Uncle Jerry had moved back to Wisconsin only a few months prior, that it would be nice to visit him, too.

With a few more phone calls, I put together a plan that had us staying with my brother Ben for the first few days at the house he'd recently bought in Anders Park. Then, on Christmas morning, we'd head up to Appleton with my mom to spend some time with Jerry and his girlfriend Becky.

I didn't want Eric to see my parents' house. I knew he'd see part of it, but I didn't want to give him ammunition to spurn me later with how shabby my childhood bedroom had been.

AT WORK I figured I'd have no problem arranging for time off. Business had slowed down considerably from the time I'd been hired. Marc explained that was the flaw in their business plan. Once an area was saturated with advertising and all the people who would be interested in their service used it, business slowed down. They had it happen before.

The following Monday morning, I was planning to ask Matt about taking a week off just as soon as I'd retrieved the phone messages from over the weekend, but before I even had the chance to do that, he called me on the intercom to come into his office.

He told me that due to business slowing down, they were going to have to lay me off, permanently. They were actually planning to close down the office within the next week or two.

I tried to hold back the tears that were forming.

He explained that even though I'd worked there a short time, I should be able to file for unemployment because they were legally dissolving the business. I took his word for it, although I didn't really know what that meant. I knew unemployment was money the government sent you if you lost your job, but I didn't have the first idea about how to get it.

Matt also tried to reassure me by promising to write me a glowing letter of recommendation for my next job. At that point, I couldn't even see as far as my next job.

I was sad that yet again I was being forced to leave a place that had become my sanctuary, due to no fault of my own.

Matt and Marc both came into my office just as I was getting ready to leave. They expressed what a great job I'd done for them and if they ever reopened that they'd hire me back without a second thought. I did my best not to cry as I hugged them both goodbye.

The drive home found me slipping deeper into sadness over the trip we wouldn't be taking now, over my job and over something that occurred to me as I got on the freeway heading towards Fern Creek.

This was my last link to Fern Valley Road. The place where I'd met Adam and had actual friends. Each day when I took the Fern Valley exit off I-65, I looked over at the Bowman Park Inn. I searched partly to see if Adam's truck was there, but mostly I was looking for any kind of connection to what I had.

Now I'd have no reason at all to even come this way.

When I got home it was only shortly after ten-thirty in the morning, so as expected Eric was still in bed. He heard me come in and called to me from the bedroom. I went in and sat on the edge of the bed.

"What happened?"

"I got laid off, permanently." I said sadly.

"Why, what happened?"

"They're going out of business; they can't afford to pay me anymore. I guess that takes care of our trip to Wisconsin. I won't have any money now."

"Won't you get unemployment?" Eric asked, skeptically.

"I guess so, Matt said I would."

"Well, there you go, there's your money. We can still go." He was sitting more upright now, looking at me with an amused look on his face, as if I was worried over nothing.

"We can?" I didn't bother to hide the surprise in my voice.

"Yeah Tate, I want to do this for you. I know you need to see your family." He said. As if there had never been a day when he'd had any other opinion of my family.

I threw my arms around his neck and kissed him on his cheek. I knew it was misplaced gratitude, but as long as I still got to go home and see my family for Christmas, for right now anyway, I was happy.

Twelve

THE UNEXPECTED GIFT

TIME SEEMED TO fly by with all I had to do for our impending trip. I had to shop, pack, make phone calls, and sign up for unemployment – which ended up being easier than I thought, it was just another phone call.

Finalizing our arrangements with Jerry and Ben went smoothly. We were all set to stay at Ben's and when we went to Appleton, Eric and I were staying in a hotel room that Jerry reserved for us. He said it might get a little crowded in his little two bedroom house.

A phone call to Lana to arrange a visit went okay, too, once we got past the awkwardness of not having spoken in such a long time. The phone call was short, but she sounded really happy that we'd be visiting. Once we made plans, we hung up and I dialed the next number.

The call to Jennie was next. So much had changed for her. She'd moved to Green Bay to live with Janelle – basically just to get out of Anders Park – and it seemed the change of scenery helped. Not long after she got there, she met her new guy, Travis. She sounded really happy with him. She was even talking about getting married. I told her I couldn't wait to meet him.

That's when the disappointing part of the call came; as we realized that while Eric and I were heading to Wisconsin, she'd be leaving for Minnesota to spend the holidays with Travis's parents. The revelation that we were going to miss one another eventually put a damper on our conversation, so once we'd both offered the obligatory wishes for warm holidays and safe travel, we hung up.

Thinking about Jennie and her new life made me remember another thing I needed to do: get my birth control pills refilled.

That meant a trip to the clinic.

A FEW MINUTES into a typical exam, the nurse was at the part where they listen to your breathing and feel around on your throat. She abruptly dropped her hands from my neck.

"I'm not going to be able to give you any pills today, Tate."

"What? Why?"

"Because your thyroid is enlarged, I think it's probably overactive, but without lab tests we can't be sure. I can't give you birth control pills until you have that checked out and corrected."

"Where do I do that?" I asked impatiently.

"All I can do is give you the name of the physician that we typically refer to."

She handed me a business card with a doctor's name and number on it.

"Thanks."

When I called the number from the card and explained my situation. The woman on the phone made my decision easy. The lab tests alone would be two hundred and thirty dollars and I'd have to pay up front. I thanked her for her time.

I started to think about the fact that from everything that I'd heard, women typically have a hard time getting pregnant after they'd been on the pill for a long time. I'd just get the tests done after we came back.

Besides, it's not like we ever have sex anyway.

In the interest of full disclosure, I told Eric about not being able to get any pills and that I planned to find a new doctor as soon as we got back from Wisconsin. Without much discussion, he seemed to agree with my opinion that the likelihood of me getting pregnant was nil.

— 244 —

On our way to Wisconsin, we traveled mostly in silence, taking in the scenery. Eric was amused as the landscape changed from high-rise buildings and intersecting freeways to a country winter wonderland. It seemed that Chicago was the landmark that stood between the fickle winter weather, with its mixed precipitation and patches of snow and the deep freeze that gripped the northern portion of the Midwest during the winter months, creating a backdrop of white ground and grey skies.

When we pulled into the driveway at my parents' house, dusk was already approaching and my mind was instantly flooded with memories.

Like a movie on fast forward, memories floated by: leaving that driveway so many times with Jennie as my co-pilot, Darrin on his motorcycle, the fateful day I moved to Kentucky, even childhood memories of playing outside.

My eyes traveled up to the window of my old room and I found sadly that despite all the memories, I had really accepted that this was no longer my home.

I was pulled from my bittersweet reverie by the appearance of my parents walking towards the truck. My heart floated in my chest, buoyed by seeing them. It had been so long.

Too long.

Over the next seven days we spent time with my parents, my brothers, Lana and Alex, and finally Jerry and his girlfriend Becky. Each day consisted talking and laughing, exchanging gifts and eating too much. Throughout all of it, Eric was polite and sweet, even during the times we were alone and there was no one to put on a show for.

I relentlessly found myself thinking if only he could be that way all the time.

Our trip even featured a night out, with no jealousy and no possessiveness, just fun. After dinner on Christmas, Jerry decided that we should all go out for a drink. He sold on us on going to a little bar close to his house and it didn't take long before our revelry was in full swing: Becky and I dancing to the songs Lilly picked out on the juke box, while Eric and Jerry played dice with the bartender.

When we finally decided to call it a night – at nearly midnight – the happiness of the day, mixed with just enough alcohol had Eric and I in rare form: pawing at each other before we even got to our room.

The next morning was quite the opposite. We were both hung-over and cranky. That was all I needed. Our trip had been everything I could have hoped for, but I was ready for it to end.

Saturday morning as we stood outside Ben's loading up the truck I was dreading the long ride almost as much as I was dreading the person I'd have to deal with when we got there. Eric's façade was too good to last. It was already starting to crack, like a mask that just couldn't take the pressure of what was behind it. By the time we hit an unbelievable amount of traffic in Gary, Indiana, the normal Eric was back.

He was rude, bossy and fault-finding and seemingly *convinced* that the traffic was somehow my fault.

Easy come, easy go.

ERIC'S ATTITUDE CONTINUED to go down hill after we got home. He treated me as if because I'd gotten something I wanted, he now had the right to be especially mean. I didn't even care; I just tuned him out, which was easy because I was sick. Besides, the trip was worth it.

I'd been feeling nauseous and drained ever since we left Wisconsin. I called my mom to see if anyone was sick up there, but she said no one was.

She was overly concerned, as usual, and made a bunch of suggestions, some ominous, some not.

"Maybe it's jet lag" she suggested.

"Mom, I think you have to actually fly to get jet lag."

"What about food poisoning? Did you eat anything that tasted bad?"

"If something tasted bad, I wouldn't eat it." I retorted.

"Oh. Well then maybe you're pregnant." She teased, sounding a little too optimistic.

"Don't even say that! Okay, that's enough maternal diagnosis. I am hanging up now. I just called to see if anyone else was sick. I'm going to go rest. I'm sure it's just the flu."

"Okay, well take care of yourself and get plenty of rest."

"Bye Mom, love you."

I'm hanging up now...

"Bye, Tate, I love you, too." She said in a motherly tone, which left me feeling guilty for being annoyed with her.

She means well...

TWO WEEKS LATER, I was standing in my bathroom, holding a pregnancy test in my shaking hands. My period was two days late and I couldn't wait any longer. I needed to know.

The directions were simple enough: pee on the stick, wait two minutes, if you get two lines, you're pregnant, one line, you're not.

I peed on the stick, set it on the cabinet and washed my hands, refusing to look at the test, but by the time I'd dried my hands, my resolve was gone.

One line.

I picked up the test and stood there holding it, staring at it. Before my very eyes, a faint second line started to appear, increasing in brightness until it was as vibrant as the other.

"Oh, shit."

I kept looking at the test.

Two lines. Two lines means pregnant.

I'm pregnant.

In a trance, I walked back to the living room, carrying the test with me, and sat down on the couch. I couldn't take my eyes off that test. My head was spinning with all the different implications of having a baby growing inside my body.

Part of me was elated and in awe. There was a person growing inside me, a tiny, little person, made on Christmas Day, in Wisconsin of all places.

Another part of me was terrified because that tiny little person was going to continue to get bigger and had to get out.

Finally, hanging over all the other emotions like a cloak was the devastation over what this meant. I was now permanently linked to Eric. I'd just given him a hold on me that would last for at least the next eighteen years.

I set the test on the end table next to the phone.

I spent the next two hours on the phone. First to know was my mom, who was ecstatic – as expected, then Jennie, who was more cautious about her congratulations. She understood – better than anyone – that this was a mixed blessing to say the least.

They both offered their love and support, which helped. As I kept saying the word 'pregnant', reality was hitting me like a ton of bricks.

My final call was to Anna. That was the hardest. Her and Tom were getting closer to adopting, it just seemed like such a twist of fate. She desperately wanted a baby, whereas mine was completely unplanned.

After I hung up with Anna, I laid back on the couch and thought about how Eric was going to react. My only guess would be that he wasn't going to be happy.

I wanted to stay awake so I could get it over with, but, being emotionally overwhelmed on top of the physical ailments that now made perfect sense, I dozed off.

"Tate."

"Tate, wake up." Eric's voice penetrated my foggy dream as I was pulled back to consciousness.

"What is this?" he barked.

I turned to look at what he was referring to, but before my eyes focused on the thing he was holding in his hand, I remembered.

"Are you trying to tell me you're pregnant?" He sounded like I'd just accused him of something.

I was still groggy, it was hard to focus.

"I was trying to wait up, but... "

"You did this on purpose." He said quietly.

Suddenly all my senses came into focus.

"What?"

"Oh right! Tate, it seems awfully funny we just move into this house and right away you end up pregnant. You saw that I'm starting to get some where and you figure you'd latch right on, huh?"

"You're fucking crazy." I snarled at him, hot stinging tears flooding my eyes. "If you honestly think I'd purposely link myself to you for the rest of my life, you are crazy!"

"Oh don't hand me that shit, Tate, I know better. How'd you get pregnant on the pill? We barely have sex, is it even mine?"

"Hello? You knew damn well I wasn't on the pill because of the thing with the doctor. I didn't lie to you, Eric. I didn't trick you into *anything*. We had sex in the hotel in Wisconsin remember? Christmas night?"

His look softened just a bit as the validity of my words struck him.

"Yeah, I remember, that doesn't mean you didn't plan this."

"You know what? Fine. No, it's not your baby, Eric, it's mine. It's MY baby and all you have to do is say the word and I will raise this baby by myself without a *damn thing* from you. If this is my fault, then I don't ever want to hear you lay claim to *my* baby."

With that, I left him standing in the living room and went to bed. Mercifully, sleep came quickly.

⌒

IN THE MORNING, Eric was just as cold as he'd been the night before and what made it worse was that over night, his hatefulness had a chance to settle over me. Despite my desire to stay strong, I was letting him hurt me in a way that was different than anything I'd felt before.

For him to treat me with disdain *now* was cold, even for him.

I kept thinking about how *that* moment - when he accused me - would forever be the first memory that we share of our child's life.

Sadly, I could see a lifetime of those memories; moments ruined by the dreadful relationship we lived.

I went to a clinic to take another test, just to be sure. When the nurse walked back in the room after the test, holding a pair of yellow baby booties, I knew. It surprised me that I was genuinely happy.

When I got home Eric was genuinely *not* happy. He'd been hoping I'd made a mistake, that I wasn't really pregnant.

Neither of us spoke a word to each for two days.

A week went by before we told his parents. For the first time he seemed positive about the pregnancy. I thought it was a breakthrough, for a moment I finally felt excited to share it with him, but when we got in the car to leave, he eliminated the notion from my head.

"Don't think I'm happy about this." He said flatly.

"Then why did you act happy in there?"

"Because they're happy and really, I just didn't want to listen to them bitch."

"Eric, if they're worthy of a deliberate act, then aren't I at least entitled to decency?"

"I didn't want this! I didn't want to be saddled with a kid, not with anyone, especially not with you!" he snapped.

I felt like I'd been punched in the gut. The anger just came bubbling out.

"You think *I* wanted this? Why don't you just let me go?" I screamed, hot tears streaming down my face. "I hate you, why don't you just let me go?"

"You're not going ANYWHERE!" He bellowed. "You're the one who got knocked up! You put yourself in this situation!" Then, in a viper like tone he hissed "Whether we like it or not, we're stuck together Tate. If you ever even *think* of taking my kid away from me, I will kill you. Do you understand?"

"I understand." I mumbled.

"WHAT? I didn't hear you?"

"I understand."

⌒⟶

THE NEXT FEW weeks passed in fog. On top of the emotional turmoil, the physical symptoms that started this roller coaster wore on. I was exhausted, nauseous and depressed. I laid around, struggling just to keep the house clean.

I did manage to go downtown to sign up for medical assistance. Without insurance, I had no choice. Still on unemployment, I qualified easily, but they told me to notify them when I got a job. They gave me a list of what doctors I could go to and sent me on my way.

⌒⟶

MY FIRST APPOINTMENT with the doctor I'd chosen from the list was surreal. Right off the bat, there were four pregnant women in the waiting room and one was really, really pregnant. It hit me hard.

I'm going to look like that.

Once I got back to the exam room, the nurse listened to my lungs, took my blood pressure, asked me to pee in a cup, and stand on the scale. More or less just like any other doctor visit but now, instead of lists of cold symptoms or products to prevent pregnancy displayed on the walls, there were images of pregnant women and tips on what steps to follow when you go into labor.

Finally the doctor came in and introduced herself as Dr. Taylor. She looked over my chart then basically outlined what I could expect over the next few months from her and how often certain procedures would happen.

I had so many questions; about the changes my body would go through, how big my baby was, what senses it had and how developed it was. I had a lot of questions about childbirth.

After looking once more at the notes that the nurse wrote on my chart, Dr. Taylor asked me to lie back on the exam table. She raised my shirt, revealing my belly and squirted some clear jelly like stuff on me, which was so cold it gave me goose-bumps. She picked up what looked like a microphone and pressed it to my stomach in the middle of the gel and started to move it around until she found what she was looking for. At first all I heard was what sounded like stomach sounds and then, a loud, rhythmic beat.

"That's your baby's heartbeat." Dr. Taylor said matter-of-factly.

A heartbeat. Oh my God.

Right then, the concept of having a person inside me became extremely real. I just listened, mesmerized by the steady beat and I forgot every one of the questions that had just been buzzing around my head.

"It's so fast." I said, surprised.

"That's because the baby is so little. It sounds strong and healthy, though, just like it should."

We listened for a moment longer before she laid the microphone down and handed me a tissue to wipe off my stomach. She said she's see me in a month and that for now all I had to do was just take good care of myself and my body would do the rest. With one more look at my chart, she gave me a due date of September 7th.

After that appointment, I *really* had a lot of questions, so I was happy when Dell brought over a bag of books and magazines, all about pregnancy and babies. Eric's cousin Jodi had them from when she'd recently had her little girl.

I began reading immediately. There was one magazine in particular that had me mesmerized. It had actual pictures of a baby inside the womb, detailing the size and development at each month. Another book that held my attention detailed all the things that could be expected during each part of pregnancy and finally labor.

Labor was the part that freaked me out the most. Unfortunately, it was the one topic that was honestly not made better by knowing what to expect. The whole thing looked incredibly messy and painful.

As WINTER TURNED to spring and spring gave way to the early signs of summer, I struggled with the reality of what was coming. At the same time though, developing a love that I never knew was possible. There was the all consuming, unconditional love that really hit me when I heard the baby's heartbeat, then as time went on, I began to develop a fierce sense of protective love, some of which I suspected came from my situation.

Not since Eric and I first met, had I truly considered these people to be a part of my permanent future. Now they were, and they'd be permanent in my child's life as well. There were times I wished I could just run away before the baby was born. Then somehow I wouldn't have to share with Eric or his family.

I thought about it a lot. I knew that I should have gotten out, that bringing a child into a relationship like this wasn't what was best for anyone.

Why hadn't I? What kept me here?

Money.

I wanted to get out, but how could I? My parents' house wasn't an option and I didn't have, or make enough money to make it on my own.

Now any chance was gone. If I couldn't make it on my own, I damn sure couldn't pay for myself *and* a baby. Even if I could, Eric would never let it happen. He reminded me often that leaving would be a mistake. Once the baby was born he'd have the law on his side and I definitely could not afford a custody battle, so none of it mattered anymore.

I'm stuck.

OVER TIME, ERIC'S anger slowly turned to indifference. He acted like the proverbial expectant father whenever anyone else was around, but in reality he took no part in the pregnancy. He didn't talk about it, didn't buy anything for the baby and hadn't accompanied me to any doctor appointments, I felt lonely and rejected. I had an outlet though; the more

Eric refused me the love and support I craved, the more determined I grew to give my baby all the love and support it could ever need.

Eric did do one thing that at the very least showed decency. He didn't hit me. He still got as mad as ever and screamed a lot and said really awful things, but he hadn't raised a hand since he found out about the baby.

I told myself at least it was something.

Then there was Dell. His mind-set about the pregnancy was starting to get a little creepy.

Of course he was happy; he'd talked a lot about wanting a grandchild before, but what bothered me was that he instantly laid claim to the baby. He just kept talking about 'when we have this baby…' and 'when our baby gets here…'. It seemed beyond a normal grandparent attachment.

Eventually I got a sense that he felt like this child could be his second chance, his chance to fix the mistakes that he'd made with Eric. That was going to be a problem.

Annetta, she wasn't overly possessive like Dell, but I could see she was going to have an answer for everything once the baby was born. She had never been pregnant, so she couldn't comment firsthand, but being the caring hand for a lot of siblings, nieces and nephews, she clearly fancied herself the expert in child care.

My doctor appointments continued monthly and everything seemed to be progressing normally and without issue. Dr. Taylor did comment that I was still a little small for how far along I was, so just before my sixth month, she had me scheduled for my first ultrasound. I was ecstatic. I'd been waiting for this.

I would finally get to see my baby.

Eric agreed to go along to the ultrasound appointment, but only when I pointed out how it would look to his parents if he didn't.

I wanted him to *want* to go, but even if I had to manipulate him, at least I wouldn't be showing up for such an important appointment alone.

At first it was like any other visit, but instead of the device that allowed the heartbeat to be heard, next to the exam table there was a machine attached to a small monitor.

"Will you be able to tell the sex of the baby?" I asked hopefully as the doctor squirted the cold gel onto my stomach; a sensation that was now familiar, but still impossible to get used to.

"Maybe, if it's in the right position."

"I hope it is." I whispered to Eric. He smiled a forced smile and looked around, bored.

The doctor followed the same procedure as when searching for the heartbeat, but now looking for an image. My eyes were glued to the monitor.

She settled in one spot. I searched for something recognizable, but I couldn't make anything out. She looked to me expectantly.

"Do you see it?"

"What am I looking at?" I asked, a little discouraged.

"That's your baby's face!" she exclaimed.

Still holding the device to my belly with her right hand, using her left, she pointed out an eye and then the nose.

Finally I could see it. My heart swelled.

She moved the device around and pointing out body parts, including a foot and a tiny little heart beating.

"Everything looks good, the heartbeat is strong." She told us.

As moved as I had been each time I heard my baby's heart beating, I was in absolute awe by the image of it.

I looked over at Eric. I wanted to gauge his reaction, maybe even share the moment, but he didn't look at me. He didn't take his eyes off the monitor. Instead he just stared like he was witnessing a miracle. His face had softened and in his eyes was a look of love that I'd never seen on him.

I looked back to the monitor, hungry to soak up the experience. The doctor continued to look at different parts of the baby and lightheartedly informed us that our baby must be shy.

"What do you mean?" I asked.

"Because this little baby's umbilical cord is between its legs, hiding the sex." She laughed.

"Oh. Well, that's okay." I said. Just getting to see the baby was enough.

"Actually, you may get another chance to see it. Go ahead and clean up and I will be back in a few minutes to talk to you."

Her tone worried me. What did she need to talk to me about? Hadn't she said everything looked good?

She returned a few minutes later to find Eric and I seated in the chairs next to the desk.

"Is there something wrong?" I asked nervously.

"Not wrong exactly, it's just small. I am going to send you for a specialized graphing ultrasound. They will measure your baby and determine its exact size. Your baby looks perfectly healthy, but I'm just not sure if it's growing as quickly as it should be. I would like to rule out a condition called Intra Uterine Growth Retardation."

"What?" I jumped. All I heard was 'retardation'.

"Tate, please understand that the word 'retardation' has nothing to do with the brain development, I have no reason at all to think there are any problems other than the *size* of your baby. You may just be having a small baby, but I want to rule out any problems."

"What happens if I have that? If we have that?" I asked, putting my hands to my belly.

"Simple bed rest. You stay in bed and take really, really good care of yourself."

"That's it? That will fix it?"

"Well, it's not quite that simple, but we'll cross that bridge when we get there. Let's not assume the worst, okay? I will have the receptionist schedule your appointment at Norton Hospital with the specialist and then one for you to come back here shortly after."

"How long will I have to wait? Before the appointment, I mean?"

"We'll make sure you can get right in, a few days at most." She reassured. "Do you have any other questions right now?" She looked at Eric.

Eric had been silent throughout the whole conversation. He shook his head 'no'.

"No, I think that's it for now." I responded quietly.

"Alright, let's go get those appointments made."

⟨⟩

MY APPOINTMENT WITH the specialist was four days later. Those were the longest four days of my life. Despite what Dr. Taylor said, I just kept thinking about the word 'retardation'.

I was scared to death that something was wrong with my baby.

On the morning of my appointment, I got up and got ready with plenty of time to spare. I woke Eric up and told him if he was going to go along, he needed to get up and get ready.

"Can you just go?" he asked sleepily. "I'm so tired."

"WHAT?" I snapped.

"You want me to go by myself? You honestly think it's fair that I should go through this alone? What if something is wrong, Eric? Don't you think I'd like to have someone there with me?"

"Tate, I'm sure everything is fine. Just call me after if you need to." He said, rolling over to go back to sleep.

"I hate you." I spat before walking out of the bedroom.

Norton Hospital was downtown. Without having directions, it took me longer to find it than it should have. I cried the whole way there, so when I finally pulled into the parking lot, I was glad I still had some time to fix the mess I'd made of my makeup.

I still couldn't accept that he was making me go through this alone.

Once checked in, a friendly looking woman in lab coat led me to an exam room that was dark and cozy. It was nice compared to the intrusive bright lights I expected. There was a gown and a blanket laid out on the exam table. She told me to go ahead and put the gown on and that I could cover up my legs with the blanket so I wouldn't be cold. She was very empathetic.

I felt so alone that even the slightest show of caring was appreciated.

As she began the same procedure that Dr. Taylor had done just four days before, she explained that the ultrasound would take about forty-five minutes, so I'd have plenty of time to see my baby today. She explained that she was a neonatal radiologist, so she should be able to analyze the results right away.

I was having the same overwhelming emotion at seeing the images, clearer this time – on equipment that was obviously higher tech than at Dr. Taylor's office.

"It's a pretty neat process actually. We can get really close to your baby's exact size by first measuring and then, well, it's a little like a mea-suring a loaf of bread and then weighing one slice. It's hard to explain, but it works really well." She laughed.

As the images of my baby swirled around the monitor, I couldn't really tell what I was looking at, but it was amazing nonetheless.

"So do you want to know what you're having?" she asked.

"Yes definitely - if you can tell, I mean. At the last ultrasound we couldn't tell because of the umbilical cord."

"I can usually tell." She said confidently.

A few minutes later she spoke again "Do you have names picked out?"

"Um, yeah I think so. Summer if it's a girl and Elijah if it's a boy." I said uncertainly.

I had settled on the names myself, though I knew at some point Eric would want to chime in, even if he didn't care right now.

"Well Tate, I can tell you that you're definitely having an Elijah."

"I am? Just like that?"

"See that right there?" she asked, pointing to the screen.

"Yeah?"

"That means this baby is definitely a little boy."

"A boy. I wanted a boy. I was afraid to say it out loud."

The rest of the ultrasound was a blur. I was having a boy. For a moment, I even forgot why I was there.

"Okay, all done." She said cheerfully. "And I can give you some more good news. There is absolutely nothing wrong with your baby. He is small, yes, but not abnormally so. Your stomach muscles are just tight and holding him all inside."

"So my baby is fine and I'm fine and I'm having boy?"

"Yep!"

"Thank you so very much. I was so scared. This day could have turned out so bad, and instead it is so awesome!" I felt like hugging her

"You are very welcome. I'm going to print some pictures for you to take with you. I'll do that from my office while you get dressed and you can pick them up from the front desk, okay?"

"Sounds great."

"Good luck, Tate."

"Thanks."

I quickly got dressed and went to pick up my souvenirs from the receptionist. She handed me an envelope with about ten pictures from my ultrasound, some even had little notes on them, typed in to assist in discerning what body parts they were. There was even one that read 'It's a fella'.

On the drive home, I debated on whether or not to even tell Eric the news. I thought after not coming along to the appointment, he really didn't deserve to know. I settled on telling him that the baby was healthy and fine, but not telling him the sex.

Little Eli would be my secret for a while.

When I walked into the house, Eric was sitting on the couch, looking expectantly at me for news.

"The baby is fine." I said flatly.

"It is?"

"Yeah, I guess it's small but not too small and my stomach muscles are just holding it all in."

"That's good news, huh? See, I told you everything would be fine." He said, relief giving way to smugness.

"Yeah, like you knew. I will not forgive you for missing that appointment. Not ever."

"Tate, I'm sorry. I just, well – I was just too scared to be there in case there was something wrong."

"Oh, so make me go through it alone? Did you ever consider how scared I was?"

"I know, Tate, I know. All I can say is that I'm sorry. I'm so glad that everything is okay."

"Whatever."

Later, as Eric was getting ready for work, he called to me from the bathroom.

"Tate, did you find out the sex of the baby?"

What to do, what to do?

"Maybe." I said under my breath, not sure if it was loud enough for him to hear.

He obviously heard, because the next instant he was standing in the kitchen with me.

"You did, didn't you?" he said, smiling. "You found out. You have to tell me, Tate."

"Why should I? If you'd have gone to the appointment with me, then you'd know, too." I retorted, giving way to the fact that I did know the sex.

"It's a girl, isn't it?" he said, slight disappointment creeping into his voice.

"Maybe." I kept my back to him, focusing instead on my task.

"Come on Tate!"

"Hey, you've got a fifty-fifty chance of being right, don't you?"

"You can't let me go to work like this."

"Tate."

I spun around to face him. "Eric, you have not taken one bit of interest in this baby, why should I tell you? Why do you even care?"

"What do you mean? How could you say that? Of course I care." He sounded hurt.

"You have a funny way of showing it." I snapped.

"I know I haven't been the most supportive, but, well I will make it up to you, okay? I will show you how much I care, starting today. Just please tell me."

"No."

"Fine." He stormed back to the bathroom.

Five minutes later he was back at my side, pleading again. I liked the power of having this secret, but I knew I couldn't hold out much longer.

"You're really going to do this? You're really going to not tell me? Are you going to tell anyone?" he implored.

"Yep, soon as you leave, I'm going to call my mom, and then Jennie, and Anna, too."

"What about Mom and Dad?"

"Well, I can't very well expect them not to tell you can I? So I guess, no, they'll have to wait, too."

"Tate, that is not right." He said looking playfully wounded.

I'd honestly not seen him this happy since he found out about the baby. Knowing it was a boy might actually keep him in a good mood for a little while. He'd never mentioned wanting a boy, but being the man he was, naturally he would.

I went to my purse to get the envelope of pictures. I dug through and found the one that revealed the sex.

"Here. Figure it out."

He stared at the picture.

"I can't tell, Tate, I don't know what I'm looking at. Please tell me." He whined.

"READ it, Eric."

"It's a fella." He read out loud. "A fella."

Recognition took over his features.

"It's a boy?" he asked excitedly. "We're having a boy?"

I couldn't help but be happy sharing this moment with him. It felt good to share it.

"Yes, we're having a boy and I already have his name picked out."

"You do, huh?" he challenged teasingly.

"Yeah, and since he'll have your last name, you don't really get much say."

"Well, what is it then?"

"Elijah Parker Sheppard. Eli for short."

"Eli. Eli Sheppard" he said, testing it out. "I like it." He sounded genuine.

"You *do*?"

I fully expected a fight but remembering my proclamation of decision making power, I regained my composure. "Well, that's good because that's what his name is going to be, like it or not."

THE HAPPY BUBBLE we were floating on didn't last long. When I told Eric my unemployment was about to run out the final comment of his screaming tirade was that I 'better damn well find a job, immediately'.

Dell and Annetta had already offered to help us after the baby was born, so I knew that I wouldn't be returning to work right away, but Eric refused to ask for help now, saying that I was perfectly capable of working, which I had to admit, was true.

I knew I shouldn't have waited so long, since now I didn't even know how to approach a job search, knowing that I was going to quit right away. What employer wants to train someone for four months of work at best?

I decided to swallow my pride and take what seemed the best chance I had to get a job.

When I pulled up in front of the Bowman Park Inn, a sense of déjà vu washed over me, but faded quickly as I thought about how different my life was a year ago.

I scanned the parking lot, looking for a familiar vehicle despite knowing I wouldn't find it. Anna told me months ago that the pilots no longer trained here in Louisville.

Adam isn't here...

It was actually better that way. I just needed a job, not drama. I wouldn't have come if I thought he would be. Truth be told, I preferred Adam not see me pregnant – it wasn't my most flattering look.

I climbed out of the car and silently rehearsed my speech on the way up to the looming glass façade.

Inside, Megan and Anna were behind the desk. Megan waved, looking surprised as I walked towards Glen's office. Anna simply gave me a thumbs up. I'd already called her the day before to gauge what she thought my chance would be of getting my old job back.

I knocked lightly on Glen's open door. He was sitting at his desk looking at his computer screen. He smiled warmly when he saw me.

"Tate! Come on in." he said, waving me into his office. "What's new?"

As I stepped inside his eyes traveled down to my pregnant belly.

"Oh! That's new! Congratulations. When are you due?"

"September seventh."

"That's great, that's great." He replied, obviously not knowing what else to say.

"So Glen, looking for help, huh?" I casually gestured in the direction of the large red banner once again strung up on the hotel roof.

"What? Oh, yeah we are. Jamie left us to go back to Florida, so we're looking again."

"Well, what if you had someone who could – um, help out for a few months, say, someone you wouldn't have to train?"

"Tate, are you asking for your job back?" A smile crept into the corners of his mouth.

"Yes Glen, I am, but I have to be honest - it would only be until the baby is born, I wouldn't be coming back."

"That's not a problem. Yes Tate, I will hire you back, even if it is only short term."

"You will?" I didn't bother hiding my surprise.

"Yep, you're hired. Easiest job interview you ever had, huh?" He got up from his desk. "Come on, let's go get you set up."

He walked me out to the front desk and instructed Megan to put me on the schedule.

"You can go up to housekeeping and get uniforms, I believe you know the way?" he asked teasingly.

"Yes, I do, Glen. Thank you."

"You're welcome Tate. I look forward to having you here."

With that he went back to his office and I spent a few minutes catching up with Megan and getting my schedule.

"What about Eric?" Megan asked.

"Did you talk to him?" Anna asked.

"No, I didn't talk to him because at this point, money will be more important to him than me not working here, besides, in my current state, I don't think he's too worried about guys looking at me." I laughed.

"Good point." Megan said giggling.

It was set. I'd be working second shift on Mondays, Tuesdays and Fridays. The rest of the week I'd have off. It wasn't full time, but it was something. I got my uniforms which consisted of a hideously huge jumper style dress. The only good part about it was I was told I could wear it with a simple white t-shirt. At least it would be comfortable.

Eric reacted how I thought he would. A little miffed that I'd not asked him first, but content nonetheless that I'd gotten a job.

Once I got back in the swing of things, I was actually glad to be working there again, being around people. Anna worked all the days I did; it was nice to be around someone who actually took an interest in my pregnancy. Even knowing what she knew about Eric, she couldn't believe how indifferent and absent he was.

ON MOTHER'S DAY, I called Lilly with my warm wishes for her day and we talked about her coming down to spend a few weeks with us. She planned to bring a bus down, right after the baby was born. I thought about having her in the delivery room with me, and we discussed it, but we agreed it would be hard to plan the timing of her trip that way.

I spent the rest of the day daydreaming about what my next Mother's Day would be like.

AS MY BELLY grew, so did my anxiousness to get the baby's room ready, but I needed Eric's help. I asked, but he always said we'd do it when we had to. Eli was due in a few months and the extra bedroom in our house was still just that: an extra bedroom.

One sunny Saturday morning, he woke up in a good mood so I asked again.

Apparently I picked the right day, because he agreed.

We already had a borrowed crib, he put that together first, while I cleaned out the closet making room for the baby's things.

I started to strip the covers off the full size bed that occupied the room, but Eric interrupted me as he walked into the room.

"Why are you taking those off?" he asked.

"For when we take the bed out." I replied, thinking the answer obvious.

"Why would take it out?"

"Why wouldn't we? It's a baby's room; we don't need a full size bed in here." I said.

"No, it stays." He said flatly.

"What do you mean? Eric – seriously? Can we please not leave this in here? Babies take up room, they have a lot of stuff."

"You're acting like it's just a baby's room! It's a spare bedroom, too!"

I could feel my blood start to boil.

"Oh, so you're going to have guests sleep in a room with our baby?" I asked skeptically, keeping in mind that our most likely guests were his drunk friends.

"Tate, don't be stupid." He snapped as he walked away.

I sat down on the bed, angry tears threatening to spill from my eyes.

Everything had to be his way, all the time and I hated it.

This room should be my way. I'll be the one in here with the baby, anyway!

I decided not to give up the whole day by fighting. I wanted this room done, even if I had to concede to Eric as usual.

It was again up to me to compromise at the store. I picked out a pretty baby blue color for the wall, but he wanted white. When he picked out a floral border, I just gave up.

This was a losing battle, not worth fighting.

I would just have to decorate it the way I wanted, once his part was done.

In order to salvage the day, I pretended to come around and like the things Eric picked out for the room. It seemed to work; when we got home Eric cooked us a nice dinner: Italian chicken and we sat down to watch a movie.

About twenty minutes in, I felt the baby start to move and stretch in my belly. I paused the movie and turned to Eric.

"Do you want to feel the baby move? He's moving around a lot right now – you can even see it."

His face contorted into an uncomfortable grimace.

"Tate, I really don't want to."

"How could you *not* want to? It's your *little boy*, Eric. Aren't you at least a little interested?"

"I am, but it's just weird. I just don't want to touch it."

We watched the rest of the movie and went to bed in silence.

ONCE THE NURSERY was painted and Eric's awful floral border was hung, I got to work on decorating it so that it actually looked like a baby's room. Eric wasn't concerned about my decorating because he'd already moved on to bigger, better things. He figured out all he had to do was mention how much better our house could be for the baby and Dell took over the rest.

Eric had such a way of manipulating his parents that a month later, there had been numerous improvements made to our house, all spear-headed and funded by Dell.

The biggest project was the deck.

Dell's idea from when we first bought the house came to fruition: what once was a kitchen window was now to a door that led out to a second story deck, which spanned the entire length of our house.

I had to admit, Dell was quite a skilled carpenter. The deck was sturdy and well built and with each step Dell seemed to have safety in mind for the baby. He built a swinging gate at the top of the stairs that led down to the ground and made sure the spindles were close enough together that a toddler wouldn't be able to fit through and fall.

When it was finished, Annetta decided we needed patio furniture and gave Eric money to get that, too.

With the deck, a new furnace and a remodeled bathroom, all done by the end of July, our house was in better shape than it had ever been, and thanks to the generous guests at a baby shower thrown by Annetta and Eric's cousin Jodi, we had nearly everything we needed for the baby.

I was ready, now I just had to wait for Eli to be ready.

Eric started staying closer to home on the weekends. I would have loved to think it had something to do with the proximity of my due date, but in reality, it was the new deck. Eric made sure there was plenty of beer and food for the grill, making our house the place to be once again.

I didn't mind, not even the extra cleanup. It was just nice not to be alone all the time.

Thirteen

FROM OUT OF THE BLUE

THE FIRST WEEKEND of August, I was back to being alone. There were no friends over hanging out on the deck, Eric was no where to be found. He left for work on Thursday and didn't come home until two days later.

Just before midnight on Saturday, he finally came stumbling through the door.

I was sitting on the couch, where I'd been trying unsuccessfully to lose myself in a movie. I had full view of him when he walked in. He was obviously drunk.

If he'd have looked mad, I may have backed down. If he would have been his arrogant self, I might have just gone to bed – angry, but relieved that he was home.

He didn't look mad or arrogant. He looked sorry.

"Tate, I'm sorry, I know you're mad." He flopped down onto the couch next to me.

"Yeah, I'm mad." I said, refusing to look at him, trying not to breathe in his stench.

"I just needed some time to think." His speech was badly slurred.

Red hot anger for each hour I'd spent alone, waiting, wondering when he'd come home was bubbling inside me.

I jumped up off the couch and spun around to face him.

"Where the hell have you been?"

"With Shane."

"That figures." I snorted. "All he cares about is partying and obviously that's all you care about, too!"

I was towering over him and in that moment it made me feel powerful.

"Tate, that's not true. I was just freaking out about the baby. I told you, I just needed some time to think."

"I'm going to be a dad, you know." He said, as if I'd forgotten something obvious.

"Are you out of your mind? I think it would be a little hard for ME to forget that *you're* having a baby!"

"Tate, I said I'm sorry." I could hear the anger creeping into his voice, but I ignored it.

"Oh you're sorry. Well that makes it all better, doesn't it?" My anger just kept boiling over. It wasn't just about his disappearing act; I was angry for his behavior through the entire pregnancy, through our entire relationship.

"So you're panicking, huh?" I asked sarcastically. "How do you think I feel Eric? What? This is easy for me? You're a fucking genius, I swear. Do you get that everything you're going through, I'm going through – times ten? Do you get that it's happening to MY body?" I grew more agitated the more I yelled. "Have you ever considered that? Have you ever considered that I'm scared, too?"

"You are the one who got us into this!" he roared.

"Then let me go." I said matter-of-factly. "It's not too late. You can just let me go and I will have this baby around people who actually care and you'll never have to be bothered by me again. Just LET ME GO!"

All at once, the slur was gone from his speech, the remorse from his eyes and he was standing, his face inches from mine with his hand at my throat.

The stench of alcohol and stale cigarettes made my stomach churn as panic seeped upwards inside my chest

"I already fucking told you that you're NOT going anywhere! I will fucking kill you if you even think about taking this kid from me. You think I'm going to let you take this baby and have it around your fucked up family? So it can turn out just as fucked up as you? I don't think so!"

Stay calm Tate. The baby...

In my most composed voice I spoke. "Eric, you need to let go. I am pregnant with your child; you do not want to do this."

"Why not?" he asked, his grip tightening on my throat. "If I kill you now, doesn't it make all my problems go away?"

"Eric, please." I choked through repentant tears. I regretted challenging him, thinking that he wouldn't hurt me because of the baby. "Please, you need to let me go."

Using his grip on my throat, he spun me around and pushed me back, hard. I landed on the couch with a thud. I knew instantly he'd made a conscious effort to throw me there, instead of on the floor.

A woman beater with a heart of gold...

"DON'T fucking tell me what I need to do. You're lucky you're pregnant."

Now he was the one towering over me.

"All you ever do is bitch that I'm not around or bitch that I don't have anything to do with this baby. I don't give a FUCK! Can't you understand that? Maybe I'll feel different when it's born, but right now it's YOUR FUCKING PROBLEM, NOT MINE! Why do you think I'm never around? You don't know, because you're too fucking stupid to figure it out!"

"I hate you, Eric," I sobbed. "I absolutely hate you. I can't believe you are being like this to me."

"Believe it! Stop whining about how hard this is for you and think about other people for once in your fucked up life. Think about that baby!"

"That's *all* I ever think about." I protested between sobs.

"Tate, I said I was sorry. You could have just taken that and been glad for it. I was even going to *touch your belly and feel the baby move*, like you were crying about, but now –"

An audible sob ripped through me. How could he be so cruel?

"Now, sorry 'bout it." He mocked.

That's when the pain started.

It felt like the false contractions I'd been having for the last few weeks, but different, stronger.

"Eric, please stop."

"Shut the fuck up."

"Eric, something is wrong."

"Yeah, you." He snorted. "I'm going to bed, you can sleep on the couch, stupid little bitch."

"Oh, I guess you're not that little anymore are you?" He sneered as he walked to the bedroom.

I got up and went to the bathroom to be sick. After, I sat back down in the living room while the contractions kept getting stronger and moved around to my back.

Walk Tate. You're supposed to walk around and see if the pain subsides.

I got up off the couch and slowly began to pace the living room, taking deep breathes, trying to calm myself down.

"It's too early for you to come out, Baby." I said to my belly, rubbing it softly, feeling the shape of my baby beneath my fingers. "We just have to calm down now. I'm sorry. I'm so sorry that I put you through that. Your daddy is just a little drunk tonight. He didn't mean all those things."

I choked up and had to take a breath before continuing.

"We just need to calm down."

Pain ripped through my back and radiated through my midsection.

"Okay." I breathed. "Think maybe we should call the doctor."

I went to the phone and dialed the number that after eight months of pregnancy, I knew by heart. I got Dr. Taylor's answering service and left a message. Two contractions later the phone rang.

"Hello?"

"Hello. This is Dr. Taylor, is this Tate Parker?"

"Yes." I answered weakly.

"Tate, can you tell me what you're feeling.

I described to her each symptom I was having and about how long I'd been having them. She asked me a few more questions, wanting to know if I was bleeding or dizzy.

"Well, I want you to go ahead to the hospital. I will see you there a little later okay? I will let them know you are coming."

"Okay, thank you."

My mind was moving at light speed. I didn't know what to do first. I needed to wake Eric up; he'd have to drive me. Did I need to take anything with me? I can't be having this baby yet, there's still so much to do. Should I take my bag, just in case?

My back and lower belly started to tighten again. I sat down.

Once the contraction passed, I was determined to focus.

"Seriously, just calm down." I said out loud. "Don't panic."

I went to the baby's room and got my bag, setting it down with my purse at the door.

That was the easy part.

I opened the bedroom door and was overwhelmed by the alcohol stench that hung in the air.

Walking over to the side of the bed, I said a quick prayer.

"Eric."

He just snored.

"Eric." I said louder.

"Hmmm."

"Eric you need to get up. I have to go to the hospital."

"What?"

"I might be in labor, the doctor told me to go to the hospital. You need to take me."

"I can't Tate. I can't." he mumbled.

"What?"

"I can't drive you, Tate. I'm too drunk to drive you." He said, fake concern dripping from his tone. "It wouldn't be safe. Just call me if anything happens."

"Don't worry, I won't." I snarled as I walked out.

I'll just have to do this on my own.

Audubon Hospital was located in the wealthier part of Louisville, the east end. The drive normally took about a half an hour, but less this time due to little traffic at one o'clock in the morning. It went smoothly enough, despite the contractions, which I now knew were four minutes apart. I was nervous, but at least driving gave me something to focus on.

It was when I got there my nerves kicked in again. The instant I was in the care of medical personnel, I put myself in their hands and got back to being scared.

Twenty minutes later I was in a hospital bed with monitors in three places: one on my finger, one around my belly and blood pressure cuff around my arm. The one on my belly was attached to a monitor, enabling me to see the technical results of my contractions. The glowing green line moved up and down with the wax and wane of the pressure.

I'd been examined, told that I was in labor, my contractions were two to four minutes apart and I was dilated to one and a half, which meant that I was still a long ways from giving birth.

A short while later, a different nurse appeared and reported that they'd talked to Dr. Taylor and she'd ordered a medicine that would stop my labor. I was given shot in my arm and told I'd be monitored for a while to be sure it took effect. Once it had, I'd be given oral medicine to take and sent home.

Finally, the fading contractions gave way to exhaustion and I fell asleep, worrying about what would happen when I went home.

The room was much brighter when I opened my eyes.

"Tate, how are you feeling?" Dr. Taylor asked.

The strange surroundings took a moment to make sense.

"I'm feeling better, but very tired."

"That's to be expected." She said soothingly. "You were in premature labor, but it looks like we were able to stop it. Given the size of your baby I really want you to stay pregnant for a while longer."

"I know." I let the guilt wash over me.

If I just would have stayed calm...

"I have a few instructions for you to follow now."

"Okay." I nodded.

"I am going to give you some medicine to keep the contractions from starting again, but you'll need to take your pulse each time before you take the pill.

"How do I take my pulse?" I asked nervously.

"A nurse will show you." She reassured before continuing her instructions. "You will need to take your pulse and then one pill every four hours, even in the middle of the night. If your pulse is over one hundred, you shouldn't take the pill, wait until the next four hours, if your pulse is still high, then come to the hospital."

"That is a lot to remember."

"Or if your contractions start again, come to the hospital. I know this is a lot to remember Tate, but it is the best chance we have of keeping you pregnant for now. It is the best chance for this baby." She touched my belly lightly with her fingertips. "I will have the nurse write it all down for you, including how to take your pulse, okay?"

"Okay." I said gratefully. "When am I being released?"

Not that I really wanted to go home.

"How about we give you a few more hours to rest before we kick you out?"

"That would be good, thank you."

I got home just before eight o'clock that morning, and Shane and Andy were there with Eric. The three of them were in the driveway putting stuff in Eric's truck. They were getting ready to go fishing.

Nice. You're pregnant girlfriend is in the hospital and you're going fishing.

"So, what happened?" Eric asked as he walked into the living room where I was already laying on the couch.

"I went into labor." I said dryly.

"And?"

"And they stopped the labor and now I have to take medication."

"Tate, I'm really sorry about last night. I was drunk. I didn't mean the things I said to you. I do love you and this baby. Please don't be mad at me, okay?"

"I'm too tired to fight Eric. Just leave."

"I'm sorry, I'll leave you alone so you can rest. Do want me to pick up a movie on my way home?"

"Sure." I didn't care what he did. His attempt at being nice was trite.

"Bye, Tate." He said, leaning in and kissing my forehead.

EVERYTHING WAS OKAY until – exactly two weeks later – I woke up bleeding.

My alarm was set for six am, when I needed to take my pill, but I woke up to use to bathroom ten minutes early. I rolled out of bed and waddled in my t-shirt and underwear to the bathroom. Just before I got there, I felt a gush.

Oh God, my water just broke.

But when instinctually I looked down, I saw red streaks running down the inside of my legs.

Something is wrong.

"Oh my God. Eric!"

Amazingly enough, he was at the bathroom door in seconds. When he saw me sitting on the toilet, blood streaks on my legs, he had the same reaction I did.

"Oh God. What do I do?" he asked, his voice quivering.

"Um, get me the phone. Oh and could you get me a pad from the hall closet and some underwear from my closet."

He brought the phone back to me and then went to retrieve the other two items. I dialed Dr. Taylor's number, unsure if I'd get the answering service or not. I didn't want to wait for a call back.

"Dr. Taylor's office, this is Samantha."

I was relieved to reach a nurse, and even more so one who knew me.

"Hi Sam, this is Tate Parker. I am bleeding." I said, my words coming out in a rush.

"Okay Tate, calm down. I'm going to ask you a few questions, okay?" She spoke in calm and reassuring tone.

"Okay, how much blood is there? Would you say like a period, or more?"

"Um, like a heavy period I guess."

"Okay, are you having contractions?"

"No, I'm on that medicine to stop them."

"Okay, that's right, well are you in any pain?"

"Not really, no."

"Okay, I'm going to put you on hold for just a minute and talk to Dr. Taylor, but I will be right back, alright?"

"Okay." I said breathing deeply, trying to stay calm. I'd read and re-read everything I could get my hands on about pregnancy. Blood was *never* a good sign.

A minute later, Sam came back on the line.

"Tate, Dr. Taylor wants you to go ahead to the hospital." She will be there shortly to check on you and see what's going on. You don't have to take the Brethine anymore, but you do need to work on staying calm." She instructed.

"Okay, thank you."

"Good luck, Tate. I look forward to seeing you in a few weeks for your follow up with a healthy baby."

"Thank you"

"We need to go to the hospital." I called out to Eric, who immediately appeared at the bathroom door again with the items I'd asked for.

I cleaned myself up, brushed my teeth and got dressed. Twenty minutes after six we were walking out the door on the way to the hospital.

We made light small talk about traffic and the best route to take to get to Audubon quickly, but that ended when I had my first real contraction. It wasn't like the ones I'd had a month before, it was extremely worse. I was scared and surprised how soon after my missed dosage they started. By the time we reached the hospital parking lot, I'd had three of them.

EIGHT HOURS LATER, my nerves were shot.

I'd been strapped to monitors all day. Nurses had poked and prodded at me. I'd been given an IV, a catheter, and an ultrasound.

Still no one was any closer to knowing why I was bleeding.

All day I'd been having contractions that could only be described as feeling like someone was trying to slowly rip me in half.

Because they still didn't know what was wrong, they still couldn't give me anything for the pain.

And I wasn't dilating, I was still at one and a half, which I'd been since premature labor.

And I *still* hadn't seen Dr. Taylor.

I did have frequent visits from Beth, my labor nurse, though. She was a friendly looking woman who I'd guess was in her mid-thirties. The way her warm hazel colored eyes smiled out from behind her glasses made me feel like she really cared about what was happening to me, not just doing her job. I put my trust in her.

Eric had been in and out all day, claiming phone calls and cigarette breaks as reasons to leave. I was indifferent. I never expected any help from him anyway.

He was on his way out for another cigarette break when he met Beth at the door of my room.

"You're probably gonna want to come back in a few minutes, okay?" She said to him solemnly.

"Sure."

"Hi Tate. I need to check you again." She pulled a glove from the box on the counter and quickly did the exam. Afterwards she washed her hands and sat down on the edge of bed.

"I talked to Dr. Taylor again and I've got some news." She looked at me squarely.

"Your baby is still doing okay, but we're worried about you. You're still not dilating any further than two, your blood pressure is getting higher, and we can't tell why you're bleeding – but we do know that it is you that's bleeding, not the baby."

"So what does it all mean?"

Just then Eric came back and walked around to the opposite side of the bed of where Beth was sitting.

"Tate, Eric - Dr. Taylor wants to deliver your baby by C-Section."

Like a faucet was turned on, tears immediately sprung to my eyes.

"Why?"

I was terrified of surgery. My body was designed for childbirth, surgery was another thing entirely. I'd always been scared of surgery. Out of all the books I'd read, all the magazines I'd poured over, I never read the parts about C-Sections because I convinced myself there would be no reason I'd need one. I was a healthy, twenty year old woman whose baby was in the head down position from month seven on; there should be no reason I would have to have a C-Section.

Except, now here I was, about to have one.

"I know you're scared Honey, but this is the best way. It is not an emergency yet, so Dr. Taylor wants to get the baby before it *becomes* an emergency – for either of you."

That did make sense. That was the only goal after all: to get the baby delivered without any thing bad happening.

"Okay, well when can I have something for the pain? My back is starting to hurt really bad, too, but not with the contractions – it hurts all the time. It feels like someone is squeezing the tops of my lungs."

That sounded weird after I'd said it, but I didn't know how else to describe this new throbbing pain.

"That would be from your blood pressure. You have what is called Toxemia. It is basically pregnancy induced high blood pressure and if left unchecked, you could have a stroke."

Suddenly the C-Section didn't seem so risky when compared to having a stroke.

Beth circled back to my original question. "In a little while, Dr. Taylor will be here and we will get you prepped for surgery. When we get you into the operating room, the anesthesiologist will administer a spinal and very quickly you will be numb from the chest down. You won't be feeling any pain at all then."

"Is that like an epidural?"

"A little bit, but it is just a shot that goes in and comes out, nothing stays in like when you have an epidural"

"Will I be awake? Can Eric be in there with me?"

"Yes, you will be awake, though you may be groggy. Eric can come in if he wants to." She looked up at him "Do you want to watch the delivery?"

"Yeah, Yeah I want to be in there, for sure." He was unwavering. He squeezed my shoulder.

"Okay, then when we take Tate, be sure to tell them that you want to be in the operating room and they will get you gowned up."

She looked at both of us "Do you have any more questions?"

"Will you be in there?" I asked.

"I will."

"Okay." I said, forcing a smile.

"Alright, just hang in there a little while longer and we'll be back to get you."

After she walked out of the room Eric came over and sat where she had just been.

"Are you okay Tate?" His face showed genuine concern.

"No, but what choice do I have? You better go tell your parents and call my mom, please."

"Alright. Are you going to be okay alone?"

"Yeah, I'm okay." I promised.

Four more contractions ripped through me as I waited. By the time Beth came in with two nurses who I hadn't seen before, I didn't care what had to be done; I just wanted the pain to stop.

"Are you ready?" Beth asked.

"Not really, but I guess I have to go, huh?"

"Yep Kiddo, have to."

The other two nurses were pushing a gurney, which they lined up next to my bed. Beth disconnected everything from me except the IV and the catheter. Like a well oiled machine, the nurses lined up and by the corners of my blankets, lifted me gently from the bed and put me on the gurney. Beth then unhooked the IV bag from its pole and laid it on the gurney next to me, same with the catheter bag.

"Let's get you going." Beth said.

"Wait, what about Eric? He went to tell his parents, I don't know where he is right now."

Despite *everything*, I needed him with me.

"We'll find him, okay? I promise we'll get him in there before the baby is born." She reassured me.

As they rolled me down the hall, it felt like my stomach was filled with angry butterflies.

After a short trip through a few hallways, I was cruising through two swinging doors, then two more. The room I ended up in was drastically different. It was cold and surgical, sterile. Everything was either made of stainless steel or covered in flimsy blue fabric.

The nurses did their trick again, lifting me this time from the gurney to the operating table. Beth turned to me and explained what would happen next.

"I am going to go get Eric okay? Julie is going to stay here with you and the anesthesiologist will be in shortly. They will take good care of you and I will be back with Eric before the surgery starts."

She was confident when she spoke and it was reassuring. She was very good at her job.

"Thank you Beth." I said weakly.

"You are welcome Tate."

The nurse she called Julie came to the side of the table I was on and asked me to sit up and put my legs over the side of the table.

Just then, someone – who I could only assume was the anesthesiologist – walked in carrying a syringe.

Julie spoke as she positioned herself directly in front of me. "Okay I'm going to help you, I need you to lean as far forward as you can and arch your back, like a cat. There's going to be a big pinch in your lower back, but it will only last for a second."

I leaned forward into Julie's arms as she instructed and braced myself for the pain. My gown must have come untied in the back because I could feel it slipping down my arms. Scared to move from my arched position, I let the gown fall to the floor, oblivious to being naked this far into this day.

I felt the cool tips of the anesthesiologist's gloved fingers on my spine and then the tiniest poke. Immediately I felt the pain that had racked my body all day dissipating.

Warmth instantly spread through my midsection and down my legs.

"I feel warm." I was amazed at how fast it was working.

"We need to get you laid down Hon, right now." Julie said with an urgency in her voice. I understood her urgency a moment later when I was laying flat.

I tried to bend my toes and couldn't. I was completely paralyzed from the chest down. I couldn't feel or move a muscle.

Julie then got to work hanging a large piece of the blue paper across my chest so that I couldn't see the surgery. That suited me just fine, that was the last thing I wanted to witness. She laid my arms out flat and strapped them down at the wrists.

"What is that for?" I asked nervously.

"Oh that is just so you don't move and hurt yourself during the surgery."

She said it nonchalantly, but it still felt a little creepy to have my arms strapped down to the table, regardless of the reason.

By the time she got everything set, the room had filled up. The other nurse that transported me was there, as was a third. They each set to different tasks, getting things ready for the surgery and for the baby. The anesthesiologist returned and was checking my vitals and finally Dr. Taylor walked in, holding her gloved hands up to keep them sterile.

"Hi Tate. How about we get this baby of yours out into the world, huh?"

"Yeah, I think so."

"You know, when you called this morning and said you were bleeding, I had a feeling I would be performing a C-Section on you today. I don't want you to be scared. This is a much more common surgery than it used to be, we do these all the time."

She moved to the other end of the sheet, out of my view.

"Where is Eric?" I asked to no one in particular.

Julie piped up. "I saw him outside with Beth; they are getting him into a sterile gown."

"We won't start without him." Dr. Taylor said lightheartedly.

"Here he is." I heard her say just as the swinging doors opened again. Seeing his face was a relief.

"Hi." He said softly.

"Hi. I'm scared." I confessed. I could feel tears leaking from my eyes and rolling down my face towards the little pad under my head.

"I know Tate, I know." He whispered.

"Will you hold my hand?" I asked.

"I don't know if I can." He looked down at where my hand should be, but was covered by the end of the blue curtain.

Beth popped into sight.

"You sure can hold her hand; you just have to find it first." She said laughing warmly. She maneuvered the curtain around so that Eric could see where my hand was and let it fall back once our hands were securely entwined.

"Okay, here we go Tate. If you feel any pain, I want you to tell me right away. You should feel pressure, but not pain." Dr. Taylor instructed.

"Okay." I said nervously.

I did feel pressure, but no pain at all. It was surreal. I could hear the doctor and nurses murmuring instructions to one another, feel Eric's hand in mine and sense the anesthesiologist standing behind my head, but at the same time, it felt like I wasn't really there, like it was a weird dream.

Eventually I just sort of let my mind go blank.

Eric's voice pulled me back to reality.

"How are you doing? Are you okay?"

"I'm okay."

I really was okay, which surprised me, as terrified as I'd been of having surgery.

"Here he is." Dr. Taylor's voice rang out.

The sound of a baby's cries filled the room. In that moment my entire world shifted.

"That's my baby crying." I said, crying myself. "Eric, is he okay?" I implored, looking to Eric's face. I thought if something was wrong I'd be able to tell in his face.

I could. Nothing was wrong. Tears were streaming down his cheeks, but they were happy tears.

"He is perfect Tate. He's beautiful." Eric said in awe.

"Go see him."

"Are you sure? I can stay with you."

"No. Go see our baby." I pushed.

I could hear the nurses talking, they sounded further away. I kept hearing the numbers four and fourteen.

Four fourteen, that must be the time he was born.

"Tate do you want to see your baby?" a voice called out.

"Yes!" I cried.

Beth walked over to where I could see her. In her arms was a tiny baby wrapped up in a blanket. His face was red and his eyes were closed and smeared with clear gel, which I knew from my reading was to prevent some kind of eye infection.

He was the most beautiful creature I'd ever laid my eyes on. I wanted so desperately to touch him, to hold him and count his little fingers and toes, but the procedure that brought him into this world wasn't finished. I could feel the pressure getting stronger - it was now more pushing than anything and it was making me queasy.

"Would you like me to give you something to relax you?" the anesthesiologist asked softly.

"Yes, please." I answered immediately. It felt strange to say 'please'. In my head, I sort of laughed at myself for saying it.

He chuckled a little bit, too, at my good manners. "Okay. You are going to wake up in recovery in about an hour."

"Thank you."

I looked back over to Eric, who was now holding Eli. He stared at the new baby with terrified awe.

Once again I felt the drugs taking over my senses.

I woke up in recovery just as promised. I slowly opened my eyes as the memory of what had just happened came flooding back to me. Eric was sitting next to my gurney, but looking around so he didn't notice I was awake.

My hands instinctively moved to my stomach, where an incision now took the place of where my baby had been for the last nine months.

"Where's the baby?" My throat was so dry; it made it hard to speak.

Eric jumped a little, obviously not realizing I was awake.

He smiled. "He's in the nursery. They have him in a warming bed."

"Why a warming bed? Why does he have to be in there?"

I wanted to see him. I just wanted to see for myself that he was okay.

"Tate, he is fine, he's perfect, they're just having a hard time getting his body temperature to stabilize because he's so little. He hardly has any body fat." He shrugged cheerfully.

"How little is he?"

"Four pounds, fourteen ounces. He's tiny."

Suddenly the numbers made sense.

"I thought that was the time he was born. I heard four fourteen in the delivery room, but I didn't know that was his weight. You're sure he's okay? That's so little!"

"Tate, I promise he is fine."

"Well, what time was he born?"

Now I was curious to see how far off I was.

"Three fifty seven."

"That makes sense then."

I sat quietly for a moment feeling like there was something I was forgetting.

His name...

"Hey!" I made Eric jump again.

"What, Tate?"

"You named him?"

"Yes. I named him." Eric said.

"What did you name him?" I said suspiciously.

"What do you think I named him, you goof? I named him Elijah Parker Sheppard."

"Okay."

Then I noticed a cup of ice just out of my reach.

"Eric, can you hand me that ice? Actually, could you go fill it with water? I am so thirsty."

"Uh, sure but the nurse said you can only have slow sips." He grabbed the cup and filled it up at the water fountain on the other side of the hallway. For the first time I looked around at my surroundings and realized I was basically just parked down the hall from a nurses' station.

Eric handed me the cup and I greedily drank the whole thing.

"Tate, you need to slow down." He implored. "The nurse said-"

"I'm fine, just one more cup, please? My throat really hurts."

Julie came by just then to foil my plan.

"Unh unh, uh. Not too much or you could throw up. You just had surgery. You don't want to rip out those staples do you?"

"Staples?" I asked incredulously, setting the cup back down. "I have staples?"

Gross.

"Yep, a few layers of stitches on the inside and staples on the outside, that's pretty normal. How are you feeling?"

"Thirsty. And anxious to see my baby."

"I know, I know. I am going to check your vitals and your incision and then we'll get you moved to your room. *Then* you can see your baby. We have to take care of you first so you can take care of him."

"That makes sense." I conceded.

Two nurses got me settled into my private room; the room that Julie said would be my home for the next five days at least. She said that with my high blood pressure, Eli's size and the fact that I had the C-Section would keep us there at least that long. I had to be moved from one bed to another one more time, as the effects of the spinal still hadn't worn off, I still couldn't move my legs. Julie told me that would probably last through the rest of the night.

My room was comfortable and nicely decorated. It had a small fold out couch that Eric could sleep on and it had a nice view, although it was nearing dusk so the view was quickly fading. The room was on the back side of the hospital so instead of the typical parking lot view you got on any of the other three sides; mine was all trees and grass.

Eric came in just before the moment that I'd been waiting for finally arrived: they brought in Eli.

"Here he is." Julie sang out as she pushed the mobile bassinet into the room. "Mr. Elijah Parker Sheppard, he's little, but he's tough!"

She parked the cart right next to my bed.

I looked over at him: Eli, my living, breathing miracle and my heart actually *hurt*.

He was *so* beautiful.

He was awake, his big blue gray eyes, seemingly searching the world around him.

Julie leaned over him and gently scooped him up. She turned towards me and looked down at him.

"Are you ready to meet your mom, Little Guy?" she cooed. "I think he is. Here you go Mom."

She handed me the little bundle and I nestled him into me, he fit perfectly into the crook of my arm. I wasn't prepared for how light he was going to be.

"Hi, Baby." I purred. Tears were streaming down my cheeks. My heart felt as if it could burst open any minute and love I held for this tiny person would spill out into the world. I was overwhelmed as I stared into his eyes.

"I'm your mom, Eli. I love you so much and I'm so glad to finally meet you."

When I spoke, I could feel his little body relaxing in my arms, like he knew he was home.

In that moment everything changed. All the hatred, all the yelling, the screaming, the fights, even the violence – none of it mattered.

In that moment the world made perfect sense.

Fourteen

Perfect Timing

THE TRANSFORMATION MY life went through during the first couple weeks of my son's life was astonishing. All the pieces that made up my life shifted, like a puzzle that had been put together off kilter had now shifted into place. Not only did external pieces change, but the internal ones did, too – the big ones; the pieces that made me, me.

Things that used to matter no longer did. I saw the world in a different perspective because all things led to one goal; to keep this baby safe and loved – to keep him with me.

Emotionally, I was full, but physically I was exhausted. Recovering from labor and major surgery, plus taking care of a brand new infant was difficult physically to say the least.

Not surprising, Eric was of no real help. He got up with the baby once the first night we were home, after that I was on my own. I was too scared to take the pain pills I'd been given because I was afraid I wouldn't get up when Eli did.

It was tough, but it was so worth it. Sometimes my hormones would kick in and I'd cry just thinking about how lucky I was to have him. On some level, I felt like I finally understood the reason I'd been put on this earth: to be Eli's mom.

BY THE TIME he was two weeks old, I was feeling better, both physically and mentally. I'd been to my first check up, got my staples out and was told that I was healing perfectly. The hormones were starting to level out and I was excited for Lilly's arrival. I couldn't wait for her to see Eli.

The day before she was due to arrive, things blew up again. Eric had been getting crankier, but I could never have imagined he would sink so low.

I was sitting in bed, holding Eli in my arms, feeding him his morning bottle. Eric roused from his sleep and rolled over so that he was facing us.

"Good morning." He said sleepily.

"Good morning."

"So are you excited about your mom coming tomorrow?" There was something strange about his tone.

"Yeah, of course. Why wouldn't I be?"

"Tate, you know you can't take Eli from me, right?" he asked quietly.

I rolled my eyes. "Yes Eric, I know I can't take Eli from you."

"Sure your mom's not coming down here to get you two, take you back to Wisconsin?"

"Eric, seriously. I'm going to leave with her? What? On the bus? — Don't be dumb. She's coming down to visit and to meet Eli. In two weeks she'll be going back to Wisconsin — alone. Quit being so paranoid."

"Bitch, shut up. I'm not being paranoid, I know you have something fucking planned. I will kill you."

I was so sick of his threats, the words were out of my mouth before I could stop.

"Oh fine, then kill me then Eric. I'm so over you threatening me."

I regretted the words instantly.

In a flash he reached over the side of the bed and was back upright with a pistol in his hand - one I knew to be loaded.

He pressed the cold barrel hard against my temple.

"Bitch, don't think I won't."

In that moment I only had one thought:

If he pulls the trigger, I'm dead, if he doesn't then... I'm not; either way, there is absolutely nothing I can do.

I sat still, not talking, not crying, just staring at the baby in my arms. For what felt like a long time nothing happened.

Eric jabbed the gun forward into my skull then pulled it back. He leaned over to deposit the gun on the floor.

Instinctually, I wanted to set Eli back in his bassinet, but didn't. I worried that if I moved quickly, Eric would grab me.

Stay calm.

Eric didn't hit me like I thought he would.

Instead, he sat as still as me. When I finally looked over at him I saw tears streaming down his cheeks.

"I'm so sorry. Please forgive me, I'm sorry."

"Eric, I —"

"I had a bad dream."

"A dream." I confirmed sarcastically.

"I had a bad dream that your mom came down here and took you away from me. I just don't want to lose either of you."

"Whatever. That was nice, Eric." I spat at him as I got out of the bed, with Eli. " Real classy."

We didn't bring it up again and later that fact is what hit me the hardest. It wasn't what he did, but the idea that he could do something so heinous and we could both act as if nothing happened.

That's not normal.

Eric picked up Lilly from the bus station downtown the next afternoon. When they finally walked in the door, she was a sight for sore eyes.

I immediately went to hug my mom. Her being here was going to be like therapy for me, I could feel it. I decided right there in that moment: every girl should have her mom around when she has her first baby.

"How are you?" She leaned back from our hug to look at me.

"Fine, happy. Tired. Fat."

"Well, you don't look fat, you look healthy."

"Mom, I gained sixty pounds while I was pregnant. Eli was less than five, you do the math."

"Well, I think you look beautiful. Now speaking of Eli, when do I get to meet my little grandbaby?" She walked towards the bassinet.

"Here, sit down, sit down." I ushered her to the couch and picked Eli up out of the bassinet.

"Mom, this is Eli." I looked down at the tiny baby. "Eli, this is your Grandma." I whispered.

Lilly lovingly took Eli in her arms as I passed him to her. She sat and looked at him with a look of love in her eyes. The look was familiar now; lots of people looked at him that way when they held him in their arms.

"Oh my goodness! Hi, Eli. You sure are little. I'm so glad to meet you." She cooed.

"Oh Tate, you did so good. He's perfect." She beamed at me.

After she spent a little while holding him, I put him down for a nap and showed her where she'd be sleeping. I had to admit, it did help right now that there was a full size bed in the nursery.

She got settled and we spent the evening catching up. Eric made a really nice dinner of meatloaf and mashed potatoes. He outdid himself. I figured it was because he felt like such a jerk after the incident with the gun. Of course I would never tell Lilly what happened, but he had to feel embarrassed, in light of her being here. After dinner he excused himself and left us to catch up alone.

We did just that. We spent the next four hours talking and looking at Eli. She just couldn't get over how little he was. I told her how in the hospital nursery he made all the other babies look like they were a month old already and that he'd already gained two pounds.

She said really nothing had changed at home. That was both comforting and disheartening at the same time. I *wanted* things to change for her. I wanted better things for both of us someday.

When it was my turn to give an update, Lilly was blunt.

"So how are things really? Not the baby, I know you love Eli – that's easy to see, but how are things between you and Eric? How are his parents being to you and Eli?"

I started talking honestly with her and the flood gates opened up.

Two hours later I'd told her everything: every time he hit me, how Dell and Annetta turned a blind eye to Eric's abuse, everything except the gun and Eric's dream.

We were both crying. She looked drained. I imagined I did, too.

"Mom, you can't say anything to Eric. He can't know that I told you, it will just make it worse for us."

"I know Tate, I know. What are you going to do? What if he hurts Eli?" she pleaded.

"He's not going to hurt Eli, at least never on purpose. Eric is a woman beater, not a child abuser. He may not be the most present parent right now, but I know he loves Eli."

I did honestly believe what I was telling her was true.

"I don't know what I'm going to do yet, but right now, nothing. I don't even have a job. I have to wait until he's older, but I will get out someday – I promise I will." I said.

"I hope you do Tate. You and this sweet little boy deserve better. You have a nice house and what looks like a nice life here, but if he's hurting you it's not worth it." There was a hint of disgust in her voice.

"I know Mom, I know."

OVER THE NEXT two weeks, we didn't do really do anything special, like sight seeing or anything like that, Lilly was just happy to spend her time with Eli. There were a few times I'd almost wish she *would* put him down. It was wonderful to have help with him and to see her so happy, but I was worried she was getting him used to being held all the time. I did make good use of the time though. I caught up on all the work around the house I'd been neglecting since Eli came.

All too soon, it was time for her to go home. I wished more than anything that I could make Eric's bad dream come true; take Eli and get on the bus with her. I thought about it more than I should; just taking Eli away. I wondered what Eric would really do.

We all rode to the bus station on the sunny September morning. I said goodbye to her in the parking lot, the ride and fresh air were good for Eli, but we didn't want to take him inside the station.

"I will miss you more than you know." I whispered when I hugged her.

"Tate you hang in there." She looked at me. "Take good care of that baby, and don't be a stranger. You guys come up to visit next summer, or maybe I will just back down in spring."

"That would be good."

"Okay, I think we have to get you on the bus Lilly." Eric chimed in.

Lilly leaned over into the car to say bye to Eli. Afterwards, she turned to me and with teary eyes she forced a smile.

I watched through my own tears as she followed Eric towards the station.

When I got back in the car and looked at Eli, I vowed that they *would* be in each other's lives, I just didn't know when.

BY THE TIME Eli was two months old, we had gotten into a nice little rhythm. I was getting more and more comfortable taking care of him, knowing what he needed, getting around with him. I could do things on my own now, including errands and housework. I took Eli to his doctor appointments myself and sometimes, just to get out of the house we would go shopping or to Dell and Annetta's.

My body was healing well and I was feeling better physically so I started working out. I did simple floor exercises in the living room when Eric was at work and Eli slept. I started slow, but I was determined to get my old body back. I figured since I was lucky enough to not get any stretch marks, I owed it to myself to lose the weight.

All the little things were coming together, making me a little stronger and more confident every day.

Even Eric was more tolerable, but it wasn't that he was any nicer, it was that he mattered less. His attitude didn't bother me because I was so focused on Eli. It was like we didn't really have adult conversations anymore. We had conversations with the baby and about the baby.

Almost every day, Eric spent the hour before work with Eli. He would hold him and play with him while I got things done around the house. I figured an hour wasn't much, but it was better than nothing.

It wasn't long before I started to worry once again about money and finding a job. I just wished there was some way I could stay home with Eli and still make money. I couldn't stand the thought of putting him in daycare with strangers. Dell and Annetta felt the same, which is why they were helping us out, but I was starting to feel guilty about it. I thought maybe Annetta could watch him while I worked, but that idea felt just as wrong.

Then – like an answered prayer – the perfect situation arose from out of the blue. My old boss called me.

"Hello?"

"Hi, is this Tate?"

When I heard Marc's voice, my mind started racing, trying to figure out what he could possibly be calling me about.

"Yes it is."

"Hi Tate, Marc McKinney."

"Hi Marc. What's up?"

I knew that sounded rude, but his call just caught me very off guard.

Maybe something got goofed up with my unemployment and it's just coming up now.

"Okay, well then, I'll get right to it. Are you working anywhere Tate?"

"Um, no, I'm actually not. I just had a baby."

"You did? Congratulations! Boy or girl?"

"A little boy. Eli, he's four months old."

"That's great. Things are good then, I take it?" he asked suspiciously.

"Um, well, I could use a job if that's what you're asking, but I just don't know what would work for me right now, hours wise."

"Well Tate, I think I might have the perfect thing for you then. How would you like to do data input for me, at home?"

"I would get to work from *my* home?" I asked in disbelief. "But I don't have a computer."

"I would give you one. Let me explain. After we dissolved A Clean Slate, I started a new company called Independent Paralegal Company, LLC. I basically do the same thing, but I advertise much differently now and I do divorces and bankruptcies for people all over the country. I'm getting too busy to do all the input myself. We told you if we had an opportunity to hire you back – we would, so here I am offering you a job."

"So all I would have to do is put people's information into the templates? I could do that. How much were you thinking of paying?"

"Well, first off I should tell you that you wouldn't actually be an employee, you would be an independent contractor, which means you'd be responsible for your own taxes and there are no benefits. Are you okay with that?" he asked skeptically.

"Marc, compared to having a job and being home with Eli, those seem like pretty small details."

"I could pay you four hundred dollars a week, but you're going to want to take some of that out for taxes. It's a good idea to save for it as you go." His tone was very father-like.

"I can do that. The job sounds perfect, I'll take it. When do I start?"

"Well, why don't you swing over here to my house on Friday, whatever time works best for you will be fine. I will show you how the different templates work and give you a computer and printer to take home, and all the supplies you'll need. Sound good?" he asked cheerfully.

"Perfect. Thank you Marc. See you Friday, probably about noon."

"See you then, Tate."

When I hung up the phone, I let out a loud 'Woo-hoo!'.

*This was **exactly** what I needed. Yeah, I'll be saving up for my taxes, among other things.*

THAT FRIDAY I made the ten minute drive to Mount Washington and found Marc's house easily. I was a little nervous about what the job would actually all entail, but my worries were quickly subdued once Marc started showing me the process I'd follow.

The data entry for divorces looked simple. Marc had different templates made for each state he was currently operating in. Use of the find and replace feature in word processing allowed the clients information to be entered easily. There was a more specific program for bankruptcies, a little more involved, but still easy enough to follow.

He had a computer and printer waiting for me, stacked on a chair in the crowded sunroom he was using as an office. There was also a box filled with supplies and another filled with paper.

The process was simple, too. I would mail the documents as I prepared them and once a week return to Marc's house to get new cases, drop off the finished client files and pick up my check.

This job really was *exactly* what I needed.

When Dell heard about my new job, he took it upon himself to get me a desk. He went to a local flea market and picked up a large steel one that reminded me of a teacher's desk. It wasn't pretty, but it was perfectly functional. It was large enough to fit the computer and printer, plus file shelves, and it fit perfectly right at the bottom of the basement stairs. I put a rug down and made what ended up being a decent little place to work.

The first week went smoothly enough, even though was hard to get on a schedule. I was trying to work during Eli's naps, but would usually get sidetracked by something else that had to get done. By the third week I learned though, that if I went down to work as soon as I put Eli down for the night, I could get in about three hours before Eric got home. The dedicated time slot allowed me to be more focused and by month two, I was easily getting my work done working only four nights a week.

My only fear about the job is that it would end, just like my office position did.

WHEN I WASN'T working, my life was consumed by being a mom. At six months old, it was easy for Eli to take up most of my time because I was basically a single parent. Eric continued to play with Eli once and a while, but all of his actual daily care was done by me.

I was okay with it, really. If I was the one taking care of him, I knew it was getting done right and it meant that much less interaction I had with Eric.

He was getting irritable again.

I could see the indicators of the mood shift. He was getting more irritable with me, more demanding. He was making snide comments about me working out too much, about me not cooking him anything, and telling me that I was too focused on Eli.

I didn't help that I was still sleeping in Eli's room every night. I never intended it to be that way, it just happened. When I moved him from the bassinet to his crib, I wanted to be closer to him for the first few nights. Six months later I was still in there and Eric hated it. He said I was spoiling Eli. I knew that wasn't true. I didn't lay down in a bed with him; I quietly got into bed each night well after he was asleep in his crib.

In my head, it basically came down to who I wanted to wake up to every day.

The more Eric griped about things, the more I was determined to do them, not in order to antagonize him, but almost to separate myself from him somehow. I felt the more he disliked about me, the more I was my own individual person, instead of who he wanted me to be. The more he griped, the more I worked out and the less I cooked and I didn't even consider going back to his bed any time soon.

As soon as I started making money, Eric started asking me for it, but I'd still managed to save some. I wanted to buy a new car. Correction: I needed a new car. Mine was on its last leg. I was afraid to drive too far with Eli; afraid the car would break down and we'd be stuck. I used that thought to point out that a cell phone would really come in handy now that we had Eli, but Eric still refused.

Eric told Dell that I was looking to get a different car and within hours, they had one lined up. Eric's uncle was selling his car and they all thought it would be perfect for me. It was a ninety-three Thunderbird, slate blue. It was nice, sporty looking, but bigger than my Cavalier. I liked the tinted windows, but worried about getting Eli in and out of the deep back seat.

After I drove it I considered that the car was in great shape, it ran great, it had low mileage and he only wanted four thousand dollars for it, so I couldn't pass it up. Eric's uncle offered to let me make payments to him. That part I did pass on, because I wanted to go through a bank. I wanted to start building my own credit.

When I mentioned to Marc that I was going to try to get a car loan he suggested that I use my original start date on my application. He said he'd be happy to verify that, should anyone ask. I was hesitant at first, but with a smirk he explained that one *could* say that I was *on extended maternity leave while the company was being restructured.*

Nice.

Lying is bad, spinning is good.

Eric's uncle agreed to knock five hundred dollars off the car in exchange for my Cavalier. That money, plus what I'd saved, meant I only had to borrow two thousand dollars. The loan application process was a daunting one, but it went quickly; just two days after I applied, I was driving the Thunderbird. I felt very empowered by the whole thing and I loved my new car.

Life was back to being about as good as it was going to get for me. Eli was healthy and happy, growing and learning every day. My job was going well. I was back to the size I was before Eli. I loved my house and my new car. Everything was great, except for Eric.

He was getting meaner and meaner. I knew something was coming. When it happened, when he blew up, it was by far not his most violent overture towards me, but it was his most blatant one.

Dell was over at our house to visit Eli and take care of some odds and ends that Eric was neglecting on the house.

We were all standing in the kitchen talking when the topic of money came up. Dell said he thought our water heater was going to need to be replaced soon. Eric suggested that I should pay for it since I had so much money now.

"How do you figure I have so much money? I already spend most of what I make on bills."

"It's not my fault you had to have a new car."

Dell walked over and put his hands out to Eli, who was in my arms. Eli leaned in towards him, happy to go to his Papa.

"Guys, you don't need to fight about this. I didn't say it had to be replaced today. I will just help you when the time co-."

"No Dell." I interrupted "you shouldn't have to pay for *everything* for our house."

I said the words to Dell, but I didn't take my eyes off Eric's. I could see that he recognized the sarcasm I directed at him. It was pathetic how Eric worked his parents, manipulating them until he got what he wanted.

"You need to shut your mouth." Eric snapped.

"Eric! Don't *talk* to her like that!" Dell objected.

"It's fine Dell, I'm used to it."

In a flash Eric moved so that he was standing in front of me, pinning me against the wall, with his hand on my throat.

"Listen you little bitch, you still owe me money from when you weren't working, when I carried your ass. I'd say about a thousand dollars ought to cover it."

Dell was standing next to us, begging Eric to let go of me.

"Dell, please just take Eli into the living room."

"ERIC! LET GO OF HER!"

His yelling startled Eli, who started to cry.

"Dell *please* take Eli into the living room."

Eric's fingers were still wrapped around my throat. His grip was getting tighter. All I could think about was that I didn't want Eli to see this.

"Eric, I was off work because I was having your baby. I didn't realize I was running a tab. Now please let go of me." My words came out hoarse as his grip got tighter.

Then he snapped his head forward so that it collided with mine. Mine in turn, bounced off the wall behind me.

"ERIC!" Dell screamed. "You let go of her RIGHT NOW!"

But he already had. His face was inches from mine when he spoke again.

"You will pay me, you little bitch. I'm not gonna let your freeloading ass off on this. You can start by giving me whatever money you have now and then make payments on the rest. Add it to what you owe me every month towards the house."

"Fine, whatever." I pushed past him and walked away, leaving the three of them in the kitchen. I wanted to get Eli from Dell, but I needed a minute to compose myself. I didn't want to scare Eli even more by seeing me upset.

I went into the bathroom and locked the door. I was shaking but not from fear or pain. It was anger. I honestly felt like I could kill Eric at that moment.

How dare he do that in front of Eli? Maybe Eli didn't know exactly what was going on, but he could no doubt sense that something was very wrong and it wouldn't be long before he would understand and even emulate Eric.

I'm continuing this awful cycle. I'm raising a son who's going to end up abusing women. Just like his dad.

I couldn't. I could not allow this fate to befall my son. I was even more determined to get away from Eric, before it was too late.

<hr>

AUGUST CAME, AND brought with it two significant birthdays: Eli's first and my twenty-first. I was thinking I would talk to Anna about getting together with the girls from the hotel for my birthday. I didn't really want to go out and get drunk, but going out to some bars on my twenty-first birthday seemed only natural.

When I brought it up to Eric, basically to ask for permission, he shot me down immediately.

"Don't think that just because you're twenty-one that anything will change. You will NOT be going out to bars, not on your birthday, not anytime."

I gave up. It wasn't worth the fight.

As for Eli's birthday, Annetta suggested we have a party for him at our house. Dell and Eric were quickly on board with that. With such a large extended family the guest list quickly soared to over fifty people. The plan was to have the party in our back yard. I didn't understand the need for such a large gathering for a one year old, but with Dell and Annetta funding most of the party, I was game. I felt guilty for letting them provide so much for us, the very thing I chastised Eric for, but I told myself I wasn't manipulating them like Eric did; I was simply going along with what *they* wanted.

I was hoping Lilly could come down for Eli's party, since she hadn't been able to in the spring like she'd wanted to, but she said she just couldn't take off work. The restaurant she was working at was short staffed, so she knew without asking that time off would be out of the question. She instead said she wanted to buy Eli a really nice gift.

"I wish you could come down, that would be the best gift you could give him."

I was laying the guilt on pretty thick.

"I know Tate, believe me, I wish I could. Why don't you guys come up here? We can celebrate here after Eli's birthday party down there."

"I just don't see that happening, Mom. I don't think now is a good time."

"Has he hurt you?"

"No everything is fine." I lied. I didn't want to worry her even more than I knew she already was. I knew it wasn't fair to tell her everything, only to withhold details later, but I didn't want her to know that Eric hit me in front of Eli. That would break her heart.

"Well, maybe being a dad is really changing him, Tate."

"I wouldn't go that far. So what kind of really nice gift are you planning to get your grandson?"

"Well, what about that cute teddy bear toddler bed you said you liked?"

"Mom, that is almost two hundred dollars! You don't have to spend so much."

"I want to, besides, Carl is pitching in, too."

"Okay, well yeah, that would be an awesome gift. He wouldn't be able to use it right away, but it would be nice to have it when he is ready."

"Well I will send you the money then and you go get it for his party. You can tell him it's from his Grandma and Grandpa and that we love him and miss him very much."

A FEW DAYS before the party, Eric, Eli and I went into town to pick up the rest of the party supplies we needed. After the party supply store, Eric told me to drive to the liquor store so we could use the rest of the money that Dell and Annetta had given us.

"Eric, they gave us that money for party stuff and food."

"Yeah, and we need alcohol for the party, too."

"It's a one-year-old's birthday party."

"And?"

"And I just don't think it needs to be a drunk fest at our house!" I snapped.

"Who asked you? Is that all you know how to do is bitch? Why are you so worried about money that's not even yours? How about I give you some money worries?"

I took my eyes off the road to look over at him, puzzled by his question. I realized what he meant when I saw my purse in his right hand, held up towards the window while his left was crossed over his body, hovering over the power window button.

"WHAT are you doing?" I panicked.

"Shut the fuck up and drive."

"Eric, put my purse down."

The window started sliding down at his touch.

"ERIC!"

I glanced back at Eli, who was thankfully still sound asleep.

He dropped my purse on the floor.

"FINE! UGH!"

Then his fist made contact with the dashboard of my car, then again. Over and over he punched it as hard as he could, denting the steel and cracking the plastic that covered it.

"STOP!" I yelled. "Stop doing that! You're wrecking it! " I couldn't believe what he was doing. "Fine, I'll go to the liquor store, just stop wrecking my CAR!"

The noise of Eric punching the dash woke up Eli, or maybe it was my yelling, either way, Eli was now screaming, adding to the chaos. Finally Eric stopped.

I was crying hot, angry tears as I struggled to get my composure, drive and calm Eli down at the same time.

"Just go home; I'll go get the damn liquor myself."

I hate you.

Eric never apologized, never offered to pay to fix my car. Again, he acted as if nothing happened.

Eli's birthday party, by anyone's standard, was huge success. The weather was perfect. The forty plus people in attendance all seemed to have a great time relaxing and talking, the kids playing in the yard. The large group did make it feel a little more like a family reunion than a birthday party though. Eli got passed from family member to family member, each one oohing and ahhing over how big he was getting and how cute he was.

Eric played host to perfection as usual. He was his usual charming self, people commented over and over what a nice job *he'd* done on the house. Whenever I saw him in this mode, I couldn't help but think what a joke it was and if only people really knew.

I bustled around in and out of the house, getting drinks for people, checking on the food and eventually cleaning Eli up once he was covered in chocolate frosting from the small teddy bear shaped birthday cake I'd made just for him. We got some great pictures of him and he got a lot of new toys and clothes.

Everything was perfect except for the feeling in my gut that lingered the entire day. I felt like a fraud. Despite the smile I kept plastered on my face, I wanted nothing to do with these people and I found myself resenting them more and more as the day wore on. My only real wish for the day would have been to celebrate Eli's birthday at a small get together with *my* family, not this huge ordeal with Eric's.

I was relieved when the party was finally over and they were all gone, save for a few cousins, who sat out on the deck with Eric, drinking.

One thought continued to flit in and out of my head:

I have to get out of here. I need to start putting together a plan.

Fifteen

THE LAST DANCE

"TATE, I WANT you to move back to our room."

Eric stood in the doorway of Eli's room watching me make the bed that I'd slept in alone.

"Why?" I asked without looking at him.

"What do you mean 'why'? Because, it's time."

I squeezed past him on my way to check on Eli, who I found still playing happily on the living room floor. I started picking up some of the toys that were scattered everywhere.

Eric followed me and looked at me expectantly. Clearly he wasn't going to let the subject drop.

"Why is it time?" I asked. "Why does it matter to you?" I was being intentionally thick. I knew exactly why it mattered. We'd had sex only once since Eli was born. Eric was getting restless and wanted access to me.

I could go the rest of my life and never have sex with him again and be perfectly happy about it.

"You know why it's time." He said quietly.

"If I have to take that bed out of there in order to make you move back to our room, I will."

I knew he was right, but for a completely different reason. A month had passed since Eli's first birthday and he was starting to attempt escaping from his crib on his own. That meant I'd have to put him in his toddler bed soon, for his own safety. It still irritated me that Eric's manipulation was so blatant.

"Fine, you win. I'll start sleeping in our room again, but can I tell you something?"

I knew what I was about to say would piss him off, but I didn't care.

"What?" His tone was softened by his apparent victory.

I stopped cleaning to look directly at him, for maximum effect.

"I guess you can force me to sleep in your bed, but you'll never be able to force me to feel things that I just don't."

I was pleasantly surprised at the look on his face. Eric actually looked hurt as I once again walked past him.

Then I thought to myself:

Who ARE you?

Over the next few days, I let that conversation get under my skin; the hurt look on his face and the pleasure I took from it. I thought a lot about what was happening to me. When did I turn into someone who takes pleasure in causing someone else pain? Was that how Eric felt? Did he take pleasure in hurting people? In hurting me? I told myself that at least Eric seemed remorseful, sometimes. I felt no repentance for the stinging words I'd said to him. On the contrary, I liked it and wished I could make him hurt more. It made me feel strong.

Things inside me were shifting again and I wasn't sure I was going to like the end result.

ERIC FOUND THAT having me in bed with him did no good in his quest for sex. Every time he tried, I made up some excuse about why I didn't want to. I had cramps or my period, I didn't feel good or I was too tired. He was getting irritated but I didn't care. The longer I stalled, the more I considered it, the more the thought of being intimate with him made me ill.

There was also the fear of getting pregnant. With one kid I still had a chance of getting out. There was no doubt in my mind, with two - I would be stuck with him for the rest of my life.

ONE FRIDAY NIGHT, near the end of September, Eric didn't come home from work right away and it irritated me a lot more than it should. I didn't know why it bothered me so much, but as the minutes ticked by, I grew more and more agitated. Just before midnight, I heard his truck pull into the driveway and I mentally prepared myself for a fight.

He walked in the door carrying a fast food bag in hand and a belligerent, angry look on his face.

"Where were you?" I snapped.

"None of your fucking business."

He looked at me with steely eyes.

I was puzzled. His eyes were glazed, but his speech wasn't slurred and the familiar, sickening smell of alcohol that I was expecting to flood my nostrils as he walked past, didn't come.

I got up to follow him into the kitchen, but I stopped short, standing in the hallway, from there, I could make a quick escape into the bathroom if I needed to.

"How is it none of my business? Eric, don't you ever think that I deserve better than what you give me?"

He moved from my sight line. I heard the sounds of him opening the cabinet, retrieving a plate and crumpling the now empty food bag before chucking it into the garbage.

I stepped back as he moved past me again, carrying a plate of tacos.

"What you're going to *deserve* is a beating if you don't shut the fuck up." He snapped as he sat down on the couch.

Anger took over. "Do you know that I truly fucking hate you?"

I should have done what he said. I should have kept my mouth shut, but the rage I felt at that moment wouldn't allow it. All I wanted was to hurt him.

I walked over to stand in front him, he looked up at me, and I saw my own rage reflected back.

"Do you really want to know how I feel about you, Eric? About us? Here's the truth: If it weren't for having to be here to be a mom to that little boy in there, I would blow my own fucking head off, just to get away from you."

He flung the glass plate at me. I turned fast enough that it hit my shoulder instead of my face, where he was obviously aiming.

Instinct kicked in: get low or against something so he couldn't throw me. I dropped to my knees, instantly feeling pathetic kneeling on the floor amidst lettuce and cheese scattered everywhere.

Out of the corner of my eye, I saw a flash of movement. I turned my head just in time to see Eric jerk the end table by one leg, sending the lamp, a picture frame and my can of soda crashing against the wall and then to the floor.

I watched as he raised the small table up to chest height and my brain shut down. Instinct told me to shield my face.

I heard the dull thud of the blow, the wooden frame of the table that spanned the full width of my back, before I felt the pain.

I cried out just as Eric grunted loudly and delivered another blow: he stomped on my lower back, pushing me further into littered floor.

Work boots. You rotten son of a bitch.

"NOW CLEAN THIS SHIT UP!"

I pushed myself back up onto my knees and turned to him.

It hurt to breathe.

He was towering over me.

I spit at him, surprising even myself with the vulgar act.

"I HATE YOU!"

In an instant he was on top of me, the weight of his body pushing me face first into the floor.

Then the blows started.

He smashed his head into the back of mine. The blow landed just at the base of my skull.

He hit me again

"STOP!" I screamed.

And again.

And again.

He's going to crack my skull.

His head smashed into mine again.

"Please stop."

Tears mingled with the food smeared across my face.

His head hit mine again.

He's going to kill me.

And again.

"Eric, please." I bawled.

The more I struggled, the harder he held me down. His hands were on my shoulders, gripping my sweatshirt, which was working itself up as I struggled to get out from under him.

My bare breasts were grinding into the carpet, stinging the fragile skin.

Dear God, please help me.

He hit me again.

When that little boy wakes up tomorrow, he's not going to have a mom.

He hit me again.

The sweatshirt was working itself up around my face. It was getting hard to breathe.

He hit me again.

I was getting dazed. There was pain in so many places, yet at the same time, I felt nothing. Like my body was going numb.

Again his head smashed into mine.

"I – can't – BREATHE!"

Maybe he was getting tired, or maybe it was the lack of air that sent my adrenaline pumping and gave me a sudden burst of strength, but whatever it was allowed me to finally break free from his grip. I flipped him off of me sideways as I scrambled to get away.

I turned to look at him and saw in his eyes a look that shook me to the core. He looked like a wild animal.

He stood up and composed himself quickly. Clearly still seething with rage, but more aware of what he was doing, he spoke with quiet venom.

"Clean this shit up, now."

He walked away. I heard the door leading out to the deck open and close. No doubt going out to smoke.

Adrenaline thrust my thoughts forward.

Now is your only chance.

I made a decision in that moment that I knew could make things worse for me in the long run. But I also knew if he started in on me again tonight, he would probably kill me.

He's gotta be on something.

The only other time I'd seen him this full of rage was the night I went to find him at Melinda's, the night Andy took me to the hospital.

Only tonight, Andy's not here to help me.

Still on my knees on the living room floor, I looked over at the cordless phone on the end table that was only a few feet from me.

Not that one, he'll hear it.

I crawled as quietly as I could into the bedroom, maneuvering around the food strewn everywhere now. I grabbed the corded phone from the stand just inside the bedroom door and pulled it into the hallway where I sat.

There was no crying coming from Eli's room. By the grace of God, somehow he'd slept through the noise.

With fingers shaking, I silently pushed the three digits that would lead to help.

"Hello, nine-one-one, what is your emergency?"

"My boyfriend is beating me up. I need help." I whispered.

"I'm sorry I can't hear you. What is your emergency?"

I struggled to choke back the sobs that were threatening to erupt. Panic was rising up in my throat.

You're running out of time Tate, if he finds you on the phone...

"I'm sorry" I cried quietly. "I can't talk louder. My boyfriend is beating me up, I need help."

I heard Eric's heavy footsteps moving across the deck.

"Twenty-six ten Noble Road. Please hurry."

I hung up the phone and replaced it on the stand as quickly and quietly as I could. I got up and I positioned myself so that it looked like I was coming out of the bathroom, just as the back door closed.

The sobs were coming in full force now, as pain ripped through my back and head, fear through my whole body.

Eric stopped in the hallway, looked at the mess still scattered all over the living room floor, then over to me.

"I thought I told you to clean this up."

His tone was cold and cruel.

"I'm sorry, I will right now. I just had to go to the bathroom."

I kept my head down when I spoke, not daring to look him in the eyes. The last thing I wanted was to set him off again.

I moved slowly into the kitchen to get some paper towels. When I got back to the living room, I found him sitting on the couch, prepared to watch me clean up the mess he'd made.

The humiliation made me nauseous.

While I was carefully picking the bits of food out of the carpet, I kept an eye on the front door. I was thankful for the warm September night that allowed the inside door to be left open. Through the screen door I had full view of the road. I was trying to think of a reason to turn on the light.

Then my heart sank.

I remembered the front porch light was burned out. In the dark, our country house was almost impossible to find. We didn't even have house numbers.

They'll never find me.

Eric started berating me, apparently not satisfied with the beating and the humiliation he'd already put me through.

"Do you know how fucking pathetic you are? You're such a joke. Look at you, on your hands and knees, cleaning up your mess."

I hate you. I hate you. I hate you!

YOU'RE my mess, the mess I've made of my life.

"I can't believe I've put up with you for this long. You are such a piece of shit. Where would you be if not for me, huh? In Wisconsin, in that fucking hell-hole your parents live in, probably."

I tried to just shut out the awful things he spat at me, purposely concentrating on working as slowly as possible. If the police ever did come, if they did manage to find me, I wanted them to see the state the house was in: the lamp on the floor, the table overturned, the food…

I *needed* someone to see it.

"I shouldn't be surprised that you are the way you are. You're whole family is trash. But you – you're the trashiest of all of them. Hell, even *they've* turned their backs on you. When is the last time any of those pathetic fuckers called you? I mean besides your *mommy?*"

The more he spoke, the more numb I felt. I just kept picturing him getting arrested.

He took off his boots, and leaned back into the couch, as if he were settling in to make a night of this.

"You know, I really could kill you and not even fucking care right now. You'd shit yourself if you knew how easy it really would be and how easily I could get away with it."

I was starting to shake. He'd never talked like this.

"Really, do you know how many places I could hide your body? Hell, around here – I could burn it in the back yard. None of these country fuckers would even notice."

"I bet it would only smell for a little while."

Please Dear God let the police find me before it's too late.

"Then I could get Eli a *new* mom, someone who would actually be a good mom."

An audible sob ripped through me. I could withstand most anything he had to say, but not the thought someone else raising Eli.

He's too young. If I died now, he won't even remember me.

I stopped cleaning and just sat, sobbing.

"GET TO WORK YOU LAZY LITTLE BITCH! Stop crying! You're so fucking weak. I would really be doing Eli a favor, wouldn't I? If I got rid of you?"

"I'm a good mom." I let my words trail off.

He just stared at me.

"Yeah, you're right, that is one thing you are okay at. Eli does seem to be pretty attached to you."

Attached?

"Well, you're fucking lucky you are the mother of my kid, or I would fucking kill you, right here, right now."

Out of the corner of my eye I saw headlights on the road. My heart pounded in my chest and my hands were shaking. The car slowed and finally stopped just past our driveway. Then I saw another car pull up behind the first, its headlights illuminating the one in front. It was the police.

Oh thank God.

I jumped up from the floor and darted for the door. I didn't even look back to see if Eric was chasing me or hiding or what. I kept my sight focused on the officers approaching me.

In an instant all the tears that I'd been trying to hold back, all the pain that the adrenaline had kept at bay, all the fear – it all came out. I so overwhelmed by emotion I felt dizzy.

"He's here. He's in here, please help me."

I remembered something, most likely from TV, that the police couldn't come in your house without a warrant or an invitation. I stepped back up onto the porch and opened the screen door for them, letting them walk in first.

When I stepped into the house after them, as they surveyed the area, each with their hand on their gun, I looked into Eric's eyes for the first time since that fateful mistake of spitting at him. I couldn't believe what I saw.

Betrayal. He *actually* looked betrayed that I'd called the police.

"Ma'am, can you tell us what happened?"

"He beat me up." I sobbed.

I lifted up the back of my shirt to show them. I didn't know what it looked like, but there *had* to be marks.

"It's a boot print." One officer said to the other.

I put my shirt down and turned to look at them. They both looked at Eric, then down at the floor where his boots still lay.

"Did you do this to her?"

"I don't know what happened here Officers, I just got home from work."
He looked right in their faces and lied.

You bastard.

The officer turned back to me "Is there anyone else in the house?"

"Just my little boy. He's sleeping in his room." When I spoke of Eli, another wave of emotion crashed down over me.

He looked back to Eric and took a step towards him; the other took a step back and put his hand back on his gun.

"Stand up, you're under arrest."

"Can I at least put on my shoes?"

"Yeah."

I stood back and watched the surreal moment unfold in front of me. The officer put handcuffs on Eric and patted him down, finding only his wallet, a pack of cigarettes and a lighter in his pockets.

This was exactly what I wanted, but it didn't feel the way I expected it to. I realized this would not be the solution that I thought it would, or the one I needed.

I felt more hatred for him in that moment than ever before, yet at the same time - I felt remorse for what I'd put in motion.

In my mind, I could now see the ramifications of involving the police. The spread out like the aftershocks of an earthquake, rattling people's lives apart – namely my own.

The officers led Eric out the police car. One returned a short while later. He told me that he needed to take my statement and that he'd called for a female officer to photograph my injuries; that photos would be instrumental in making the charges stick.

I hadn't thought about charges. I hadn't thought about any of this. All I wanted was to be safe.

The officer and I moved into the kitchen and sat down at the table. There I recounted the night's events, leaving nothing out.

I cried as I told him how Eric had smashed his head into mine over and over, how he threatened to kill me and burn my body in the back yard. The officer wrote notes on the report without a word, but his face showed the disgust he felt towards the man who'd done these things to me.

When the female officer arrived, it startled me how young she was. She couldn't have been much older than me.

That could be me, I could have a job like that, I had a future once.

How did I let this happen?
I felt stupid and pathetic and weak.

The young female officer took pictures of my back, my shoulders, the back of my neck and my legs, showing me the utmost respect. Once she was finished, she showed me the images on the digital camera. There really was a boot print on my back.

"Tate, I think you need medical attention. Can we take you to the hospital?"

"No. My baby slept through all this, I am not waking him up now. Plus, I don't have insurance."

She persisted. "Well, what if we call an ambulance for you? At least the EMTs could examine you here and it won't cost you anything if we request it."

"That would be okay, I guess."

"Alright, I'll stay with you until they get here." She patted my hand.

"Thank you."

When the EMTs arrived, the police officers left, making sure I had their business cards and knew how to reach them if I needed to.

"We will see you when this goes to court." The male officer said. "We will be there to testify to what he did to you."

Court?

I really hadn't thought this through.

The EMTs were two young men, not as young as the female officer, but young enough to make me even more embarrassed about my situation. One examined me and made verbal comments while the other one wrote down the details on another report.

"You really should go to the hospital. You have a concussion."

I tried to swallow the lump that was forming in my throat. I didn't want to cry anymore.

"I can't. My little boy is sleeping and I don't want to wake him up and put him through that."

"Isn't there anyone that you could call to stay with him? Or at least to stay with you?"

I thought of Anna, then I looked at the clock: three am.

"No, there isn't anyone I can call."

Not at three in the morning.

"Well, here's the thing you need to be aware of: You have a pretty bad concussion and if you go to sleep within the next few hours, there is a good chance you won't wake up."

His tone was dead serious.

Not sleep? That's all I want to do is sleep. Go to sleep and wake up to find that this whole night was a very bad dream.

"I'm sorry, I know it's not the smart thing to do, but I just don't have any one to call. I'll be okay. My little boy will be up in a few hours. I'll just keep myself awake until then."

I figured the pain radiating through my body might help me stay awake.

"Okay, but we do have to note that you refused help against medical advice."

"That's fine. I understand."

"At least go and get checked out within a day or two, okay?"

"I will." I lied.

When they left, I sat on the couch for a while, thinking only of how quiet the house was and how broken I felt.

Despite the pain, I went back to cleaning up. I put the table back up right and replaced the lamp. Some how that managed to stay in one piece, but as I fished the picture frame out from behind the couch - where it landed when Eric upended the table – I was in awe at the symbolism in my hands.

It was a picture of the three of us: Eric, Eli and me, taken just a few months ago. The glass was still in place, but not whole. Spider web like cracks now distorted the picture.

Broken and distorted - just like me. Just like my family.

I WOKE TO the sound of the phone ringing. I was startled, but more by the fact that I'd fallen, asleep even after the EMT warned me not to, than the shrill sound.

I put the broken picture down and answered the phone.

As Dell's voice came through the receiver I wasn't thinking about his words. I was thinking about falling asleep with that picture in my hands and realizing that it was only seven o'clock in the morning and wondering why he was calling me right now and if he knew what happened.

Of course he knows. He would be the first person Eric would call to get him out.

"Tate, did you hear me?" his voice was harsh, business-like.

"What? No, I didn't."

"You need to get Eli and get out of the house so we can get Eric out of jail."

"What?" This time my question wasn't from not hearing, it was a lack of belief in what I heard. "Dell, do you know what Eric did to me last night?"

"Well, he said you two had a fight and that you overreacted and called the police. He's not mad at you Tate, he just wants to get out."

"OF COURSE HE WANTS TO GET OUT!"

"Tate please, don't make this harder on everyone, there's already been enough damage. This is going to be expensive for Eric to get out of these charges."

"And of course, you're going to make sure that happens." I made no attempt to hide the sarcasm in my voice.

"Eric is my son."

"Dell, I am hurt. I have a concussion, Eli isn't even awake yet. Where am we supposed to go?"

"You can come to our house. You and Eli can stay with us until you and Eric work this out."

"WORK WHAT OUT? Dell, he threatened to KILL me!"

"Oh Tate, you're being silly. Eric has a bad temper, maybe he was drunk if he said that, but you know he would never really hurt you. You are the mother of his child."

I felt like my head was going to explode. The bad dream didn't end, it was getting worse. I tried one more time to reason with Dell.

"Why can't you just let him sit for a while? Obviously you know he hurt me or the cops wouldn't have arrested him. Can't you just let him think about what he did for a little while?"

"Tate we would, but Eric is supposed to go to a fishing tournament with his uncle today. It's already been paid for."

"A FISHING TOURNAMENT? ARE YOU KIDDING ME?"

"Tate, I'm sorry, but that is Eric's house and in order to let him out of jail, they said you and that baby need to leave." His tone was all business again.

I was getting no where with him.

"Okay, it's Eric's house. I see how this is. No problem, I will pack some things and Eli and I will come to your house, but I can promise you one thing."

"What's that?"

"Someday Dell, you will regret what you're doing right now, as much as Eric will regret what he did last night. Maybe not today or tomorrow, but someday, I promise you."

"We will talk about this later, just get some things together for now." His voice was suddenly filled with concern.

"There's nothing more to talk about. I'll be out within an hour."

I hung up the phone, a million different thoughts going through my head, but only one emotion prevailed: anger.

I am so done here.

I got some things together, just the things I thought Eli and I would need for a few days. I didn't know if I'd be going to back to Wisconsin or what, but I'd call the police to help me get the rest of our things if I needed to.

As I moved around the house gathering stuff, I sidestepped around the remnants of food still on the floor.

Screw him, he can clean it up himself.

I changed my clothes and got our stuff loaded into the car. I poured Eli a cup of milk and carried into his room. I hadn't heard him wake up, but when I walked in, I found him standing in his crib with the biggest smile on his face. My heart melted.

How could I do this to him? Tear his life apart like this?

"Hi Sunshine."

"Mama! Out." he pleaded with me, arms up in the air.

"I know Baby, I know you want to get out. Mom's gonna change you and then we're going to Nana and Papa's house, okay?"

"Papa's house?" he smiled. "Out."

I plucked him from the crib and hugged him tight before laying him down on the bed to change his diaper and clothes, handing him the spill proof cup to keep him occupied.

He pulled the cup from his mouth. "Daddy?"

"Daddy is fishing." I said as cheerfully as I could, hoping he wouldn't notice the fat tears that were forming in my eyes.

"Daddy fishing?"

"Yup. Fishing. When you're bigger, Daddy is going to take you fishing."

I had no idea if that was a lie or not.

Once he was changed and dressed, I swooped him up off the bed and carried him straight out of the house to the car.

All the way to Dell and Annetta's house Eli chatted happily about Daddy fishing and about Papa's house and other things that made sense only to him.

I thought about how to him, the world was exactly the same as it had been the night before, when he went to bed.

My world, on the other hand, had been blown apart.

TWO WEEKS LATER, Eli and I were still at Dell and Annetta's and I was on the verge of a nervous breakdown.

I'd called Marc right away to explain that I needed a few weeks off work to figure out what was going to happen. He graciously told me to take my time; that my job would be waiting when I got things figured out. It seemed like a terribly counterproductive move, considering I needed money now more than anything else.

I hadn't been back to the house nor had I laid eyes on Eric. He came to visit Eli a few times. I stayed in the bedroom for the duration of his visits. Each time, he had Annetta ask me if I would see him, but each time I refused.

I had nothing to say.

As the days wore on, each one blending into the next, my situation became more and more stagnant.

I had no money, no way of getting an apartment and no hope of being able to take Eli back to Wisconsin since Eric asked Annetta to tell me that he would work with me on custody – if that's what I wanted – but he wouldn't allow me to leave Kentucky.

I was stuck.

And Eric's parents were driving me crazy.

Every day I heard from them how sorry Eric was and how he didn't mean the things he said. They told me he said he was drunk, that was the only reason he acted that way – which I knew wasn't true, but I didn't even bother pointing it out.

More likely he was coked up – that's where the rage came from.

I didn't bother because they wouldn't hear me anyway. They refused to hear *anything* bad about their *golden* boy.

Eli was getting cranky and asking for Eric more and more every day. I couldn't pretend this wasn't having an effect on him.

I started to think the easiest thing to do was just go back. At least Eli and I would be in our own house, not camping out at Dell and Annetta's. Eli was sleeping in a play pen and we were recycling the same clothes every few days. If we went back, things would be calm, for a while anyway. I needed time to regroup, to make some money, and to finally put together a real plan.

The final straw was the day that Dell pulled me aside to talk.

"Tate, I want to talk to you about something."

"What?"

I knew what it was about; he wanted me to go back. Yes, I was thinking about it, but I wouldn't admit it, not yet anyway.

"Tate, I think you know that the best thing for that little boy - the best thing for all three of you - would be for you and Eli to go back to Eric. You should go home."

"But that's *Eric's* home, not ours. Remember?"

"Now you know that is not what I meant when I said it was Eric's house. On paper it is his and they refused to let him out until you were gone."

"What about what he did to me, Dell? Am I just supposed to forget? Shouldn't he have be pay, at least a little?"

"Of course you shouldn't just forget. I know that Eric really hurt you, but he *is* sorry. He is paying."

"How?"

"Because every time he comes over here, I can see the pain in his eyes. I can see how much he's hurting because he misses Eli. He misses both of you. He says he's sorry – you just won't listen."

"Sorry isn't enough! Sorry just until the next time? It's just not enough, Dell."

"Well, what if I asked you to do it for me?"

"No disrespect, but if I wouldn't do it for Eric, or for Eli, or even for me – what in the world would make you think I would do it for you?"

"I could make it worth it for you."

"Oh yeah? How's that?"

I knew there was nothing that Dell could offer me that would make me *want* to go back to Eric.

"What if I paid off your car for you?"

"What?" I asked incredulously.

Dell took my disbelieving tone entirely the wrong way.

"Yeah, I would do that for you. I know it's a lot and it probably feels like too much, but I would do anything to see you guys back together and happy again."

"Too much? Are you joking? Dell, let me make something clear to right now. This has *nothing* to do with money – other than the fact that if I had enough money, going back would be the LAST thing I'd do. If it was about money, it sure as *hell* would cost a lot more than two thousand dollars!"

The look on his face clearly showed me that he was confused by my tone and did not comprehend what an insult he'd just delivered.

"Tate, I just want to help."

"By paying me to go back to your son? No thanks."

I realized there was only one thing to do to end this mess.

"I don't want your money, Dell. Don't worry, I'll go back to Eric when he makes more than a half ass effort to fix things, but it is only because at this moment I have no other choice."

I heard Eli waking up from his nap so I got up from the kitchen table to go get him, effectively ending our conversation.

I stopped halfway down the hall and looked back at where Dell still sat.

"Paying me to go back to him? Really? Dell – no disrespect – but that's disturbing, even for this family."

Sixteen

BIG MOMENTS

ERIC AND I sat alone at the kitchen table in his parents' house. Another week had passed, I'd had all I could take. So I did the thing I knew I would do. I called him. This was the part where I'd compromise myself in order to get my day to day life back. As dysfunctional of a life as it was, it was mine and at least it was comfortable.

Dell and Annetta were so very eager to help us 'patch things up' as they called it, like we'd had a simple spat, they volunteered to take Eli for the afternoon and go shopping.

I told myself that this was the right thing to do for Eli. I just needed to be strong and suck it up for his benefit, because that's what parents do. Even still – as I sat there listening to Eric tell me everything he thought I wanted to hear – I knew that in the end, the anger I felt at him wouldn't go away, it would simply be directed inward.

I wasn't going to let things go so easily this time, though. There had to be some stipulations.

"Tate, I will change. I know I've said it before, but this time is different."

"Why? What's different – that I called the cops? That you could have killed me?"

His face flushed red.

"I'm so sorry." His eyes glistened with tears.

To bad for him I was way past being moved by a little crying. I'd already cried enough for a lifetime.

"Eric, I know you're sorry, but I need to know what you are willing to do to make this right. How are you going to change?"

"What do you want me to do?" he begged.

"Um, I don't know, it would be great if you could STOP HITTING ME for starters."

His head hung in shame.

"I know. What else?"

"Stop doing the things that make it more likely for you to hit me. Stop drinking and stop doing whatever you were doing that night."

"What are you talking about?"

"Eric, I'm not that stupid. I know you were on something. Were you by Melinda's?"

"Tate, let's just focus on the future, okay? I'm here, I want to make things right, I just don't think talking about that night will help anybody. I am so sorry for what I did to you, I don't know why it happened, but I promise I won't let it happen again."

His lack of answer was as good as confirmation that I was right on both accounts: he was at Melinda's and he was on something, but he'd never actually admit it.

"Eric, how can you stop it from happening if you don't know what caused it? That doesn't make any sense."

"Tate, I've been thinking a lot and I know that I've put you through hell. You do have a smart mouth, but that doesn't give me the right to hurt you. I think one thing I could do is work on walking away when I get mad."

"Okay, that's a start."

I ignored the 'smart mouth' comment.

"What about the drinking? Are you willing to give that up?"

"All of it?"

"Eric."

"What if I promise only beer – no whiskey? Whiskey is what makes me a mean son of a bitch."

"There have been plenty of times when you've been a mean son of a bitch without any help from whiskey. What about those times?"

"I don't know Tate, but I know I need to try. I love you and Eli so much. I need you to come home."

"You have to do more than try. This is it Eric. This is the last chance you get."

I saw a glimmer of anger cross his face. Even now, he couldn't stand that I dared to be the one making rules. I knew he would never really change.

"Tate, please come home."

"I will come home, Eric – but please don't mistake this for making up. Eli needs stability and he misses you. As for me – your parents are driving me fucking crazy."

"I think it's too late for that, Tate." He retorted, laughing at his own joke.

I looked at him without even a hint of a smile and his faded.

I hate you.

I left him sitting there while I went to the bedroom to pack. I felt like an animal who escaped the cage, just to find out that's the only place the food is.

WITHIN A FEW days of coming home, a police officer served me with a notice that I was being subpoenaed to court. From what I could make of it, this would be a hearing to decide if there were grounds for a hearing. It made no real sense.

The legal repercussions that were yet to come wore heavily on me. I had mixed emotions because as much as I wanted the whole thing to just go away, I also wanted to see Eric punished.

Eric received a subpoena, too, only he got his from his lawyer, who was someone that had been recommended to him by a friend of Annetta's.

I knew who the friend was. At my baby shower, I learned that Annetta's friend Gloria had a daughter who worked in the county legal system.

On the day we were scheduled for court, I drove separately because Eric had to go to his lawyer's office first. When I got there, I found the courtroom listed on the subpoena and made my way in. A harried looking man approached me immediately.

"Are you Tatum Parker?"

"Yes, I'm Tate Parker."

"Miss Parker, I am Thomas Boyer, the Assistant Commonwealth Attorney for Bullitt County." He shoved his hand towards me.

"I'm the prosecutor on this case. I'm sorry if this seems like a waste of your time, but you probably won't be testifying today. Mr. Sheppard's lawyer has filed for a continuation that will likely be granted. However, I do still need you to stay for the hearing. You can have a seat here."

He pointed to the front bench behind the table where he'd been sitting and walked away.

Moments after I sat down, Eric walked into the courtroom with his attorney. Dell was not far behind.

They took their seats, Eric at the front table next to his lawyer and Dell in the same row as me, but on the opposite side of the court. Eric was whispering things to his lawyer with a smug look on his face. The lawyer looked unaffected.

The bailiff said "All Rise.", the judge came in, Eric's lawyer moved for the continuation and the judge agreed. He banged his gavel, the bailiff repeated the command and the whole thing was over.

Thomas Boyer spoke to me as he walked past.

"Thank you for coming. You'll receive another subpoena when the next hearing date is set."

Everything went so fast, I left feeling like didn't know what just happened.

Eric was already at home when I got back because I went to pick up Eli from Annetta's. I was determined to just let it go, I didn't want a fight, but I did have one question for him.

"Why did your lawyer do that, ask for a continuation?"

"As a stalling tactic."

"Why?"

"That is what Beth told him to do, get the case held over until after the election."

"Who is Beth? What election?" I was getting more confused by the second.

"Tate, Beth Wynn is Gloria's daughter. Remember, mom's friend?"

"Yeah?"

"She is the one who referred me to my lawyer and told him to get the case postponed. She is running for Bullitt County Judge."

Elizabeth Wynn won the election.

The next subpoena never came.

By NOVEMBER, I was beginning to think Eric really had changed for good. He hadn't raised a hand to me, not once, and even more amazing he hadn't so much as threatened to. He drank less. He spent more time with Eli. He was just a little nicer and even seemed to laugh more.

Maybe he felt like he dodged a bullet with the way the case against him disappeared, or maybe he scared himself by how brutal he'd been, but whatever it was – things were actually better.

Together, we watched our baby turn into a walking, talking little person. Once Eli was mobile, there was never a dull moment.

He was constantly on the move and I was always on his trail. It was tiring, but so fun. My whole heart felt full each day that I would spend playing with him, reading to him and watching him learn. I started working with him, teaching him things like saying 'please' and 'thank you', and picking up his toys.

Eric took more pleasure in spending time with Eli too, now that he was older and could interact more, but he still limited his time to play. No meals, no baths, no diapers – just play – the rest was left for me.

I was glad I'd gotten into the habit of doing my work at night, since now that was the only time I had. I picked up my job right where I left off. I apologized to Marc about ten times and promised not to let my personal life get in the way of my job again. He said he would rather that I took the time to get things figured out than try to work when my head wasn't in it.

I pushed my idea of 'someday' to the back of my mind and tried to live life the best I could. I had everything I wanted, or at least as close to it as I was ever going to get.

⟨⟩

THE DAYS PASSED, the holidays came and went and Kentucky's mild winter finally burst into spring.

The calm prevailed and I was happy; at least that's what I kept telling myself.

This is what you wanted.

Eric really was trying. He was still Eric of course, conceited and chauvinistic as ever, but he was different in ways that mattered and the changes seemed to be sticking. I was impressed and thankful for all the efforts he made.

Still, the improved state of our relationship didn't undo all the pain and anger that lay beneath the surface. Better? Yes. Enough? I wasn't so sure.

A funny thing started to happen: the less strong I *had* to be, the stronger I *felt*.

Not thinking about the constant threat of violence all the time allowed me to see more clearly what my life *could* be like.

I grew appalled at how much time I'd wasted, at what I let happen to myself.

It was a big moment, when I finally realized that it was me. I was the one who allowed Eric to hurt me because I was the one who stayed.

So if it's up to you, what are you going to do about it?

Just like that, months of the thought process culminated with the concept of 'someday' pushing its way back from where I had buried it.

Pop – there it was.

I welcomed it. I felt as though I was looking at it with new, more determined eyes.

Hello, Old Friend.

As I grew stronger, I could feel that the balance of power had shifted, just a little. Eric was clearly still the dominant and ruling force of our relationship – of my world – but things were changing.

Around the beginning of April, I tested it.

"I want to go to Thunder over Louisville."

We were in the living room; Eric was putting on his boots, getting ready to leave for work.

"What brought this on?" he asked.

"I've always wanted to go, and I think this year, you should take me." I was curious to see which way this would go.

"Oh really?"

He looked both surprised and amused.

Without a word, he walked over to where Eli sat on the floor - happily playing with toys - and kissed him on the top of his head. Then he came over to kiss me.

Before he walked out the door, he looked back at me, smiling.

"Well, maybe I will."

The balance was definitely shifting.

ERIC CAME HOME from work one night wearing an expression I'd not seen on him before. I couldn't decide if it was guilt or trepidation.

"Tate, I want to talk to you about something."

"What's up?"

"There are some guys at work who are organizing a deep sea fishing trip for the end of June and they invited me to go. I would love to do it, but I didn't want you to be mad. I'd be gone for a week and it's pretty expensive. What do you think?"

I was in shock. I could not believe he was in effect, *asking* me if he could go.

A week without him would actually be wonderful, but I didn't want him put off by being indifferent, so I played along.

"A whole week? Well, where would you be? Do you have to fly somewhere?"

"No, no flying. We would drive to Gulf Shores, Alabama, get on a boat and head out to sea about a hundred miles and fish there. We'd stay on the boat for four nights, then come back to shore and drive home. Six days, seven max."

"Well how much does that cost?"

"The entire trip costs about fifteen hundred dollars. That's gas, food and everything."

He seemed to brace himself.

"Fifteen hundred dollars? That sounds like an awful lot of money to spend fishing."

"I know Tate, but this is like a once in a lifetime experience."

He was pleading. It was weird.

"Yeah, sure I guess when you put it like that. I don't mind if you go. Eli and I will be fine for a week."

THE SECOND TO last Saturday in April arrived, bringing with it the kickoff to the Derby festival. I had not mentioned the fireworks again. In a way, I wanted to see what Eric would do. Either way, it wasn't worth a fight the likes that Derby brought before, so I just waited.

I was at the sink doing dishes when Eric came in the kitchen, Eli at his heels.

"Dad is going to pick up Eli about one o'clock."

"For what?" I asked casually.

"I figure we'll leave about two. That will give you time to get ready. We're going to Thunder over Louisville."

I let the plate in my hand sink back into the soapy water.

"Are you serious?" I challenged incredulously.

"Well, if you don't *want* to go..."

A smile crept onto his face, he obviously felt he was being extremely generous.

"Yes, I want to go! Where are we going? Where are we watching from?"

"The best place to see it - in Indiana."

"Indiana? Why is that the best place?"

"Because then you have the city of Louisville as your backdrop. It is pretty amazing."

I tried not to think of the years that he'd probably seen it while I sat at home alone.

"Well, where in Indiana? And why are we going so early?"

"Shane's girlfriend lives in Jeffersonville. We were invited over there for a big cookout and then later we'll walk down to the river front."

"Wow. That sounds awesome. You planned all this for me? Why?"

Momentary suspicion floated through my mind.

Now he's being a little too nice.

"I know you really wanted to go, Tate. You've always wanted to go. I never took you and I should have."

"Thank you, Eric."

Dell picked up Eli right on time, leaving me an hour to get ready. In itself, getting to shower and do my hair and makeup without stopping to check on what Eli was doing was a treat.

As we got ready to leave, I was still a little shocked. I thought *maybe* Eric would take me, but I never expected him to plan a whole day of it, complete with babysitter and all.

The cookout was a lot of fun. Because there were so many people that we didn't know - including a lot of guys, Eric was charming and attentive all day. I knew it was just acting, his way of guarding what was his, but the effect was the same either way.

Just as dusk was promising to settle in, someone announced it was time to go. Everyone grabbed their jackets, blankets and whatever drinks they wanted and as one large group, we all walked to the river. It was quite a hike - over two miles - but when we got there it was worth the walk.

I'd never seen anything like it. Thousands upon thousands of people were packed on either side of the Ohio River. Music was blaring from huge speakers, food and beer tents were everywhere. It was one giant party.

The energy of all the people was amazing. Contagious excitement seemed to hang in the air. I was infected on contact.

Eric had the opposite reaction. As we neared the crowd, he tensed up. He tightened his grip on my hand.

"Stay close to me." he barked.

I laughed.

"Relax Eric, I don't think anyone is going to try to steal me."

"Don't be so sure, Little Fish."

We fought our way through the crowd, breaking up into smaller groups as people found places to sit. The spot Eric, Shane and I chose was small, but had a perfect view of the water, thanks to the slope of the embankment. I spread the blanket out and we all sat down to wait the half hour before the show would start.

I got lost. Looking all around me, I was in awe of the sights and sounds.

I watched as floodlights sent colorful streaks of light into the ever darkening sky and realized there were helicopters hovering above us.

"Eric, what are those helicopters for?"

"People watching the fireworks."

"People? What people?"

"Very, very rich people who have their own helicopters."

"Wow, I guess *that* would be the best seat in the house, huh?"

The river in front of us was empty except for two barges. Further into the distance though, the water was packed with boats of all sizes. I thought to that would be a pretty awesome place to watch from, too, though not as good as a helicopter.

Finally, a warning blast was shot off one of the barges.

The crowd roared with excitement as people everywhere scrambled to get to their spots.

I turned to Eric.

I was a little mad that he hadn't allowed me to come to this before.

Think of all the things you could do if you weren't under his thumb Little Fish. Who knows the places you could swim!

I tried to ignore that thought and the anger that provoked it. I was here now, enjoying the day.

"Thank you for bringing me here."

"You're welcome, Tate."

He put his arms around me and held me close to him. It felt nice – strange, but nice.

As soon as the fireworks started, everything else seemed to disappear. Watching Thunder over Louisville on TV was absolutely not even close to seeing it in person.

I thought of all the fireworks displays I'd been to as a kid. This had the effect of getting all the fireworks from one of those small town 4th of July displays and setting them off in the sky at once.

The twin barges shot blast after blast into the sky, at least twenty at any given moment, lighting up the massive crowd on either side of the river. Making it even more amazing was the fact that the whole thing was choreographed to music.

Eric was right: having the city lights as a backdrop was gorgeous.

The finale was, of course, the best part.

Fireworks continued shooting up from the barge, exploding into huge colorful blasts in the night sky, while the I-65 bridge that connected the two states lit up. A waterfall-like effect was created as streams of white light shot off the bridge and down into the water below. At one point the sky was so bright; it was actually hard to look.

Then it was over. The sky grew dark once again.

We stood up right away and for the first time I was nervous about the size of the crowd. The excitement that filled the air was gone, only to be replaced by the urgency that people felt when leaving a large event. Everyone was moving away from the river into darkness at the same time.

As we trudged along amongst the sea of people, I found myself glad this time for Eric's tight grip.

The high from that night lasted longer than I expected it to. Even though Derby festival itself, we were good. Eric went to the Oaks, as always, with Dell. This year, he was home by nine o'clock, drunk, but happy. He joked a little, ate then went to bed without any problems. The next day, we had a few people over to our house for a small Derby party, mostly Eric's cousins, plus Andy and Shane.

'SOMEDAY' FLITTED IN and out of my mind depending on how each day went. My strength and independence grew a little more each day, but so did my belief in Eric's changes. I needed advice.

I dialed Jennie's number with a little trepidation. We hadn't talked in so long, I wondered if the connection would still be there.

"Hello?"

"Hi Stranger, remember me?"

"Hmmm, the voice sounds familiar?"

"Ha, ha very funny." I giggled.

"How ya been?" she asked, dropping the silliness. I knew what she was asking.

"Good. A little too good, that's the problem. I need advice."

"Is there a such thing as too good?"

"When it's something you're trying to walk away from, there is."

"Okay, enough with the metaphors – talk."

I filled her in on everything that had taken place over the last eight months – since the last time Eric hit me. I told her all about that night and how much he'd changed since then.

"So that's my problem. On the surface it looks like I have everything I wanted, but underneath, I'm still mad as hell and I don't think that will change no matter how long I'm with him or how much he changes. I mean, he's still kind of a dick, but at least he hasn't hit me or threatened to since last September. So what do I do?"

"Geez Tate, I don't think I can answer that for you. That would be hard. If you can see he's making an effort, it would be hard not to let yourself love him even more for trying so hard."

"Oh that's not a problem." I said, interrupting her. "I don't love him more – sometimes, I actually love him less. Isn't that weird? I guess I'm getting to the point that I don't want to end up like my mom has. I don't want to wake up one day forty and realize that I wasted my life being with someone who I really didn't want."

"Then you need to go. Maybe not today, maybe not even tomorrow, but you need to keep it in your mind that you want to go. You sound so different Tate. I can tell things are changing for you. You sound more like the real Tate Parker than you have since you moved down there. Remember what I said to you when you told me about the violence?"

"Huh?"

"I told you it was like he was inside your brain. Sounds to me like you kicked him out of there."

"Oh, yeah." I laughed. "I definitely did that. My thoughts are definitely my own now. I think Eli has a lot to do with it. Like the older he gets, the more I think I really could do this on my own."

"Tate, I know you could! If I can do it, you can do it. How is Eli, by the way?"

"Perfect. He's so big! He's almost two already. It's crazy how fast life goes when you have a kid."

"Tell me about it."

"Yeah, I bet Brandon is really big!"

"He is. He'll be starting kindergarten next fall."

"What? That can't be right."

"It is, Tate. You are absolutely right; time does go faster when you have a kid."

"So you think I should go huh?"

"Yes, and it has nothing to do with the fact that I am selfishly hoping that you'll move back to Wisconsin so we can raise our kids together."

"Oh, okay." I was laughing again. "Well, I don't know if that will happen or not, but thank you so much for your honesty and impartiality."

"Anytime Tate, anytime."

"I'll be in touch soon. Love ya.

"Love you, too. Be strong."

"I will."

As I hung up the phone, I had an epiphany; at least I thought it must be an epiphany because I'd never had such a profound realization in such a profound way before.

Staying here doesn't mean you're strong, it means you're too weak to leave.

Going through the violence, the degradation, the abuse – I always felt like I was strong because of what I went through to be with Eric, how much I could withstand. In reality, I was doing what was easiest. I was literally taking the path of least resistance. The *exact* thought I used to justify coming back after the last time – that no matter how dysfunctional of a life it was, it was comfortable – was the *exact* problem. Staying was comfortable; it was definitely easier to stay. The hard thing, the thing that would take real strength would be to do what I was most afraid of: to strike out into the world on my own.

The only problem left was the matter of how.

ERIC SEEMED TO pick up on the tension that was growing inside me. He kept switching back and forth between being cranky and being clingy.

He seemed to be getting more and more possessive, something I didn't even think was possible.

I wanted to stop it in its tracks. I needed to do something that would push Eric, just a little but not over the edge. I needed to see how he would react.

My plan backfired, but only a little.

I decided that as a twenty-one year old mother who worked and made her own income, there was no reason in the world that I shouldn't have a cell phone.

I chose carefully. I didn't want to get locked into a contract - that seemed counter productive - so I opted for a pre-paid phone, but I did want it to have national service, just in case.

It was Saturday afternoon. I was sitting out on the deck while Eli napped. I made no attempt to hide the phone from Eric. I left it on the table, in plain sight.

When he came out onto the deck, he saw it immediately.

"What is this?" He picked up the phone and looked at it as if he literally didn't know what the object was.

"It's my phone. I just got it."

"Who told you that you could get a phone?"

"No one told me. I guess I told me." I kept my tone light, but firm.

"I think you're getting a little big for your britches."

"Eric, I am not your child. I am an adult raising a child of my own. I wanted a phone for safety reasons, I paid for it and there is no reason that I shouldn't have it. I honestly don't think it should be any of your concern."

"Well it is!"

"Why? What horrible thing are you convinced is going to happen? I'll talk to a friend? Call someone to come and save me? Let me tell you - no need to worry because you win!"

He looked puzzled.

"Win what?"

"Me! I'm clearly not going anywhere. I've accepted that." I lied. "But *you're* going to have to accept the fact that I am an ADULT!"

I honestly couldn't tell by his expression which way it was going to go.

"So I win? Really? Well guess what, Tate? I don't want the fucking prize."

He pushed his chair back, scraping the legs of the chair against the wood loudly. It startled me. I thought for sure he was going to hit me, but he didn't. He turned and walked back into the house. "You want to go? Fine, you'll go. NOW. Let's get your shit packed."

My heart sank.

What is he going to do?

I jumped up to follow him into the house, before I even got all the way inside, I could see he had the hall closet open. My closet.

"What are you doing?" I yelled.

He appeared from behind the door with an armload of my clothes.

"You want to go? Get going then."

He carried the clothes away and I stepped into the hallway and watched in horror as he threw my clothes out the front door.

"Eric, please don't do this. Things have been really good with us, please don't do this now."

"YOU'RE doing it. You want so much damn independence and want to be an adult, here's your chance. Go be an adult!"

He grabbed another armload. I wanted to stop him, but I knew better than to get in his way, then he probably would hit me. I was going to have to talk him down.

"This is not fair! If you are really going to let me go – you know damn well I can't just jump in my car and leave. I don't have any place to go. Not like this."

"Guess you should have thought of that before you wanted to be so grown up!" he spouted as he carried another armload.

"What about Eli? Are you going to throw Eli's clothes out on the yard, too?"

Eric stopped in his tracks.

"Eli's not going anywhere. You want this, not me, not him, *you*. You want to leave, you're going to leave, but you're NOT taking my son."

"Eric, please don't do this. I don't want things to be like this."

Instead of coming back to the closet for more, Eric sat down on the couch. I went into the living room and knelt on the floor in front of him: the perfect submissive position.

"I'm sorry I got the phone. I didn't do it to make you mad."

"It's not the phone, Tate."

"Then what is it?"

"I don't understand why you can't just be happy. I have tried so hard to be better and you don't even see it." He was crying.

"I do see Eric, and I appreciate it so much. I'm sorry I upset you, I don't want things to be like this."

"Neither do I, Tate." He cried, leaning forward into my arms.

I held him and for a moment, I almost felt sorry for him. *Almost.*

"Let's not fight, alright Eric?"

"Alright." He conceded tearfully.

I hugged him for a minute longer before getting up to retrieve my clothes. I wanted them in before anyone saw them outside.

The whole thing was embarrassing, but I definitely learned from it. I knew now that in order to leave, I needed a plan that could stay one hundred percent secret until the last minute possible, like I needed to leave while he was at work or something. I needed to have everything lined up ahead of time. I still didn't know how or where to start.

But he didn't hit me AND I still have the phone.

Later that night I made a decision. I might have to play the victim to get what I wanted, but I would never be the victim again. Eric had played head games with me for a long time, it was my turn. I was taking back control of my life.

I started looking in the paper for apartments. I figured out I could afford to live on my own, as long as my job held out; the problem would be getting started. Having to pay for the first month's rent, the security deposit and furnish an apartment would most likely wipe me out. I'd been saving for my taxes like Marc suggested, and then some, I had almost two thousand dollars saved. I was originally hoping I'd have enough to move out without dipping into the tax money, but I'd use it if I had to and worry about the taxes later.

I was feeling really positive for a few days, but there were so many things to think about, I got easily overwhelmed.

How can I line up an apartment, buy furniture and move, all by myself, all the while taking care Eli?

It was easy to slip back into compliant contentedness when faced with all the challenges. It really was easier to stay.

ON MEMORIAL DAY, Eric's parents came over to spend the day with us. It wasn't like we never saw them, but the fact that they were coming to our house made it feel like an event. Annetta and I sat on the deck under the big umbrella chatting while Dell chased Eli around the yard and Eric cooked dinner on the grill. It was a beautiful day; it felt good to take advantage of it before the weather turned sweltering hot.

After dinner I laid Eli down for a late nap and Eric's parents got ready to leave.

"I'm really glad to see you two getting along so well." Annetta commented as she helped me clear the patio table.

"Yeah, it's about time." Dell chimed in.

Eric and I looked at one another and just smiled. Things weren't perfect, but it was easy enough to let Dell and Annetta think they were.

After they left we returned to the deck. It was quiet, and late afternoon was the best time to be out on the deck, once the sun had moved passed the house.

"I wish you were happy."

"I am happy Eric, what are you talking about?"

"I can see it. I know Mom and Dad can't, but I can see you're still not happy. What more do you want from me?"

"It's not that I'm not happy Eric, it's just that, I just wish things were different. I wish the violence never would have happened. You have been really great for a long time and I'm really impressed with the changes, but it doesn't just make the past go away."

Why am I even telling him this?

"So if I said you could go – would you?"

That was clearly a trick question. The truth could be disastrous, but a lie wouldn't work either.

"I honestly don't know, Eric."

"You know…"

"Eric, I'm sorry. I don't know what else to say. Right now, I'm just taking things day by day I guess. Today has been good, let's keep it that way."

I walked into the house to use the bathroom. When I opened the bathroom door to come back out, Eric was standing in my closet again.

"Eric, what are you doing?" I sighed. This was seriously getting old.

"I think you want to go. I think you'll be happier if you just leave, it's written all over your face."

"Eric, I –"

"No, Tate, don't deny it any more. I think you should leave today."

He was getting more and more agitated.

Hot, angry tears flooded my eyes. I didn't have the energy to keep doing this.

"Eric, please."

I moved into the bedroom and sat down on the floor in front of the phone.

Maybe if I call his parents… maybe they can calm him down.

"What are you doing?" he snapped. He clutched fifteen or so hangers in his hand, my clothes swaying back and forth.

"I'm calling your parents. Maybe they can talk some sense into you. This is ridiculous!"

"No Tate, it's simple. Do you or do you not want to leave? If you want to leave, you're doing it now." He shook the clothes at me as if to gesture what he meant by 'now'.

What did he expect me to say?

In that moment, I made a decision with perfect clarity.

In one month you're going to be a hundred miles out at sea. When you get back, we'll be gone.

"DO YOU WANT TO LEAVE?"

"No." I cried.

I knew what I had to do.

It was a decision that felt four and half years in the making, now made in an instant.

"No WHAT?" He stood there, towering over me. The symbolism was overwhelming.

I swallowed every bit of pride I had left and looked into his eyes. With absolute conviction I told the most blatant lie of my life.

"No I don't want to leave. I love you and I want us to stay together."

His face relaxed and his arm fell dragging my clothes on the floor.

I felt defeated. I sat there, tears still streaming down my cheeks when I heard Eli's door open. He walked over to where I sat, looking sleepy and confused, and plopped down in my lap.

"Why you crying, Mommy?"

"It's okay Baby. Mommy's okay. I was just a little sad, but I'm okay now."

He looked up at me.

"Sad?"

"Yeah, but I'm okay now. You make me happy."

"You make me happy." He echoed as he snuggled back into my chest.

I looked up to where Eric still stood, painful realization settling over his face.

"Can we stop this now?" I asked quietly.

"Yeah." He turned and walked back to my closet and hung my clothes back on the rod.

Seventeen

THE COUNTDOWN

I WOKE UP the next morning and the decision settled over me in a light, comfortable sort of way, like a warm sheet. It always did that when I let myself get caught up in thoughts of a life free from Eric.

Hope replaced hopelessness.

I was easily swept away creating pictures in my mind, planning out details, thinking about what real freedom would feel like.

But this time was different.

The longer I thought about it, the more determination and absolute conviction fueled the fire. There was no doubt in my mind that when Eric returned from his fishing trip, Eli and I would be gone.

I didn't know how I was going to do it, but I did know where I needed to start: reality.

The fatal flaw in all my plans and made up worlds was that when I did dare to dream, the result was always the same. Like bubbles, my hopes would grow and grow until they got too big, leaving them no choice but to pop and disappear.

I had to make a plan – *really* make a plan. It had to be secret, it had to be realistic, and it had to be in place by June 29th.

A sense of control over my own life goaded me on and I spent the morning with thoughts racing.

Where do I start?

A place to live. I need to know where I'm going before I plan how to get there.
. . .
Wisconsin, that's the only way.
I had phone calls to make.
Isn't it time for him to leave YET?

In order for this to work, I needed to use all the resources that I had. That meant going back to Wisconsin where there were people who loved me. I believed in my heart that they would welcome me back - even be glad to help me - I just needed to ask.

That was the hard part. I held on to the feeling that I got myself into this so I should be able to get myself out, but it was clear now that would be impossible. Just the sheer logistics of moving made it impossible to accomplish alone.

Going back to Wisconsin meant that there were going to be legal obstacles. To take Eli out of the state without Eric knowing was probably nothing short of kidnapping, regardless of the reason.

I need to talk to a lawyer, that's the realistic first step.

I made sure to put Eli down for his nap in time that he would be sleeping when Eric left for work. The moment his truck was out of the driveway, I got a notebook, a pen, the phone and phonebook and sat down on the couch. I opened the phone book to 'A' for attorneys.

I punched the numbers in to the first one listing family law that I found.

"Johnson and Ford Attorneys at Law, how may I help you?"

"Hi, I have a question regarding child custody and removing a child from the state."

"Okay. Would you like to speak with one of our family law specialists?"

"Does that cost me anything?"

"No Ma'am, the initial consultation is free."

"Okay, well then yes, I would like to speak with a family lawyer."

"One moment please."

"Randy Ford."

"Hi, Mr. Ford. I have some questions about custody. I would like to take my son out of the state of Kentucky and move back to Wisconsin, where I'm from."

"Okay."

"I'd like to do that without his dad knowing. We aren't married. What do I need to do to avoid kidnapping charges?"

"Are you still with him?"

"Yes."

"Have you been to court to establish paternity or child support?"

"No, there was never a need to; we've been together since the birth of our son, although we did sign a form in the hospital naming him as the father."

"Well that document is useless in the eyes of the law. If you haven't established paternity in court, then legally you are that child's only parent and can take him anywhere you want without telling anyone."

"Really?"

"Really. Be advised that doesn't mean there won't be custody implications by doing what your asking, but you will not be charged with kidnapping.

"Thank you, that's all I needed to know."

"You're welcome."

I called two other law offices, scribbling down notes about what each one said. Three different lawyers all gave the same answer. That was good enough for me.

This might actually be possible!

Next I wanted to call Marc. I needed to give him notice that I wouldn't be working for him – I owed him that.

"Hello?"

"Hi Marc, it's Tate."

"Hi, Tate. What's up, have a question on a case?"

"No Marc, work is fine. I just need to talk to you. I'm not going to be able to work for you after the last week in June."

"Oh." He sounded dejected. "Did you find a different job?"

"No, I will need to – I mean, I'm leaving Kentucky, I am moving back to Wisconsin. I need to get away from Eric, for good."

"Good for you, Tate. I'm proud of you, as much as I'm sad that I won't see you anymore, I think getting out of there is what's best for you."

"Thank you Marc."

Every little bit of positive energy helped.

"Tate, is there anything I can do to help you?"

"Well, I was wondering if there is any other work that I could pick up from you to earn a little extra. I don't know how long it will take me to find a job in Wisconsin."

"Tate, would you be interested in doing *this* job in Wisconsin?"

My mind raced with the possibilities.

"Marc, what do you mean?"

"There is no reason that we couldn't keep up the same arrangement that we have now when you're in Wisconsin. You take the computer with you and we can do everything by mail and e-mail, I will pay for your internet service when you get there. I will just mail you the client questionnaires and your paychecks; you prepare the docs and continue to mail them out. I think it would work out fine.

"Marc, you would really do that for me? Let me take your computer?"

"Of course, Tate. You can consider it yours, whether you work for me or not."

"I WILL work for you!" I couldn't contain my excitement. "But I might need a week or two to get settled."

"Plan on three and I'll give you one week pay anyway, like a paid vacation."

"Well, I'll get back to it sooner if I can."

"It's a deal."

"Marc, you don't know what this means to me. To be able to plan this move and know that I still have a job…"

I choked up.

"That was my biggest obstacle. What you're doing might just be the thing that makes this actually happen. I don't know what to say."

"You've said enough, Tate. I am glad to help you out, both you and Eli. There is also the fact that I have never had a single complaint about your work. The documents you send out are always done right and on time, I don't want to lose you!" He laughed.

"Still need extra work? I think you're going to have a lot of other things to think about right now."

"No, you're right; I do have a lot of plans to make. I'll just stick with what I'm doing now and I'll get back to it as soon as I can when I get to Wisconsin."

"Thank you, Marc."

"You're welcome. Please let me know if there is anything that we can do for you."

"Alright, I will."

I meant it.

"Good luck. Bye."

"Bye Marc."

In matter of an hour, the two biggest hurdles I was facing were cleared. I was ready to bounce off the walls.

Focus, Tate. You still need a place to live and a way to get there.

As I sat looking around the house, I thought about the fact that everything was Eric's. It was going to cost a lot more than I had to furnish a new place to live. That was a problem.

Why should it all be his?

I paid every penny I had into this place. Granted I didn't make the house payment, but I paid the utilities. And I was the one who took care of the place, kept it clean. Shouldn't that be worth something?

He'd say that was the price of living here, not owning anything.

What did I own? My car, that was it.

That *was* it.

Eric owed me; he took value off my car and never paid for it. I should get to take furniture equivalent to the damage he'd done.

A simple justification at best, but it worked. I decided I'd get an estimate on what it would cost to fix it, so I'd have proof.

I started to look around, trying to decided what I would need versus what I could actually take.

There will be time to think of that stuff later, make the next call.

"Hi Ben, it's me."

"Hi Me." my brother answered sardonically.

I ignored his typical brand of humor and got right down to business. "I need your help."

"With what?"

"Um, I need you to come down here and get me, but I will pay you."

"Are you in trouble?" His tone softened.

"No, everything is fine right now; I just have to get out of here – for good."

"Okay, but why would you want to pay me?"

"Because it's time I started standing on my own two feet. By paying you I can feel like I am doing that.

Just saying that out loud felt good. I felt strong.

"Okay Tate, I get it."

"Plus, it's going to cost you money to come down here. Do you want to know what it entails?"

"Sure." He sounded hesitant.

"Okay, here goes. Eric is going on a deep sea fishing trip for a week, he's leaving on June 28th. On that day, I want you to get another guy to come with - preferably Danny – and drive down here. You'll stay in a hotel that night and in the morning you'll have to pick up a trailer that I will have rented, help me load my stuff, then take our stuff back to Wisconsin, while I follow with Eli in my car."

"Wow, it sounds like you've got this all figured out."

"Actually, it's all kind of falling in to place as we speak." I laughed nervously. Everything was moving so fast.

"Okay, I can do that. What if Danny can't make it?"

"Then bring Joey, bring someone who can lift furniture."

"Okay, so where are we moving your stuff to? Back to Dad's?"

"NO. I can't go back there, I need to get my own place. Any ideas?"

"I should let you rent my place."

"What are you talking about?"

Ben's house would be perfect. We'd be less than a block from the playground!

Excitement rose in my chest. A clear visual of what my place would look like would definitely be of great help to me.

"But why would you want to move?" I was confused on his intentions. "And if you did, how much would you want for rent?"

"Well, I could just use a change. I could rent it out to you for a year or so and just rent someplace else."

"Yeah, but are you going to have a different place by the time we get there?"

"Good point – probably not."

"Tate, why don't we do this: you plan on coming here, you and Eli can stay with me for a while and we can figure out then if you're going to get a different place or I am."

"Is there room for all of us?"

"Yeah, I don't use the upstairs at all, I have my bedroom downstairs, the two up there would be perfect for you guys.

"Okay then. It sounds like a plan. Now we just have to figure out money. How much to move me up there and how much for a month's rent?"

"Um, how 'bout three hundred for everything and you cover my hotel stay."

"Done."

Another connection I can hopefully use.

"Talk to you soon, Ben."

Next I called the trailer rental place. I learned that for $189 I could rent an enclosed trailer that would hold an apartment's worth of furniture. That sounded big enough, we would have Ben's truck and the trunk of my car, too. I reserved it, promising to have the full amount paid well in advance. I made a request with my reservation: No phone calls or letters could come to me. I said that it could create a dangerous situation for me. The woman assured me that was no problem and I wasn't the first who'd made that request. She ended the phone call with 'Good luck, Honey.'

I'd made so much progress that I was on a high and wanted to keep going. I called the hotel, hoping Anna was there.

Anna and I hadn't talked much since Eli was born, but I did know she'd managed to move up the ranks. Megan moved on to a different hotel and Anna now held the Front Desk Manager position. When she'd told me about it, I thought of how that could have been me. I started right after her.

"Hi Anna, it's Tate."

"Hi Stranger! How are you?"

"I'm good, hopefully really good. I need your help."

I was getting used to saying those words. It was actually starting to feel good.

I told her about my plan, how I'd finally made up my mind and things were falling into place. She was excited for me and wanted to help in any way she could, just like Marc and Ben. I told her what I needed was a discount on a room for my brother to stay in so we could get a fresh start in the morning. I couldn't risk him staying at my house. His truck being there would be impossible to explain, should someone see it.

"No problem. I won't just give you a discount, I'll comp the room for you. Absolutely."

"Oh Anna, thank you."

"Anything to see you get away from him. I'll miss you though. I know we don't see each other much anymore, but I'll still miss knowing you're here."

"I know. I wish it wouldn't have taken this to get us back in touch. There aren't very many people I'm going to miss here, but you are the one I'll miss the most."

We set up the details of the reservation and promised to talk again soon. Just like Marc, she made me promise to let her know if there was anything she could do to help me.

Amazing what can happen when you ask for help.

When I hung up with Anna, I sat back and looked around my house, the place that would only be my home for another month. Sadness tried to settle over my excitement, but it didn't last long.

I knew I had so much more to do, little things to plan, but for now this was enough. Three hours earlier I wasn't sure where to start and now I had a date set, a job lined up, a place to live and a way to get there. Every major piece was in place.

Now I just had to focus.

Thirty-one days. After four years of living with him, in a month it will finally be over.

I wanted to call my mom and Jennie, but I heard Eli waking up so I knew it was time to leave well enough alone for the time being and take care of life.

As the night went on, guilt started to settle over me. How could I do this to Eli? To take him away from his dad, no matter what the reason, seemed cruel. I knew that Eric loved Eli very much and Eli thought Eric hung the moon. Who was I to rip them apart?

He's left you no choice. You need to swim home, Little Fish.

I thought it was a little ironic that I'd been worried that a month wouldn't be long enough to plan everything, since after the way things fell into place, I was starting to realize that it was actually going to be a lot of days to act like nothing was going on.

The reality was that Eric was going to return from vacation to find his girlfriend and child both gone, along with half of his furniture and I couldn't give the slightest impression that anything was off.

It was going to be hard, I knew that. Emotionally I would want to do things to prepare to leave, like have Eli spend as much time with Eric as possible, but I couldn't push things now. In the past, when I thought about leaving, it was written all over my face. Sometimes I even hinted to the fact that I was thinking about it, for effect, to get Eric's attention; that simply *could not* happen this time. I *had* to maintain the perfect poker face.

It created unique concerns.

For one thing, I wouldn't be able to pack anything. The best I could do was sort through our stuff and say I was collecting items to add to the next rummage sale Jodi had. That way, at least the sorting could be done ahead of time.

It's a lot to think about. One day at a time.

The next day when Eric left for work, I got on the phone right away again. The logistics were in place. I needed my support system now. Lilly and Jennie needed to know I was coming home.

"Hello?"

"Hi, Mom."

"Hi, how are you?"

"I'm fine. I need to tell you something."

"You're not pregnant again?" her tone was somewhat less than enthusiastic, but no more than mine in return.

"God, no. No, no, no."

Thank God, no.

"Okay, good, well what is it?" she asked impatiently.

"Eli and I are moving back to Wisconsin. I'm coming home."

"Tate, I –"

"Oh – not to *your* home. I'm getting my own place, I have to."

She laughed. "I kind of figured that. When? Where?"

"Ben is going to come and get us, and then we are going to stay with him – maybe rent his place or find a different place. And I get to bring my job with me, so that is covered, too. All the pieces are in place – I just have to take care of things on my end and be patient."

"Wow, when is all this happening?" her tone was more insistent now, like she realized I was serious.

"Oh, I forgot that part. June 29th is the day we will be there."

"Tate, that's only a month!"

"I know, it's crazy to think about it – in a month Eli and I will be living up there. I don't know what will happen from there, but I am taking all the steps I can to be safe and do things right. I talked to lawyers and everything. Because Eric and I never went to court, it's fine for me to take Eli up there without him knowing ahead of time. I will have to let him know where I'm going, but I am just going to leave him a letter.

"Tate, do you think you'll stay this time? If not, maybe it's better if you —"

"I AM staying this time, Mom. My mind is made up. I can't stay here, I can't raise Eli like this. If I do – do you know what will happen? Someday I will be the mom getting a phone call from her son saying that he is in jail for beating up his girlfriend. I can't let that happen, this awful cycle needs to end here. I have to be the one to do it."

"Tate, I am very proud of you right now. You will make it, I know you will. You are going to have a great life and whatever we need to do to help, we will do."

"Thank you. I finally wised up about asking for help, and about having the control to make this decision. I was letting Eric make decisions for me. I know now that it's up to me. I am an adult and I can do this. There is nothing that Eric can do to force me to come back to him, nothing. I know I'll have to let him see Eli, but that doesn't mean I have to be with him, or be in Kentucky."

"That's right. Tate, you've made my day. I can't wait to have you and Eli here."

"Me neither, Mom. Can I talk to you in a few days? Eric left for work a while ago and have a lot to do. I still need to call Jennie and tell her, too."

"She'll be happy, that's for sure. Are you going to call Lana, too?"

"Absolutely not. I can't risk telling her, I'm pretty sure her loyalties lie with Eric. I just can't take that chance."

"Yeah, that's probably better. The fewer people that know, the less chance Eric or his parents will find out."

"That was my thinking, too."

"Okay, I will talk to you soon. I love you, Tate. I can't wait 'til you're home."

"I love you, too, Mom. Bye."

One more call. The one I was looking forward to the most…

Jennie's voice filled the receiver.

"Want to know a secret?" I asked.

"Yeah, what is it?" she asked in her best super sneaky voice.

"Can you keep it secret?" I teased.

"Better than anyone." She whispered.

"I'm moving back to Wisconsin."

That's where the whispering ended.

"Oh. My. God! Are you REALLY? You're not kidding? You are really and truly coming back, to live? For GOOD?"

She was squealing with excitement. It was exactly what I was looking forward to, pure unabashed excitement about my return.

"Really, really, I am, to live, for good. The end of this month Eli and I will be there."

"Tate, I am so happy. How are you doing it? What happened that got you to this?"

Again I recounted the details. I got more unabashed excitement, and it was contagious.

"I can't wait. It's going to be so awesome. I am totally coming down at soon as you get here. Maybe I will stay with my parents for a few days to help and to visit. I can't wait just to sit and talk."

"Yeah, I can see it now. Ben's house has this big ol' screened in porch, we can sit in there and hang out. We can go to festivals together and take the kids to see fireworks and go to the pool. Jennie, I'm so excited! But, I'm scared, too."

"I know, Tate, but you're gonna be fine. You have so many people who love you and care about you here, and you're strong. You're going to just do what it takes to make it."

"I'm glad you believe in me, Jennie. It helps."

"Tate, you listen to me. If there is any time during the next month that you get scared or feel like you might change your mind, you just call me. I am going to see that you get through this — not just for my own selfish reasons, but for you. Even if it meant I would never get to see you again, I would still want you to get out of there and be free. I love you. You deserve to be happy."

Free.

"I love you, too Jennie."

"And if we have to, if he comes up here and starts trouble, we'll just see to it that he gets a good old fashioned Yankee ass-kickin'!"

I laughed. "Thanks Jennie."

She sounded more like a Rebel than a Yankee.

The rest of the week was spent mentally preparing. I had errands to run, but I needed an excuse to get out of the house. I didn't want to drag Eli with me from place to place, so when I thought of tanning – it seemed like the perfect cover, with the added benefit of feeling better about myself, too. I hadn't gone since Eli was born, so I could definitely use the boost.

When I step into my new life, I should look my best.

ON MONDAY I went to a salon in Mount Washington. I picked a tanning salon there because that is where the trailer rental place was. The first time I just went tanning and scoped out the area. I needed the trailer place, the post office and an auto shop, but I would take care of just one thing each visit, so Eric wouldn't be suspicious of the amount of time I was gone.

The post office and trailer rental were easy and quick to take care of: fill out a change of address, not to be effective until June 29th and pay cash upfront for the trailer, which was from a national company, so it could be returned in Wisconsin. With both of those things done, I turned my attention to the auto shop. That wasn't a necessity, but I wanted to try. There was a shop across the street from the salon. I'd just check, if they told me it would take more time than I had, I would just skip it.

On Saturday, June 8th I stopped there after tanning. It ended up being faster than I could have imagined. I simply told them I wanted a written estimate as to how much it would cost to fix my dash board. The technician looked at it for a few minutes, checked some figures in a big book, and then scribbled on piece of letterhead for me. Ten minutes and I was out, estimate in hand.

Twelve hundred dollars.
Well, that entitles me to quite a bit, I think.

When I got home, Eric seemed miffed.
"What took you so long?"
"Oh, they were overbooked. I had to wait about ten minutes to get into a bed."
"Oh. You've been tanning a lot, don't you think it's a little much?"
I looked down at my skin, now several shades darker than it had been a week ago.
"Yeah, I know – I think I got back into it too fast. I'm going to stop for a while now. Maybe I will just lay out on the deck, cheaper that way." I laughed.
Three more weeks.
My light and casual tone was easy to pull off because now I'd accomplished what I needed to.
Now it would just be work inside: inside the house and inside me.

The more I thought about my plans, the guiltier I felt, but still I never considered abandoning them – that was the thing about asking for help, you were letting a lot of people down if you didn't follow through.
I couldn't get over what I was doing to Eli. Even putting him in the car for eight hours seemed like a hurdle to get over. I let it bother me a lot. Then finally I considered it from a different point.
I wouldn't think twice about it if we were going on vacation, this is no different, it's the same drive.
As the day approached, faster and faster, my self doubting thoughts fought to make themselves heard, creating a kind of dialogue in my own head.
How can you do this to Eli?
He'll adjust and he'll be better off in the long run.

How can you do this to Eric?
He is the one who pushed me to this. After all he's done; he has no one to blame but himself.

You really think you can make it?
I have no choice, so yes, I do.

I got down to the business of figuring out what I was going to take with me. I knew this was going to be adding insult to injury for Eric - the fact that I had the gall to take the things he considered his - but I had to push myself. Not only did I deserve some of the household items, but he owed me for the car.

That twelve hundred dollar estimate is what pushed me over the guilty hump.

Besides, his parents will just buy him new stuff.

I walked through the house picking out the things I'd take. I didn't want to seem greedy, that could look bad when we went to court. I'd have to stick to the least expensive items, the spares and hand-me-downs where I could. I focused on the basics to put together a new place.

The less I had to buy, the better.

The TV was mine. I bought it when the one he had died.

There was a spare DVD player for the little TV in the basement; Eli loved his movies, so I'd take that for sure.

The living room furniture was off limits, as was the entertainment center and the bed. That left me with the spare bed that was now set up in the basement, having been finally moved out when we put Eli's toddler bed up.

The kitchen table I could take, and the microwave, I thought I remembered buying that, too.

The dresser and chest in Eli's room - they had been Dell and Annetta's; they went with the extra bed. I was the one who asked for them when they were being discarded. Eric didn't need them, we did. That made them fair game.

For the little stuff, there wasn't much to figure out. I didn't have much in terms of decorations or mementos; over the years Eric had broken most that stuff. I figured dishes and towels could easily be split when I actually packed. The holiday decorations in the attic would need to be separated so I could move things down the garage faster when the time came. That was at least one thing that could be done ahead of time.

Eric never went into the attic and if he did, he'd never notice if things were moved around.

I got my notebook from its hiding spot, I kept it hidden as if my life depended on it, because it did. In it I jotted down everything I planned to take organized by room, so I could figure out what I would still need.

Kitchen: Table and chairs, microwave, some dishes.

My bedroom: Spare bed, dresser & mirror from Eli's room.

Eli's room: Toddler bed, dresser, toys.

Living room: TV, DVD player from basement.

Misc.: Towels, sheets, DVDs, CDs.

That pretty much took care of it. All that I would need to get, as far as big stuff, was living room furniture. I'd talk to Jennie and Ben, see if either of them knew where I could get some for cheap. That wouldn't be a problem.

Once I decided what I was taking, I wanted to get everything in as good of shape as possible. Extra cleaning would help pass the time and would go unnoticed.

Cleaning and sorting took me through another week and the weekend. By Monday, June 17th - Eric's birthday – I was physically as ready as I could get.

Now I just had to wait.

Waiting was hard.

Waiting led to thinking.

On his birthday, I thought about how his twenty-fifth would be the last one I would spend with him.

Each day when I saw him with Eli, I thought about how horrible it was going to be for him, how horrible I would feel if he took Eli from me.

When I was working I thought about what would happen if the work slowed down again and I lost my job.

I thought about what would happen in court.

I thought about what I wanted to say in my goodbye letter.

I was stressing myself out and it was getting harder to not let it show.

I need something, some encouragement or an outlet, something.

I called Annetta to see if she could watch Eli for a little while, that I had some shopping I wanted to do. She happily obliged.

After I dropped him off, I went to the mall. I didn't know what I was looking for, but it was relaxing just to get out of the house and window-shop; let myself dream about the someday that was less than two weeks away.

When I came to the bookstore, I went in. At the very least I could find something in there for Eli.

I made my way slowly to the back of the store, where the children's section was, but I stopped short when I came to the self-help section.

Some encouragement maybe?

I looked slowly through the titles, not sure what to look for. I doubted they'd have a book called 'How to leave your abusive boyfriend and steal his child away while he's on vacation.'

Then one book caught my eye. It's slate blue and ivory cover stood out amongst the bright books around it.

I picked up and read the cover.

'Encouragements for the Emotionally Abused Woman.' By Beverly Engel.

I flipped through the book stopping at random points.

The book was set up with quotes and advice about recovering from abuse. Each page had a quote at the top, an explanation of its relevance. I looked at the Table of Contents; it basically looked like a step by step manual on figuring out and admitting that your being abused, deciding whether to leave, things to help you leave and what to do after.

I tucked the book under my arm and went to find a journal. That would serve as the outlet I was looking for.

Once I purchased the books, I called Annetta to let her know I'd be there in few minutes to pick up Eli. She asked if she could just keep him overnight, that she and her sister wanted to spend the afternoon with Eli and Jodi's little girl.

Perfect timing.

She said she had plenty of clothes and diapers there, so I didn't even need to worry about stopping back unless I wanted to.

I wanted to. I needed to tell Eli that I would pick him up in the morning. I left him there with a promise to be back in a little while; I didn't want to break a promise. I *never* wanted to break a promise to that little boy.

After I covered him with kisses and we exchanged 'I love yous' three times, I peeled him off me and left. He wasn't crying – he was laughing and being silly, hanging on my leg.

As I drove home, I felt an odd mixture of guilt and relief.

Guilt for taking him away from Eric, yet relief for what I was saving him from. Guilt because I was relieved to be away from him for the night.

I went home and dove headfirst into my new book. Two pages into the introduction I stopped reading to get a highlighter. This book made total sense to me.

I kept reading and reading, highlighting things that really hit me, the quotes that would become my mantras over the next few weeks, and some for the foreseeable future.

The first quote that really grabbed me was by R. D. Laing.

'The way out is through the door you came in.'

There were pages that specified the benefits of anger, and releasing it, in order to deal with the pain hiding underneath. That made a lot of sense to me. It was why I could never forgive Eric enough to stay with him. I covered the pain with anger. Now there is too much anger to ever get past.

In the chapters that dealt with deciding whether or not to leave I read about needing to trust yourself and that even if you make a mistake, it's okay.

Another quote would have sealed the deal, had it needed sealing. It was by Stephen Thomas: '*If you had six months to live, what would you do, and if you're not doing that now, why not?*'

I skipped over the chapter that detailed what to do if you decide to stay.

I finished the book. Then I hid it away, laid down on the couch and cried for over an hour. It wasn't just little crying; it was a full on, feel-like-you're-heart-is-getting-ripped-out-of-your-chest kind of cry. The kind that makes you physically feel the emotional heart.

I cried for Eric, because he'd be alone, I cried for Eli, for uprooting his life and taking him from his dad, and for myself. I cried because I was sad; I had to admit to myself that I was going to miss him. As much as I hated him, I loved him, too. I felt bad that I was going to inflict so much pain onto him. Bastard as he was, he was still human.

I cried from fear.

I was terrified that something was going to go wrong. What if Ben didn't make it down? What if he got a flat tire? What if Eric doesn't go? What if Eli freaks out on the ride? What if Dell stops here while I'm packing?

Nine days, Tate, nine days. It's going to be fine.

A quote from the book came back to mind, the one that stood out the most.

'You must do the thing you think you cannot do.'
That was it, plain and simple.
You're right, Eleanor Roosevelt, I do.

I went to bed before Eric came home, but before I climbed into the bed, I kneeled on the floor and leaned against it.

I need a higher power.

I prayed to know if I was making the right decision and I prayed that nothing bad would happen, but in the end, I mostly I prayed for strength.

The next morning I got up and prepared to go to Marc's house to pick up my new files before going to pick up Eli.

I knew that Marc was going to be giving me some extra supplies to take back to Wisconsin with me and a better printer.

He was also going to give me some boxes. He saved some for me, I'd take just enough to fill my trunk so I could keep them hidden.

I didn't show any signs that anything was unusual about my trip to Marc's, at least I didn't think I did, so it freaked me out when Eric *decided* to go with me.

"Maybe I'll ride over to Marc's with you today."

Even weirder was he said it super nice.

WAY too nice.

"Why would you do that?"

"I don't know, I just want to. What, don't you want me to?"

"I just don't know why you would want to go with me, basically to my job. It's a little odd."

"Well I think it's odd that you don't *want* me to go. What's the big deal? It's not like you work for a real company or anything."

I make real money, asshole.

Think Tate, THINK!

. . .

Guilt trip.

"There isn't a big deal. It's just that, uh it would be a little embarrassing. You know I had to tell him why I was off work for those few weeks."

"I don't give a fuck what he thinks of me!"

"Whoa, Eric, calm down, I didn't say *he* thinks anything about you, it's just that I feel embarrassed about letting my personal life interfere with my work. Having you show up there with me feels like I'm doing that again."

He sat and just looked at me for a minute.

"You know if I didn't want you to go, I could just go out and slash all your tires right now."

"What?"

"Yeah, then you couldn't go anywhere, I'd have to *take* you to Marc's."

Dear God

"ERIC! This is almost as bad as hitting me! You can not threaten to do stuff like slash my tires! I thought you changed!"

Calm down, don't blow this now.

I was scared. Did I go too far? Would he really slash my tires?

He sat motionless. That was either a good sign, or a very bad one.

"Eric?"

He was starting to freak me out again.

Finally, he spoke.

"I'm sorry. Go to Marc's. I'm going to get ready for work.

"Thank you, Eric."

"For what?" He looked miserable.

"For not doing anything to hurt me, for stopping."

It was way too little, too late, but it was appreciated anyway.

As I drove to Marc's, I thought about what just happened. I took it as a sign, it felt a little presumptuous, but it seemed like a bigger fail not to recognize it for what it could mean.

It proved to me that Eric is never going to stop being an abuser. One way or another, as long as I'm with him, he will always abuse me.

Thank you God, I understand. Leaving is the right thing to do.

I turned to my book, my journal, and to God a lot in the next eight days as they ticked down – in surreal fashion – from eight to one.

Eighteen

SOMEDAY

I woke up on Friday, June 28th with a knot in my stomach. Today was the last day that I would ever see Eric, as his girlfriend at least. Every time we saw each other for the rest of our lives from this day forward would be as parents only. I was sad, nervous and happy all at the same time.

Eric was leaving at ten o'clock. He was driving his truck to Lexington and meeting up with his ride from there. He insisted on us eating breakfast together, so after he loaded his truck, he made a traditional southern style breakfast, complete with biscuits and gravy. I'd grown to hate biscuits and gravy.

I just wanted him gone. I felt like I was going to jump out of my skin.

"Tate, you seem upset." He said sweetly. "I'll only be gone a week, it's okay."

If you only knew, you self centered asshole, like I'd really be sad if it were only a week away from you.

"I know it's just a week, Eric, but me and Eli are going to miss you."

I learned well over the years. Eric was a good teacher: I was lying as skillfully as he did now. It wasn't a complete and total lie though – we would miss him, it would just take more than a week.

"Hopefully I will bring back lots of fish. That grilled fish you like? I can make that for you when I get back. I'll make it Cajun style."

I thought about how good the fish would be. Eric was such an excellent cook.

Tate! You're not going to be here to eat the damn fish!

I looked at the clock: nine fifteen.

I had to get away from him. I was going to have a nervous breakdown. All I wanted to do was start packing.

I got up to start clearing dishes from the table.

"Could you get Eli out of his highchair and get him dressed?"

"Sure. I'd like to spend a little time with my buddy before I go."

My heart panged with guilt.

You must do the thing you think you cannot do.

I wondered if Ben had left yet and who he was bringing. He was right in his prediction: Danny couldn't make it down.

Suddenly another mantra popped into my head, a baseball reference, no doubt prompted by thoughts of Ben and Danny

Keep your eye on the ball.

That was perfect.

But what was the ball?

Me. I was the ball. My life, the life I wanted for Eli and for myself. That was the ball, that was what I would focus on.

Finally, it was time for Eric to leave. My heart pounded in my chest as he moved to hug me goodbye.

The last hug.

I swallowed against the lump forming in my throat.

"I'll miss you Tate. Be good."

Do not cry.

"I'll miss you, too, Eric."

Emotion crashed over me. It took everything I had to choke back the tears. Tears would be such a dead giveaway; he'd know a week separation would not warrant them, not after all that had already been shed for much, much worse things than this.

It took a lot for him to make me cry these days. I cried in private, but not for him, not anymore.

It was a sign of weakness I would not give.

Eric released me from his grip and moved to say goodbye to Eli. I had to turn away. I could not watch the final moments Eric had living with his son.

The moments crawled past. Everything felt significant: the last day, the last hug, the last 'I love you'.

As he walked out the door, I sat back down on the couch. From there I watched through the picture window as his truck pulled out of the driveway.

Then the tears came.

Quiet tears rolled down my cheeks and cooled quickly; they weren't the hot, angry tears that I usually cried, these were borne of sadness and relief.

Step one: done.

I sat there watching Eli play on the living room floor for one hour. That's how long I gave him to possibly forget something and return to get it. I figured once he was a half hour into his trip, he would replace the forgotten thing rather than make the drive back.

That was the slowest hour of my life.

When I got up off the couch it would be the last time I'd rest until almost midnight. That's when I'd gotten everything that I could move down into the garage. I figured Ben could just back the trailer right up to the door and we'd load up. I was thankful for the big sliding door that connected the basement to the garage; it made the logistics much easier.

I sorted and folded and packed all day. I felt guilty for leaving Eli to play most of the day by himself, but he was content with toys and the TV, and I told myself it was only one day. Today was one day and tomorrow was going to be one more. After that, it would be hard, but at least I could start to build a new life for him.

I made quick work of it, especially while Eli was asleep, but there was a lot more to move than what I thought. I hadn't really considered how much stuff we really had.

I packed the clothes, towels and toys in garbage bags and used the boxes for kitchen stuff and smaller things. It was easy to let things go rather than move them, so I ended up adding a lot more to the rummage sale pile.

When I was done, I went to bed right away. The sooner I fell asleep, the sooner I could wake up and get this over with. Ben called; he made it to the hotel, he had directions to the trailer place and to my house. Everything was set. He was by himself, but I didn't even care – there was nothing that he and I couldn't carry anyway.

I was glad it was all falling into place, but I was scared as hell, too. This could still get ugly. If Dell came over unexpectedly while we were loading up, I didn't know what he'd do, but if Eric came back for any reason, I'd be dead.

Going straight to bed also kept me from having to look at my house in its current state.

It's not your house anymore Tate, get used to it.

Keep your eye on the ball.

My alarm went off at seven-thirty am. That gave me time to shower and get Eli up, ready and fed and get the rest of our stuff packed and into the car by ten o'clock when Ben was due to arrive.

Everything went smoothly enough, though I was sore from all the lifting and moving the day before, but I found that was the least of my worries. Despite being right on schedule, I was a nervous wreck.

Keep your eye on the ball.

Ben got there right on time and he backed the trailer down the curved driveway to the garage like he'd done it a million times.

We said quick 'hellos' and got right to work. I pointed out what things I thought all had to go, told him I'd put my computer in the trunk of my car and that the rest of my car would need to be left empty for us to sit in and for our overnight bags. I didn't want to make that drive smothered in boxes.

We worked quickly and efficiently together. Eli sat in his playpen upstairs. I told him we were going away but we had to do some work in the basement first. Cartoons on TV again kept him entertained.

Geez Tate, it's like the TV's a babysitter.

The sardonic thought brought to mind the time I'd thought the same thing about Lana and Alex, when this whole thing started.

So much time wasted. I got my little boy out of it, but four and half years of my life, gone.

Four and half years, to the day: our anniversary was on the 29th.

In less than an hour, we were done.

"You ready?" Ben asked.

"Uh yeah, I just have to pack up Eli's play pen and check the house one more time."

"Okay. I'll wait outside."

"'Kay, thanks."

He was obviously trying to give me privacy.

I did want to say good bye to my house - whatever that meant - but as I walked through the naked looking rooms, I realized that Eli was the only good thing to ever come out of this and other than the ones of him, there were no memories I wanted to take along. This was no home for me, it was a prison.

You're finally free, so quit searching for ghosts. GO!

I double checked the closets, made sure my letter to Eric was in plain view on the counter, got Eli and the rest of our stuff.

Then, just like that, we left.

Half an hour into the ride, Eli was asleep.

See, why didn't I think of that? He'll probably sleep most of the trip.

The miles passed under my feet like a clock being wound backwards, in a way – undoing some of the wasted time, but also winding back the years on me. As I kept my eyes trained on that trailer hauling all my worldly possessions I started to feel younger and younger, like the seventeen year old child that made the decision to move to Kentucky in the first place.

I can't do this.
I can't make it on my own. Who am I trying to kid?

I can't do this. I'm going to have to get Ben's attention to pull over.
I looked back at Eli.
I have to go back.

Despite the panic in my heart, I let my mind prevail. I did not do anything to get Ben's attention and I did not pull over. I just kept my eyes trained on that trailer.

"Keep your eye on the ball. Keep your eye on the ball."
I looked back again at my sleeping child.

Keep swimming Little Fish, you can make it.

WE FINALLY CROSSED into Wisconsin, I worried less about today, but felt overwhelming worry about the distant future. I kept a few CDs handy, ones that had songs I found to be inspirational. When talking out loud to myself didn't do the trick, I popped in a CD and let the lyrics bolster me. We *were* making good progress when Ben took a wrong turn. Near Milwaukee, he stayed on I-94 heading towards Madison instead of taking Highway 45 towards Fond du Lac. I panicked a little and flagged him down. When he stopped, I was a little hysterical because I didn't know how to get to Anders Park from where we were. I did *not* appreciate the irony of getting lost.
Really? How full circle does this have to be?
He reminded me of the number one rule I learned from him: don't panic, then he very calmly told me that he knew right where we were *and* how to get home, it would just take a little longer.
Crisis averted.

As we came into Anders Park - ten hours after we'd left Eric's driveway – it was surreal. I'd seen this moment a hundred times in my head.

This time it's real.

The lump in my throat was back.

Ben parked his truck and trailer in front of the house. I pulled around it and parked in the driveway, next to Carl's car. I was relieved that my parents were there.

I was so still so nervous, my hands were shaking.

I got out of the car and went around the other side to get Eli out. It was almost his bed time.

I need bedtime.

Lilly greeted us before we'd made it ten steps out of the car. She pulled me into tight hug.

"You're so skinny!"

"Yeah, I haven't been eating much."

"Well, stress will do that to you."

She turned her attention to Eli.

"Hi Sweetheart."

Eli looked to me, slightly confused.

"Eli this is Grandma, you remember Grandma? From the phone and pictures?"

A tired smile took over his whole face. My heart panged with guilt.

Poor little guy. He has no clue what's going on.

"Hi Grandma." He wrapped his arms around her as she bent to meet his hug. She'd been talking to him on the phone a lot since I started planning to come back. She didn't want him to be scared of her when we got here.

Ben walked out to where we were gathered.

"Tate, what else do you need brought in the house tonight? Your bed, Eli's bed and his toy box are all upstairs."

How long have I been standing here?

Everything was moving so fast, I couldn't think straight. I hadn't even noticed them carrying stuff in while we'd been talking.

"Um, can you give me just a minute? I'll come in and get my bearings. I need to see the rooms."

"Gotcha. I'll be in the house."

"We're coming."

"Ready to go into Uncle Ben's house? We're going to stay here for a little while." I said cheerfully to Eli.

"Home?" He looked at me, again in confusion.

"No Baby, we're not going home tonight, we're going to stay here."

"Why?" he whined.

I swooped him up and carried him with me into the house, planting kisses on his cheek and whispering reassurances in his ear.

When I got inside the house, the scene took moment to settle in. I saw that both Joey and Danny were there. I also saw that Ben's house was a lot more cluttered than the last time I'd seen it. It wasn't gross or anything, just cluttered.

I introduced Eli to his uncles and his grandpa. He was out of sorts and it was starting to show. He was getting cranky and clinging to me. I looked around the house and my heart was sinking. How could we fit here? There was no room for any of our stuff.

We climbed the steep, narrow stairs and ended literally in one of the bedrooms. To the left was the other bedroom, it had its own door. That meant it had to be Eli's. I couldn't put him in a room with no way to keep him from the dangerous steps. I could at least put the baby gate up in the door frame of the second room.

Ben must have had the same thought, as my bed was in the first room, while the toy box and the bed with the blue, teddy bear shaped headboard was in the other.

The house was so different than how I remembered it. It felt small and stuffy, cluttered and run down. I didn't want to seem ungrateful, but this wasn't what I was expecting.

Not even close.

I went back downstairs and found Ben.

"I didn't remember those stairs being like that."

"Yeah, they're steep."

"Ben, are we going to fit here? I don't know if there is room for our stuff."

"Well, were not going to fix anything tonight." He snapped. I couldn't blame him, he was no doubt as exhausted as I was.

Still, his remark was all it took to send me over the edge.

I looked up the staircase and called to Lilly.

"Mom?"

"Yeah?" she poked her head out of Eli's makeshift room to look down at me.

"Can you just watch him for a little while?" I could barely get the words out.

"Sure. Are you okay?"

I couldn't hold back the tears any more.

"I'm fine." I choked.

I went to sit on the front porch. I was horrified when I saw what it had become.

It was filled with junk. Instead of old fashioned wicker that it used to have, it was cluttered with a desk, various mounted animals, magazines and newspapers; none of it in any particular order.

So much for late night talks on the front porch.

I turned around and went for the side door; I just needed to get some air; I needed to be alone.

I sat down on the side steps and let the tears come.

I was crying because I was disappointed. The pictures I had in my head didn't match what this place looked like, not even close. It set me back, reeling with thoughts that I'd done something horrible.

I shouldn't have come here.

I cried.

Quiet tears worked into uncontrollable sobbing. For a while, I literally could not stop, even when I tried. For what must have been fifteen minutes, I sat there on those wooden steps with the faded red paint and as dusk settled all around me, I cried until I didn't think I could make another tear.

When the tears were gone, so was the disappointment. I still didn't like the house, but I realized that what just happened was an unavoidable release. All the worrying, the fear, all the planning, everything that had led me to this moment, culminated in those tears. I felt like I'd been holding my breath and was finally able to exhale.

We were really here, I made it.

Welcome to your new life Little Fish.

WHEN I WOKE up in my strange new setting, I knew exactly what I had to do. I couldn't stay here with Ben. I needed a fresh start and an empty apartment with clean white walls would fill that need. It was the only way I'd be able to move forward.

I wanted to plan to be out by the middle of July. Partly because I didn't want anyone spending their July 4th weekend moving my stuff into a new place and partly because I had two weeks before the trailer had to be returned, so the timeline was set.

It was a motivating factor into finding a place quickly.

I got up and got Eli up. He woke up happy and smiling, not screaming and angry like I worried he'd be. He was fine. We ate breakfast and he chatted happily to me about Grandma and Grandpa. They had made quite an impression on him the night before. I couldn't wait to get him out to their house and let him run free in their big back yard.

I knew I needed to call Jennie to let her know we got here okay before I did anything else. I wanted to see her, but I thought maybe we could just wait until the 4th. There was so much going on in my head already.

She startled me by answering the phone with rapid fire questions.

"Are you here? Are you okay? Did Eric find out?"

"I'm here. I'm okay."

Emotion came crashing down over me when I said the word 'okay'.

Was I?

"Oh my God! I can't believe you're here!" she screamed into the phone. "Wait – are you really okay? You're not going back, are you?"

"No, Jennie, I'm not ever going back there." I said with conviction.

"Good. I'm coming down. Can I come down today? I want to see you in person!"

"Well, I was thinking maybe we could take the boys to the fireworks on Thursday. Maybe you could spend the weekend at your parents and we could hang out. I've got to look for an apartment. I don't want to waste our time together doing boring stuff."

"Yeah, that would work out great actually. I have off all weekend, so I will bring Brandon down. Maybe Saturday night the G-mas could watch the boys and we could go out."

"Out?"

The thought of Jennie and I cruising Cassden didn't hold the same appeal as when were teenagers.

"Yeah, out. Have you heard of it? Out, for a beer or something. You know we're both old enough to get in the bars now, right?"

Right, out.

I could go in to a bar. I could do whatever I wanted. Eric wasn't here to tell me I couldn't. The freedom was momentarily terrifying.

"Hmmm, out. Out? What is this *'out'* that you speak of?"

"You nut!" she laughed. "We *are* going to go out and you're going to feel what it's like to be free!"

I broke down.

"Tate. Hey, are you alright? I can be down there in a few hours, you just say the word."

"No, no – it's okay." I composed myself.

"It's all just a little overwhelming, that's all. Ben's house is really crowded with stuff and all of my stuff is still in the trailer outside. I am just anxious to get settled, I guess. I am happy though, Jennie, I really am."

I didn't want her to think I was having doubts. I wasn't.

"Do you miss him?"

I thought about her question before answering.

"Honestly? No, I don't. I am sure I will, but I don't yet."

"Good. Do you think he knows you're gone?"

"No, he's out at sea until Thursday, I think. I am sure his parents know, though."

"How do you think they're going to take it?"

"Bad. They'll be crushed to not be around Eli, but I can't help it. Believe me, I've spent the last month feeling as much guilt as I'm going to feel. I just keep reminding myself of the times they turned a blind eye to what Eric did to me. I feel bad for them, but they only have him to blame, not me. I don't owe them anything."

"Good attitude, Tate. You are so right. The only people you owe are yourself and Eli. Well, and me, you owe me a fun weekend!" she laughed excitedly. "I can't wait!"

"Me either, Jennie. I can't wait, just to see you, to talk in person, gain some perspective."

"I gotcha. Well, you can count on me."

"I suppose, I should get to my apartment search. I think I'll feel better once that is done. Right now, it's like I'm juggling too many plates."

I remembered the furniture.

"Oh, hey – I almost forgot – do you know anyplace I could get some hand me down living room furniture for cheap?"

"Great timing."

"Why's that?"

"My parents are getting new furniture next weekend. Their old stuff isn't bad; but they were just going to donate it. Couch, loveseat, end tables and a coffee table. Consider it yours."

"Awesome! You're the *best*."

"Well, I wouldn't be a very good *best* friend if I wasn't!" she laughed. "I'll call you when I get to my parents' house on Thursday, probably about three, 'kay?"

"'Kay."

"Tate, you hang in there and be strong. I know you can do this and you call me if you need to, anytime, day or night. Love ya."

My heart felt like it was overflowing.

Why didn't I do this sooner? Why did I wait so long to let these people help me? They want to help, they love me.

"I love you, too, Jennie. You *are* the best friend, *ever*. See you soon."

After we hung up I went to check on Eli. I followed the sound of his happy little voice and found him in the living room, playing with Ben. I quickly scanned the room looking for kid hazards, but took a step back before Eli saw me.

Okay, it's not necessarily how I would keep things, but he's with Ben. It will be okay. Let people help you.

I got down to my apartment search by approaching it with the same technique I used to build my plan to move here. I sat down at Ben's kitchen table with a newspaper, my secret notebook – that didn't have to be secret anymore – and the phone. I started making calls.

That notebook felt profound. As I held it in my hands I thought of Eric and how desperately I'd guarded the notebook from him.

I thought of how I would never have to hide things again.

The initial apartment search was frustrating to say the least. There was only one available place in Anders Park that fit my needs. I needed a two bedroom place in a security locked building and I would prefer a second floor apartment because it felt safer. I didn't know what Eric was going to do, but I didn't want him to be able to get anywhere near me, should he try.

In the end, it was my credit that kept me from renting the place in Anders Park, at least that's what I was told. I thought it was more like age discrimination because while the manager waited on the phone with me for my credit report to process, she told me three times that parties weren't allowed.

I explained to her that I had a two year old; there would be no parties in my apartment.

She denied me anyway.

Two steps forward, one step back.

I went into the living room by Eli and Ben and collapsed in frustration onto the couch.

"This sucks. I really wanted to live here, in Anders Park."

"You know Tate; anything that doesn't kill you makes you stronger."

"Well then I must be one hell of a strong person." I replied sardonically. As got up to leave the room, I heard him faintly say "You are."

I GAVE UP on finding a place in Anders Park and opted for Cassden. After two trying days of phone calls and driving around to look at places, I finally found one that might work. It was a little more expensive than I would have liked, but it was nice, clean and secure. The complex was on a quiet end of town, and across the street were elderly apartments. Perfect.

Lilly, Eli and I went to look at the place. As the manager walked us through, I kept trying to picture it with our stuff. It had a big bright master bedroom with walk-in closet big enough to live in. The second bedroom was much smaller, but fine for Eli, as he'd most likely play in ample living room. The bathroom was nice, too – it was huge, and the kitchen and dining area were more than ample for what the two of us would need.

After a few minutes, I realized we wouldn't really have a dining area – that would have to be my office.

The unit even had a few perks over some of the others. The elderly woman explained that because it was an end unit, it had two bedroom windows instead of just one and the balcony was covered, but those two features cost an extra ten dollars a month.

I wanted one more look around the apartment to make sure. The light in the master bedroom was beautiful and the mature trees outside both windows made it feel extra private. When I walked out on to the covered balcony I thought of Jennie.

Late night talks on the balcony would be okay, too.

The manager pointed out that they did have others units available, without the added fee or features.

The window and the balcony were well worth ten dollars.

What's ten measly dollars when you're already spending over five hundred?

In the end, I decided the apartment would be perfect for us.

I agreed to rent the apartment and made plans to move in on July 13th. I wrote her a check on the spot for the pro-rated first month's rent and the security deposit which was equal to a full month's rent. I worried momentarily that she wouldn't want to take the starter check from my brand new checking account, but she told me a lot of people pay for their first months rent with them, that it was fine.

The check was almost nine hundred dollars. It was the biggest check I'd ever written. Spending that much made me nervous, but I told myself this is what I'd been saving for.

Then it was time to sign the year lease. That made me nervous, too. *Now it's permanent.*

As we drove back to Anders Park, the nervousness floated away, leaving only optimistic anticipation. I had an apartment; a place of my very own. As cliché as it was, I told Lilly I felt like a huge weight had been lifted off my shoulders.

"Tate, I am so happy for you. I wish I had a nice clean apartment like that to move into."

Her comment made me a little sad for her, but happy for myself. I'd told Jennie that I didn't want to repeat the mistakes that Lilly made, spending her life in a physically, then emotionally abusive relationship. This was me, not repeating.

"I wish you did, too, Mom."

IN THE COMING days, I got to the tasks of setting up a home phone, electric and internet. I talked to Marc to touch base and tell him that I'd start working the week of July 14th, keeping my promise of shooting for a two week hiatus instead of three.

He still wanted to give me a week of vacation pay, despite the fact that I wasn't really an employee. I didn't argue. I wanted to, but instead I graciously agreed.

Let people help you.

That was it. Again, I was back to the part where all I could do was wait. The apartment was rented and the utilities were set up. They were in my name, for the first time in my life, which had a validating effect on me. I felt very grown up. Now I just had to wait until moving day. Carl, Ben, Danny and Joey were all on board to help and Lilly volunteered to keep Eli so we wouldn't be tripping over him.

I was thankful for the holiday and the upcoming weekend. I needed a distraction.

THE MOMENT I saw Jennie, the feeling of waiting dissipated. This was enough for now. Being with Jennie would keep me plenty distracted.

"You're too skinny!" was the first thing out of her mouth.

"Yeah, I've heard."

She pulled me into a big hug.

"I'm so happy you're home, Tate."

"Me, too, Jennie, me too."

In that moment, everything was right with the world.

We spent the better part of the four days together; sometimes with our boys, sometimes on our own. We went to the fireworks, and from beginning to end, that experience was surreal. Even the simple act of getting ready without worrying about someone critiquing my outfit was different. It all came down to having control over my own life.

The small town fireworks only made me a little sad, as I recalled the experience of Thunder over Louisville.

Jennie never did get me into a bar. I told her that I just wasn't ready for that yet. I joked about it, telling her I needed to get my bearings first before I go out carousing around, looking for men.

She laughed and agreed that was the *last* thing I needed to worry about right now.

We went to a movie instead, a comedy. Afterwards, I decided laughter really was the best medicine.

Sunday afternoon when it was time for her to head back up to Green Bay, I was sad to see her go. I felt so much more confident with her around.

"Can't you just stay? Just keep staying with your parents!"

She shot me a look of mock loathing.

"Uh, no thanks."

"Okay, well better yet, you three should move down here. You can rent an apartment in my building, but I'm sorry; the unit with the extra window and covered balcony is already taken."

Jennie laughed at my silliness. "I will come back as soon as you get settled, okay?"

"Okay." I said dejectedly.

"You know, basically, I just want to get out of helping you move."

"That figures."

We both laughed.

"Oh, and don't forget – you can pick up that furniture from my parents house anytime. They said they'd be home all weekend."

"Like I'd forget a room full of furniture? I might notice the absence after sitting on the floor for a day or two."

"Good point, good point. See? That's why you're the smart one." She tapped her finger on the side of her head.

"I love you, Jennie. Thank you for everything and for just being my friend."

"Yeah, yeah you're stuck with me. I guess I kinda love you, too." She teased.

"Good."

We shared a tearful hug, standing there in Ben's driveway. She joined Brandon in the car and I rounded up Eli. I figured we'd head out to my parents'.

The hurry up and wait mentality that I'd had for the last month and half was wearing on me. Now I just wanted to get into my apartment, get back to working and making money, most importantly just to get back to a routine.

When I got out to my parents' house, Carl had some news for me. He approached it comically, which I couldn't understand since I found it extremely distressing.

"There was a sheriff here looking for you."

"What?"

My mind raced with thoughts of kidnapping.

"They left this for you." He handed me a large brown envelope.

"The officer laughed when I explained things. I told him that you weren't living here but that Eric knew where you were. He said that as long as he knew, then things should be fine."

I had a feeling Carl may have missed some of the details.

I ripped open the envelope with shaky hands and scanned the legal documents. I knew the format well, so it was easy to discern the basics quickly.

"Well, this is just great. Eric is suing me for full custody of Eli, based on the fact that I am mentally unstable and stole him without any word as to where I was going, AND, he wants *me* to pay *him* child support."

"Well, that certainly all sounds fair." Carl said sarcastically. "Don't worry about too much right now, Tate. Things will be fine, I'm sure."

He was sure, but I wasn't. I was scared and seething mad.

I'll show you mentally unstable.

The next day I went to the government building in Cassden. I knew from talking to Eric's insurance company that Wisconsin was out of their network, so they would only pay fifty percent of any medical costs. I thought maybe I could get medical aid to pick up the rest. I also needed to file for child support.

I was able to meet with a case worker almost immediately. We talked about child support first. She told me that since Eric had already filed papers in Kentucky, I would be unable to file up here, due to the Uniform Child Custody and Jurisdiction Act. She explained that it stated that a child needed to live in state for six months before that state could make determinations on issues of custody, and since he had mentioned support in his papers, I couldn't file my own.

She told me the best thing I could do would be to hire a lawyer in Kentucky and go from there.

The topic of insurance went much more my way. She took a look at the statement I provided, showing how much money I made, then showed me that according the charts, not only would state medical insurance pick up whatever Eric's insurance didn't for Eli, but I would be covered, too.

After I'd signed all the required forms, she told me that with my income, I was just under the limit to receive food stamps as well.

I thanked her but told her unequivocally that help with medical was all I was looking for. I did not want any other kind of assistance.

She seemed to admire my resolve.

I admired my own resolve.

WHEN MOVING DAY finally arrived I was nervous and excited and couldn't get started fast enough. Ben told me it might take two days and if it did, we'd have to do it without the trailer because it needed to be returned that night. I didn't care about the details, I just wanted to get down to business. I asked that our bedroom stuff be moved in first so Eli and I could sleep there. He *promised* to oblige.

I laughed to myself.

He'll probably be happy to have his house back!

By ten o'clock my brothers and Carl were all at Ben's and I'd already dropped Eli off with Lilly.

We jumped right in.

Unfortunately, it was scorching hot and a few times, tempers flared. It made the day longer for everyone, but by the end of the first day, it all got done. They even retrieved the furniture from Jennie's parents.

I got Eli's room done first. It was getting late and I needed to pick him up, but I wanted his room to be put together so he would feel some sense of home. I could work on the other rooms after I got him in bed for the night.

The drive back to Anders Park went fast. When I got to my parents'
house, Lilly had Eli all ready to go.

"How did everything go?" she asked.

"Okay. It was hot, but we're done, that's all that matters."

"Well, Carl and I are going to come over tomorrow to see how you're
doing. I figured you might need a few things yet, we could go shopping."

"That sounds good."

"Okay, well I guess Eli and I are going home."

Our eyes met and there was a peaceful happiness there. Matching
smiles grew across of our faces.

Home.

"Congratulations, Tate. I am so proud of you."

TWO WEEKS PASSED quickly, but peacefully. I hadn't heard anything more
from Kentucky since the papers came. Lilly told me that Annetta called
and tried pumping her for information, but Lilly didn't budge. She said
she'd told Annetta only that we were fine, Eli was doing great and that
she would have me call when I was ready.

I had a lawyer in Kentucky working on the custody case. It was
someone Marc had recommended and while I wasn't positive, I thought
he was taking pity on me, because he only charged me five hundred
dollars for a retainer and told me that could very well cover the whole
case. That seemed awfully cheap for a lawyer, but I just took it as a gift
and was thankful. As far as I knew, he was busy handling my case, as I'd
only spoken to him twice. During the initial phone call he told me there
would be a time when I would need to return to Kentucky for court, but
he would take care of as much of it as he could without me.

I got my office set up in the dining room and got back to work right
away, relieved to have money coming in steadily again.

Eli was adjusting well. He was happy and playful and seemed to love
our new place. It was obvious he missed Eric, but the crankiness that
took over him when we'd stayed with Dell and Annetta never came.

In my heart, I knew he'd be fine.

Another thing that never came was the overwhelming sadness that I expected. I'd mentally prepared myself to miss Eric deeply, but I didn't. All I felt was relief from being away from him. I wrote a lot in my journal, and still turned to the encouragement book quite a bit, but I was healing, albeit slowly.

I knew I'd be fine, too.

IT WAS SUNDAY afternoon and Eli was with my parents for the day. I was taking advantage of the free time to attend to some odds and ends.

Only two weeks had passed since we'd moved in, but because of the pro-rated half month, it was already time to pay rent for August.

May as well take care of that now, too.

As I wrote out the check I realized that in two days, a full month would have passed since we'd moved here. We were fine. I survived and I never even considered going back.

I was doing it. I was living my life, free.

I put the rent check in an envelope and walked across the street to put it in the drop box, located inside the foyer of the elderly apartment building. As I walked slowly back to my own building, the symbolism of what I'd just done overwhelmed me.

I *really* was doing it.

For the first time in my life, I paid rent on my own place, with my own money. It wasn't my parents' place or Eric's, it was mine. It wasn't child support or state assistance; it was just me, standing on my own two feet.

I got back up to my apartment and closed and locked the door safely behind me. This was my sanctuary.

This is *my* place.

I'm free.

I sat down on the floor in the middle of the living room and looked around at the bare walls and hand me down furniture.

I wept quiet tears. They were happy tears.

In that moment I knew there was a long journey ahead of me. A lot had to be taken care of before this would be completely over and before

I was really healed, but I knew if I could make it this far, I could make it the rest of the way.

You did it Little Fi-

Suddenly, the moniker no longer fit. I wasn't Little Fish any more. I'd navigated treacherous shark infested waters and survived, swam home against the current, and now I was treading water, all on my own.

That horrible part of my life was really over. I'd grown up, struck out on my own and most importantly, I mattered here. People cared about me.

In Eric's world, I would have always been Little Fish, forever.

In this pond, I was one of the big fish.

The kind that gets away.

The End

Acknowledgements

VERY SPECIAL THANKS to...

Jacob. For always pushing me to be the best I can be, for being proud of me, for sharing a love of books and for using big words, for being every single thing that a mother could ever want in a son. My pride, my love. I thank you.

Mom. For always being there, no matter what, for believing in me, even when I didn't believe in myself and for loving me only the way a mother can, for solving the mystery of where the words come from. It's not your childhood pages lost, but I hope it's the next best thing.

And...

Debbie. What else but this; for sharing a friendship with me that was the most fun to write about, you know – you were there. ;) It's not a job for Hallmark writing greeting cards, but your encouragement kept the spark alive way back when. Couldn't have this, if I didn't have that.

Jill. For believing in my writing before anyone else and with a conviction strong enough to keep a dream alive.

Mara & Jade. For... wow, so much. For bearing with me when this whole thing started. For encouraging me all the time (well, except for that one time ☺), for proofreading, for caring and for being incredible friends.

And to Cindy, Jeremy, Amy, Steph, Ginny, Juli, Kevin and Dr. Steve; For all encouragements, big and small.

Made in the USA
Monee, IL
16 March 2022

92973557R00221